THEOLOGY AND SCIENCE AT THE FRONTIERS OF KNOWLEDGE

1: T.F. Torrance, *Reality and Scientific Theology*.
2: H.B. Nebelsick, *Circles of God, Renaissance, Reformation and the Rise of Science*.
3: Iain Paul, *Science and Theology in Einstein's Perspective*.
4: Alexander Thomson, *Tradition and Authority in Science and Theology*.
5: R.G. Mitchell, *Einstein and Christ, A New Approach to the Defence of the Christian Religion*.
6: W.G. Pollard, *Transcendence and Providence, Reflections of a Physicist and Priest*.
7: Victor Fiddes, *Science and the Gospel*.
8: Carver Yu, *Being and Relation: An Eastern Critique of Western Dualism*.
9: John Puddefoot, *Logic and Affirmation — Perspectives in Mathematics and Theology*.
10: Walter Carvin, *Creation and Scientific Explanation*.

THEOLOGY AND SCIENCE AT THE FRONTIERS OF KNOWLEDGE

GENERAL EDITOR - T.F.TORRANCE

GROUNDS FOR REASONABLE BELIEF

RUSSELL STANNARD

SCOTTISH ACADEMIC PRESS
EDINBURGH
1989

Published in association with the
Center of Theological Inquiry
and
The Templeton Foundation Inc.
by
SCOTTISH ACADEMIC PRESS
33 Montgomery Street, Edinburgh EH7 5JX

First published 1989

ISBN 0-7073-0581-0

© Russell Stannard 1989

All rights reserved. No part of this
publication may be reproduced, stored in
a retrieval system, or transmitted in any
form or by any means, electronic, mechanical, photocopying,
recording or otherwise, without
the prior permission of Scottish Academic Press Limited

British Library Cataloguing in Publication Data
Stannard, Russell
Grounds for reasonable belief.
1. Theology
I. title II. Series
230

ISBN 0-7073-0581-0

Camera-ready copy prepared by Pam Berry
Printed in Great Britain by Bell and Bain Ltd., Glasgow

To my wife, Maggi
in gratitude for her support
and encouragement of this work.

CONTENTS

General Foreword ix
Preface xiii

Chapter
1. Introduction 1
2. The Viewpoint of Classical Physics 7
3. The Exclusion of God 15
4. Towards the Modern Physical Viewpoint 25
5. What of the Physical World-in-itself? 45
6. The Inadequacy of Nothing But... 69
7. The Exclusion of the Mental 77
8. Explanatory Frameworks 88
9. Inferring the Physical from the Mental 106
10. Relating the Mental and the Physical 129
11. Other Minds and the Concept of Oneself 157
12. The Inner Religious Experience 168
13. Other Experiences of the Numinous 175
14. The Otherness of Religious Experience 189
15. Religion and the Unconscious 199
16. The Spiritual Interaction Framework 224
17. What of God-in-himself? 248
18. Relating the Spiritual to Other Frameworks 259
19. Theology as Science 295
20. Theology beyond Science 310
21. Review 325

Index 357

GENERAL FOREWORD

A vast shift in the perspective of human knowledge is taking place, as a unified view of the one created world presses for realisation in our understanding. The destructive dualisms and abstractions which have disintegrated form and fragmented culture are being replaced by unitary approaches to reality in which thought and experience are wedded together in every field of scientific inquiry and in every area of human life and culture. There now opens up a dynamic, open-structured universe, in which the human spirit is being liberated from its captivity in closed deterministic systems of cause and effect, and a correspondingly free and open-structured society is struggling to emerge.

The universe that is steadily being disclosed to our various sciences is found to be characterised throughout time and space by an ascending gradient of meaning in richer and higher forms of order. Instead of levels of existence and reality being explained reductionistically from below in materialistic and mechanistic terms, the lower levels are found to be explained in terms of higher, invisible, intangible levels of reality. In this perspective the divisive splits become healed, constructive syntheses merge, being and doing become conjoined, an integration of form takes place in the sciences and the arts, the natural and the spiritual dimensions overlap, while knowledge of God and of his creation go hand in hand and bear constructively on one another.

We must now reckon with a revolutionary change in the generation of fundamental ideas. Today it is no longer philosophy but the physical and natural sciences which set the pace in human culture through their astonishing revelation of the rational structures that pervade and underlie all created reality. At the same time, as our science presses its enquiries to the very boundaries of being, in macrophysical and microphysical dimensions alike, there is being brought to light a hidden traffic between theological and scientific ideas of the most far-reaching significance for both theology and science. It is in that situation where theology and science are found to have deep mutual relations, and increasingly cry out for each other, that our authors have been working.

The different volumes in this series are intended to be geared into this fundamental change in the foundations of knowledge. They do not present 'hack' accounts of scientific trends or theological fashions, but are intended to offer inter-disciplinary and creative interpretations which will themselves share in and carry forward the new synthesis transcending the gulf in popular understanding between faith and reason, religion and life, theology and science. Of special concern is the mutual modification and cross-fertilisation between natural and theological science, and the creative integration of all human thought and culture within the universe of space and time.

What is ultimately envisaged is a reconstruction of the very foundations of modern thought and culture, similar to that which took place in the early centuries of the Christian era, when the unitary outlook of Judaeo-Christian thought transformed that of the ancient world, and made possible the eventual rise of modern empirico-theoretic science. The various books in this series are written by scientists and by theologians, and by some who are both scientists and theologians. While they differ in training, outlook, religious persuasion, and nationality, they are all passionately committed to the struggle for a unified understanding of the one created universe and the healing of our split culture. Many difficult questions are explored and discussed, and the ground needs to be cleared of often deep-rooted misconceptions, but the results are designed to be presented without technical detail or complex argumentation, so

GENERAL FOREWORD

that they can have their full measure of impact upon the contemporary world.

Professor Russell Stannard is a high energy nuclear physicist, who has been the Head of the Physics Department at the Open University in Britain since 1971, and is Vice President of the Institute of Physics. He has also been a Reader in the Church of England since 1966, and has for many years been actively interested in working out the relations between science and theology. This bore fruit in the publication of *Science and the Renewal of Belief* in 1982, in which he sought to offer a wide-ranging discussion of the issues in a manner that would be accessible to the non-specialist. It was widely acclaimed by scientists and theologians alike, and quickly gained recognition by the Templeton UK Project Award 'for signal contributions to the field of spiritual values; in particular for contributions to greater understanding of science and religion'.

In writing this new work Russell Stannard has once again brought to it his own experience of working in the multi-disciplinary environment fostered by the Open University, and has deployed his remarkable gifts of devising fresh ways of presenting the ideas of modern physics in non-mathematical terms. *Grounds for Reasonable Belief* is a lucidly clear and beautifully argued work in which he compares the foundations of belief in science and theology, and assesses the reasonableness of religious belief for non-believers as well as believers. His book has a powerful apologetic character which is charmingly and convincingly presented. He takes up many of the questions that arise in people's minds, but which they may not know how to frame properly, or how they may be answered reasonably. In so doing he shows how science, far from disproving God's existence, actually faces rather similar problems when addressing the really fundamental questions of existence and knowledge. Hence he does not find it surprising that science and theology have insights to offer each other as they tackle their respective difficulties in analogous ways. His distinctive stress is on the need for appropriate modes of understanding within hierarchically arranged frameworks of explanation, in which theological questions move up to an even higher framework than that which can be provided by the physical sciences; but he is acutely aware that in both science and theology there are aspects of reality which we cannot put into words and are not to be encompassed in any system of articulated explanation.

Thomas F Torrance
Edinburgh,
Advent, 1988

PREFACE

THE idea for this book originated from a series of consultations held at St. George's House, Windsor Castle, U.K., at which theologians, scientists, psychologists, and philosophers were brought together to discuss the interrelationships between their different subject areas. Michael Mann organized these sessions, and I am grateful to him and to the other participants for the stimulation of their views.

The book was written during a sabbatical year spent at the Center of Theological Inquiry, Princeton, U.S.A., a research institute having a special interest in relating theology to contemporary thought, particularly modern scientific thought. My gratitude to Jim McCord for providing me with this opportunity. Thanks are due to Princeton Theological Seminary and Princeton University for the use of their libraries. I am indebted to the Open University for releasing me from my duties as Chairman of the Physics Department for the year, and to the Institute of Physics in respect of my position there as Vice President.

Finally, I wish to thank those who so generously gave of their time to discuss this project with me. The coverage of the wide field here attempted would not have been possible without the cooperation of others, especially those from discipline areas other than my own. Invidious though it is to single out certain people and not others, the following were particularly helpful through the critical reading of early draft chapters: Gerhard Adler, Diogenes Allen, Enrico Cantore, Jack Hawley, Eric Hutchinson, Jim Loder, Dan Migliore, Ernst Monse, Harold Nebelsick, Jim Neidhardt, Edward Nelson, Lesslie Newbigin, Bill Placher, Victor Preller, Derek Stanesby, Anthony Stevens, Martin Stone, and Tom Torrance. It goes without saying that these persons are in no way responsible for any remaining errors, nor should it be assumed that they necessarily subscribe to the views expressed.

CHAPTER 1

INTRODUCTION

THE aim of this book is to examine critically, with the help of modern scientific thought, how one might justify a belief in God.

The approach will be to compare the grounds for believing in God with those that underpin beliefs in other aspects of human existence - beliefs to do with one's physical body operating in a physical environment, one's mind engaging in social interaction with other minds, and there being an unconscious part to the mind that interacts with the conscious part. Only by comparing the argument for God's existence with the corresponding arguments concerning these other aspects of existence can we assess its reasonableness.

Normally, of course, we do not think to question these latter beliefs; we simply 'know' that this is how things are and get on with the business of running our lives. But do we really 'know'? It comes as a surprise to many to learn that, among physicists who have thought most deeply on the latest developments in physics, there are those who believe that the correct answer to the question 'Does the physical world exist?' is - No! Others do not go quite as far as that. They hold that the world does exist - however, there is nothing, absolutely nothing, that can be said about it. Yet others, you might be relieved to learn, continue to believe that the world is there and that the job of science remains what we always thought it was: to describe and explain it - but this is a minority view. One of the tasks of this book is to explain how this extraordinary state of disarray among physicists has come about.

1

It is important that you be clear as to the nature of the task before us. We are not attempting to explain how in practice we come to acquire a particular set of beliefs. Rather, the aim is to establish a reasoned, critical assessment as to how well founded those beliefs are, and thus, whether we should continue to hold them or not. In the process, we shall clarify our understanding of these realities and deepen our appreciation of the role each has to play in human existence.

And what of the result of this investigation? First we shall find that there is no deductive proof of the existence of God - not the kind of proof that would compel a tough-minded philosopher to abandon a position of scepticism, should that be the chosen standpoint. But then again, there is no such proof of the existence of the physical world, of minds other than one's own, or of the unconscious part of the mind. In other words, the demand often made that one should prove God's existence as a prerequisite for taking religion seriously, makes no sense. Which leads into the main discussion of the book: how it is that, despite the lack of water-tight proof, we are yet able to draw plausible inferences as to the existence of physical, mental, and spiritual realities. In setting out the grounds for such beliefs, we shall discover that one can justify a belief in God in much the same way as one justifies a belief in the other types of reality. This is not to claim that the evidence for God will strike everyone as equally convincing; many people remain unpersuaded of the existence of God, while happily accepting that the physical world exists. The point I am making is that the *type of justification* one seeks for beliefs in the two cases is the same. Contrary to popular opinion, belief in the physical is not to be regarded as founded on incontrovertible proof, whereas that in God relies on uncritical faith.

We shall make a start with physics. Having seen how far we can get with the question of physical existence and what might be said about the physical world, we go on to consider other types of existence, culminating eventu-

INTRODUCTION

ally with the question of the existence of God and what might be said of him. Why begin in the physical domain? Because the concepts used in science are relatively clear and unambiguous. This will allow us to pose the problems in a sharply focussed manner. Were we to begin with the problem of inferring from conscious mental experience, the existence of the unconscious, or the existence of minds other than one's own, one might be inclined to think of the exercise as rather pedantic and unnecessary. Similarly, if we began with the problem of knowledge as it arises in connection with the unknowability of God, one might suspect this to point to nothing more profound than woolly-mindedness or defensiveness on the part of the theologian. But with the problems of existence and knowability as they arise in physics there are no such easy get-outs. When trying to infer from physical interactions that there is a physical world-in-itself, one becomes enmeshed in paradoxes that are stark and unavoidable - to the extent, as already indicated, that some scientists have lost their belief in the reality of that paradoxical world, or alternatively have given up hope of describing it. A study of the problems as they arise in physics underlines the need to take seriously the related questions in other areas.

But before launching into this programme, there is a preliminary issue to be settled. One often hears the view expressed that the question of God's existence no longer arises: 'Science has disproved religion.' If this claim can be justified then we might as well save ourselves a lot of effort by setting out the argument. Thus the first few chapters are devoted to examining the claim - and seeing what is wrong with it. It is an instructive exercise in its own right, but in addition introduces many of the ideas we shall later need to call upon.

The investigation before us is a broad one. It encompasses not only science and theology, but also psychology. One cannot assess the reliability of the evidence for God based on religious experience, without examining the role that might be played by the unconscious in the production of such experiences. Likewise, the investigation must take on board the fruits of philosophical discussion. Though the problems that have arisen in physics might strike physicists as startlingly novel, they would not appear so to philosophers; the latter have long wrestled with just these sorts of difficulties. Breadth of investigation, including a willingness to make comparisons across a number of discipline areas, yields insights that elude the more narrowly focussed type of study.

But the same wide scope of the investigation can also be its weakness. For good reason it is customary to work within the safe confines of a single discipline, there being so much for any individual to learn in a given subject area. Those of us who attempt to span from one's own discipline to another cannot but lay ourselves open to the charge of not doing justice to the field that is not their own. How much more this must be true of the present endeavour which tries to build bridges between several disciplines. But I believe the attempt ought to be made, even though it fall short of the desired mark. At the very least it might spur others to do a better job of it.

I have deliberately refrained in the main from attributing ideas and views to particular people. This is not, of course, to take credit for ideas that are not my own. The problem is that, even at the best of times, it is not easy to represent accurately and faithfully someone else's opinions. In the present work, where the range of topics to be covered would have allowed only the shortest quotations from other writers, taken out of context, the difficulties would have been especially severe. The book is not in any case intended as a history of ideas; its concern is limited to presenting the contemporary situation as I see it.

What else ought I to say before we get started? I should mention that I have written mainly from the Christian standpoint; much of the material, however, is of relevance to any religious faith. The book is intended to be of interest to religious believers and non-believers alike.

The former in the context of how to reflect upon faith and how to justify its reasonableness to others; the latter in regard to determining whether religious belief can be held with intellectual integrity, and thus be deserving of sympathetic consideration. I have tried to pitch the book at a wide readership, consistent with doing justice to the subject. To this end I have assumed little or no prior knowledge of physics or theology, or indeed of psychology and philosophy. From which it should not be assumed that the discussion of each topic remains confined to the elementary level at which it is introduced. Professionals working in these various fields will, I hope, find something of interest to them. Theologians, for example, could well find value in the approach I offer to an understanding of the spiritual domain - an approach consonant with the mind-set now adopted in physics. Physicists might be chastened to learn how some of their latest ideas were anticipated by theologians long ago. Philosophers will doubtless be gratified to learn of the new relevance of their work in the discussion of the significance of the findings of modern science.

Finally, I would like to draw attention to the final chapter: 'Review'. This is intended as a succinct summary of the argumentation of the book. All chapters are subdivided into numbered sections, each making some contribution to the argument. Each section is summarized in a few sentences in the 'Review'. It is up to you how you use it. You might like to read it in sequence in the normal way. On the other hand, you might find it helpful to refer to it throughout your reading of the book, refreshing your memory of where we have got to at any particular point, and perhaps looking a little ahead to see where we are heading. Non-scientists experiencing difficulty with any section of the initial seven chapters can, if they wish, settle for the summary version - at least on a first reading. They can return to these sections once it has become clearer how the scientific topic fits into the later theological argument. Of course, another way of using the 'Review' is to look at it now to see whether you wish to read the book at all!

CHAPTER 2

THE VIEWPOINT OF CLASSICAL PHYSICS

A RECENT opinion poll revealed that of those people who do not believe in God, one in three are under the impression that 'science disproves religion'. Why is this? The kind of science that most people have in mind is what I shall be calling *classical physics*. Broadly speaking, it is the physics that held sway prior to the 20th century - that plus a few modern ideas such as an elementary notion of atomic structure, and the knowledge that the universe began with a Big Bang. Very little of the theory of relativity, and virtually nothing of quantum physics has yet seeped into public awareness, so for the time being are excluded from the discussion. Our first task is to remind ourselves of the assumptions that underpin classical physics, and to make clear the mindset it encourages. This will prepare the way for the next chapter in which we examine why this type of thinking, if applied to areas beyond the study of the physical world, can lead to conclusions that appear damaging to religious belief.

1. Classical physics takes it for granted that there is a physical world; this assertion goes unchallenged. It is a reality in which the setting is that of a three-dimensional space. This space acts as a passive arena, much like a stage on which a play is to be enacted. The actors in this drama are physical objects: the Sun and Earth, tables and chairs, balls and stones, human bodies, etc. These objects are distinguished from each other by the properties they possess (size, shape, position, electric charge, and so on). They generate fields of force that extend over space, and through these they can affect each other's

motion; the objects change their position with time. Time is regarded as existing in its own right. It flows inexorably, whether anything is changing or not - just as space is there whether or not there is anything in it.

Space, time, objects, properties, fields of force; granted that such types of entities exist, it becomes the task of science to elaborate on which particular objects, properties, and forces there are, and on the particular characteristics of space and time. This information is gathered together and organized within what we shall refer to as an *explanatory framework*.

An explanatory framework is an example of a language system. Language systems, or language games as they are often called, come in many forms. Each is concerned with a particular activity in life and fulfills a particular function. Some are concerned with the explanation of a non-linguistic type of reality; these I call explanatory frameworks. Thus, for example, there will be a mental explanatory framework concerned with the discussion of mental experiences, and a spiritual explanatory framework for the discussion of God and our relation to him as spiritual beings. Our present concern is with a framework for explaining physical reality.

Though it would be wrong to think that language systems in general have to be representational of features of a non-linguistic reality, the intention behind these particular systems is that they should. The terms employed in the framework must somehow be hooked onto the reality to be described. These days we know better than to subscribe to a naive 'naming' theory of language whereby a concept used in the language stands in a simple one-to-one relation with the physical object or property to which it refers. We now accept that a concept is partly read off from the reality, but also partly read into the reality as a particular way of conceptually ordering reality in our minds. However, classical physics acknowledges none of this. Accordingly, in the spirit of the current exercise, we lay aside this insight and accept the one-to-one relation. Thus, a billiard ball is said to be hard because it *is* hard; a nylon shirt on being withdrawn from the tumble drier is said to have an electric charge because the shirt really does carry a certain something extra that it did not have when placed in the drier.

The classical framework refers through *concepts* to particular physical entities that are believed to exist, and through *laws* to describe the behaviour of those entities. It 'explains' what is going on by showing how some state of affairs must logically occur, given that other events have taken place and that there are laws connecting the events. Because the laws of classical physics are held to govern immutably everything that happens, the framework describes all behaviour as fully determined. Given complete information on the state of the universe at any particular time (the positions and motions of all the objects and the nature of the forces operating between them) one could, in principle, predict the state at any future instant.

2. In order to gain knowledge of the world, one must interact with it; one must observe it. This is done through experiments. Although the scientist has thus to interfere with the world, the effects of this interference are negligible - either that, or they are of such a nature as to allow one to make a suitable correction. The equations and laws, therefore, apply to the world itself without reference to the act of observation. Accordingly, the scientist is to be regarded as detached from that which is being observed - a mere spectator of the drama.

3. The universe is to be regarded in much the same way as one would think of an enormous machine. The job of the scientist is to take this machine apart (in imagination), examine its various components, discover what each part is, how it affects its neighbours and is in turn affected by them through the operation of scientific laws. The pieces are then reassembled.

Normal everyday objects (our own bodies included) are to be regarded as composites made up from more fundamental entities. The wide diversity of materials we find in nature can be accounted for in terms of their being built up from only 92 different chemicals, or types of atom. This is a great simplification. Atoms themselves are found to consist of a central nucleus surrounded by electrons - a miniature solar system with the planets (the electrons) arranged about the sun (the nucleus). The various nuclei are then found to consist of neutrons and protons stuck together, and these in turn consist of even more fundamental particles: the quarks. So, everything is to be understood as being made up from a small number of different types of basic particle: electrons and quarks. These constituents have properties which determine the interplay of forces between them. For example, they carry electric charge and this brings about electric and magnetic forces.

The aim is always to reduce to a minimum the number of basic entities in terms of which all else is described. This applies not only to the types of particle that exist, but also the types of force. Thus, for example, there are electric and magnetic forces. Originally they were looked upon as separate and distinct from each other. Closer examination, however, revealed them to be but different manifestations of a common force: the electromagnetic force. The hope is that eventually we shall be able to see connections between all the basic types of force and, as a result, reduce them to one.

It is held that once one knows all the basic particles that make up a composite body - their positions, their movements, and the forces that act between them - there is nothing more to say about the nature of that composite body; one has a complete understanding of it.

4. Such then is the basis of the classical physical viewpoint. But there is more to an explanatory framework than concepts and laws of behaviour. In addition there are *rules of discussion*. How do these come about? In fact, they have already begun to creep in. I said just now that when one had succeeded in understanding how a composite object is made up from component parts and the forces between them there was nothing more to say by

way of explanation of that object. It might have occurred to you that there was a great deal more that one might have said. Suppose for example, the object were a violin. Does a mere description of the layout of the atoms constituting the violin really provide one with all that one might want to know about what a violin is and why such objects are made? An advocate of the physical viewpoint would rule such considerations out of order because they all begin 'Why...?' It is a characteristic of normal scientific discourse to exclude why-type questions. Curiosity about the physical world can take two forms: One can be interested in *how* things are, or in *why* things are the way they are. It is the former kind of question that is the concern of science. This presumably arises from what most people regard as the ultimate goal of science: the manipulation of the environment to one's own ends through the medium of technology. In order to change the environment one must understand the basic laws governing how it operates. Only then can one see what options are open and how they might be achieved. Hence the preoccupation with how-type questions.

Not that it is always immediately obvious what kind of question is being asked. Take, for example: 'Why is the kettle boiling?' This sounds like a why-type question. In the scientific context, however, it is not. This is because of the nature of the answer being sought - one in which we talk about an electric current passing through the heater element, how this causes the molecules that make up the element to vibrate, how the energy of vibration is then transferred to the molecules of water, how bubbles are formed, and how they rise to the surface. The answer makes it clear that, despite its opening word, the question is of the how-type. In another context the answer might be: 'Because I was thirsty and thought I would make a cup of coffee'. This is an answer concerned with purpose, with motivation. If this is the kind of answer expected then the question is indeed of the why-type, but it is not a scientific one.

Within the scientific enterprise it becomes a rule that one disregards why-type questions. There are sound reasons for this. But note the danger: If scientific ways of thought are brought to bear on problems that science was not originally set up to address - for example, a discussion of the existence of God, this same rule is liable to be carried over into the wider discussion. In this context, however, the exclusion of why-type questions might be wholly inappropriate. This is a point we shall need to bear in mind.

A second rule of scientific discourse is the assumption that all physical phenomena admit of a purely physical explanation in terms of law-like behaviour. Though currently one might not possess that explanation, there is the expectation that a physical explanation will one day be forthcoming. In other words there is to be no resort to talk of miracles and supernatural interventions. I well remember a cartoon I once saw. It showed two scientists contemplating an enormously complicated formula stretching the length of a blackboard. In the middle of the formula there was a small gap. Over it had been written 'Then a miracle occurs'. One of the scientists is saying to the other 'I think you should be more explicit here in step two'. That I believe sums up the attitude of a scientist. If the task is to understand how the basic laws of science operate, one cannot, as soon as the going gets tough, opt for the easy way out and ascribe the difficulty to a miracle. There must be the conviction that a rational, scientific description can be given to each step. For normal scientific work, this is a necessary prerequisite. But again, that is not to say that the same rule is to be carried over unquestioningly into a wider discussion of God's existence and how he might on occasion operate - a context for which the rule might not be appropriate.

A third rule is Ockham's Razor, so named after William of Ockham who in the fourteenth century was influential in helping to lay the foundations of the modern scientific approach. It arises from a guiding principle we have already noted: the search for simplicity. Not that it is a straight-forward matter to define 'simplicity'. Obviously it has something to do with invoking the least number of concepts and the least number of scientific principles and laws. But that is not to say that the simplest theory is necessarily to be preferred. Newton's ideas of space, time, and gravity are simpler than those of Einstein. But, as we shall be seeing later, Einstein's theories gain the edge over Newton's inasmuch as they address a wider range of problems - the added complexity being more than outweighed by the greater scope. So 'simplicity' is to be defined in relation to how much is to be explained. When competing theories set out to explain the same range of phenomena, however, one clearly goes for the simpler. Thus, we speak of one type of force rather than several, and a few fundamental particles rather than many kinds of object. Ockham's Razor excludes unnecessary hypotheses. It is a rule that works fine in the scientific context - but yet again, as we shall need to remind ourselves later, this does not mean it necessarily has universal validity for investigations of wider scope.

5. Such then are the rules of the discussion. They might not be specifically stated and acknowledged as formal rules, yet they are nonetheless an integral part of the mind-set of those who engage in scientific investigation. They have therefore to be added to the concepts and laws to complete the classical physics explanatory framework. Together they add up to a viewpoint that can be described as 'classical materialistic reductionism incorporating representative reality'. What does such a daunting mouthful mean? The viewpoint is classical because it does not take into account the findings of modern physics. Although it is happy to take on board the idea that atoms are made up of quarks and electrons, it does not take account of the more philosophically demanding aspects of modern physics - relativity and quantum theory. It is materialistic because it is couched in terms of physical entities only; reductionist because it sees composite bodies as nothing but their constituent parts

and the interplay of physical forces between them; it is representationally realist because it holds that there is a one-to-one relationship between the symbols appearing in the scientific equations and the features that constitute the real physical world.

A particularly extreme form of this view, but one that some find seductive, holds that eventually we shall reduce everything to a single equation, and moreover we shall at that stage come to recognize that this is the only possible equation - in other words, the world we live in is how it is because it could not have been otherwise.

Though few people would care to use such a phrase as 'classical materialistic reductionism incorporating representative reality' to describe their viewpoint, it is nonetheless how most people do regard the scientific view of the world. Indeed it closely conforms to the way many scientists regard their work. For most scientific purposes, one does not need the full panoply of relativistic and quantum mechanical thinking. In designing a bridge or sending a space probe to a distant planet, classical physics is perfectly adequate - and a good deal simpler to handle. It is a powerful way of marshalling information, the triumphs of technology bearing eloquent testimony to its continuing usefulness. For this reason classical physics and not modern physics is taught in our schools. It is classical physics that people have in mind, and will continue to have in mind, when they endeavour to think out the implications of scientific thought for other areas of human concern.

CHAPTER 3

THE EXCLUSION OF GOD

WHY does acceptance of the classical physics viewpoint, its assumptions about reality and the rules that govern its discussions, lead some to reject God's existence?
1. We begin by examining what might be said of God's role as Creator. The universe appears to have had its origins 15 000 million years ago in the Big Bang. At that instant all the matter in the universe was concentrated into a point. There was a great explosion. Today, the distant galaxies of stars are still hurtling apart in the aftermath of that momentous event. It is believed that the Big Bang marked the creation of the universe.
But why did it happen? Is this where we must invoke God? No. A physical explanatory framework - that is to say, *any* physical explanatory framework, classical or modern - takes the existence of physical reality for granted. Its task is not to account for why this reality is there, but merely to describe its structure and behaviour. Postulating God as the source of the world would, in any case, only raise another question: Why was there a God in the first place? Such why-type questions, so it can be argued, get us nowhere. That is the reason for ruling them out of the discussion. Better to accept the existence of the world as a fact - the prior assumed basis of discussion - rather than to invoke some unknown origin for it, which is then given a name: 'God'. One does not solve problems by giving them names. A discussion wholly conducted within the physical explanatory framework automatically rules out the question of the origin of physical reality. As for the argument that God is required in order that a decision be made over which kind of world it should be, that is taken care of by the extreme

view that holds that one day we shall be able to demonstrate that the world is the way it is because it is the only kind of world there could have been.

2. That is one way of excluding God the Creator. There is another: We have said that the galaxies are rushing apart. But there is a gravitational attraction between them tending to slow down the rate of expansion. Is this gravitational attraction strong enough to slow the expansion down to a complete standstill? If so, the galaxies would subsequently be pulled together into a Big Crunch. The answer depends on how much matter there is in the universe - this being what controls the strength of the force of attraction. The present assessment of the contents of the universe indicates that there is not sufficient to halt the expansion. But this is not a firm conclusion. Astronomers have the habit of discovering new types of matter out there to add to their inventory. Who knows, when the accounting is complete there might indeed be enough to apply the brakes hard enough to bring the galaxies to rest, and thereafter produce a Big Crunch. If this proves to be the case, what would happen next? It is anybody's guess. One possibility is that there would be a Big Bounce, leading to a further stage of expansion, another contraction, and so on. Our universe might be of the oscillating type, with alternations between expansions and contractions continuing indefinitely. Such a universe has no beginning and no end. Again there would be no need of God as Creator.

3. How about God, the Sustainer of the Universe? God is supposed not only to have created the universe in the first place, but actively sustains it - keeps it in being - from moment to moment.

A person of a sceptical frame of mind finds this idea equally unconvincing. Continuity of existence can be regarded as the *normal* state of affairs; it requires no agency. In the scientific equations and laws there is no term or concept corresponding to a sustaining agency. The hypothesis is unnecessary. So, one of the rules of the discussion - Ockham's Razor - gets rid of it.

4. What of the Argument from Design? The components of the animal and plant worlds fulfill their functions so well it is hard to resist the idea that someone must have designed them for those purposes. Just as the discovery of a watch on a beach would point to the existence of a watchmaker, so, it would appear, the discovery of the wonderful mechanisms at work in our bodies and elsewhere points to a mind that designed them.

This once popular argument no longer convinces. The Theory of Evolution by Natural Selection provides a satisfactory alternative. According to this theory, the physical characteristics and behaviour of animals are to some extent governed by genetic make-up. The genes are inherited from the parents, thus explaining why offspring largely resemble their parents. But off-spring are not identical; though resembling their parents and each other, they show variations. Some will be able to run faster than average, or have a thicker protective hide, or sharper claw, or greater intelligence. Others will be less well endowed. The former have an advantage when it comes to surviving to an age when they can mate. Those that succeed in mating are, therefore, not truly representative of their generation as a whole; they will include more of those that happen by chance to have a genetic make-up that confers some advantage on its owner in terms of being well-adapted to survival within the particular environment. As a consequence, this type of genetic make-up has a greater than average chance of being passed on to the next generation. As generation succeeds generation the species become better and better adapted. The end result is animals that appear to have been deliberately designed for life in this environment. But the impression is false. These animals, ourselves included, have arisen through a process of natural selection.

The mechanism by which all this is carried out is now rather well understood. The genetic coding is to be found in the DNA molecule. This is shaped like a double helix, consisting of long chains of smaller constituent molecules. It is the specific sequences of these smaller molecules that make up the genetic codes that determine the physical characteristics and behaviour. Novel codes come into existence through mistakes in the copying process whereby DNA molecules are produced for the new off-spring. Mutations can also be caused by radiation impact, and possibly other accidental occurrences. These novel codes give rise to the random variations upon which the process of natural selection gets to work. There is no need for a Designer to help this process along; it happens automatically. So again, by Ockham's Razor, the God hypothesis is eliminated as unnecessary.

The Argument from Design, having in this way seemingly been delivered a mortal blow, has in recent years suddenly and unexpectedly received a shot in the arm. Just when religious believers had come to accept that evolutionary biologists had pulled the rug from under the argument, astronomers and physicists have lately come up with indications that appear, on the surface at least, to argue towards a Mind that has fixed things. The new-style Argument from Design centres upon a consideration of those characteristics of the physical world that are the prerequisites for producing the right conditions under which life - any kind of life - can come into existence. Of course, in one sense the world we inhabit must be one in which life can evolve; otherwise we would not be here to observe it. But when one examines the conditions that the universe had to satisfy in order for life to put in an appearance, it is found that the constraints were exceedingly narrow. If one of a number of factors had been out by very much, life could not have got started.

In the first place, the conditions of the Big Bang had to be just right. If the violence of the explosion had been greater, the matter of the universe would have dispersed before the stars and planets could have condensed. If on the other hand it had been less violent, the universe would have re-collapsed into a Big Crunch before life on the planets could have developed to the point at which human beings could have put in an appearance. Between these extremes there lies a narrow band of conditions conducive to the eventual production of life, and that is where our universe happens to lie.

Secondly there needs to be a very careful balance between the values of the constants that determine physical behaviour - constants that govern, for instance, the strength of the gravitational attraction between objects and of the force between electric charges. If these had not been just right, stars of a size conducive to the formation of planets hospitable to life would not have formed. Not only that, but no carbon nuclei would have been produced. Carbon is the essential raw material out of which the basic building blocks of living matter are constructed. But on studying what came out of the Big Bang, we find only the two lightest chemical elements, hydrogen and helium. To produce carbon, these light elements had to be fused together. This is done in the fiery interior of a star. The carbon having been manufactured in this way, the star explodes spewing out the newly synthesised material. This later collects together under the influence of gravity and recondenses to form a second generation star (like our Sun) and accompanying planets (such as the Earth). The carbon on the surface of the planets is then ready to be incorporated into living tissue. It is when astrophysicists examine the conditions under which the carbon synthesis had to take place they discover just what a knife-edge situation it was. Had the fundamental constants been slightly different, no carbon would have formed, or had they been slightly different in another way, the carbon once formed would have been used up in the formation of other elements. The conditions had to be right with remarkable precision.

Thus, in a variety of apparently unconnected ways, there seems to have been a conspiracy to fix the conditions. Hence the temptation to resuscitate the Argument from Design. Not this time the design of living creatures - that much has been conceded to the evolutionary biologists - but the design of the fundamental fabric of the universe. However, before anyone jumps to the conclusion that here indeed is proof of God's existence, let me advise caution. Recently a theory has been put forward which, if correct, would account for the rate of expansion of the universe being right. I shall not go into the details. Sufficient to say that it is a candidate theory for explaining the expansion rate of the universe as a natural and inevitable outcome of physical processes, rather than something happening fortuitously. As to why the fundamental physical constants should be arranged the way they are, no-one has yet come up with a proposal. But I think it premature to conclude that there will never be a solution. There might in the future be some discovery that forges unexpected links between these constants and gives us new insight into why they relate to each other in the way they do.

But even in the absence of such a development, one is still not justified in regarding this latest version of the Argument from Design as conclusive. A counter-proposal already advanced is that our universe is only one of an infinite number of universes. Each has its own set of physical constants, and only a small proportion of the universes are such as can lead to the production of life. Our own existence as living creatures dictates that our universe belongs to the latter class.

The first worry one has about this suggestion is that there appears to be no way to test it - the universes do not interact with each other. This means we are dealing with a metaphysical speculation rather than a proper scientific hypothesis. Secondly, the invocation of an infinite number of universes is, of course, the last word in extravagance! What of Ockham's Razor now? Would not the acceptance of the existence of God be a simpler alternative? Many of us might think so. A sceptic, however, could still prefer to settle for the infinite number of universes.

5. If God's existence cannot be conclusively demonstrated in terms of his being outside the world operating as its Creator, Sustainer, or Designer, how about his

operation *within* the world? Down through the ages, when confronted with a seemingly inexplicable type of phenomenon, it was customary to attribute it to God's intervention. Thus, God was once thought of as the instigator of thunder and lightning, these being regarded as manifestations of his wrath. Nowadays we know that this phenomenon arises quite normally through the operation of electricity and magnetism. Again, it was thought that he was responsible for life - it was he who at a particular point in the history of the world injected into ordinary inanimate matter a special ingredient called 'life'. But today, most biologists see the word 'life' as nothing more than a convenient collective term for describing various patterns of physical behaviour exhibited by certain complicated arrangements of matter called 'organisms'. Starting out from simple inanimate chemicals, these arrangements of matter, and the patterns of behaviour that accompany them, have arisen quite naturally and spontaneously in the course of evolution.

In these and other ways, we see that the process of pointing to gaps in scientific knowledge, and claiming them to be proof of the working of God, is not helpful. As science progresses, the gaps in knowledge shrink. More and more of the workings of nature come to be understood as the natural, inevitable consequences of the regular operation of laws; less and less room is left in which a God of the Gaps can continue to manoeuvre.

6. There is still, however, a second way in which God could work within the world - through the interruption of the laws, that is to say, through miracles performed on special occasions. Many people point to the miracles of Jesus, for example, as proof of his divinity. The occurrence of present-day miracles is likewise regarded as proof of the on-going work of the Holy Spirit. Unlike the God of the Gaps, who was always vulnerable to further systematic advances of science and the progressive closing of the gaps, the God of miracles is not so threatened. He can intervene at will in a non-systematic way.

How ought we to respond to this? Firstly it should be pointed out that the original understanding of biblical miracles was that they were events - any events - through which God revealed himself in a particularly striking manner. God was held to be at work everywhere and at all times, but especially did he reveal himself in certain out-of-the-ordinary events. For people unconcerned with scientific questions, it was of little significance whether the occurrence violated what we would now call a law of nature. It needed solely to have been a marvellous happening - one that prompted a sense of awe and wonder, and from which a religious believer could learn something about the nature of God. Only later, under the growing influence of scientific attitudes, did it become important to establish whether miracles, besides revealing God, had also on occasion violated the newly-discovered physical laws. The word 'miracle' in popular usage came to be associated specifically with those events which, if they had occurred exactly as relayed to us through the Bible, would have entailed a violation of a physical law. The significance of the miracle story was now seen differently. Instead of it being primarily a means of learning something of the nature of God - a God whose existence was taken for granted - the emphasis shifted towards using the event as a *proof* of God's existence. The events interrupted the normal operation of the laws of nature, and only God, as the originator of those laws, had the power to do this.

Regardless of how convincing these law-breaking miracles might be to certain people - especially those who believe they have first-hand experience of them - they cannot be part of any discussion based on the physical viewpoint. The scientific enterprise is founded on the underlying assumption that the world is understandable in terms of orderly behaviour governed by laws. This rule of discussion automatically excludes all talk of miracles.

7. Finally, one might ask about the *purpose* of the universe. Doesn't God have to be invoked in this connec-

tion? No - not if one has conceded that other rule of the discussion: the one that claimed that only how-type questions were meaningful. Let us go into this in a little more detail because it is not immediately obvious that science is indeed only concerned with how-type questions. We have already seen one way in which a question beginning with the word 'Why' (Why is the kettle boiling?) is in fact a how-type question because of the nature of the answer expected. But there is a second way a how-type question can masquerade as a why-type question:

Suppose for the sake of argument you had been brought up all your life within the confines of a single room. You know nothing of what might lie outside. Being scientifically inclined you investigate the laws of nature as best you can. You discover that objects fall to the ground and you examine *how* they do this: the rate of acceleration, the effects of air resistance, and so on. But you have no idea *why* they fall; your scientific experiments do not address that problem. One day you are released from the room. You learn, among other things, that the room is situated on the Earth. Moreover, you learn of the law of gravity. You are told that the answer to your question as to why the objects in the room fell to the ground was that they were being attracted to the centre of the Earth in accordance with the law of gravity. So, in a way, the why-type question originating in the narrow confines of the room is answered in a how-type manner in the wider context. The falling objects in the room become part of a wider picture of how objects behave in accordance with a law. Suppose next you investigate how gravity varies over the surface of the Earth. You discover that the Earth is not exactly spherical; it bulges outwards at the equator compared to the poles. If the Earth were permanently and completely covered in cloud so as to exclude contact with the outside world of Sun, Moon, and stars, you might find this strange shape intriguing. Having understood *how* the distance to the centre of the Earth varies with latitude, you might want to ask *why* it varies in this manner. The answer comes one day when, at last, the clouds clear and you see for the first time the heavens passing by. The Earth is spinning. Investigation of how spinning bodies behave leads you to the answer to your original question as to why the Earth bulged at the equator. Once again, the why-type question in the restricted context becomes a how-type question in the wider context. Such why-type questions are only pseudo-why-type questions; they are really how-type questions that take on the appearance of why-type questions when one artificially constrains the situation. They are to be regarded as an indication that one ought to be widening the scope of the investigation.

But what have why-type questions to do with the universe as a whole? The universe already embraces all that is physical so there cannot be a wider physical context in which such why-type questions can be converted into the normal how-type question. An adherent to the view that all description must be in physical terms takes the lack of a wider context as signifying that *global* why-type questions have *no* meaning. They must be excluded from the discussion. Thus, the universe has no purpose; it is simply there, and that is all there is to it.

8. In these various ways, therefore, we see how acceptance of the implicit assumptions of the physical viewpoint concerning the conceptual basis and rules of discussion - particularly the rule associated with Ockham's Razor - automatically preempts the outcome of any debate on the existence of God. A discussion built on such foundations must conclude that there is no room for God.

CHAPTER 4

TOWARDS THE MODERN PHYSICAL VIEWPOINT

WE have seen how the uncritical acceptance of classical physics, and the type of thinking that normally goes along with it, appears to rule out all consideration of God. But how valid are its assumptions? What right has it to be regarded as the only approach suitable for examining what exists? Before assessing its credentials for pronouncing on realities in general, we first examine how well it accounts for its prime concern: the physical domain. In doing so we introduce the modern scientific outlook - the ideas that will play a large part in our later work.

1. As a preliminary, we first dispose of the extreme version of the classical point of view - the one that holds that eventually everything will be understood, and that we shall then see how this is the only type of world that could have existed.

At its deepest level science becomes physics. The natural language of physics is mathematics. It is impossible to disentangle physics from mathematical ideas. This being so, we can learn something of the fundamental nature of physics by studying the underlying structure of mathematics.

Historically the study of mathematics arose from observations of nature. Mathematics came to us in embodied form. But this does not mean that mathematics is indissolubly wedded to physical reality and has meaning only to the extent that it models that reality. We now know of many kinds of mathematics, most of which have nothing to do with the description of nature. One can, therefore, regard mathematics as a field of legitimate study in its own right.

In such studies, mathematical symbols are to be regarded as purely abstract; they represent nothing. The symbol 4, for example, does not mean the quantity 'four' (four apples, four pigs, or whatever); it is merely a squiggle on a piece of paper. The symbol + does not mean 'plus'. It is simply another empty squiggle - but a different kind of squiggle to 4. How do we know it is of a different kind? Because of the precisely defined rules for writing down the squiggles. A rule might say that the following combination of symbols is OK: 4+4=8; whereas the combination 4+= is not. In this way one divides up the symbols into different classes according to the positions in sequences of symbols they are allowed to occupy. Another rule might be concerned with the generation of further symbols: 1+1=2 introduces the new symbol 2; 1+2=3 introduces 3, and so on. Pure mathematics is not only abstract, it is also formal in that the validity of mathematical demonstrations lies in the structure of the statements rather than by reference to any particular subject matter. It is all rather like a game of chess, various pieces being manoeuvred according to the rules. The pieces, though bearing names such as 'knight' and 'bishop', have no actual association with those objects in real life. The names signify nothing. What matters are the rules of chess and how these govern the way the pieces are to be arranged on the board and subsequently moved about. This purely formal way of looking at mathematics is not one that commends itself to everyone, but most mathematicians see it that way.

What has this to do with our discussion? Mathematics becomes of relevance to physics when one takes the purely abstract symbols and associates them with aspects of physical experience. Thus in connection with the symbol 4 we physically indicate four apples, four houses, four blasts on a whistle, four pricks from a pin - that is to say, groups of objects such that the only property common to them all is their number. In a similar way one gives meaning to the symbol + by associating it with the act of adding objects together, and so on. The rules for manipulating the symbols are chosen to mirror the ways in which the entities in the real world relate to each other.

Not only do we need a number system for counting physical objects, we also require a suitable mathematical model for physical space; we have to adopt a geometry. This involves choosing a basic set of axioms. One of these postulates might be that only one straight line can be drawn through two points; another, that only one straight line parallel to some other straight line can be drawn through a given point. From axioms such as these, one then deduces consequences called theorems - for instance, Pythagoras' Theorem. There is no question of having to seek confirmation of these theorems from outside, by experimental observation; the internal deduction from the axioms is sufficient. Given the chosen set of axioms as a foundation, the superstructure of theorems is an inevitable consequence.

The claim that one day we shall be able to demonstrate that only one form of physics is possible entails proving that there could be only one relevant form of mathematics. But how is this to be done? Take, for example, the mathematical model of space. Is only one foundational set of geometrical axioms possible? For a long time it was thought that this was the case. Only one type of space was conceivable - that of Euclidean geometry - so physical space must be like that. But then Riemann demonstrated that one could, in theory at least, imagine all kinds of space, the Euclidean type being but one of them. For instance, one could have a space in which on leaving a given point and travelling in a straight line, one eventually found oneself back at the starting point! It is, therefore, not at all obvious which geometrical space one should use as a model for physical space. Experiments must be performed with actual objects in physical space to discover, empirically, which mathematical space is the appropriate one. And in practice, as Einstein showed in his General Theory of Relativity, nature's choice of space is not that which most readily comes to mind. Instead of the passive Euclidean arena assumed by classical physics, space is such that its properties are dependent on the nature of whatever objects are put into it. It is one of the additional spaces dreamt up by Riemann. What is true of geometry is equally true of other branches of mathematics. There is no self-evidently relevant mathematics: it is impossible by making deductions within a given mathematical structure to justify the original choice of axioms upon which that structure is built; for such justification one needs to look outside.

This poses a problem for someone wishing to argue that one day we shall be able to demonstrate that there could only have been the one form of physics. Whatever type of physics applies, we know that it will be paralleled by a mathematical structure of some kind. But the choice of axioms underpinning that mathematical structure cannot in any internally self-evident way be demonstrated to be uniquely determined. It follows that the choice of physical laws modelled by that mathematical structure also cannot be internally self-evident.

And that is not the only problem for this overly optimistic viewpoint. A recent development in the understanding of the foundations of mathematics has thrown further doubt on the claim. This has come about through the work of Kurt Gödel.

As we have already noted, geometry is characterized by a set of basic axioms, together with the theorems that can be derived from that basis. Over the past 200 years this way of regarding geometry has been extended to other branches of mathematics, including elementary arithmetic. In each case one identifies the set of axioms or initial assumptions upon which all the other true statements within that branch of mathematics can be deduced.

That at any rate was the hope. But then in 1931 Gödel derived a proof that this axiomatic approach suffered from fundamental limitations. Firstly it was impossible to prove from within the methods open to many important areas of mathematics (including elementary arithmetic), that the initial choice of axioms upon which those areas were built were consistent - meaning that they could never lead to contradictions. In other words, one could not prove that having argued through to a particular theorem by one route from the axioms, a contradictory conclusion could never be reached via some other route. Secondly he showed that, even were it possible for a particular mathematical system to prove consistency, that same system would not be complete. By this is meant that within such a system it would be impossible to prove the truth of all the true statements contained in that system. A possible example of this is Goldbach's Conjecture. This states that every even number can be represented as the sum of two prime numbers (a prime number being one that cannot be divided by any whole number other than by itself and one). Thus, for example: 4=2+2; 6=3+3; 8=3+5; 10=3+7; 12=5+7; etc. Though no exception to this rule has been found, a proof that it holds universally has yet to be devised. If the conjecture is true, then it may be one of those intrinsically unprovable statements referred to by Gödel's proof.

The problem essentially stems from self-reference. For example, consider the following:

'This statement is untrue.'

Though superficially this sentence appears to make sense, closer examination shows that it defies logic; it is nothing more than a meaningless jumble of words. The trouble arises from the way the statement refers to itself. So it is with mathematics. When one tries from within a branch of mathematics to establish the truth of all its true propositions and the consistency of its axioms, one inevitably finds that the mathematics has to refer to itself. This is what causes the difficulties, and as Gödel demonstrated, the difficulties are insuperable. Like it or not, there can be no final, complete systematization of many important areas of mathematics.

This fundamental limitation on mathematical theory - coupled with the earlier observation that, from within a mathematical structure, it is impossible to justify the initial choice of axioms - disposes of the extreme view of the comprehensiveness of any final mathematical theory of the universe, and hence, the comprehensiveness of any final theory of physics. The best one can hope for is a physics that explains the most number of things in terms of the least number of inexplainables. One's understanding has of necessity to be built on a basis that is *given* rather than deduced, and even then, it will not be complete.

2. Having dealt with this preliminary, we now turn to our main critique of the classical view of physics. We begin by taking a look at the physical objects of the world - the actors in the drama. What can really be said about them and their properties?

First we examine the ideas of size and shape. Ordinary everyday objects like chairs and cups have both size and shape. But what do these properties mean and how do objects come to have them? We have seen how objects consist of quarks and electrons. The overall size and shape of the object is determined by the arrangement of these constituent particles - how far apart they are and how they relate to each other. But what of the constituents themselves - how do they acquire size and shape? They don't! Quarks and electrons appear to be point-sized; they have no dimension, no size, and hence no shape. No matter how closely they are examined, using the most powerful tools of modern physics, they reveal no structure whatsoever.

How about other properties - mass, for example? How do we determine how heavy an object is? We might weigh it on a pair of scales, placing the object in one pan, and seeing how many weights we have to place in the other pan to achieve a balance. Or we might allow the object to collide with some other object, measuring their speeds before and after. Note that in each case one is dealing with spatial relationships. In the first, we are looking at the positions of two pans; in the second, we are observing speeds (which, of course, again involves position measurements). All mass determinations are comparative. The concept of mass reveals itself only in the context of our relating one object to another. A hypothetical universe consisting of a single object would be one in which it would be impossible to give the concept 'mass' any meaning.

How about electric charge? The electrons in an atom stay close to the atom's central nucleus; they do not drift off into space. We explain this in terms of a property called electric charge. It comes in two kinds: positive and negative. Electrons carry the negative kind, the nucleus the positive kind. We further postulate that there is a force between these charges - an attractive force that confines the electrons to the vicinity of the nucleus. The explanation sounds plausible. But note we do not at any time directly observe this extra something called 'electric charge'; we cannot look at a charged object and see it carrying something extra that uncharged objects do not have. The rationale for introducing the concept of charge is entirely invested in trying to make sense of the spatial positions of objects and how these might change in time.

And there are several other properties I could mention. Most manifest themselves only at the subnuclear level, in highly sophisticated laboratory experiments. For example, there is the oddly named property: 'strangeness'. When high energy collisions take place between subnuclear particles, some of the energy of the collision can be transformed into matter - a possibility allowed by Einstein's relativity theory. In this way, new types of fundamental particle can be produced - particles made up of quarks not normally found in nature. Examination of the collisions reveals that some of these new types of particle are never formed singly; they are always accompanied by a second newly created particle. Why? The suggested explanation is that the new particle carries a hitherto unrecognised property of matter. This property, like electric charge, comes in two forms: positive and negative. Moreover, the sum total of this property must remain constant (just as the sum total of positive and negative electric charge always remains the same). This new property is called strangeness - for the simple reason that the behaviour it gave rise to was initially considered strange! Nowadays, however, physicists are happy that they understand what is going on. Because it carries some strangeness - let us say +1 unit of it - the creation of the particle would mean a change in the total amount of strangeness, and that is not allowed. If, however, at the same time a second new particle carrying -1 unit of strangeness could be produced, then the law of conservation of strangeness would be obeyed; the net sum of strangeness would not have altered: +1 -1 = 0. So that is how physicists explain the mysterious way in which these particles come to be produced together; the solution is to postulate a new property of matter. But note that at no time does anyone observe the actual property itself: strangeness. Like the other properties we have considered, it is to be regarded as simply a convenient way of explaining relationships in space and time - in this case, why two particles are always produced at the same point in space at the same instant of time.

In this way we begin to appreciate the shadowy nature of the ultimate constituents of the physical viewpoint. They are quarks and electrons - particles having no size and no shape. Their point-like positions in space are defined relative to each other. These positions change with time. The correlations and regularities exhibited by these changes are accounted for by attributing properties to the particles. But at no time are these properties directly observed; their existence has to be inferred. All we ever do observe are spatial and temporal relationships. *The concept 'electron' or 'quark' has, therefore, to be defined through a cluster of spatial and temporal relationships.*

Such a view of the constituents of the universe cannot help but strike one as odd. At a stroke the familiar, reassuring, tangible, solidity of the physical world evaporates. One is left simply with relationships between structureless points in space and time, the constituent

particles of nature being the end points of those relationships.
3. What of space and time? The relationships we have been considering not only occur *in* space and time, but it is the relationships themselves that *create* the space and time. Consider: earlier I mentioned that the concept 'mass' would have no meaning if applied to a hypothetical universe in which there was only one object. If we now consider that object to be a fundamental particle, such as an electron, so that it has no size, then the concepts of 'space' and 'time' would also have no meaning in that universe. In order for 'space' to make an appearance there needs to be at least two fundamental particles. An imaginary line drawn between these two points will then constitute a space - a one-dimensional space - and we can begin to talk about a spatial position along that direction. We say that what distinguishes one point from the the other is a difference in the property 'spatial position'. Without the second point there would be no distinction to make, and so no way of meaningfully referring to the property. Having in this manner defined the one-dimensional space, one can now envisage further fundamental particles placed in it at different positions along the line. The introduction of a particle off the line will incorporate a second dimension of space; points can now be accommodated in a plane, as on a sheet of paper. Finally, the appearance of a point outside the plane will introduce the third dimension of space. Thus, the meaning to be accorded to 'space' ultimately derives from the relationships to be found among the point objects in that space.

What is true of 'space' is true also of 'time'. Suppose the collection of fundamental particles in space have positions that never change. Under these static conditions, the concept 'time' has no meaning. It is only when the positions of certain of the particles change relative to others, so that we go from one state of affairs to another, that time puts in an appearance. In drawing a distinction between the two states, we say that they differ in a certain property. One state is characterized by one value of that property, the other by another value. The property is called 'time'.

Thus, the classical physical viewpoint is incorrect in presenting a picture of reality as consisting of tangible physical objects situated in an independently existing passive arena of space, acting out a drama in an also independently existing flow of time. Rather, the stuff of reality is better pictured as positional relationships that alter in time. 'Physical objects' are the end points of the relationships, and the 'properties' we assign to them are defined in terms of the manner in which the positional relationships evolve in time. Moreover, it is these same relationships that give rise to the concepts of 'space' and 'time' themselves. Without the spatial and temporal relationships there would be no objects and no properties; equally, without the point objects there would be no space and no time. Objects, properties, space and time - all four are mutually dependent on each other.

This is what I call *reciprocal definition* of concepts. Recognition of one is, by that same act, recognition of the other. Each concept simultaneously invests the other with meaning. This is a most important idea which will recur later in various contexts. Thus, for example, we shall find that the definition of oneself as an individual person will depend on the simultaneous recognition of other persons; the recognition of one's innermost being will, at one and the same time, mark the recognition of God.

4. The shift towards an emphasis on relationships, rather than on things that exist in their own right in isolation from anything else, is reinforced when we come to consider two outstanding developments in modern science: relativity and quantum theory. Both theories are concerned with the role of the observer. According to classical physics, the observer is thought of as someone capable of gathering data without materially affecting that which is observed. But relativity and quantum theory show this not to be the case. The observer must be

MODERN PHYSICAL VIEWPOINT 35

brought into relationship with whatever is being studied, and makes his own contribution to the findings.

5. First we consider how this comes about in relativity. According to Einstein's theory, there is no single space and no single time. Depending on their relative motion, different people have different spaces and different times. Take, for example, a space-craft flying at 9/10ths the speed of light. According to the astronaut, his craft might be 200ft long. But according to the mission controller at Houston on the ground, as he observes the spacecraft go by, it is only 100 feet long; the length is reduced by a factor of ½. The faster the craft travels, the shorter it becomes, according to the mission controller. As far as the astronaut is concerned, the length remains fixed at 200 feet. The difference in length as perceived by the two observers arises because space (i.e. distance) for an astronaut is not the same as space for the mission controller. Only when the space-craft is stationary on the ground, so that the relative speed of astronaut and mission controller is zero, do they share the same space and agree on the length of the craft.

The same is true of time; it also is affected by relative motion. To the mission controller all processes occurring in the space-craft flying at 9/10ths the speed of light are slowed down by the same factor of ½: the clocks on board the craft, the astronaut's pulse and breathing rate, etc. This is not to say the astronaut will be aware of this strange state of affairs. According to the mission controller, the astronaut's brain processes have also slowed down by the same factor, and hence the rate at which the astronaut thinks. A slow clock looked at by a slowly functioning mind appears to keep good time. Again, the disparity between the two perceptions increases with increasing speed, and disappears only when the craft is stationary on the ground. Except for the case of zero relative speed, time for the mission controller is not the same as time for the astronaut - they each have their own.

It is not my intention to explain in any depth how this comes about; that would be unnecessary for our purposes, and in any case would take too long. Suffice to say, these various effects arise because space and time are not to be thought of as separate entities existing in their own right - a three-dimensional space, and a one-dimensional time. Rather, the underlying reality consists of a four-dimensional space-time in which space and time as we experience them are inextricably interwoven into a seamless union. The events we observe occur in this four-dimensional space-time. The vantage point from which we observe the events depends upon our motion relative to what is being observed. Two observers with different motions are, in effect, seeing the events from different points of view; for this reason the appearance of the events is not the same. Both the three dimensional spatial projection and the one-dimensional time projection will be different in the two cases. Despite these differences, however, both observers agree as to the nature of the four-dimensional 'object' they are both observing. (The situation is somewhat analogous to the way one might regard a three-dimensional object, such as a chair, from different angles. The two-dimensional projections of the object onto the respective lines of sight are not the same. But this does not prevent there being agreement over the nature of the chair itself - the three-dimensional object responsible for producing the differing two-dimensional projections.)

The relativistic effects we have been discussing, although always present, only show up to any significant extent under extreme conditions of very high speed. Though strictly speaking one's watch runs a little slow every time one travels in a car or train compared to a watch belonging to someone who does not undertake the journey, the effect is so tiny that no-one would ever dream of re-setting the watch at the end of the journey to bring it back into line with those that have remained stationary. But in modern physics laboratories where high speeds are commonplace, relativistic effects are large; physicists like myself are, in a manner of speaking, re-setting our watches all the time.

Thus we find that the concepts of time and space are tied to a particular standpoint - the standpoint of a particular observer; they cannot be defined in any absolute, independent sense; they take on meaning only when the particular observer has been specified. To some extent, therefore, an observer helps to control what is observed. If, for example, I decide to get up out of my seat and pace up and down my study, I automatically change to a different space and time. As a result, the distance between myself and everything else, as measured along the direction of my motion, instantly shrinks by a factor that depends on how fast I am moving. And I really do mean everything; distant galaxies lying at the edge of the visible universe are instantaneously closer to me now than they were when I was sitting down. Not that anyone living in such a galaxy would experience a sudden jerk in my direction or anything of that sort; it is rather that my motion has altered my conception of the distance to that galaxy. Equally my conception of time undergoes an abrupt change. As soon as I start pacing up and down, all time processes occurring in the universe are instantaneously altered. But once again, this is only according to me; no-one else experiences any change consequent upon my decision to switch to a different space and time.

The fact that the observer can in this way exercise some influence over what is observed needs to be handled with caution - especially in trying to think out the possible relevance of relativistic ideas for other fields. 'All things are relative' is a statement often intended as a well-meaning, popular summary of the theory. It sends shivers down the backs of physicists! It is potentially very misleading. The impression it creates is that of physics retreating into subjectivity: reality is what the individual decides it will be. This is not the case. Though it is true an observer's choice of motion relative to what is observed must be taken into account in a manner previously unknown to classical physics, the actual amount by which space and time is affected by this motion is objective; it is given by the mathematical

formulation of relativity theory - and the observer has no control over that. Moreover, the outcome of an observation will, as one would expect, continue to depend in part on the characteristics belonging to whatever is being observed. The time interval between two events - the successive striking of a bell, for instance - depends not only on how fast the observer decides to move relative to the bell, but in part on how rapidly the person striking the bell decides to perform the action. Thus within each spatial and temporal measurement *there is an input both from the observer and from that which is being observed.*
6. The second way in which the observer becomes an active participant is through quantum theory. Earlier we spoke of electrons as particles. There is much experimental evidence for this. For example, when two electrons collide with each other they are known to rebound from the collision just as one would expect a couple of tiny billiard balls to behave. Thus, the picture one initially has of the electron is that of a solid little ball carrying properties, such as mass and electric charge. We have already seen how closer examination refines this view: the electron shrinks to a point-like object with properties defined only by relationships.

But then, in the 1920's, there came to light a new set of experimental results. These revealed that under certain circumstances electrons behave, not like particles, but as waves - long undulating waves like ripples on the surface of a pond. This behaviour manifests itself when one examines how electrons move in space - for example, how the beam of electrons in a TV tube passes through the intervening space between the electron source at the back of the tube, and the fluorescent screen at the front. By saying the beam behaves as a wave, one means, for example, that were the beam to pass through a small hole in a barrier, it would spread out in a manner very similar to the way a water wave spreads out when it passes through a gap in a sea wall. The spreading phenomenon is known as diffraction, and is a clear indication of wave behaviour; it cannot be explained in terms of particles.

But this being so, what has happened to the particle-like nature of the electrons? This shows up at the beginning and the end of the electrons' journey through the tube. The electrons start out as constituent particles of the atoms belonging to the material out of which the source is made. Heating the source ejects the electrons; they are emitted as particles. Particle-type behaviour does not then manifest itself again until the electrons arrive at their destination - on the fluorescent screen. Though behaving like waves throughout the intervening period, the electrons hit the screen with a series of tiny impacts characteristic of a hail of particles.

How can this be? How can an electron at one and the same time be both a localized point-like object, and also a long extended wave-like object? The way out of the difficulty lies not in finding a solution to the question, but in recognizing that there is something wrong with the question itself. The study of science is simply not geared to answering questions that begin: 'What is ...?' Science has no answers to questions such as: What is an electron? It can speak only of behaviour. It is concerned with how entities *behave*, not with what they *are*. Thus, electrons behave like particles when they interact (when they are ejected from a source, or strike another electron, or when they hit the TV screen); they behave like waves as they travel from one interaction to the next (from the electron source to the screen, or through holes in barriers). As far as behaviour is concerned there is no paradox; either one is interested in the behaviour of the electrons *between* interactions, in which case one uses wave behaviour and there is no call to speak of particle behaviour, or alternatively one is interested in the behaviour of electrons *at* the instant of an interaction, in which case one is dealing with particle behaviour and there is now no call to speak of wave behaviour. It is in this way the physicist is able to keep the seemingly paradoxical ideas of wave and particle separate; each situation encountered demands the use of one or other of the concepts - never both at the same time. By the choice of question asked, the observer determines the kind of answer received: wave or particle. In this sense the physicist helps to shape what is observed. What we have been talking about is by no means confined to electrons. Light behaves in exactly the same way. While travelling from one place to another (for example, between these written words on the printed page and your eye) it behaves like a wave; once it arrives at its destination, (the retina at the back of your eye) it switches over to behaving like a particle. Wave/particle duality, as it is called, is a universal phenomenon. It affects electrons, light, and indeed everything in the world. It even affects macro-sized objects like tables and chairs, you and me. According to quantum theory any object interacting with another (my colliding with a door post, for instance) has to be described in terms of collisions between particles - collisions in which energy and momentum are exchanged. But if one is concerned with how objects move through space in between successive interactions (my passing through a doorway) then one switches over to a description couched in terms of wave behaviour. At least, strictly speaking, one ought to. In practice, where macro-sized objects are concerned, we do no such thing. This is because the angle through which an object is diffracted depends upon the ratio between its wave-length (the distance between successive humps or troughs in the wave train) and the dimensions of the gap through which the object is passing. For an object like myself, the wave-length associated with my motion is so tiny compared with the dimensions of the doorway, that to any detectable level of precision, the wave behaviour predicts that I will carry on undeflected in a straight line. This being so, it becomes natural to think directly in terms of objects travelling in straight lines (unless they are otherwise compelled to do so by an interaction). This indeed is the thinking incorporated into classical physics. It is only in the light of quantum theory we come to recognize that the underlying principle for all motion, whether of sub-atomic particles or everyday objects, is that associated with waves. The straight line behaviour of classical physics is but a particular manifestation of this wave behaviour.

Before leaving the subject of wave/particle duality there is one further point I need to make. The observer gathers his knowledge about the world through experimenting on it, in other words, by interacting with it. But interactions are governed by particle behaviour. So does that not mean the observer ought always and exclusively to find particle behaviour? In a sense, the answer is yes; particle behaviour lies at the root of all observation. Thus, the ejection of the electron from the source is an event that can be recorded - it is observed. Likewise the subsequent arrival of the electron on the fluorescent screen can be recorded - it shows up as a little flash of light, one of many that go to make up the TV picture. But what of the electron in the intervening space between the source and the screen - that period when it behaves as a wave - how is that observed? It is not, at least not directly. During that period it coasts along unseen. How then do we learn of its wave behaviour? From the *distribution* of electron impacts on the screen. We must examine how the various impacts are positioned relative to each other, rather than the characteristics of any particular event. If the beam has passed through a hole in a barrier, we find that instead of the sharp shadow of the hole expected of straight-line motion, the pattern of impacts is spread out in the manner characteristic of a diffracted wave beam. It is in this way we infer, in retrospect, that the electrons must have been behaving like a wave during the period they were not being observed. It is an inference based on the observation of point-like particle events - the distribution of many such events. So, it is perfectly correct to say that all that is ever observed directly are point-like events. These events are called *quantum events*. They are characterized by the exchange of energy and momentum, as expected of particle behaviour. The wave behaviour comes into its own when we ask, not what the events will be like, but where they will occur. Then we must switch over to the mathematics associated with waves. Whether we use the concept 'wave' or 'particle' depends upon the type of question being asked.

7. Yet another unfamiliar feature of quantum theory, and one that has excited much interest and controversy, is that it introduces an unavoidable element of uncertainty - that embodied in the famous Heisenberg Uncertainty Principle. For instance, having observed the electron being emitted from the source, one cannot with certainty predict where it will interact on the screen. According to wave behaviour, a beam of electrons will be spread out on its arrival on the screen. With a beam made up of many electrons, it makes sense to speak of a certain proportion of them arriving in one region of the screen, another proportion arriving somewhere else, and so on - in conformity with the requirement to make up the diffraction pattern. This much is predictable. But now suppose we are dealing, not with many electrons, but with a *single* electron. What will happen if only one electron is emitted from the source? Where will it go? Presumably it cannot spread out into the characteristic diffraction pattern, smearing itself all over the screen, because its interaction has by its very nature to be a point-like quantum interaction. This expectation is born out in practice; the electron arrives at one specific location. The problem concerns the choice of location. This is governed by probability requirements. These are such that if additional electrons are released from the source, each one travelling individually through the apparatus to the screen as the first one did, then in the course of time, as more and more impacts are recorded, the normal diffraction pattern builds up. The overall structure of the pattern is predictable, but the fate of any individual electron is not. Thus, in the context of quantum theory, when one speaks of waves, what one has in mind are *probability waves*. That is to say, one is referring to the need to use the mathematics normally associated with wave

MODERN PHYSICAL VIEWPOINT   43

behaviour, in order to predict the relative probabilities of the various possible quantum outcomes.

One way of trying to understand this is the following: Suppose one were to insist on regarding the electron as being at all times a particle - which is the situation in classical physics. In order to predict where the electron will be at any future instant, one would need to know both its present velocity (i.e. its speed and direction) and its present position. To gain this information it would be necessary to take a look at it, that is to say, one would have to shine a light on it. But it has already been noted that all interactions are quantum interactions, involving the exchange of energy. The action of the light on the electron is no exception. At the instant one 'sees' the electron - the moment when the particle of light strikes - the electron abruptly changes its motion because of the energy received in the collision. Moreover, this happens in an uncontrolled manner. Whatever the electron's motion might have been immediately before the light struck, it is now something different, and one has no way of telling what it is. So, by taking a look at the electron one has found where it is, its position, but not its velocity. Because one needs both, there is not enough information to predict the future state of the electron.

To get round the problem one might try changing the nature of the illumination. The impact of the light on the electron depends upon the wavelength associated with the light. By a suitable choice of wavelength one could use a form of light that would not disturb the electron's motion. In this manner one could determine the electron's velocity, the information that was previously missing. The difficulty now, however, is that such light has a very long wavelength; in a sense, it is 'spread out'. This in turn means that it is incapable of providing a precise estimate as to where the interaction with the electron took place. The price to be paid for gaining the knowledge of velocity is that one loses the knowledge of position. Again we lack both pieces of knowledge essential for making the prediction of the future state of the electron. This is a manifestation of the Uncertainty Principle. No matter how one tries to circumvent it - and there have been many, many attempts - it cannot be done. As with the ideas that stem from relativity theory, the reason quantum theory does not impress itself more forcibly upon us is that the effects to which it gives rise are generally not all that obvious in everyday life. The quantum uncertainties arising out of the Uncertainty Principle, for example, are tiny compared to the quantities that usually interest us. Thus, it remains adequate for most purposes to continue to treat the world as though it were deterministic. But strictly speaking, it is not so, and we must not lose sight of this. The lack of determinism shows that again the thinking behind classical physics is fundamentally flawed.

8. A summary of our critique of classical physics, as it has so far developed: First we noted a subtle interdependence between space and time and the objects contained in them. The basic constituents of the world, quarks and electrons, turn out to be point-like objects possessing properties that ultimately manifest themselves only as spatial relationships varying with time. These same relationships define the space and time themselves. According to relativity theory, the single, independently existing spatial and temporal arena has to be replaced by a multitude of spaces and times, the choice being determined by the observer. The very geometry of space is dependent upon whatever is placed within it. Later we saw, from insights afforded by quantum theory, that quarks, electrons, and light are not to be thought of exclusively as particles. The constituents of the world assume a strange Jekyl and Hyde behaviour: wave/particle duality. They are hidden behind uncontrollable quantum interactions. The raw material of physics - the basic data that needs to be described and understood - are quantum interactions. Moreover, interactions subject to the Uncertainty Principle.

CHAPTER 5

WHAT OF THE PHYSICAL WORLD-IN-ITSELF?

As yet we have only brushed the surface of how radically quantum theory calls into question traditional classical ideas of what physically exists. We have seen that the basic material in which science deals consists of an observer's interactions-with-the-world. The words of that phrase have been hyphenated deliberately in order to emphasize that it refers to a single entity. This contrasts with normal usage in which the word 'interaction' implies the existence of three entities: the interaction itself, together with the two objects between which the interaction takes place. But in the present context, this begs a crucial question: *Does the physical world, considered as something in its own right, exist independently of any interaction with the observer?* If we only ever deal with interactions-with-the-world, how can we, in a manner of speaking, get behind those interactions to verify that we really are 'interacting' with something, namely, with a world-in-itself? From here onwards we draw a clear distinction between 'interactions-with-the-world', the existence of which modern physics takes for granted, and the 'world-in-itself', the existence of which we are about to question.

1. Intuitively, of course, we feel there *must* be a world out there, and that its existence has nothing to do with anyone observing it. Intuition has an important role to play in science. It does not show up in the final formulation of its laws, but it does feature in the on-going process of scientific discovery. In deciding which experiments and theoretical postulates it might be productive to pursue, a scientist often has no recourse other than to rely on hunches. A physicist advocating that the ultimate goal of

science remains that of reaching beyond a quantum theoretical account of interactions-with-the-world to a description of an independently existing world, is being guided by an intuition. It might be a sound one, leading to fruitful lines of investigation; on the other hand, it might be pointing down a blind alley, creating false expectations as to the nature of the eventual explanation that science might have to offer, and leading to wasted time and effort in the search for it. How is one to judge the reliability or otherwise of this particular intuition? It is hard to say. But at least one ought to try and uncover its origins; coming to terms with how this instinctive feeling arises might give some indication as to whether it should be trusted. There could be several influences at work:

2. In the first place, we are conditioned from birth to think in terms of what happens in the environment of everyday life - a world where there is no call for the theory of relativity because all speeds are slow compared to that of light; neither is there a need for quantum theory because all objects are macro-objects for which the effects of wave/particle duality can be neglected. In other words, it is an environment that conforms to the expectations of classical physics. It is the presuppositions of that type of physics, therefore, that appear 'natural' to us.

But the environment could conceivably have been very different. Suppose, for example, the speed of light had been much smaller, say 30 miles per hour instead of 186,000 miles per second. Then it would never have occurred to anyone that there might be a single observer-independent space or time. It would be normal to think in terms of many spaces and times. The automatic resetting of watches after every journey, for instance, would be a matter of routine.

Or suppose the physical constant governing wave/particle duality (Planck's Constant, h) were much larger than it is. Under those circumstances macro-objects, such as cups, desks, and human bodies, all these would manifest the same kind of quantum behaviour at present found only (to any significant degree) at the sub-atomic level. It would be obvious to all that we could not exercise continuous surveillance of the world; rather, our observations would consist of intermittent, quantum snapshots. The discontinuity of existence of these instantaneous events might well lead one to regard continuity of existence (of inferred objects lying behind the quantum events) as a strangely counter-intuitive idea. In such an environment the uncontrollable nature of the quantum events would be obvious, the future inescapably uncertain. On passing through a doorway, one would be noticeably diffracted, and thus unable in advance to predict more than the relative probabilities of various possible destinations. The rules governing social life would have to allow greater flexibility over the keeping of appointments! Under such conditions, it would be considered odd were anyone to think of the world as consisting of permanently existing particles, moving about in straight lines in a predictable, deterministic fashion.

A brief consideration of imaginary worlds such as these, where certain physical constants assume different values, quickly highlights the importance of these constants in shaping our intuitive feel for what the world is like, and in creating certain expectations regarding the type of explanation of the world that science ought to provide.

3. A second possible reason why we incline towards classical ideas, is that our thinking about the world is associated with a special instrument - the brain. Why did we evolve a brain in the first place? Certainly not to solve philosophical problems. So how can we be sure that it is a suitable instrument for such an activity? Could it be that the very nature of the processes built into it tend to bias the conclusions of philosophical debate?

In the context of our being a particular form of evolved animal, the brain is to be seen as part of our survival kit. It is the means of processing information received from the senses, and of initiating actions in response to those signals - actions conducive to survival. Signals from the environment denoting the proximity of food, and from one's body denoting a lack of it in the stomach, initiate the action of eating. Similarly, signals indicating the presence of a predator, initiate the actions known as taking cover, fighting, or fleeing. But in order to achieve the desired ends of eating a meal, and of not being eaten oneself, one needs to know what the appropriate actions should be. How does one decide what the choices are? Clearly the brain must perform operations such as gauging the distance and direction to an object (food or predators). It must be able to work out how the situation would change as a result of altering one's distance or angle relative to the object. If the brain were an electronic computer, one capable of generating drawings of alternative views of some object, there would be no problem in understanding how this could be done. The equations of projective geometry are fed into the computer programme, and the machine works through them in order to calculate how each line of the drawing changes in length and angle as one changes the perspective. But that surely is not how the brain works. How could the complicated equations have been input? No, I would suggest that the brain has more in common with an analogue computer, than a digital one. In other words, it works on the basis of an analogous model, rather than with numbers and mathematical equations. This model consists of theoretical 'objects' set in a theoretical 'three dimensional space'. In a manner we do not understand, the brain works with this model to anticipate the likely result of taking various courses of action. In this it is very successful. But the success of the model in no way guarantees that it faithfully represents the nature of external reality. The model is an heuristic one; experience has shown that with its help one can arrive at the correct solution to the problem of how to survive - that and that alone. But, for all we know, both the objects and the space could be wholly imaginary; they could bear little resemblance to external reality.

4. Another factor contributing to our reluctance to let go of a real physical world-in-itself is our use of language. Even when discussing modern physics, we continue to use a language which was constructed with the needs of the classical view of physics in mind. Thus, for instance, at this moment I am having an experience which I have to describe as 'I see a desk'. It is an interaction-with-the-world. The very structure of the sentence, however, implies the existence not only of the interaction but also of myself and the desk. The word 'desk' appears to have a perfectly sensible meaning outside the context of a sentence such as 'I see a desk' - an impression reinforced by the fact that I can look up the apparent meaning of the word in a dictionary. How can one, therefore, possibly throw doubt on the meaningfulness of a word like 'desk', and all other words relating to the constituents of the world-in-itself? And yet many physicists are now doing just that; they doubt whether such words have meaning outside the context of their forming part of a phrase such as 'I-see-a-desk'.

Not that this is a wholly novel idea peculiar to physicists. There are grounds other than those provided by modern physics for believing that words gain their meaning from their use in the wider context of a phrase or sentence, and from the actions associated with such utterances. A well known example is the exclamation: 'Fire!' Here the word 'fire' is being used on its own, and it is obviously meaningful. But what in fact *is* the intended meaning? Does it mean 'Pull the trigger!', or 'Evacuate the building!', or 'Dismiss him from his job!' Unless we know something of the circumstances accompanying the utterance, we cannot say. But whatever the situation, we note that the word 'fire' is being used as a shorthand way of referring to a whole sentence. Thus one can argue that it is the sentence that carries the meaning rather than the individual word. Indeed, the sentence might have to be viewed in the still wider context of the language as a whole. The dictionary definition of the word, therefore, is not so much telling us the 'meaning' of the word, as indicating the way it is used in sentences referring to particular situations.

5. In summary, we find several possible sources of the intuition that there is a real world-in-itself existing independently of our interactions with it. None of the reasons for having such a belief appears particularly sound. This is not to claim that the belief is thereby shown to be false. Despite the spurious nature of its origins, the intuition might still happen to be correct. All I am saying is that if it does turn out to be wrong, we ought not to be too surprised.

6. In considering how we come to acquire this belief in the world-in-itself we have been digressing. As I said in the Introduction, the main aim of this book is not that of accounting for how we arrive at our commonly held beliefs about reality, but one of critically justifying those beliefs. So without more ado, we return to that task. Why is it that some physicists, through considered reflection on the findings of quantum theory, have come to deny the validity of this innate belief in the world-in-itself? Why do they hold that the world does not exist independently of our observation of it? The argument proceeds as follows:

The basic data given to science consists of interactions-with-the-world. These are entities such that observers themselves play a significant part in determining what is observed. This participation comes about in two ways. From relativity theory, we learn that the results of measurement depend upon the observer's choice of spatio-temporal reference frame - his motion relative to what is being observed. Secondly, from quantum theory we find the results of measurement depend on the choice of whether to concentrate on gaining precision of position or of velocity. One's own role in the measurement process cannot be circumvented; information about the world cannot be gained other than by an interaction with it, and the choice over how to interact plays a part in determining what is found. Any inferences drawn about the world from observations of it cannot be checked out with information gained by some more direct means. One is not in the position of a cartographer. He is able to verify the accuracy of the map by comparing it directly with the terrain itself. The physicist has no such independent way of examining the world-in-itself to see whether the description of it emerging from the interactions-with-the-world is a good representation or not. Any world-in-itself can be examined only *through* interactions-with-the-world; there is no way of by-passing these intermediaries.

So, what do we think we see when we try to look through the interactions at the world that lies on the other side of them? It is hard to say. Sometimes we seem to be dealing with particles, at other times, waves. But these are fundamentally contradictory notions. In quantum theory, velocity (or momentum) measurements are closely tied to wave-type observations. It can be shown that a precise value of velocity implies a precise value of the wavelength of the wave. That in turn implies that the wave train has to be infinitely long so one can verify that the distances between successive humps and troughs do indeed all have the same well-defined value. But an infinitely long wave train, by its very nature, cannot have a well-defined position; it is spread throughout space. At the opposite extreme, one might opt to measure precise position. In this case, by a different measurement process, one finds that one is dealing with something localized - an infinitesimally small point. Now, however, no meaning can be ascribed to the wavelength, there being no successive humps and troughs. These conflicting requirements cannot be reconciled. One cannot conceive of a single entity that is everywhere throughout space, and at the same time, localised at a point.

Intractable problems arise whenever one tries to visualize the world-in-itself. Essentially they originate with this dilemma of how something can be both localized and not localized. The idea that the world is made up of constituent particles - moreover, particles behaving as 'common sense' would have them behave - simply does not hold. Let me illustrate the difficulty: A beam of electrons passes through a slit in a barrier. It spreads out into a characteristic diffraction pattern on the fluorescent screen on the far side. The impact of the electrons on this screen is in the form of individual localized particles. Could the distribution of the impacts also be explained in terms of particle behaviour - the electrons having previously scattered off the rim of the slit in the barrier, again as particles? That would yield a neat unified picture. But wait. A second slit in the barrier is opened, one that is parallel to the first and very close to it. What happens? A second identical pattern, overlapping and slightly displaced from the first? No. The overall pattern is radically different. It displays a number of light and dark bands. The dark bands are particularly interesting. They show that, with the second slit open, electrons no longer go to certain parts of the screen that a moment ago were accesssible. Whyever not? Why should an electron passing through the first slit now be denied access to certain parts of the screen? Being infinitesimally small it can only encounter the one slit; the opening of the second cannot be of any relevance. But it is! The particle description is at a complete loss to account for this. It is only in terms of wave behaviour that the pattern for two slits becomes understandable. With the second slit open, waves from the second slit interfere with those coming from the first. In certain regions, humps from one coincide with troughs from the other, so leading to cancellation, and hence nothing on the screen. Previously, with a single slit open, there was but the one wave and there could be no cancellation. Only wave behaviour accounts for the distribution of electron impacts on the screen. Extended waves and localized particles - both are necessary ingredients to a description of electrons.

It is because of such difficulties, that many physicists have abandoned all hope of giving a sensible description of the world as it might be outside the context of an observation. In the above case they would say it is a waste of time trying to account for what might be happening between the instant the electron is observed to have been emitted from the source and the later observation of its interaction at the screen. The interactions are particlelike, their distribution wave-like. But this says nothing about the nature of what might exist between the interactions - particle, wave, or whatever. According to this view, the reason why paradoxes are encountered when trying to think through what happens between interactions, is that *the very conception of a world-in-itself, existing independently of an interaction-with-the-world, is meaningless.* Attempted descriptions of such an unobserved world inevitably involve a misuse of language, the paradoxes being symptomatic of that misuse. This standpoint is known as the Copenhagen Interpretation of quantum theory, so named because Neils Bohr and several other leading pioneers of quantum theory worked there in the 1920's. Today this view is accepted by the majority of physicists. Even among its opponents, it is regarded as the standard, or orthodox interpretation of quantum theory.

Let me elaborate a little more on what one means, in the context of physics, by the misuse of language. All physical concepts arise out of our description of the class of entities known as interactions-with-the-world; they do not arise out of a description of the world-in-itself. Thus, the concept 'position' does not refer to a property existing 'out there in the world' possessed by something such as an electron. It is a word that is part of a phrase that defines a 'position-type' observation or measurement. It helps to distinguish this type of observation from another which is a 'velocity-type' observation - the word 'velocity' likewise not referring to a property that exists outside the context of that type of measurement. Neither does the word 'electron' signify anything existing in the world-in-itself; it too is a word that helps further to specify a particular type of observation, for instance one known as a 'position-of-an-electron-type' observation as distinct from, say, a 'position-of-a-proton-type' one.

(Apologies for the ugly proliferation of hyphens, but they are necessary in order to make the point).

Words such as 'position', 'velocity', and 'electron', having arisen out of the context of observations, cannot be meaningfully used outside that context. Correctly used, they do not lead to paradox. A wave (or velocity) type measurement is mutually incompatible with a particle (or position) type measurement; they physically cannot be performed at the same time. Paradox arises only when the words, 'wave' and 'particle', or 'position' and 'velocity', are taken from their natural context and applied inappropriately to the gap between the measurements, i.e. to a supposed world-in-itself divorced from the act of making an observation. The trouble that one then encounters is of one's own making because of the misuse of the language.

It is so easy to succumb to such misuse. I was myself guilty of it a little earlier. Remember how I spoke of the act of observation uncontrollably affecting what one was trying to observe? I said that if one wished to measure the precise position of an electron, one had to knock it hard with an energetic particle of light and thereby could not determine what its speed was; alternatively, if one wished to learn of the speed of the electron, one had to use gentle long wavelength light that did not disturb the electron's motion - but under those circumstances, one could not learn of the electron's position. In talking in this manner I was explaining the operation of the Heisenberg Uncertainty Principle in the way Heisenberg himself first understood it. Originally he did not doubt that there was such a thing as an electron and that it did possess a well defined position and a well defined velocity; it was just the ham-fisted uncontrollable means we had of looking at the electron that resulted in our gaining only part of the information invested in the electron itself. But according to the Copenhagen Interpretation this description of the situation is a total misuse of language from beginning to end. Heisenberg was himself soon persuaded of this. A deeper understanding of the Principle comes from the recognition that the imprecision of measurement does not arise from the supposed clumsiness of the act of measurement, but from the fact that precise position and precise velocity *do not exist together* - they simply are not out there in the first place. A precise position is not something waiting to be measured, it is a *creation* of the act of observation; similarly the precise velocity is not out there waiting to be measured, it too is created in an act of observation, but this time a different type of observation.

According to this view, it does not help to postulate the existence of the world-in-itself. Classical physics dealt with a form of reality which consisted both of objects-in-themselves and the interactions, or forces, between them. It was this type of physical reality it set out to explain. Quantum theory, on the other hand, assumes the existence of a different kind of physical domain. It deals with a reality that has but one type of entity: an observer's interactions-with-the-world.

The situation is analogous to what might happen in a theatre. As we watch the drama being acted out on stage, we are vaguely aware that we are having to look at it through a thin gauze curtain filling the proscenium arch - the type of veil used by directors to create special atmospheric effects. The drama represents the world-in-itself, the veil is the medium through which we observe that world, namely, our interactions-with-the-world. Classical physics, like quantum physics, accepts that there is this veil between us and the world, i.e. we do indeed have to interact with the world in order to learn about it. However, classical physics holds that the veil is transparent so its presence can be ignored; what we see through it provides a completely faithful understanding of what lies beyond. Quantum theory, on the other hand, says that the veil is far from transparent. Peering through this partially opaque gauze of quantum interactions, it is impossible to make out all the details of what lies on the other side. Thus, if one knows an actor's position, one cannot know what he is doing, and vice versa. Not only that, but the shapes are indistinct and puzzling. Is that object over there a wave or is it a particle? Indeed, the closer one examines the stage action, the more puzzling and paradoxical it becomes. In the end, certain members of the audience - those belonging to the Copenhagen school - declare that, no matter how hard one tries, it is quite impossible to make any sense of what is observed. At least, it is impossible as long as one continues trying to understand it in terms of a conventional stage play. Thus they make their revolutionary proposal: There is no stage, no actors - only a screen with moving images on it. Once it is recognized that we are in a cinema, not a live-performance theatre, and that we are looking *at* the screen, not *through* it, the paradoxes and difficulties disappear. The magic of the silver screen!

Thus, the Copenhagen interpretation discounts all reference to the world-in-itself; it finds no value in postulating the existence of objects as they might be divorced from an observation. Such objects are redundant to an explanation of what is considered to be the physical domain, namely: interactions-with-the world and nothing more. Being superfluous, the entire conception of a world-in-itself should be removed - by Ockham's Razor.

The irony of the situation will, I am sure, not be lost on the reader. The self-same weapon wielded earlier by the atheistic classical physicist in order to get rid of the conception of God - there was no need of the hypothesis - has now lopped off the very roots of the classical physical viewpoint. If one is to use Ockham's Razor consistently, then one has to accept that as far as explaining our physical experiences is concerned, one has no more need of the world-in-itself than one had of God.

7. Not everyone goes along with this. Though the view described is regarded as orthodoxy, there are plenty of enthusiastic heretics! In the first place there is a school of thought that is not too distant from the standard interpretation. It is one that is reluctant to give up the idea of a world-in-itself, but is yet prepared to accept that quantum

theory is saying something profound about the limitations on scientific knowledge. Accordingly, while holding that the world-in-itself does exist independently of our observations, it goes on to maintain that we cannot, and never will be able, to say anything meaningful about it. Quantum theory brings one up against a fundamental barrier that will never be crossed. This is not because we have yet to perform some crucial experiment, or that the performance of such an experiment lies beyond our physical resources; nor has it anything to do with the limitations of human intelligence in conceiving of the ultimate theory. No, we are talking here of a boundary to knowledge which by its very nature cannot be crossed.

If one is for ever denied the possibility of saying anything meaningful about such a world-in-itself, why believe it is there in the first place? What advantage does this view have over the standard interpretation? Its adherents would argue that in an interaction-with-the-world, the observer knows that an element of the outcome of that interaction is directly attributable to his own input - we have already discussed this. But in addition, he cannot help but be aware that there is an 'otherness' to the interaction. By this I mean that *there are features of the interaction that are not under the control of the observer.* Thus, the observer might decide to make a precise position measurement of an electron - that much he controls; but he does not control the actual value he measures. Indeed he does not control whether it is possible to have *any* electron-type measurement at that particular instant (in common parlance, he does not determine whether there is any electron out there waiting to be measured). Or he might decide to measure the velocity of the electron, and from that calculate its energy. From a comparison of this result with previous measurements of energy, he finds that the total energy of the system he is examining remains the same - in accordance with the so-called law of conservation of energy. He is not responsible for this law; it is something he has to discover by experience. In these ways, his observations have the power to surprise him. Conscious of his own responsibility for certain aspects of the outcome of the observation, it becomes natural for him to enquire what might be giving rise to the other aspects. Thus, the world-in-itself comes to be postulated as the agency responsible for those additional aspects. This world imposes on the interactions both the general laws governing all behaviour (such as the conservation law of energy), and the contingent features (such as whether it is currently possible to have an electron-type measurement, and if so, what particular value one obtains for the electron's position or velocity). The idea of a world-in-itself acting as an agency in this manner, satisfies the intuition we all have that when one is having an interaction, one is indeed interacting with something.

By way of rejoinder, an advocate of the straight orthodox view would say that the intuition, for the reasons we have already elaborated, is not to be trusted. Certainly there is an otherness to the interactions - an otherness indicating that interactions-with-the-world constitute a form of reality that is something other than the observer. The objectivity of science, with its right to be regarded as the study of something other than the imaginings of one's own mind, is thus already guaranteed by that form of reality. Where is the advantage in postulating a second form of reality, an unknowable world-in-itself, as the supposed origin of the otherness to be found in the first? Such a suggestion will only in its turn invite speculation as to the origin of the otherness of the second form of reality, and so on. Why not simply accept that interactions have an otherness about them, and leave it at that? Such are the lines along which one would expect the Copenhagen adherent to argue.

8. A second group of dissidents holds that to claim there to be no world-in-itself, or if there is one, that it lies beyond human description, is to give up the struggle for understanding too easily. Quantum theory, as currently formulated, cannot be regarded as a satisfactory, complete theory. We must learn the lessons of history. This

is not the first time that physicists have felt they were almost at the end of the line. At the close of the last century, many held the view that science, as it was formulated at that time, was on the threshold of a complete understanding of nature. Today it is hard to credit such unfounded confidence. (Relativity and quantum theory had yet to put in an appearance!) How dare physicists make the same complacent, extravagant claims, so soon after that previous debacle? Indeed, have not the astonishing advances of the past half century in high energy nuclear physics, astrophysics, and solid state physics already proved how false these claims are? According to those dissatisfied with the orthodox standpoint, it is premature to give up the task of seeking to explain a world that exists independently of our observation of it. Despite admitted difficulties currently facing physics, the goal of science remains unchanged: an understanding of the world-in-itself.

Those who think along these lines are to be further subdivided into two broad camps: The first aims not only to arrive at a description of the world, but is intent on reestablishing strict determinism, i.e. determinism not only for macro-sized objects, but also at the sub-atomic quantum level. According to this view, for a scientific theory to be accounted as such, it has to be able to do better than deal in probabilities. As far as measurements are concerned, one may indeed find that the Heisenberg Uncertainty Principle can never be circumvented - though not all would concede that. The important point is that, behind the partial knowledge revealed by our interactions, the world-in-itself is to be thought of as acting in a deterministic manner. The earlier conception that Heisenberg had of his principle - that measurements only were subject to its restrictions, the electrons themselves possessing precise positions and velocities - would be a version of such a deterministic world operating behind the indeterminism of the observations.

The second of these camps, one to which Einstein came to belong, is not over-worried about determinism; its sole concern is with realism. Provided that one can give a description of a real world-in-itself, existing independently of the observer's interactions with it, adherents to this view would be satisfied no matter how strange and unfamiliar that description might turn out to be. While those who belong to the first camp see themselves as trying to re-establish former standards as to what is required of a good scientific explanation, those in the latter camp, in seeking scientific explanations that go beyond those of current quantum theory, regard themselves as adopting an even more radical stance than that of the Copenhagen school.

Followers of the orthodox school would counter the above by saying that their view has been misrepresented. They have never asserted that there were no more important discoveries to be made in science - that science was close to the ultimate theory of everything. Rather than claiming, like certain turn-of-the-century scientists, that science was nearing the end of the road, their contention was to the effect that science was on a *different* road to that which everyone had previously thought it was on (the recognition that science is concerned solely with interactions, not with the world itself). Moreover, there is no other road for science to be on. Therein lies the sweeping nature of the claim, and none of the recent discoveries in science have in any way shaken it. Sixty years have passed since the gauntlet was thrown down, challenging those who believed in a real world-in-itself to describe its nature; no-one has yet managed to propose a convincing model. As year succeeds year, the orthodox are confirmed in their belief that the task is inherently impossible.

9. These then are the various stances adopted by physicists in the face of modern quantum theory. Where do I personally stand on the issue? Over the years my views have shifted; for all I know they might shift again. I can tell you only how I currently feel about the situation:

I accept that all we ever deal with directly are interactions-with-the-world. There is no first-hand evidence of the world-in-itself, nor could there be such evidence. Even if there really were a world-in-itself, it could disclose itself to us only through interactions acting as intermediaries. The lack of so-called 'direct' evidence signifies *nothing*. A belief in the world, if we are to have one, must be based on *inference* - a judgement to the effect that our understanding of interactions-with-the-world is enhanced by the postulate of a further type of reality. In making such a judgement, we cannot, by the very nature of the problem, back up our conclusion with a clear, water-tight, deductive proof - the kind of proof that would convince the deliberate sceptic. Acceptance of the inference must stand or fall by its perceived explanatory power.

So, what then are the features of interactions-with-the-world, that might be taken as indicators of the existence of a world-in-itself? Attention has already been directed to the characteristics of the interactions that are not under the control of the observer - those covered by the term 'otherness'. Otherness as such, however, is hardly sufficient grounds for positing a real world. As said earlier, otherness is a property of the interactions themselves, and might not have any explanation beyond the reality domain to which the interactions belong. But this is to leave out of account a second feature of the interactions which, taken in conjunction with otherness, does, so I believe, begin to build up a case for the existence of the world-in-itself.

I refer to the discontinuous nature of the interactions. Quantum interactions occur instantaneously. Though a sequence of interactions takes a finite span of time to be completed, each interaction by itself takes up no time at all. This being so, most of the time, no interaction is occurring. In other words, apart from these isolated instances, *nothing exists* in the reality domain of interactions. So what? The problem is that the isolated events are *correlated*. The interactions obey laws. If, for example, one measures the energy of an electron, and then soon after, the measurement is repeated, one gets the same value. This is in accordance with the law of conservation of energy. But if nothing - absolutely nothing - existed in between the observations, how are we to understand how this is done? Where was the information on the energy of the electron preserved in between the measurements? It is difficult enough to imagine how the law itself, considered as a general rule of the game, is held in existence. But when one considers the contingent features of the interactions - for example, whether there is an electron around or not, and if so, what the particular value of the energy was for this electron - then it becomes especially difficult to see how this information is to be stored in the interval between interactions if, during that period, nothing at all exists. It cannot, for example, be invested in the observer because both the lawlike and contingent natures of the interactions lie outside his control. Although it might at first seem reasonable to say that the otherness buck can stop with the interactions, rather than with a world lying behind the interactions, I do not see how this remains a tenable position once one realizes that in the domain of interactions-with-the-world for much of the time nothing actually exists there.

It is the correlations manifested by successive discontinuous interactions that inclines me to accept the existence of something additional to the interactions themselves - a form of reality that possesses continuity of existence and which can thereby serve as the on-going source of information needed for the correlations. It is this additional form of reality we call the 'world-in-itself'.

But having accepted that there are persuasive grounds for believing in a world-in-itself, the next question is what, if anything, can we say about it. Personally I find the conflicting demands stemming from the problem of localization so daunting that I hold out no hope of our ever being able to give an account of the workings of the world-in-itself, deterministic or otherwise. I have no objection to others continuing the search for a description; it would be good if they were able to prove the rest of us wrong, but I suspect they are engaged on a fruitless task.

Does that mean I align myself with those who, whilst accepting the existence of the world-in-itself, assert that one cannot say anything meaningful about it? I used to think this way. However, there is a problem. We have defined the world-in-itself as being whatever it is that is responsible for the otherness of the interactions - but we are not able to say anything meaningful about it. The same idea can be expressed the other way round: We cannot say anything meaningful about what is responsible for the otherness of the interactions, but whatever it is, we call it the 'world-in-itself'. In this latter formulation it looks suspiciously as though the expression 'the world-in-itself' is little if anything more than a name for our ignorance! But, of course, as I have said in a previous context, one does not solve problems by giving them names. For this reason I earlier described this viewpoint as being not too distant from the standard interpretation of quantum theory.

It now seems to me that in order for the world-in-itself to be regarded as a meaningful concept, one has to say more about it than simply defining it as that which causes the correlated otherness of interactions. So, we have to ask: Is there anything - anything at all - we can in fact say about it? My response is a guarded yes. I believe there are a few statements one can make about its nature. They are of a very general character and not very informative. Nevertheless, they might be adequate enough for the limited purpose of endowing the concept of a world-in-itself with meaning.

In the first place we have noted that the otherness of the interactions incorporates the laws of physics. That lawlike behaviour owes its origins to the postulated world-in-itself. That in its turn, would appear to imply that the world-in-itself must, overall, be lawlike rather than chaotic. (I include the word 'overall' because from our experience of nature we know that lawlike behaviour, in a statistical sense at least, can arise out of a large number of chaotic, random processes. As far as we know, the lawlike quality of the world-in-itself that is responsible for the lawlike quality of the interactions, could be of a statistical nature, owing its origins to underlying random processes occurring in the world-in-itself.) I should make it clear that in describing the world-in-itself as lawlike, I do not mean to imply that the same laws that are operative among interactions-with-the-world also hold in the world-in-itself. For example, just because interactions manifest a conservation law of energy, does not mean that energy is conserved in the world-in-itself, or even that there is any such thing as energy in the world-in-itself. 'Energy' is a concept arising out of the domain of interactions, and might therefore be applicable only to that domain. No, what I am saying is that there is a certain lawlike character of the world-in-itself (whatever form that might take) which corresponds to, or translates itself into, the law of conservation of energy in the domain of interactions.

There is also in the otherness of interactions the element we have been referring to as contingency. Today one has an observation known as 'I look in a box and find an electron'. Tomorrow when I look, the electron is no longer there. The manner of making the observation is the same; the box is examined exactly as it was done first time, so my input to the interaction is identical. But the outcome of the observation is different; the otherness of the interaction has changed. This means there must now be something different about the cause of that otherness: the world-in-itself. Let us be clear; the interplay between lawlikeness and contingency is a subtle one. In physics one is always examining contingent events: particular particles at particular positions moving with particular velocities at particular times. There is an ever-changing variety of these events. But beneath them all there continuously operate a few simple laws. We arrive at the formulation of those laws through the study of the ephemeral, the transitory, the changing. It is from the contingent that the laws are distilled. So it must be in the world-in-itself; in addition to lawlikeness, it too must incorporate contingency. Not that this contingency must take the same form as that which appears in the interactions, any more than the laws operative in the domain of interactions must apply to the world-in-itself. Just because we talk of an electron in a box today and not one there tomorrow does not mean that we are implying that in the world-in-itself there is such a thing as an electron, one that comes and goes. Rather, there is some unknown passing contingent feature of the world-in-itself such that, when it translates its information into the reality domain of interactions, it will be manifested there as an electron-type interaction. Can we go so far as to say that if there are two electrons detected in the interaction domain there must likewise be two contingent features in the world-in-itself, one for each of the electrons? Not necessarily. As we shall have cause to note in the next chapter, under certain circumstances it might be preferable to think of the two electron interactions as corresponding to a single, common, contingent feature of the world-in-itself.

Besides lawlikeness and contingency another feature of interactions is their consistency over time. By this I mean that physics is not changing. As far as we can tell, the laws of physics do not alter; energy is conserved today, we expect it to be conserved tomorrow and into the indefinite future. We find electrons and quarks around today; we expect to be dealing with the same kinds of entities in the future. The force of gravity has a certain strength today; we expect it to be the same tomorrow. This consistency over time argues that the world-in-itself, as its source, must also be consistent over time.

The next point to note is that it appears we can alter the world-in-itself; we can have an effect on it. An observer finds that when he has an interaction, and then follows it up with a second interaction, the result of the latter can be affected by what happened earlier. Thus, for example, if he makes a precise measurement of electron velocity, and then immediately after, another precise measurement of velocity, he gets the same value. But if between the two velocity measurements he performs a precise measurement of electron position, then the second measurement of velocity is unlikely to give the same value as was obtained first time; the intervening position measurement has resulted in a changed velocity measurement. It would seem natural to conclude that the difference in the velocity measurements reflects something that is different between the two states of the world-in-itself as it was at the times of those measurements - a change that came about at the time the observer made the intervening position measurement.

Finally, one must point out that the world-in-itself is publicly accessible; the world you interact with is the same as the world I am interacting with. This we know not only because the laws you find are the same as mine, but more importantly, the contingent events you find are related to those I find. For example, if I look and see an electron in a box, I expect you to find the same; if tomorrow I look and find none, I expect you to find none. It is therefore not just a question of your world operating to the same general laws as mine; the world I interact with has the same passing ephemeral features as yours; it is therefore likely to be the same one.

There may well be other things one can say about the world-in-itself, but I think enough has already been said to make the point that there appear to be a number of meaningful statements one can make about it. Admittedly they are of a very general nature only, concerned as they are with law-likeness, contingency, consistency over time, the possibility of it being affected by our interactions, and it being publicly accessible. These are not the kinds of statements that would satisfy those physicists who continue to seek a detailed description of the world-in-itself, a description that is complete and provides a rationale for all our interactions. It is, if you like, a typically English compromise, lying between the extreme on the one hand of saying there is no world at all (or if there is one, we can say nothing about it), and on the other of saying that there is such a world and that it is the job of scientists to describe it in all its detail. It is a compromise that at least has the virtue of putting a little flesh on the idea of a world-in-itself that holds in existence the information necessary for establishing the observed correlations between the instantaneous quantum interactions.

10. Such then is the nature of the fundamental disagreements that pervade the scientific community over the question of the existence of the world-in-itself, and over what might be meaningfully said about such a world if it does exist. Normally the scientific community succeeds in presenting a united front, creating the impression that it only ever deals in incontrovertible facts, and verifiable objective truths. It comes as something of a surprise to learn that at the deep philosophical level, there are fundamental divisions, views are polarized and seemingly irreconcilable, and beliefs are stoutly and passionately defended.

But although this is so, I would not like you to get the impression that science has retreated into subjectivity - one person's views having as much, or as little, claim to truth as any other. This is not the case. Regardless of one's own favoured position, scientists are agreed that either there is an independently existing world or there is not; either it is possible to say something meaningful about it or it is not. Thus, one of the current standpoints is the correct one, the others are wrong. And that fact is not altered by our not knowing which is which, and indeed may never know.

There are surely here some interesting parallels to be drawn with the controversies encountered in theology. As we shall be seeing later, our knowledge of God (if he exists) comes to us through our interactions with him, just as our knowledge of the physical world-in-itself (if it exists) comes to us through physical interactions. Our interactions-with-God are inevitably coloured by our own input, just as are our interactions-with-the-world. How much of our interactions-with-God should we attribute to God and how much to our own making? It all hinges on the otherness of that interaction. Without the recognition of that component of the interaction that is not our responsibility, we slip into total subjectivity. Just as it must be the explanatory power of the perceived otherness of the interactions-with-the-world that finally convinces one that there is a world-in-itself, so it must be the explanatory power of the otherness of religious experience that decides the issue of God's existence. Just as physicists at this point break up into different schools of thought, so do theologians. There will be those who believe that there is nothing beyond the religious experience itself, others who are persuaded that the experiences are indicative of a God. Among the latter we shall find those who believe God to be such that one can say nothing meaningful about him, others who believe that we can say certain things about him. In discussing the various options open to us in addressing the questions of God's existence and knowability, we shall find it helpful to look back to this chapter and the discussion of the close parallels to these questions that have now arisen in modern physics. But all this is for later.

CHAPTER 6

THE INADEQUACY OF NOTHING BUT...

EARLIER I described the viewpoint we are discussing as 'classical materialistic reductionism incorporating representative reality'. We have seen that the classical materialistic concepts will not do, neither will the notion of representative reality (the one-to-one correspondence between, on the one hand, symbols in scientific equations, and on the other, entities out there in the physical world existing independently of the observer's interaction with them). How about the element of reductionism? Is it really true that having described an object in terms of its component parts, the quarks and electrons, their positions and velocities, and the forces between them (or more strictly speaking, having restructured our understanding of the object in terms of a set of individual quark-type and electron-type interactions) - having done that, have we thereby arrived at a complete and exhaustive explanation of all that could be known about that object?
1. If so, the consequences for our understanding of human existence are not encouraging. According to this view, each of us is nothing more than a physical body - a pile of chemicals. This body behaves like any other physical object; it passively obeys the laws of physics. As with any other large physical object, its future is determined (the uncertainties introduced by quantum theory being negligible). We are no different from robots. Although the body is referred to as 'living', this term is no more than a convenient way of classifying objects that exhibit a certain combination of behavioural characteristics (respiration, reproduction, nutrition, etc.). There is no clear-cut dividing line between the living and the

non-living. It is difficult, for example, to decide into which category to put viruses; they almost satisfy the criteria to be classed as living, but not quite. As for the structure of the body and the functions it performs, these have arisen from processes based on chance; only those bodies that fortuitously had characteristics conducive to survival were preserved under the pressures of natural selection, and thereby provided a base for further evolution. Thus, the development of humankind from its earliest beginnings as inanimate chemicals to its present highly complex and sophisticated form has come about purely through the normal operation of the laws of nature.

What of the ultimate meaning and purpose of human existence? According to this way of looking at things, there is none. Recall that why-type questions are excluded by one of the rules of discussion.

Our natural inclination is to resist such an assessment of human existence. Even so, it has to be admitted that certain aspects of it are to be commended. The study of human physiology, for example, would never have got off the ground in any effective way had there not been a willingness to treat the heart as a pump and limbs as levers - and many have been the benefits to flow from that development. Personally I have no quarrel with the idea that we are evolved from inanimate chemicals by chance processes, and that in physical terms there is no qualitative difference between living and non-living matter. The shortcomings of the reductionist picture of human existence lie not so much in what it says about us, as in what it leaves out and, moreover, denies.

2. There has always been a straightforward reason why reductionism is suspect: Suppose, for instance, we are examining a lump of rock. It is rectangular and has certain dimensions. We analyse its chemical composition; from this we learn why it is yellowy grey in colour. We imagine ourselves locating every constituent sub-atomic particle and evaluating all the forces

between them. Have we thereby exhausted all there is to be said about this rock? To answer this, we take a step back. The rock is seen to be embedded in the wall of a house. That is why it is rectangular and why it is the size it is - if it were otherwise it would not fit and its size would have been altered to make it fit. We take a further step back. The house is situated in the square of an old city - one subject to strict planning regulations. Only houses made of local yellowy-grey rock are permitted - that is why the rock is yellowy grey and not a red brick colour. This reason why the rock is the colour it is, does not in any way conflict with the reason given earlier in terms of its chemical composition. The original explanation is still correct. But seeing the rock in this wider context lends further understanding - understanding that is not forthcoming from a study of the rock considered in isolation. An object is the way it is not only because of its internal structure and composition but also because of boundary conditions, that is to say, the way it relates to other things - including, in defiance of the arbitrarily imposed embargo on why-type questions, the matter of its purpose.

3. It has always been easy in this way to highlight inadequacies of the reductionist approach. But a crucial body blow was delivered recently from a most unexpected quarter: quantum theory. I say unexpected because quantum theory finds most of its applications in the study of the very small: the sub-atomic particles reached only by the progressive breakdown of objects into their constituent parts - surely the quintessential example of reductionism at work. But closer scrutiny shows this not to be the case. It is a little difficult to explain, but the reasoning goes something like this:

Imagine two electrons, conceived of in the classical sense as two entities existing in the world. They collide and move apart. They continue moving apart a great distance - so great that there is no longer any mutual force between them; they are in effect cut off from each other. An observer decides to do an experiment on electron number 1. Either he can determine the electron's precise position, or alternatively its precise velocity; it is impossible, by the uncertainty principle, to measure both. Suppose he opts to measure the electron's position. Having done so, he can use the value obtained, together with a knowledge of the conditions of the original collision, to calculate the present position of electron number 2. By prior arrangement, a second observer, over at the location of electron number 2, checks this out. The result obtained on electron number 2 confirms the prediction made by the first observer on the basis of the measurement on electron number 1. As an alternative, the first observer could have opted to measure the velocity of electron number 1. In this case the value found would have allowed him to calculate the velocity of electron number 2. Again, the second observer could have confirmed the correctness of the prediction.

Thus, electron number 2 seems to 'know' how to respond to whatever measurement is to be carried out on it. How does it do this? The electrons as they move apart from the collision cannot know in advance what type of measurement is to be made. Moreover, it can be arranged for the confirmatory measurement on electron number 2 to be carried out so swiftly after the occurrence of the measurement on electron number 1 that no information as to the nature of that first measurement could be conveyed to electron number 2 in time for it to affect the outcome of the second measurement.

The obvious way round the problem - the classical answer to it - is that the second electron leaves the collision armed with full knowledge of both position and velocity - in other words, the electron *has* both a well-defined position and a well-defined velocity. It is thus ready for any eventuality. But this suggestion goes against the view of most physicists. They hold that the significance of the uncertainty principle is not so much that one is unable to measure both the precise value of the position and the precise value of the velocity, but that a precise position combined with a precise velocity do not *exist* together. So, could it be that the situation described above proves that this view is wrong and the classicists were right after all?

Fortunately there is a practical way of deciding the issue one way or the other. Not so fortunate is the fact that it is extremely difficult to describe adequately to a non-scientist the nature of this experimental test. The explanation necessarily involves detailed argumentation and a mathematical treatment. But briefly, the experiment consists in studying a large number of events. This is done with one's detecting apparatus set at a variety of orientations. A statistical analysis of results gained at the different orientations allows a determination of whether or not one is dealing with two isolated electrons, each possessing full information on its own position and velocity independently of what might be happening to the other electron. The result? The angular correlations show that the electrons are *not* independent of each other. It is *not* the case that the first observer is interacting with one physical system (electron number 1), and the second observer is interacting with a different physical system (electron number 2). In truth both observers interact with the *same* physical system - one in which electron number 1 and electron number 2 are inextricably bound up with each other as a two-electron system, rather than each existing as separate, autonomous one-electron systems. The reason that the measurement made by the second observer confirms that made by the first is not that some ghostly message has been passed from one system to the other; it is because both observers have interacted with one and the same system, and all the information needed is somehow invested throughout the whole system and not shared out piece-meal among its component parts.

All of which is nothing short of amazing. This experiment has only been carried out in recent years. But it has already been repeated a number of times and seems to be right in its conclusions. Physicists are still trying to come to terms with it. What is so difficult to understand is the nature of whatever it is that is responsible for 'cementing' the two electrons together into a single system; certainly no physical force (gravitational, electrical, etc.) can be regarded as the agency. How is it that something happening in one location can have an immediate consequence for something happening at a distant location? Instantaneous communication defies one of the consequences of relativity theory: nothing can travel faster than the speed of light.

The conflict with relativity turns out to be more apparent than real. What relativity denies is the possibility of being able to transfer energy from one place to another instantaneously. Radio and sound signals, for example, entail the transfer of energy, so are subject to this restriction. But in the experiment we are considering, once the electrons have physically separated from each other, no energy is being transferred between them; the requirements of relativity, therefore, are not being violated. Yet 'information' of a sort does seem to pass, and we are left with the question of how to account for it.

The resolution of the problem, it would seem to me, can only be sought through drawing a clear distinction between what happens in the reality domain of physical interactions, and what happens in the domain of the world-in-itself. Relativity theory applies to the domain of interactions. It is based on the concepts of space and time and these, like all our other physical concepts, apply to the reality domain in which science deals, namely, interactions-with-the-world. The concepts, and the theories in which they are embedded, such as relativity theory, apply to this domain. They do not necessarily apply to any world-in-itself that might lie beyond those interactions. It could well be that space and time as incorporated into the theory of relativity do not exist as such in the world-in-itself. Belief in a world-in-itself entails no more than the acceptance that certain states of affairs in that domain translate themselves into phenomena in the domain of interactions that we recognize in the latter as measurements taking place in space and time. As for the measurements in the experiment we have been considering, just because they are spatially isolated from each other and no forces operate between them, does not deny the possibility that they continue to relate to each other through their being associated with one and the same entity existing in the world-in-itself. You will now appreciate why earlier, when talking about what might be said concerning the characteristics of a world-in-itself, I was reluctant to accept that two electrons in the domain of interactions-with-the-world would necessarily correspond to two contingent entities in the world-in-itself. I had in mind this experiment which could well be indicating that, under certain circumstances (for instance, those where a prior collision of the two electrons has taken place), a single contingent feature of the world-in-itself can be associated simultaneously with two spatially separated phenomena in the domain of interactions. The 'cement' binding the two isolated events together is, therefore, not to be found within the domain of interactions, and it is fruitless to search for it there. Rather, it resides in the manner in which these two events relate out of the domain of interactions to a single common entity in the other domain of reality.

We shall be saying more about how one reality domain relates to another in Chapter 10. There we shall introduce the concept of a mapping link between reality domains - an idea that might assist you to gain a firmer grasp on these difficult matters. As for the relevance of these physical concerns to our overall argument about God, we shall see in Chapter 17 how they provide a powerful analogy for illuminating the Christian doctrine of the Trinity. As in the case of the two electrons, we shall there be faced with the problem of trying to understand how individuals (the three Persons of the Trinity), despite their manifest distinctness, are yet to be regarded as one (the One God). Again we shall find the answer to lie in the recognition of there being two reality domains - in this case, two spiritual reality domains, one to do with interactions-with-God, the other with God-in-himself. In the first of these domains, God is represented as three 'individuals', in the second he is unitary. The link between the Persons in the one domain is forged through their mapping to the One God in the other. But again we must not get ahead of ourselves. I mention this only to reassure you that these deep and rather daunting physics questions do have relevance for our later discussions of theology.

4. To summarize this chapter, we began by noting that the reductionist sees a composite object as consisting of nothing but its constituent parts held together by forces, all of which can be accounted for in physical terms. But there have always been deficiencies in this approach - especially when the reasonableness of excluding the why-type questions is challenged. Now there has emerged an additional reason for dissatisfaction with this viewpoint. Quantum theory shows that the very simplest composite system imaginable - namely, two physically isolated fundamental particles - this simplest of all composite systems is emphatically *not* simply one particle and its properties added to the other particle and its properties. In addition there is a connectedness that results in the whole being different from the sum of its individual parts.

If this is true of two electrons with no physical force operating between them, how much more must it be true of the human body - a physical system of great complexity consisting as it does of a vast number of fundamental particles, all of them inextricably bound together by physical forces. Note further that quantum theory is holistic not only in the sense that it can bind together two apparently physically isolated electrons into a single two-electron system, but also in the sense that even this combined two-electron system is not to be considered in isolation - it can only be meaningfully spoken of in the context of how it further relates to an observer.

So to the previously described deficiencies of the classical viewpoint, we now add those associated with its reductionist features.

CHAPTER 7

THE EXCLUSION OF THE MENTAL

THERE really is very little left to say in favour of the view with which we began. Not a single feature of it has withstood criticism. But have we been entirely fair to the person who wishes to adopt an exclusively scientific outlook on life? After all, it could be argued that the viewpoint we have been examining is particularly simplistic - a mere Aunt Sally. Agreed it is the one a layperson generally has in mind when arguing that 'science disproves religion'. For that reason it merited attention. But it is not the view of someone who is acquainted with modern science. Suppose one were now to take into account all that has so far been said: one accepts the findings of relativity and quantum theory, attaches the concepts of space and time to particular observers, deals in interactions rather than entities in themselves, and adopts a suitably holistic rather than reductionistic approach. Could one not in *those* physical terms yet arrive at an explanation of all that there is - an explanation that would still not require the hypothesis of God or of anything other than that which belongs to scientific study?
1. We have already begun to cast doubt on whether a purely scientific way of thinking can adequately account for everything we want to know about reality. The mention in the last chapter of planning permission being the reason why house bricks were of a certain colour clearly took the discussion outside the realm of pure physics. And why not? The ban on questions beginning 'Why...?' might well be justifiable in the specific context of progressing scientific understanding, but where is the justification for making it a universal rule of discus-

sion? If science cannot handle such questions, perhaps other forms of discourse can.

There is to my mind a further and convincing reason for holding that a discussion founded on the prior assumption of physical entities alone can never be a complete description of all that there is: the fact that I have mental experiences. I experience love, pain, and anger; I make decisions. Of this I can have no doubts. But, granted that one starts out by assuming the existence of nothing more than physical interactions involving quarks and electrons, how is talk of mental experience to be incorporated? There is nothing arising from the laws of physics to indicate that a particular collection of such interactions - those attributed to my physical body - are anything special. Why should they be associated with consciousness? Yet I *am* conscious, and any outlook that does not encompass that fact, cannot be regarded as all-inclusive. And if such a viewpoint is unable to embrace mental experience as an integral part of its description of what exists, how is one supposed to take seriously its claim to be able to rule on the question of the existence of other possible non-physical realities, in particular, the existence of God?

But is it really true that the physical viewpoint cannot take account of consciousness? Let us look into this in more depth:

2. Certainly the outlook does not look promising. Take, for example, the argument one often hears as to whether a robot fitted with a computer could, one day, reach such a level of sophistication that it would be able to experience feelings and emotion. We imagine it being built to duplicate everything a human body does. It responds to the environment and to stimuli in exactly the way we do. When asked, 'Are you conscious?' it replies 'Yes, of course I am'. It replies in this manner because it has previously been programmed to respond to the recognised speech pattern in that way - just as you and I from an early age have been programmed, or taught, to do. When struck a blow, the robot cries 'Ouch!' It does this because

a pressure transducer detects the impact, sends an electrical signal to the central processor, this automatically initiates a sub-routine which ultimately causes a loud speaker to emit the appropriate sound - just as we emit the identical sound when struck a severe blow. But this is not to conclude that the robot actually *felt* anything - i.e. experienced a pain. Everything is perfectly understandable in terms of electromagnetism and mechanics; there is no *need* to invoke consciousness.

Speculating as to whether robots could be conscious, and if so, at what level of computer sophistication consciousness puts in an appearance, is but a modern variant of a much older problem: the status of animals. It has long been an open question as to whether animals are self-aware and experience anything. What of a worm that is cut in two? It writhes about as though in agony. But is it really in pain? Cut the worm up into several sections, prior to feeding it to the goldfish, and all its sections writhe. Does each section of the worm have a mind experiencing pain? Or are we witnessing mere muscular spasms initiated by certain electrical currents induced by the act of cutting? There is no way of finding out - short of being the unfortunate worm. Many have wrestled with this problem, but a watertight proof that animals have mental experiences has yet to be devised.

And what applies to the minds of animals, applies even to the minds of other human beings! As we shall be seeing in Chapter 11, if one adopts a deliberately sceptical stance, the best one can do in determining whether there are minds other than one's own is to argue by analogy: My mind is somehow associated with my body. I see other bodies like mine, so it becomes reasonable to assume that they too are associated with minds. In addition one can argue on the basis of information one receives from the supposed other mind. Someone says 'Watch out! That kettle is hot'. I stupidly ignore the warning, touch the kettle, and suffer pain. It seems reasonable to assume that the source of this information about a mental experience was a mind like mine - particularly as there appears to be no reason for assuming otherwise. But none of this constitutes *proof*; all the behaviour we observe is physical behaviour and so could conceivably have been reproduced by unconscious matter.

3. This lack of success does not stop some people from retaining the hope that one day, eventually, the study of physical behaviour will yet reveal consciousness to be an inescapable feature of matter organized at some high level of complexity and sophistication. They speak of consciousness as an 'emergent property'. What does this mean?

Consider an atom. By itself it cannot be regarded as either a solid or a liquid or a gas. Put lots of atoms together, however, and they will interact on each other with forces. If these are sufficiently strong the ensemble will be rigid and we will regard it as a solid. If on the other hand the forces are weak, so that the ensemble cannot resist deforming forces, we regard it as a liquid; weaker still and it becomes a gas. Thus the property 'solid', 'liquid', or 'gas' characterises the ensemble; it does not apply at the level of the individual atom. It has emerged out of the ensemble at the higher level of complexity.

Or take the case of temperature. As you sit here reading this book you are surrounded by air. It is hot, warm, or cold - it has a temperature. But what is temperature? Air is made up of molecules. These move about in random directions with a range of different speeds. The temperature of the air is based on a certain average value of these speeds. At any given instant, each molecule will have a particular speed; it can be moving fast or slow. A short while later, because of collisions that have meanwhile taken place with other molecules, it is likely to have changed its speed. The average speed of all the molecules, however, will not have altered; the temperature remains the same. The decision as to whether to turn up the heating rests not with what has happened to an individual molecule; it is the temperature that counts - hence the usefulness of the concept. Note that the idea of temperature does not apply to the individual molecule; it is an average, and averages imply more than one value of the property to be averaged. It is to be regarded, therefore, as an emergent property, like liquidity and solidity.

Life, as we have already seen, is yet another example of an emergent property. In earlier days there were arguments as to whether the difference between living and non-living matter derived from the former having some special ingredient that the latter did not have, an ingredient derived directly from God. This so-called vitalist viewpoint has now been more or less abandoned by biologists. Instead, they regard 'life' as a convenient term for describing a certain set of complex behavioural characteristics. It can be applied, therefore, only to a large collection of chemicals; it has no meaning at the level of the individual atom.

These then are various examples of what one means by an emergent property. Materialists argue that the concept of mind is but a further example. They hold that the study of the chemical structure and operation of the brain will eventually lead to an understanding of mind.

Plausible though this approach might seem at first sight, it suffers from an important defect. By this I do not mean the purely practical difficulties involved in relating particular brain functions to particular mental experiences. These are undoubtedly severe, there being some 10,000 million nerve cells in the central nervous system, each with many connections. Keeping track of the detailed electrical and chemical activities occurring at all these junctions is likely to remain forever beyond our capabilities. But for the purposes at hand that does not matter; in principle, it could be done.

That being the case, one can imagine taking each mental activity - be it the experiencing of a pain, having a brainwave, loving, hating, choosing a course of action, praying, or whatever - one takes each of these mental activities and correlates it to the appropriate pattern of physical activity occurring in the brain. We assume that to every mental state there is a corresponding physical state, and that we are able to discover which corresponds to which. The question is: Having done this, has one thereby *explained* mental phenomena in physical terms? No. The problem lies in the manner in which the association of mental to physical states has to be carried out. One cannot look down a microscope at the physical processes occurring in the brain and observe the thoughts and feelings that go along with them; one sees only the physical processes. The association is done by observing the state of the subject's brain and then asking him what he is thinking at that particular instant. In other words, the information on the mental state has to be injected from *outside* physics. Admittedly, once the correlation between a particular brain state and a particular mental state has been established in this way, one can then learn something about mental states through the study of brain states. Thus, if one recognizes the same brain state repeated on a future occasion, one can immediately anticipate what the mental state will be. But in order to do this, the correlation does need to have been established on a prior occasion, and as we have seen, this is by a purely empirical process rather than one involving some inevitable consequence of the physics of the situation.

Herein lies the reason why it is invalid to treat mental phenomena as though they belong to the class of emergent properties. Solidity, temperature, and life are *defined* in terms of physical behaviour and physical structures. As we have learnt, when a physicist speaks of the temperature of the air, he has in mind a formula incorporating a particular average speed of the molecules; the temperature is nothing more than that - a convenient label to attach to a certain average physical behaviour of an ensemble of molecules. Likewise, in biology, life is a term that refers to patterns of physical behaviour that are often found occurring together; it too is a useful label for behaviour manifested by certain ensembles of molecules (living organisms). It is because these concepts allow us to speak conveniently of the physical behaviour, structure, and interrelationships manifested by ensembles, that they become an integral part of the physical explanatory framework.

But in speaking of consciousness we are doing more than use a convenient shorthand way of referring to the physical behaviour of complex systems. It is true that human bodies repeatedly manifest the same combinations of behaviour characteristics, so much so that it is convenient to use a single word to refer to the whole combination of characteristics. Thus, for example it is found that an elevated blood pressure, a high pulse rate, heavy breathing, dilation of the pupils of the eye, perspiration in the palms of the hands, a tightening of the stomach muscles, an increase in the flow of adrenaline, and several other effects, generally occur at the same time. Accordingly, this combined behaviour comes to be associated with a single all-embracing word - fear. But the prime intention lying behind the use of this term is not that it should refer to physical behaviour. Rather, it denotes the mental state that accompanies such behaviour. Behaviour and emotion generally go together, so that the former comes to be regarded as a natural expression of the latter, and an integral part of what is meant by 'fear'. But they need not: A brave person can be fearful, without betraying it in outward behaviour; an actor on stage can simulate fear, without feeling it. A distinction must, therefore, be drawn between the two, with the recognition that physics has nothing to say about the mental experience.

I suppose in one sense it could be argued that consciousness *is* a kind of emergent property. Looking back over the course of evolution, one can infer that it is quite likely that consciousness arose in conjunction with the increasing complexity of the human brain. In that sense it has 'emerged'. But this is not to say that it is an emergent property in the sense relevant to our discussion. Just because it arose as a *correlate* to the increasing complexity of physical processes in the brain, does not mean that it has to be *equated* to the complexity of those processes. But more of this in the next chapter.

4. There is yet another way in which one might hope to bring the mind within the scope of scientific description. This approach is often referred to as an 'interactionist' approach; it envisages the mind as somehow interacting with matter, and making its presence felt in that way.

Take for example the raising of my arm. How are we to account for this action? One alternative is to claim that the various processes going on in my brain are no different from processes occurring in inanimate matter. They are invariably governed by the laws of physics. In the course of time, this brain activity leads to electrical and chemical changes elsewhere in the body, culminating in the contraction of a muscle and the raising of the arm. That is the explanation. It so happens that the brain activity is accompanied by thoughts to do with deciding to raise one's arm, and subsequently those of being aware that the arm is going up. But this is by the way; the physical action of the arm can be comprehensively accounted for purely in physical terms and in accordance with the normal operation of the laws of physics.

That is one point of view. An interactionist sees the situation differently: The thoughts in the mind directly affect the physical working of the body and must be included in the physical description. Thus, while the arm lies still, we can think of the physical processes in the body proceeding in accordance with the normal laws of nature. But suddenly, the orderly sequence is interrupted; the arm starts to rise. What has happened? A mental decision has been made to raise the arm. This thought intrudes into the physical domain and affects the physical state. It brings about a break in the physical causal chain.

A modern variant of this interactionist viewpoint invokes quantum theory. Heisenberg's uncertainty principle, as we have seen, offers some leeway on how future events will develop; it is possible to predict only the relative probabilities of various allowed outcomes. A suggestion has been made that the mind might be able to take advantage of these uncertainties to distort the statistical probabilities in such a way as to change the outcome from that which would probably have resulted on the basis of normal statistics. In this way one could allow the mind to exert an influence on the physical world without violating a physical law; it is behaviour permitted by quantum theory.

Regardless of which of these two procedures the mind might adopt - the interruption of an otherwise predictable chain of events, or the use of quantum uncertainties - its effects would be verifiable. In the latter case, although individual events would not be other than that permitted by the quantum uncertainties, the study of a large number of events could betray the operation of peculiar statistics. Close study of the physical processes should, therefore, reveal that some new agency had come into play. In this way an examination of physical processes could reveal the action of the mind.

To date no convincing evidence has been found that the mind does intervene in either of these ways. Not that this is a strong statement; I am unaware of any work at the sub-microscopic level capable of revealing whether or not brain processes do sometimes fail to follow normal physical laws. But, even supposing, for the sake of argument, one were to discover such an agency at work, what then? What does this tell us about the mind other than it is some otherwise unknown agency that distorts the operation of normal physics? It does not tell us that it is an entity associated with experiences of emotion, pain, love, etc. It would simply manifest itself as a new physical force of some kind.

Finally, I ought to mention a version of the interactionist argument in which the mind is thought of as an agency interfering with the physical, not in any specific and particularised way, but rather through the exercise of a general holistic control over the totality of events. The suggestion at first sounds persuasive. After all, we have earlier noted that two colliding electrons can exhibit a form of connectedness that is not associated with any physically recognisable force. Could not the mind reveal itself through such a connection? It would appear not. The physicist, in adopting a holistic approach to the electrons - treating them as a single system of two electrons, rather than as two isolated systems each consisting of one electron - is in no way implying that the electrons are conscious, or are exerting telepathic powers on each other, or anything of the sort. All that has been shown is that the purely physical behaviour of matter can be sometimes holistic rather than reductionistic. It says nothing about whether matter organised in one way has consciousness, whereas organised in some other way it does not.

5. In summary, there appears to be no way that an explanatory framework relying exclusively on physical concepts and physical laws as its assumed basis, can demonstrate the need for there being mental experiences. For mental experiences to put in an appearance they would have to arise as a natural and inevitable consequence of physical behaviour. They do not. A disembodied intelligence contemplating our universe from some other realm, so to speak, could conclude that a purely physical description of it perfectly accounted for everything observed down to the smallest detail. There would be no need to include the extra hypothesis of consciousness.

So, according to the rules of the game, Ockham's Razor must put in yet another appearance. The last time it was used, you recall, it got rid of the world-in-itself. That was distressing for classical physicists, to say nothing of those modern physicists reluctant to go along with the standard interpretation of quantum theory, but it was a matter of no concern to Copenhagen adherents. But when the desire for economy gets rid of consciousness, then surely we are all agreed: something is wrong! Though, from the point of view of physics, consciousness is an 'unnecessary' extra, it is something we do nevertheless happen to have. Any world-view seeking to explain all that exists must be equipped to take it on board.

6. So, our critique of the physical viewpoint - both that based on classical physics and that which incorporates modern physics - at last draws to a close. For all its undoubted value as a source of understanding, one has to accept that as an explanatory framework, its scope has its limitations. There are realities, such as consciousness, that lie outside its domain and about which it is able to say nothing. There are why-type questions and questions to do with feelings, motivations, values, etc., that physics is powerless to address. This being so, it is impossible to take seriously the claim that science has, or will one day have, all the answers. In particular, it is absurd for anyone to assert that 'science has disproved God's existence'. This it could never do.

CHAPTER 8

EXPLANATORY FRAMEWORKS

WE have now reached the point where we can begin to address our main task: how belief in God's existence might be justified. As indicated in the Introduction, this is to be done in the context of how one might similarly attempt to justify beliefs in other aspects of human existence - physical and mental.
1. We have in mind the challenge posed by a sceptic. But first it must be recognized that even the toughest sceptic cannot adopt a position of initially assuming the existence of nothing. Any attempt to understand and explain what exists is *in itself* a mental activity. Understanding is always understanding as it is for a conscious being. The mere fact that one is engaged in discussion at all has already subsumed an implicit assumption that mental occurrences exist.

So let us take our cue from this and make our prior assumption: There is a mental reality. Instead of starting with the physical domain, as we did in the earlier chapters, we now try to build up an understanding of what exists on a foundation of mental experience. The contents of one's mind have long been held to constitute the only reliable basis from which to start a discussion of what else might exist. Thoughts alone are given in direct awareness, so only they are beyond doubt. Other types of existence cannot be got at directly; they must be inferred.

On the face of it, the position appears reasonable. An understanding of what exists must clearly be grounded somehow in experience - conscious mental experience. Our perception of what exists is constantly being reworked in the light of experience. But does that mean that a person's mental experience constitutes a raw set of

EXPLANATORY FRAMEWORKS

empirical data, uncontaminated by any prior assumptions of the existence of anything other than the experiences themselves? For a long time this was accepted without question. Further reflection, however, discloses this to be most unlikely. For example, when we think of our mental experiences we conceptualize them. We distinguish one from another, we categorize them, and relate them to each other. Some are regarded as 'sensory observations', others as 'emotional experiences', others as 'decision making', etc. Concepts such as these belong to the language of an explanatory framework - that which we shall be calling the mental explanatory framework. But language, *any* form of language, arises from social interaction (a topic to be pursued later). The mere fact that one is structuring one's thinking about mental experience in this manner, therefore, could mean that one has from the outset unknowingly smuggled into the argument certain additional presuppositions - those to do with the existence of people other than oneself, to say nothing of the physical interactions by which social interaction is mediated. Whether it is possible, even in principle, to isolate a set of empirically given data free from all assumptions about other realities turns out to be highly problematic.

But, for the purposes of the present argument, let us lay aside these reservations. Provisionally at least, we concede to the sceptic his traditional starting position: he may take for granted the existence of his own mental reality and nothing more. The question then becomes: On such a basis, what might be concluded about the existence of other types of reality? Because the starting point involves a mental reality, the discussion begins within the mental explanatory framework. This is not to say that we have finished with the physical framework. It will again put in an appearance at a later stage. Anticipating the way the argument will develop, we shall there find that the way of handling different types of reality is to make use of *several* explanatory frameworks. Explanatory frameworks and the distinctions between them will assume increasing importance. So much so, I propose to devote the rest of this chapter to clarifying the nature of frameworks in general, and their relation to the reality domains to which they refer.

2. An explanatory framework is built on the prior acceptance of a certain kind of reality. As far as this framework is concerned, all discussion takes it for granted that there is such a type of reality. No attempt is made to describe the ontological nature of this reality - the essence or 'stuff' of which it consists. A metaphysical discussion of the underlying essence of a mental experience, or a physical particle, or an interaction-with-the-world, or God, is fruitless and possibly meaningless. We are concerned not with what the reality *is*, but how it operates, how one aspect of that reality relates to another. In the classical physics framework, for example, no attempt was made to explain what a material particle, or electric charge, or force, or space, or time was in itself; one came to understand what these terms meant from the way they were used in relation to each other and to experimental observation. Always with explanatory frameworks one is devising explanations in terms of basic concepts which themselves refer to that which is intrinsically inexplicable. The fact that the whole system of explanation is thus founded upon basic entities that are inherently inexplicable throws doubt on whether it truly *explains* anything. It might be more appropriate to speak of such frameworks as 'interpretive' rather than 'explanatory' frameworks. However, we shall stick with the present terminology.

Because the framework takes for granted its underlying type of reality, the existence of that reality can be called into question only from within some other framework - one based on the prior assumption of a different domain of reality. Ultimately, the justification for *all* assumed existences refers back to the domain of conscious mental experience. In the final analysis, explaining conscious experience is what it is all about. So, for example, we shall be seeing how certain mental experiences (those associated with the senses) have features about them that cannot be satisfactorily explained without the assumption of there being a non-mental type of reality - the physical domain. Similarly there are aspects of conscious experience that most readily lend themselves to explanation in terms of there being an unconscious part of the mind, and others that indicate that there is a spiritual domain. Unlike talk about the essence of a reality, an argument conducted within the framework associated with one type of reality as to the need to postulate the existence of some further type of reality is to be accounted a legitimate form of metaphysical discussion.

An explanatory framework consists of concepts and procedures for handling those concepts, together with rules of discussion. We have already dealt at length with the last of these. We saw that explanatory frameworks are set up to address certain questions, and the rules of discussion facilitate the finding of answers to those questions. But at the same time, these rules, if strictly adhered to, can exclude the consideration of other questions that might be equally important.

The concepts are intended to signify particular features of the assumed reality. In the scientific context these might include the concepts 'particle' or 'interaction-with-the-world', depending on which variety of physical framework, classical or quantum mechanical, is involved. In a psychological or mental explanatory framework, the assumed reality would consist of mental experiences, and the concepts would refer to mental processes, such as feeling an emotion, hearing a sound, having a brainwave, and so on.

The procedures for handling the concepts are intended to reflect, in some fashion, the manner in which the features of the reality relate to each other. In terms of scientific discussion, these procedures are to be identified with the laws of nature. In the mental framework, though it is not customary to think of 'laws' operating, nevertheless, there are ways in which the individual mental experiences relate to each other - they occur in temporal sequence; the quality of an experience will be affected by whether one has had a previous experience of a similar nature; past experiences can be recalled; taking a decision can affect the course of later experiences; etc.

Though for some purposes it might be helpful to try and draw a distinction between the concepts and the procedures for handling them, in general this cannot be done in any clear-cut manner. As mentioned earlier, one must not succumb to a simplistic 'naming' theory of the relationship between a concept and that to which it is supposed to refer. The proposal that there is a property of matter - for instance, electric charge - goes hand in glove with the proposal that there is a force acting between charges. It is the combination of electric charge concept and the law specifying the force between charges (i.e. how the charges relate to each other) that accounts for the observation one is attempting to explain - namely two particles repelling or attracting each other. In such a case it is preferable to say that it is the combination of concept and the mode of handling it that is intended to describe what is happening in the reality domain, rather than the concept and mode individually signifying different aspects of the reality.

I stress that this is an *intention*, there being no guarantee that any explanatory system does faithfully describe actuality. In response to improved knowledge gained through greater experience, the suggested concepts and procedures can evolve over time; they can be refined, or indeed abandoned and replaced by others. But although ideas may change as to the exact features of the reality domain, as I said just now, there can be no questioning of the existence of the *general* type of reality that underpins all discussion within that framework. In a scientific discussion conducted along classical lines one may argue about which kinds of particles exist (electrons, quarks, etc.) and what their properties are (mass, electric charge, and so on), but no-one questions that there are particles of some sort and that they have properties. Even when there is a wholescale revision of physical theory (classically conceived particles being replaced by quantum interactions, for instance) there yet remains the conviction of there being a physical reality of some sort - a reality to be explored with the techniques and procedures employed by physicists. Classical and quantum physics are but different versions of the physical explanatory framework. Similarly, in a discussion on psychology, one may argue about the interpretation of dreams, or the importance of the role played by childhood experiences, but no-one working with a version of the mental explanatory framework would call into question the existence of dreaming as such, or of mental experiences in general.

3. So much for explanatory frameworks in general. We have already seen something of physical frameworks in action. It will soon be time to turn to the mental explanatory framework. But are the mental and physical frameworks really addressing different kinds of reality? Before going further, it would be as well to look into this in more detail. It is essential that you be thoroughly satisfied of the need for more than one framework. Certain things previously said might have left lingering doubts about this. I can think of three reasons why you might still regard the physical and mental realities as inextricably mixed with each other, and thus possibly open to description in terms of a single comprehensive explanatory framework:

4. The first arises from the use of the word 'observer'. In both relativity and quantum theory, the observer, as we have seen, has become an active participant in what is observed. But presumably the observer is a conscious being, whereas that which is being observed is physical. So, the argument runs, consciousness has entered the physical domain.

This, however, does not follow at all, and most physicists would strongly deny such a suggestion. In relativity theory what counts is that the measurement of a distance requires the use of a ruler, and the measurement of a time interval the use of a clock. It is the readings on these instruments that specify the meanings to be attached to the concepts of distance and time interval. The ruler and the clock are themselves physical objects, so will have a certain specifiable motion relative to that which is being measured. As already noted, the length recorded on the ruler and the time interval recorded on the clock depend on that motion. But for the purposes of relativity theory, it is quite immaterial whether a conscious being (i.e. an actual observer) is around to take the readings. What matters is that the values of the distance and the time interval are those appropriate to the coordinate frame of reference in which the ruler and clock are at rest. Relativity theory is thus exclusively concerned with physical matters. The fact that we as conscious beings show an interest in the readings is neither here nor there.

The same is true of quantum theory. We have spoken of interactions-with-the-world. But whose interactions? Presumably some observer's interactions. Again, however, one is easily misled by such talk. What quantum theory actually refers to are measurements - measurements of position or velocity. These are recorded on measuring devices of one kind or another. A digital read-out indicates a loss of electric charge at the electron source of a TV set and this is a sign that an electron has been emitted. Later a flash of light is given out from the fluorescent screen indicating the arrival of the electron at a particular location. But here again one is talking exclusively of physical events. Quantum theory is relating one physical occurrence to another. As far as the theory is concerned, it is of no consequence whether a conscious being comes along and notes, through his senses, the value of the readings. Quantum theory does not deal in conscious observers agonizing over whether to set up an experimental arrangement that will measure a precise position, or alternatively one capable of measuring a precise velocity. It simply states what is physically likely to happen given either physical situation. In passing, I should perhaps point out that this has not always been acknowledged. When physicists first tried to come to terms with the significance of quantum theory, a suggestion was made that the consciousness of the observer might play a part in the measurement process. The idea was followed up by one or two physicists, but led nowhere, so today is largely disregarded.

If quantum theory is solely concerned with relating one physical event to the next, why have I been calling these events 'interactions-with-the-world'? Why not simply refer to them by the term most often used in standard physics text-books: 'quantum measurements'? Because the emphasis of the present book, seen in its totality, is on how a conscious being gains information about other realities - realities with which one interacts. Quantum measurements are of interest to us for the way they provide information about one particular form of reality: the physical. They form the indispensable link to the physical domain. Thus, a bundle of light energy will strike the retina of the eye. In physical terms quantum theory describes this event as a quantum measurement, the retina acting as a measuring device. But then this impact of the light on the retina is accompanied by a mental experience: the seeing of a flash of light. What the nature of the connection might be between the two events - the one physical, the other mental - it is impossible to say. One can only note that, for whatever reason, there is a conjunction. And it is because of this conjunction, the quantum event of the light arriving on the retina acts as the conscious being's window on the world. Not only that, but quantum events allow the further exploration of the physical. On examining in detail the nature of the light pattern seen, one can infer that the light arriving on the retina originated in some other quantum measurement - the emission of light from a particular point on a fluorescent screen. That in turn can lead to a further inference, i.e. an electron has been emitted from the electron source in the TV tube, and it was this that gave rise to the subsequent emission of light from the screen. In this manner, the conscious being is able, through chains of quantum events, to explore the physical and learn of it. For this reason I have chosen to call these quantum events 'interactions-with-the-world'. But in using this term one must not lose sight of the fact that ultimately these physical chains stop short of entering into consciousness. Between the arrival of the light on the retina and the conscious act of observation there lies a seemingly unbridgeable gap in our understanding - a boundary that marks off one type of discourse from the other.

5. So that was the first reason why one might erroneously think of the physical and the mental as being bound up in the one descriptive framework - the constant reference physicists make to observers. The second has to do with *time*. One speaks of physical events occurring in time and mental events occurring in time. Are they not, therefore, inextricably linked up in this way? The answer is no. To appreciate why, we must take a closer look at the nature of time as it enters into the discussion of physical and mental occurrences.

With regard to physical events, we saw in Section 4.5 that relativity theory describes space and time as forming a seamless union: a four-dimensional space-time. As Einstein himself once said, it is now more natural to think of physical reality as 'a four-dimensional existence instead of, hitherto, the evolution of a three-dimensional existence'. No space-time point in this continuum has greater significance than any other. Not only do all spatial locations have the same status, as we are accustomed to think, but also all instants in time. A consequence of this is that there is no special moment of time called 'now' - that which divides past from future and acts as the focus for the process of 'becoming'. The equations of space-time physics simply do not single out such a special instant. Relative to any temporal instant there are earlier and later times. But that is all. The distinction is relative only, and applies equally to each and every instant. This even-handed treatment of all points in space-time has the effect of making time look more like space than we would have suspected from our very different perceptions of the two. It would be wrong, however, to push the similarities too far. There remain essential differences. For instance, the two directions along the time axis can be distinguished from each other; the two directions along any spatial axis cannot. If there are two photographs, one showing a cup on the table, the other the same cup smashed on the floor, it is clear which was taken first, i.e. which event occurred closer to the end of the time axis labelled 'earlier', which closer to the end labelled 'later'. In contrast, one does not know from looking at the cup which direction (relative to the stars, for example) the handle points. The spatial axes are symmetric in a way that the time axis is not.

Another point to note is that physics does not recognize a 'flow' of time. The Second Law of Thermodynamics states that disorder (such as smashed cups) increases in one direction along the time axis and decreases in the opposite direction. But there is nothing in this law, or in any other aspect of physics, that says that we *experience* time in one direction rather than the other. Though it would strike us as absurd that fragments of crockery lying on a floor should suddenly and spontaneously assemble themselves to form a cup, which then leaps off the floor and comes to rest on the table, there is nothing - absolutely nothing - in the laws of physics which tells us that this does not happen. For all we know, there could be another universe somewhere, governed by identical laws of physics, in which such behaviour is the norm, and the reverse process - cups getting smashed - quite unknown.

The truth of the matter is that in space-time nothing changes at all; time evolves in *neither* direction. Not only does all of space exist, but also all of time - including those instants we customarily think of as lying in the future. According to relativity theory, physical reality simply *is*.

That being the case, where do the additional features we associate with time come in: the special instant called 'now'; the act of 'becoming'; the 'flow' of time; and the seeming uncertainty of the future? Indeed, how is one supposed to understand the use of the present tense in the last sentence of that previous paragraph - the application of the word 'is' to a physical reality embracing what we customarily think of as past and future events, as well as present ones?

To answer this, we leave the domain of the physical, and enter that of consciousness. We have to enquire how time is involved in mental events. States of the mind occur in sequence. But what exactly separates one state from the other along this sequence? We say they are separated in 'time'. These separations, or intervals, of time can be estimated and compared, semi-quantitatively at least. This is possible without reference to a physical clock. How it is done is hard to say for sure. The vividness with which one recollects an event could presumably have something to do with it. The earlier the event, the less vivid and clear the recollection. In judging how long ago it was perhaps one is forming a judgement as to the degree of fading that has taken place. But the vividness of recollections cannot be the whole story. It is well known that older people can more easily recall the events of their youth than they can more recent happenings. This could be due to the younger mind paying greater attention - the novel situations encountered then leaving a deeper impression than the more familiar experiences of later life. Perhaps it has something to do with how often earlier events have subsequently been recalled into the conscious mind - one's recollection today being more a recollection of the last time one was consciously thinking of the event, rather than the recollection of the original event itself. Despite all this, however, older people do know that these vividly remembered experiences did take place a long time ago.

This points to there being some other way of determining a lapse of time. It probably has something to do with the number of thoughts, or mental experiences, that have taken place since the original event. Clearly, 'the number of thoughts' is a crude notion. Thoughts do not come in well-defined units, nor do they come equally spaced out. Nevertheless, we do know whether we have experienced a little or a lot since the occurrence in question.

These suggestions as to how one might mentally estimate a lapse of time should not be taken too seriously. I do not know which of the two methods is used in practice, whether it is a combination of the two, or some entirely different approach. All I am saying is that there are at least two relatively plausible ways in which the mind could be making its semi-quantitative judgements about time.

But here we come to the important question: Is the time we speak of in the mental domain the same as the time we speak of in the physical domain? The answer appears to be no.

In the first place, we note that physical events are located not only in time but also in space; one cannot think of physical occurrences without thinking of them as happening somewhere. That is true of classical physics - it is even more so in relativity theory. As far as relativity is concerned, the link between time and space becomes indissoluble through the manner in which the two are interwoven in space-time. But what of mental events; do these occur in space? No. It makes no sense to think of a thought as located somewhere in space. It may be a thought *about* space, but the thought itself does not have a spatial location, nor does it possess spatial dimensions.

Secondly, one finds that it is only in consciousness that it becomes meaningful to single out a special instant of time - that which is called 'now'. It is that instant distinguished from all others through the way it marks the most recent occurrence - the direct experience situated at the end of the sequence of mental events. As mentally experienced this moment is special. Only this event exists. Events prior to this in the sequence have ceased to exist. Events beyond this point do not yet exist.

Thirdly, it is only through the acceptance of a second type of time that it makes sense to say that all of physical time *is*. The word 'is' does not refer to a particular instant of physical time; it refers instead to the 'now' of mental time. In other words, all of physical time is to be thought of as existing now in mental time (and equally at each other instant of mental time).

Finally, there is the 'flow' of time we experience. What does one mean by 'flow'? One means the change in something with time. The flow of a river, for example, is the volume of water passing a given point in a given time. But what then can it mean to speak of a flow of *time*? The change in time in a given time? That means nothing - unless one is talking of two different types of time.

In this way we begin to appreciate that the same word 'time' is applied to two quite distinct things: physical time and mental time. These are so different from each other, I would go so far as to say that it is unfortunate that the same name is applied to both. The reason they are both referred to as 'time' is because there exists between them a close correspondence. Thus, an experience in the mind (for instance, the hearing of a bell chime now), is correlated to a feature of physical reality (the impact of a clapper on the rim of a bell at a particular point in space-time). The 'now' of mental time is correlated to a particular instant of physical time. Although, as said earlier, all of physical time exists now - not just this one instant - this one particular instant is singled out as having special significance for the now of mental time. Not that this state of affairs persists. A short while later (according to mental time, that is), the 'now' correlates to a different physical time. The difference between this new physical time and the former one, judged on a clock, when compared with the perceived lapse of mental time

Unlike the two previous objections to the idea of there being one reality rather than two, this last one, based on the intrinsic unknowability of the substance of a reality, is not one that can be dismissed. There might be two realities, or there might be only one. We have no way of deciding. An advantage of assuming a single reality is that one has a ready explanation of certain correlations that exist between the physical and the mental - the correlations between physical processes going on in the body (the chemical action of an aspirin, for example) and mental processes going on in the mind (the relief from a headache), or the correlations between mental time and physical time. According to the common reality hypothesis, the frameworks are talking about the same thing so, of course, it is only natural there should be correlations. A disadvantage of the common reality hypothesis is that each framework *appears* to be addressing a quite different form of reality. As we have seen, if one starts out from a consideration of physical concepts alone, one cannot bridge the gap to the mental concepts. Concepts devised for use in one framework cannot be transferred meaningfully into the other.

If one is inclined to accept the hypothesis of a single reality, then the two frameworks are to be regarded as *complementary* ways of addressing that reality. The word 'complementary' has a variety of meanings, so let me be clear as to how I shall be using it. In the first place the complementary modes address one and the same object. This is not to say that each necessarily is concerned with the totality of the object (the physical description accounts for all kinds of things going on that have no correlate in the mental description of consciousness). Secondly, each has something to say about the common reality that cannot be said by the other. Thus, both are necessary for a complete description of that reality. Thirdly, the descriptions are mutually exclusive of each other; they cannot be reduced to a single way of speaking - they are incomensurable with each other. Finally, there can be correlations between one mode of description and the other, as well as an indication within one description of the need for the other.

We can illustrate the nature of the complementarity between explanatory frameworks by drawing attention to the way complementarity can sometimes operate within the confines of a single framework. In Sections 4.6 and 5.6 we came across two complementary ways of regarding an electron: wave and particle. Both descriptions refer to the same object, namely, the electron. When asking *how* an electron interacts we must speak of it as a particle; when asking *where* it will interact we use the language of waves. Both descriptions, therefore, are equally necessary for an exhaustive explanation of electron behaviour. Neither description can be reduced to the other. The fact that the particle description shows only how the energy will be delivered, but not where this will occur, points to the need for the other description.

Complementarity defined in this particular way can also be regarded as 'orthogonality'. Here we have in mind the helpful analogy of an architect's drawings of a building viewed from two directions at right angles to each other (the front and side elevations, for example). The two drawings refer to one and the same building; each contains information not available from the other, so are both indispensable and point to the need of the other; certain features of one - a rectangle representing a wall seen face on, for example - are correlated to certain features of the other - a line representing the same wall seen end on. (The fact that this analogy is not complete without the plan view of the building will be exploited later in Chapter 18 when we discuss the need for a further orthogonal explanatory framework - the spiritual.)

Summing up: The ontological nature of the physical and mental realities is intrinsically beyond definition, so there is no way of ascertaining for certain whether we are dealing with two distinct realities or one reality looked at in two complementary ways. But in a sense this does not matter. *What does need to be emphasised is the requirement for two explanatory frameworks, rather than two distinct realities.* These are frameworks that address their respective reality bases in such ways as to make those bases appear utterly dissimilar to, and incommensurable with, each other. The inadmissability of fusing concepts from one description to those of the other is perhaps best kept to the forefront of our minds by speaking of the physical and the mental as two distinct realities, each with its own explanatory framework, even though the truth of the matter might be that there is only the one reality viewed in complementary ways. This, in fact, is how I shall continue to speak of them. However, you ought not to lose sight of the possibility of there being a common reality undergirding those that we speak of, and indeed we shall return to this point later when introducing the spiritual explanatory framework. There again we shall be confronted with the problem of whether a new framework referring to what appears to be a new type of reality really does address a new reality, or whether it is yet another complementary way of viewing the one reality.

CHAPTER 9

INFERRING THE PHYSICAL FROM THE MENTAL

FROM the initial assumption that there is a mental reality, what can be said about other types of reality? For a start, can we establish the existence of the physical domain?

1. Before trying to answer that, we must first be clear about the contents of the mental domain - the basis from which later inferences are to be drawn. On looking out of the window, for example, one might have an experience known as 'observing the Moon'. But what exactly does this mean in terms of what exists in the mind?

'Common sense' might say that, somewhere in the mind, there is a visual sensation - 'a picture' showing a round white patch of light on a dark background. The centre of consciousness, the ego, examines the visual image and decides that it is the Moon. To do this, it must remember what the Moon looks like, so it has to call up a memory of a past sighting of the Moon, and compare it with the visual sensation. Accordingly, the mind contains several different kinds of entity: sensations, memories, an ego, and a means by which the ego can examine such things as sensations and memories. This view is reinforced by the way we talk about our mental experiences. We speak of 'mental pictures', 'the mind's eye', and so on.

Or take the example of listening to a clock chiming. On hearing the third chime, what is to be found in the mind? An auditory sensation, plus individual memories of the two previous chimes, plus an ego capable of listening to the new sound and to the sound of the memories.

INFERRING THE PHYSICAL 107

Credible though this might at first seem, closer examination reveals that none of this actually makes much sense. In the case of the Moon observation, where exactly is this mental picture with the round patch of white on it? What is the form of the memory - another sort of picture? What is the nature of the ego? How is the internal 'seeing of the picture' done? How is the comparison made between the sensation and the memory? In the same vein, when listening to the chiming clock, how is the sound of the memories generated? By what means is the ego able to hear these sounds?

Though much thought has been given to such questions, no satisfactory answers are to be found. This is taken to be an indication that so-called common sense is misleading us. The mind is not at all the way we have described it. During the past fifty years, the philosophy of the mind has undergone a revolution - one as radical as anything that has occurred in quantum physics. Indeed, the character of the two revolutions parallel each other to a remarkable degree.

In quantum physics we discovered that we had no direct access to objects-in-themselves. Instead, we had to be content to deal in interactions-with-the-world. That and that alone. While there was consensus over the existence of interactions and what could be said about them, the conception of an object capable of existing independently of having an interaction was regarded as a separate, less immediate issue - a subject for continuing debate.

In the same way, an examination of the contents of the mind confronts us with *mental experiences*. That and that alone. We do not have direct access to sensations or memories - the kinds of entity we earlier took for granted. When observing the Moon, for example, what we can say with certainty is that there is in the mind an experience: one referred to as 'myself-observing-the-Moon'; on listening to the chiming clock, an experience known as 'myself-hearing-the-third-chime'. Just as the quantum physical framework deals in interactions that include the participation of the observer, so the mental framework deals in experiences involving the ego. Whether beyond this veil of mental experience there lie sensations, memories, and such like - entities capable of existing independently of their being involved in a conscious experience - this has to be regarded as more problematic. In view of the aforementioned difficulties of trying to make sense of what such entities would be like and how they would interact with each other, the tendency today is to dismiss such notions as having little or no explanatory value. The idea of a passive, raw sensation sitting there in the mind regardless of whether any attention is being paid to it is unhelpful. Instead, *the input from the senses is to be thought of as indissoluably integrated into an act of observation involving the active participation of the ego.* Likewise, there is nothing to be gained by thinking of a memory as something that sits in a store waiting to be taken out and compared alongside some new sensation. It is not that one hears the third chime, hears the memories of the other two, recognizes that they are similar, counts them up, and concludes: 'This is the third chime'. Rather, the experience of hearing the third chime is a *different* experience to that of hearing the first chime. It is an experience accompanied by an expectation that was absent in the other. Hearing and recognizing the third chime is a single integrated experience - one not to be broken down and analysed in terms of component parts and activities.

Thus we find there has been a transformation in the theory of the mind very similar to that which has occurred in physics. In both cases the direction has been away from thinking of entities that have an independent existence of their own, and towards the acceptance of *a relational, interactional type of existence.* In the same way as the concept 'electron' has no meaning in the physical interaction framework outside the context of it being part of the specification of an interaction such as a 'measurement-of-the-position-of-an-electron', so the concept 'sensation' means nothing outside the context of helping to specify an experience of the ego when making an observation, 'memory' means nothing outside the ego's experience of recollecting, and 'ego' means nothing outside its being involved in conscious experiences. I repeat: In the reality domain of the mental explanatory framework, the only existent entities are conscious mental experiences.

This is *not* to rule out the possibility that beyond the domain of mental experiences there might lie a second mental domain of some kind. Indeed, in much the same way as some physicists see value in postulating a world-in-itself, so, it can be argued, there is value in proposing that there is a mental domain which we might call 'mind-in-itself'.

Recall how earlier, in connection with our discussion of physical reality, I expressed concern that not to postulate a world-in-itself meant that most of the time nothing at all existed. (This was because quantum interactions occur instantaneously.) Without some form of continuity it was difficult if not impossible to understand how there could be any consistency across the gap between one interaction and the next. The law of energy conservation, for example, appears to require an energy measurement to 'remember' the value given by the previous measurement. But if nothing, absolutely nothing, exists between the two measurements, how is this to be accomplished? A world-in-itself fills this need.

In the same way, there is a problem of continuity in the mental domain. What happens to me when I am not having conscious mental experiences - during a dreamless sleep, for instance? Do I cease to exist as a mental being? Possibly, but that gets us into trouble: If I cease to exist for a time, what assurance is there that what reappears is the same me? If by way of answer one says that I behave and think now exactly as I did before, one still has the problem of how the similarities have been preserved. Where was the 'memory' in between? Considerations of this sort point to the need for a second domain of mental reality - one that remains continuously in existence. This is the mind-in-itself. It is responsible for the interelatedness of my experiences; it provides for the identity and continuity of my personhood. It has the same relationship to my mental experiences as the world-in-itself bears to physical interactions. Just as the properties of the world-in-itself contribute the consistencies and law-like characteristics exhibited by physical interactions, so the qualities of the mind-in-itself are responsible for endowing my mental experiences with their enduring character traits. Just as contingent changes to the world-in-itself show up through the contingent features of interactions, so changes to the mind-in-itself lead to altered mental experiences. A moment ago, for instance, I might have been startled by the chime of a bell; now the repeated sound is recognized as the third such chime and occasions no surprise. The sound is the same, but the mind-in-itself is not. It has been affected by the first experience and now responds differently. This is not to say that in the mind-in-itself there are separate memory traces of the first two chimes. All that can be claimed is that the previous experiences somehow dispose the mind towards a different experience next time round. This is similar to the physical situation in which today one observes an electron in a box, yesterday there was none. This is not to say that in the world-in-itself there is an actual electron, one that was not around yesterday. All that can be safely asserted is that today there is something different about the world-in-itself - whatever form that difference might take - and it is this difference that reflects itself in the changed physical interaction.

This talk of mind-in-itself might strike you as unfamiliar and rather speculative, but it ought not. Mind-in-itself refers to something mental not included under the category of conscious mental experience. As such, it comes within the province of the unconscious mind - a conception most of us are happy to accept. The unconscious is a topic we shall treat more fully in Chapter 15.

2. The features of conscious mental experience that point towards the existence of the physical world are, of course, those associated with the senses - sight, hearing, taste, smell, and touch. These experiences we shall be calling *observations*. Incidentally, I should perhaps say that for the time being at least I shall be laying aside the insight afforded by quantum theory that, strictly speaking, we ought to be asking how we establish the existence of the domain of physical interactions-with-the-world rather than the physical world-in-itself. As we have seen, it is this, rather than the world-in-itself, that lies immediately beyond the senses. Only having established the existence of the domain of physical interactions ought we then to go on to argue about the world-in-itself lying a further step removed from direct experience. But in order to avoid sounding pedantic, I shall refrain from labouring this point and will pose the question in its traditional form: How do we know the physical world exists beyond our observations?

At first it appears absurd that anyone should question the belief that the sensory input to the experience of having an observation has a cause, and that the cause is physically based. Surely the hearing of a sound is due to a clapper striking a bell, a pleasant taste to the eating of strawberries, the seeing of the Moon to light coming from the physical Moon. But if this is so, how are we to envisage the *mechanism* by which something physical causes something mental? We have already briefly alluded to this question. Let us look at it again in more depth:

The subject of causality has always created difficulties - even in the case of one physical event causing another physical event. The fact that one such event is invariably followed by another does not necessarily mean that there is a causal connection between them. Take, for example, two toy boats on a pond. Boat A bobs up and down and immediately afterwards boat B bobs up and down. This sequence is repeated again and again. Every time boat A moves, a short while later boat B does the same thing. And never does Boat B move unless Boat

A has done so a little earlier. Does this sequence mean that Boat A bobbing up and down is the cause of Boat B bobbing up and down? Not necessarily. What I have in mind is a little boy squatting by the side of the boating pool and from time to time hitting the surface of the water near him with a stick. The ripples move outwards, reaching first Boat A, then Boat B. It is the boy's action that is the cause, not the motion of Boat A; the bobbing of Boat A is as much an effect, as that of Boat B.

In this example we see that a constantly repeated sequence of events does not necessarily imply a causal connection. This could be established by setting Boat A in motion in some other way (hitting it with a stone, for instance) and observing that Boat B is unaffected, or by the boy changing his position so that he is now nearer to Boat B, so causing this boat to be set in motion first.

But now suppose we have a clear-cut case of cause and effect: A ball hits a window; the window smashes. We are all agreed (including the culprit) that the effect is a smashed window, and this was brought about by the cause - a blow from the ball. But what is it about the arrival of the ball that actually *causes* the breaking of the window? We cannot say; the nature of the causal link is a mystery. All we see are two physical states - ball approaching window, immediately followed by flying glass and rebounding ball. But, you might complain, such a description is far too crude. If one were to examine the collision in its finest detail, surely then one would be able to discern the causal mechanism. The answer is no. The most detailed study one can make of a collision is that between two elementary sub-atomic particles - between two electrons, say. When such an examination is carried out one finds that, because of the inherently discontinuous nature of quantum events, all one ever deals in are isolated 'snapshots'. First a set of snapshots showing the electrons approaching each other, then a set showing the electrons moving apart. All that can be learned is what the state of affairs was before the collision, and what it was afterwards. Never does one see the crucial incident itself - that instantaneous moment when two infinitesimally small particles actually interact. It is, therefore, impossible to tell what it is about this fleeting incident that converts the first state of affairs to the second. One has to rest content with simply noting that the first is always followed by the second. This being true of collisions between sub-atomic particles, the same must be true for interactions between large composite objects: a ball approaching a window, followed by the window shattering. Such large-scale collisions can, in principle, be analysed into the interactions of the component sub-atomic particles and these, as we have just seen, offer no clue as to the nature of the causal link.

If this is the case in respect of like entities - namely two events both of which are physical - it goes without saying that the difficulties involved in establishing the nature of the causal link between entities as dissimilar as a physical event on the one hand, and an accompanying sensory input to a mental observation on the other, are likely to prove insuperable. Without that link it becomes impossible to *prove* from observations that there *must* be a physical world acting as their cause.

3. Is there some other way of proving the world's existence - one that does not rely on the senses? After all, the mind does entertain thoughts other than those of experiencing observations. Perhaps among these other kinds of thought there will be some that will provide a means of establishing the existence of the physical world independently of the information conveyed through the senses.

For example, are we not born with an innate understanding of the nature of space? We saw in Sections 4.1 and 4.5 that this was not so. The 'common sense' 3-dimensional Euclidean space is not the one adopted by nature. It is 4-dimensional and can be 'warped' by the presence of the matter within it. In order to know the kind of space we live in, we must experiment and observe - we *cannot* arrive at such knowledge by a mind unaided by the sensory input that conveys the results of those experiments.

To this it might be objected that the idea of a space with more than three dimensions had been around prior to the discovery, through the senses, that space-time was indeed of such a kind. The possibility had been suggested by Minkowski. Not only that, but the properties of non-Euclidean geometries had been explored by Riemann long before it was discovered that such a geometry had relevance to the description of space-time. On such grounds, can it not be argued that the human mind has an innate capacity to *anticipate* the revelations of the senses?

What we see at work here is the imaginative faculty of the mind - the ability to extrapolate from what is already known to that which might also be the case. Thus, for example, having observed a cow, then a horse, one's imagination comes up with the conception of a unicorn - a horse to which one of the characteristics of the cow has been transferred. But does this new concept correspond with anything in the physical world? This is a matter that can only be settled by resort to further observation. If the existence of the unicorn is thus confirmed, it can indeed be claimed that the mind anticipated the revelation of the senses. But note, until the unicorn is detected through the senses, the concept remains a hypothesis only - one possibility among many. Not only does the mind require the process of observation to assist it in the formation of the hypothesis in the first place (the prior observation of the horse and of the cow's horn), it also depends on observation to establish the correctness or otherwise of the hypothesis. It is the confirmatory observation, not the imaginative faculty, that converts the hypothesis into genuine knowledge. In the case of the unicorn, of course, there is no such confirmatory evidence - the hypothesis happens not to be correct. But in other cases, a hypothesis does happen to be correct. The proposal that space has 4 dimensions appears correct, whilst those that hold that there are 3, 5, 6, etc. dimensions appear wrong. (I say 4 dimensions 'appears' correct because the exact number of dimensions is still the

INFERRING THE PHYSICAL

subject of debate; a theory currently attracting attention suggests there might be 10!) In summary, therefore, we conclude that the imaginative faculty is not in itself a source of knowledge.

4. But if a knowledge of space cannot be arrived at *a priori*, how about mathematics and logic as potential sources of knowledge? Do these not originate solely in the mind, and yet allow us to make discoveries about physical reality - discoveries that are independent of the senses? The nature of mathematics was discussed to some extent at the beginning of Chapter 4. There it appeared that mathematics as such told us nothing about the physical world unaided by the senses. Some would dispute this conclusion, so let us look into it more deeply. The essential point, as I see it, is that there is more than one type of mathematics - there are an infinite variety of them. This is not generally understood because the only type of mathematics one is introduced to at school is the one that happens to be useful in describing the physical world. How do we know that this is the useful form of mathematics? By observation - through the senses. We have already seen how this is the case with geometry. It is true for other branches of mathematics, even simple arithmetic. There is more than one kind of arithmetic. For example, it is perfectly possible to imagine a world in which 0+1=1, 1+1=2, but then 1+2=1. On a limited scale one can see this sort of arithmetic at work at the top of those illuminated cylinders of coloured oil where the heat of the light bulb applied to the base results in the formation of bubbles that rise to the top of the column. First one bubble moves to the top, then a second to give two, but then when the next joins the other two they coalesce to form a single bubble: 1+2=1. Who knows, we might have inhabited a universe where this kind of behaviour was the norm: two objects when put together with a third, coalesce to form a single object - regardless of what type of object they are. Or take the kind of arithmetic which governs angles expressed in degrees: 3-1=2, 2-1=1, 1-1=0, but

0-1=359. Once again, we happen not to inhabit a universe where it is the norm that if you take something away from nothing you end up with a lot! But such a universe is conceivable - just. We know not to apply such a type of arithmetic to the world in general, not through the examination of the mathematics itself, but by observation of the world through the senses. Concrete experiences lie at the basis of our understanding of all mathematical operations. This, of course, is not to say that one needs a concrete experience of all mathematical propositions in order to understand what they mean. I do not need to handle 246 apples and 107 apples in order to know that 246 + 107 = 353. The manipulation of numbers eventually becomes a matter of following rules rather than the laborious handling of actual objects. But our understanding of numbers in the first place and how they are used is ultimately rooted in the handling of actual objects.

The next point to note about mathematics is that we must be wary over the suggestion that it is possible to make mathematical 'discoveries'. From the time when, as a child, we first proved Pythagoras' theorem, we were encouraged to think that from the basis of a few simple assumptions (the axioms underlying Euclidean geometry) we could gain in knowledge by proving more and more theorems - each of which could then be independently checked out against observations of the physical world. Thus, for example, having proved Pythagoras' Theorem, one draws a triangle, constructs squares on its sides, measures the area of the squares, adds the areas of the two smaller squares and compares it to that of the larger. Lo and behold, they are equal - just as the theorem had predicted. But what are we to conclude from this? Does the proving of a theorem constitute a genuine discovery about the world - a discovery made by means of geometry alone? In a sense, yes. Mathematical deductions do allow us to become aware of features of the world that we had not previously appreciated, and these features can be anticipated before we have direct physical experience of them. But in an important sense, the answer must be, no. Having deduced the theorem, we can at that stage see it as an inevitable consequence of having initially adopted the axioms. Acceptance of the axioms was, in effect, acceptance also of the theorem, and this is not altered by the fact that we did not at the time recognize the theorem to be one of the consequences. Axioms and theorems together form a single interlocking mathematical system. If one part of the system is an assumption, then so is the rest.

So much for mathematics - how about logic? Once again, the matter is open to dispute, but the generally held view is that logic unaided by the senses, like mathematics, is sterile in its implications as to the kind of world we live in. Just because a statement is logically true, does not mean it necessarily conveys useful information. For example, the statement 'It is either raining outside or it is not raining outside' is perfectly correct; no-one would argue with it. Moreover, it is true under all circumstances. But that is the trouble with it. It is true regardless of the state of affairs in the world, and therefore tells us nothing about the world; it is a tautology. There are other statements of logic that are always incorrect: 'It is raining outside and it is not raining outside'. This is a logical contradication, and also tells us nothing about the physical world.

5. Neither mathematics nor logic nor prior notions of space can provide us with *a priori* knowledge of the physical world; we have constantly to refer back to our sensory input. This should not be construed to mean, however, that we enter life with a completely blank mind, knowing nothing until we make our first observations. We are evolved animals, and as such, are invested with a genetic inheritance:

Observation of other animals reveals that certain aspects of their behaviour are genetically based; they do not have to be learnt by the individual. Following its birth, a baby kangaroo will immediately head up its mother's fur and locate the pouch which is to be its new home - it does not need to be taught this. Many animals are born with a fear of potential predators; again, this does not have to be learned. It is common for the newly-born promptly to form close bonds of attachment to mother-figures. Indeed, the list of examples of genetically determined behaviour can be extended indefinitely. This being so for other animals, it is only reasonable to presume that the same must be true for human beings; we too must have our own genetically based behaviour patterns - forms of behaviour that help us cope with our environment, but which do not have to be learned through our own individual experience.

Does the fact that animals and human beings come into the world to some extent already pre-programmed, necessarily imply that this knowledge - if we may call it such - stems from a source other than sensory observation? To answer this we must enquire how these behavioural patterns arose in the first place. They come about through the process of evolution by natural selection. As an example, consider how it might have happened that newly born birds immediately know how to relate to their mother as she returns to the nest. At some time in the past, we presume that some baby birds happened by chance to possess an innate tendency to open their beaks wide. This was lucky for them; it attracted the attention of their mother who responded by giving them the worm. The others were not so fortunate; they happened not to have this tendency and so got overlooked. There being a general shortage of food, those possessing the tendency had the better chance of surviving. On reaching maturity, they passed their genetic characteristics on to their off-spring - including that which manifests itself as the tendency to open the beak wide on sensing the return of the mother to the nest. The birds that lacked that characteristic had a reduced chance of surviving to maturity, and so had less chance of passing on their own genetic make-up to the next generation - a genetic make-up lacking in the characteristic. Thus, on average, it is more common in the next generation for the young to manifest the beneficially appropriate behaviour than it was in the immediately prior generation. In this way, we see how the pressures of natural selection could have worked towards the creation of succeeding generations more suited to survival within the physical environment in which they find themselves. But note that this inherited information, though not obtained through the individual's own sensory experience, is not independent of the senses. The beneficial behaviour patterns have been moulded through the interaction of previous generations with the environment - an interaction involving the use of *their* senses. The information available to the individual through the genes is therefore of the same *type* as that which will later come through its own senses.

To speak of genetically determined behaviour is, of course, to use the language of science. This you might have found confusing; after all, are we not now supposed to be talking about what happens in the mind rather than in the world of physics and biology? There is in fact no problem. The same idea is present in the language of psychology. It appears for example in the work of Sigmund Freud. As is well known, he maintained that much of our thinking is governed by basic instinctual drives, particularly that associated with sex. Carl Jung in his theory of archetypes, has since taken up essentially the same notion, greatly expanding it to embrace a whole range of innate tendencies. This is a subject to be addressed in some detail in Chapter 15. Suffice for the present to note that there do exist psychological correlates of the biologist's genetically determined behaviour patterns. The mind is therefore to be thought of as coming into existence to some extent already pre-programmed - but not with knowledge independent of the senses.
6. So it is that we are repeatedly thrown back on the use of our senses. But as we have already seen, the lack of any clear picture of the mechanism of the supposed causal link between the physical and mental, renders sensory information incapable of providing *proof* of the existence

of the physical domain. What do I mean by 'proof'? I remind you of the aim of the current exercise: that of trying to convince an avowed sceptic. 'Proof' in the present context, therefore, is *deductive* proof. In a deductive argument one begins from a set of premises that for the sake of the argument are assumed to hold. One then demonstrates that a particular conclusion *unavoidably* follows. For instance, we might start from the two premises: (i) Neutrons have no electric charge; (ii) This particle is a neutron. These lead to the conclusion: This particle has no electric charge. The conclusion is inescapable. What we have found is that, if for the sake of argument one grants the sceptic his initial position, namely, an empirical reality base consisting solely of mental experiences, then a demand for proof of the existence of the physical domain - absolutely undeniable, deductive proof - *cannot be met*. It is important not to lose sight of this. Later, from the self-same starting position, the sceptic will demand water-tight proof of God's existence. We shall conclude no such proof is to be had. But this is hardly the damaging admission it appears to be - not when it is realized that proof of that sort is not available even in respect of physical reality.

Notwithstanding this lack of proof for a physical reality, no-one in practice embraces the conclusion to which the argument seems to point - the adoption of an idealist standpoint. Why is this? What is it about our observations that encourages even those of a sceptical turn of mind to draw the inference that there is a physical world lying beyond the senses - this despite the absence of proof? Perhaps there are useful insights here as to how to argue later in respect of a spiritual reality. In short, we ask: What are the grounds for *reasonable* belief?

Before trying to answer that, I should perhaps make clear what I mean by 'reasonable'- the word, after all, crops up not only here but in the very title of the book. A conclusion is reasonable if it constitutes a position that can be held with intellectual honesty, that is to say, if it incorporates reasoning *as far as that is possible given the nature of the problem,* if it does not ignore contra-indications, and if well-balanced judgement points to it being the more plausible of the various possible alternatives. As such, a reasonable conclusion is to be distinguished from a reasoned conclusion. The latter is deduced infallibly by reasoning alone from some accepted starting point; the former is the best conclusion available on the evidence, but one that leaves open the possibility of one's being mistaken.

Reasonable belief is founded on *inductive* arguments. An inductive argument is such that acceptance of a given set of premises, while not leading inescapably to a particular conclusion, can lend support to it. Thus, for example, a set of premises might be: (i) 60% of the children in the school science class are boys; (ii) An individual named X is in the school science class. Conclusion: X is a boy. The conclusion does not follow inescapably; X could still be a girl. But the argument lends a measure of support to the conclusion. The conclusion is now more likely than it seemed in the absence of that piece of information (60% probability now instead of 50%). One should note also that inductive arguments can be cumulative. Thus, a further argument about X might be built on the premises: (i) Boys are twice as likely as girls to have dirty fingernails; (ii) X has dirty fingernails. Conclusion: X is a boy. Again the conclusion is not inescapable, but more probably true than not. Taken in conjunction with the first argument, the odds begin to mount that X is indeed a boy.

There are many situations in life where reasoning unaided will get one only so far. On the threshold of marriage there is no way of rationally deducing that one will be happy. Nevertheless, a study of the other person's characteristics, interests, temperament, previous behaviour, etc. can indicate that the choice of partner is a reasonable one. One weighs the evidence and exercises judgement. The arguments do not coerce, but they do have the power to influence and persuade. Indeed, it is rare to encounter *any* situation in life open to unaided deductive reasoning. Inductive argument is not the exception, but the norm. The fact that there is no deductive proof of the existence of the physical domain or of God is not in the least embarrassing. A demand for proof of that nature has no foundation; it is the last, unworthy, refuge of the inveterate sceptic. The inductive form of argument is not the apologetic 'second best' it is often taken for. It is normally the *only* type of argument there can be.

7. In justifying a belief in the physical world on the basis of what is found in the domain of mental experience, we are in much the same situation as modern physicists trying to decide, from a study of interactions-with-the-world, whether or not there lies a world-in-itself beyond those interactions. As before, we find ourselves locked into the particular domain of reality that underpins the type of discussion we are having. On the basis of what is found there, we try to argue that there is explanatory value in the postulate of a further type of reality - one that lies beyond that with which one is currently dealing, but is somehow related to it. As we seek to argue that a study of mental experiences (specifically the sensory observations) leads to a reasonable belief in the existence of a physical domain, we shall see parallels with the physicists' endeavour to argue on the basis of physical interactions that it is reasonable to believe in the existence of a world-in-itself.

We begin once more from the idea of otherness. Sensory observations, like the physical interactions we considered earlier, possess the quality of otherness. That is to say, they exhibit features that are not attributable to one's own input, and for which there appears to be no explanation - at least not within the reality domain with which one is dealing. Thus, for example, I can choose to open my eyes. To that extent I control the situation and understand why there should now be a visual observation. But having decided to open my eyes I do not control what I see. Not that one should take this to mean that the act of observation is wholly objective. It is not. I do not mechanically record the scene laid out before me and then only later, by an act of the will, interpret what was seen. A good deal of interpretation is built into the very act of observation itself. When looking at the Moon on the horizon I might immediately think of it, incorrectly, as being larger than it is when high up in the sky. Nevertheless, the observation does carry a strong element of objectivity. I might be led to the wrong impression of how large the Moon is, but whether the experience is one of observing the Moon or something else is not in itself a matter of subjective interpretation. So that then is the first aspect of otherness: an observation has features about it that cannot be explained in terms of an input from me; it has the power to surprise me.

The second arises when I compare one observation with another. The process of observation is inherently discontinuous. It is discontinuous not only in the sense that I can open and close my eyes repeatedly, but also discontinuous in a fundamental way at the quantum level of description. Quantum theory reveals that even when the eyes are kept open I do not keep the scene before me under constant observation. What I see corresponds to the arrival of tiny packets of light energy on the retina. These quantum interactions, like all quantum interactions, occur instantaneously. The receipt of visual information is, therefore, a discontinuous process. (Not that I am aware of this, the situation being similar to what happens in a cinema - the viewing of a succession of still pictures leading to the illusion of a continuous phenomenon.) Despite this discontinuity of vision, however, the separate acts of seeing can be strongly correlated to each other. Having made an observation of the Moon, if I close my eyes and immediately re-open them, I expect to observe the Moon again. On the other hand, if I found no Moon, closing and re-opening the eyes ought again to reveal no Moon. In either case, the second observation is correlated to the first. But why? There does not appear to be any mechanism within the mind for holding in being the potentiality for there being either a Moon or alternatively no Moon, whichever is appropriate, during the period when no observation is being made. Invoking memory - the past experience dictating what one observes the second time - does not help. On that hypothesis, one would not be able to explain why sometimes the second observation is *not* consistent with the first (a passing cloud now possibly obscuring the Moon). If the *changes* in what I observe are to be attributable to some agency lying outside the mind, then it appears only natural to attribute to the same agency the *consistency* between observations. Thus I am led to the inference that during those periods when no observations are being experienced, something beyond the mind does continue to exist and hold in being the potential for producing the characteristics of my future observations.

The correlations between observations go far beyond the rather crude notion that if I observe a Moon now, I am likely to observe the same if I briefly close and re-open my eyes. Repeated observation over long periods of time reveals more sophisticated patterns of correlation. It is found that the likelihood of observing the Moon varies in a systematic way over the course of a month. Moreover, the phases of the Moon vary in a systematic fashion. None of this law-like behaviour is attributable to myself; I do not create these patterns - I discover them. This is where the postulate of a physical reality again comes in. If I am prepared to accept that there is a physical Moon, illuminated by a Sun, and circling an Earth which itself is spinning, I have a remarkably simple explanation of the otherwise inexplicable patterns of observation.

The belief in a physical reality is further strengthened by noting that not only can there be correlations between consecutive observations, there can be correlations between concurrent observations from different senses. The sight of an apple can be accompanied by the characteristic feel of the hardness and roundness of an apple, by the smell of an apple, and by the sound of one's teeth going into it. Why should the inputs from these very different senses be correlated in this way? The simplest explanation is that there is a common source - an actual apple belonging to the physical domain.

8. *Thus we see that, although one begins from a base consisting solely of conscious experiences, this does not mean that one is thereby imprisoned in the mental domain, unable to accept there being other realities.* The key to the escape from idealism into the realm of the physical lies with the otherness of the observations. There are features about observations that cannot be explained purely in their own terms. It is in order to provide some explanation of those features that the physical domain is postulated. The justification for making this inference lies in its perceived *explanatory power*.

What does 'explanatory power' mean? It is not easy to say. One can begin by noting that explanation has something to do with being able to predict the future. The ability to anticipate what is likely to happen is an important characteristic for the evolutionary development of animals. It is not surprising, therefore, that humankind is endowed with an in-born tendency towards trying to make sense of what is happening, and thus being able to make predictions relevant to preservation. The first characteristic to look for in a good explanatory theory, therefore, is its capacity to marshal data in such a way as to allow predictions to be made.

But we cannot leave it at that. Darwin's theory of evolution by natural selection is held to have much explanatory power, but its ability to predict how evolution will progress in the future is decidedly limited. In any event, if all one is interested in is the ability to predict, one does not need a theory. With regards predicting future sightings of the Moon, the overall pattern of past sightings is in itself sufficient to allow one to anticipate what will happen in the future; one simply assumes the pattern will be repeated. Likewise, in deciding when it will be possible to sunbathe on the beach, one reaches for the table of the tides, not for a physics book to explain the dependence of the movements of the seas on the gravita-

observed patterns and regularities among the observations become a natural consequence of it. Moreover, it is a model that can interrelate observations based on the five different senses in a particularly simple manner. Finally, it is one that is found to be intuitively satisfying.

9. Let me end by reiterating a point made in the Introduction. None of the above should be mistaken for a description of how we as human beings, developing from babyhood, in practice came to acquire a belief in the physical domain. We instinctively accept the existence of the physical from the moment we are born. From the very outset we live our lives as physical beings in a physical environment. This mind-set emerged through the course of evolution and has been preserved and passed on to us in our genetic inheritance (Section 5.3). It is easy to see why. On making an observation indicative of the presence of a predator, any animal that had to work its way intellectually through the kind of argument that we have just been through, before deciding it was prudent to take the appropriate avoiding action, would have been eliminated. There is survival value to be had in instinctively accepting the existence of the physical. It is this instinct we have temporarily had to lay aside in seeking to justify our belief in the physical.

CHAPTER 10

RELATING THE MENTAL AND THE PHYSICAL

THE existence of the physical can be inferred on the basis of its ability to explain certain features of mental experience. This implies a link of some kind between the two reality domains. But as already noted, we do not understand the nature of any causal connection between the two. Indeed, we previously insisted that mental experiences and physical interactions be dealt with separately. We are in a predicament: Something happening in one type of reality can have relevance for what happens in another, yet the distinctiveness of the two reality domains is to be respected. How are these competing requirements to be handled?

1. At this point we introduce the idea of a *mapping*. It is a concept important not only for our discussion here, but generally whenever we consider how one type of reality relates to another. In Chapter 18, for example, we shall be discussing how spiritual realities relate to ourselves as conscious mental beings, and also how they might affect the physical domain.

By a mapping, I mean that there can be a correspondence between a particular state in one reality domain, and a particular state in another reality domain. The two are correlated such that if one occurs, the other occurs. For example, in the physical domain we might have the physical state consisting of a thumb trapped under the head of a hammer, together with the appropriate chemical and electrical occurrences that customarily take place in the brain on such occasions. In the domain of mental experience there is the feeling of a painful thumb. We say that the particular state of the body maps itself onto this corresponding mental state.

This is not to say anything about *why* there should be this correspondence, or *how* the link between the two kinds of reality operates. I am not saying that the state in one reality domain 'causes' the state in the other to occur because of some action that takes place through the link between them; one state is not to be thought of as active and dominant, the other merely reacting passively. Rather, the two realities are to be thought of as being on the same footing.

Earlier we saw that it was impossible to say anything meaningful about the intrinsic nature of the entities to be found in the physical and mental domains. Now we must acknowledge that it is equally impossible to say anything meaningful about the intrinsic nature of the link between the two types of reality. Obviously, if one subscribes to the 'common reality hypothesis', whereby the physical and mental explanatory frameworks are to be thought of as complementary ways of addressing the same reality, there is no problem. The physical arrival of light from the Moon on the retina of my eye is correlated to the mental experience of observing the Moon because the two descriptions refer to one and the same feature of the common reality. This approach to reality does, of course, have its own difficulty: why the same event should lend itself to two such radically different types of description - a problem as intractable for this viewpoint as that of correlation is for the two-reality hypothesis.

Because the question of there being one or two realities is inherently insoluble, I have deliberately opted for the neutral word 'mapping' to refer to correlations between the reality bases of the two explanatory frameworks. It is neutral in the following sense: An ordinary map is associated with a certain geographical terrain. The map and the terrain are obviously very different from each other in terms of one consisting of paper and ink, the other of earth, rocks, trees and houses. But there are correspondences between the two. Related to certain features of the terrain, there are certain features on the map. The way features of the terrain relate to each other has a bearing on how the features of the map have been drawn relative to each other. This is not to say every feature of one has its representation in the other. Not all the physical objects to be found on the landscape are shown on the map, neither does the terrain show all the information that is on the map - political boundaries and who owns which plot of land. There is no causal link between the terrain and map; they may never have come into physical contact with each other. One cannot even say that the map is the way it is 'because' of the characteristics of the terrain; for all we know, the map might have come first, the terrain later being laid out according to it.

The idea of a mapping is used in mathematics. There it is given a rather strict and formal definition inappropriate to the present context. But even as used in that context, it conveys the same sense of neutrality as regards the nature of the link between the two domains - in this case, domains consisting of mathematical entities.

I should add that whenever I talk of mappings between the physical and the mental, I do not mean to imply that these are necessarily mappings between particular aspects of the thoughts one has at any one time, and particular component features of what is occurring in the brain - which is doubtless the impression given by the analogy of the map and the terrain. It is preferable to think of the *total* experience of the mind at any one time correlated by a one-to-one mapping to the *total* activity of the brain, including any other part of the anatomy that might be relevant. Thus, by speaking of the domain of mental experience, we do *not* mean the state of the mind at one particular instant, with the entities in the domain being identifiable elements that make up the total experience at that time. Rather, it is a domain consisting of a collection of total experiences of the mind as they are at different instants of time. Just as the physical framework has the task of relating successive physical states, and must therefore address a domain consisting of physical states as they are at different instants of physical time, so the mental framework relates successive total experiences, and must therefore address a domain consisting of total experiences as they are at different instants of mental time. The manner in which the consecutive mental states relate to each other in the mental domain reflects in some way the manner in which the correlated states of brain activity relate to each other in the physical domain.

2. The idea of a mapping is sufficiently important to our discussion that it is worth spending a little more time clarifying the way we shall be using it. To emphasise its wide applicability, we consider an example that has nothing to do with maps as we ordinarily understand them - one that serves as a particularly suitable analogy for the relationship between the mental and physical.

Imagine contestants competing in a TV quiz game. Each progressively amasses a point score according to the rules of the game. Corresponding to the points gained, there are prizes to be won. At any stage of the game the contestants can opt to collect whatever prize corresponds to their current score, or if they prefer, they can carry on accumulating more points in the hopes of later winning a more valuable prize. To each prize on offer there corresponds a particular number of points. But until they have opted to collect a prize, they do not know ahead of time what it will be. That would be information additional to that which is to be found in the rationale of the game - information to which the contestants do not have access.

Behind the scenes, the situation is different. Here we have an assistant whose responsibility is to despatch the prizes to the studio as and when they are needed. She is positioned out of ear-shot, so cannot hear how the game is progressing; she therefore depends on the producer's instructions as relayed over headphones. For the assistant, unlike the contestants, there is no mystery over the prizes and why these particular ones are on offer this week. She herself was responsible for their purchase in advance of the show. She knows the budget she had to work to, what was available from the suppliers, what discounts were to be had, which prizes have proved popular in the past, etc. For her the unknown element concerns, not the nature of the prizes, but which ones will be called upon, and when exactly they will be required. She cannot learn this merely from a study of the prizes themselves or from what she knows of the rationale that went into their purchase.

The contestants in the studio and the assistant behind the scenes deal in different entities - points in the one case, prizes in the other. The points constitute one domain, the prizes another. Each domain has a rationale of its own. In the studio, the rules of the game and the skills of the contestants determine the development of the point scores over time and how the individual scores relate to each other. Behind the scenes, the budget to which the assistant had to adhere, among other factors, determines the nature of the prizes. The separate rationales have an integrity of their own. A quiz game can be satisfactorily conducted without the incentive provided by prizes, and goods can be purchased without the need to give them away.

The idea of mapping comes in when we note that to each prize there corresponds a point score; we say the prize maps to the point score, and vice-versa, the score maps to the prize. It can be a one-to-one mapping with a different prize for each score, or a one-to-many mapping if several scores (all those lying within some range) correspond to the same prize. The mapping concept implies that there can also be a correspondence between the rationales operating in the two domains. Although, as we have seen, these rationales are very different in character, nevertheless, the characteristics of the one are to some extent reflected in those of the other. This comes about through the systematic manner in which the mappings between the states are established. The point scores are not associated with prizes in a haphazard manner; the higher the score, the more valuable the prize to which it maps. As a consequence, the range of possible point scores becomes related to the purchase of prizes of

markedly differing value, and the fact that it takes time for the contestants to amass the higher point scores accounts for the more valuable prizes not being required until later in the show.
  Such then is an example of a mapping. How can we use it as an analogy for the relationship between the physical and the mental? The point scores are to be likened to the entities belonging to the physical domain, the prizes to those belonging to the mental domain. The point scores evolve in accordance with the rules of the quiz game; physical phenomena are governed by the laws of physics as incorporated into the physical explanatory framework. As far as the conduct of a game is concerned, there is no necessity to have prizes; indeed some games do not have them; contestants learn of prizes only when they appear from behind the scenes. The point scores constitute a self-contained system. Likewise, according to the view we have so far consistently followed, as far as the study of physics is concerned, there appears to be no need to invoke the existence of mental phenomena. The knowledge that physical activities of the brain are associated with mental experiences, is additional information injected from outside the physical explanatory framework.
  Behind the scenes there is a certain way of thinking about the prizes that is independent of any quiz show that might be going on - various considerations that went into their purchase. Similarly, the mental explanatory framework incorporates ways of thought that make sense in their own terms. Humans were rational beings long before they became aware that their thoughts were reflected in brain activity.
3. But in contrast to what happens in the quiz game, not everything about the prizes can be understood solely in their own terms. While certain aspects about them are subject to a self-contained rationale, not all are. The prizes disappear from time to time, and in a systematic order. How is the assistant to account for that? If she is restricted to a study of the prizes themselves, she cannot.

To make sense of what is going on, she has to refer out to the game. Only by asking the producer what happened in the studio can she gain the necessary additional information. Thus, in order to understand everything about the prizes one must refer to the point scores, whereas it is never necessary to refer to the prizes in order to understand everything about the point scores. This asymmetry is one that is widely thought to apply to the physical and mental domains. Take first an attempt to explain the following sequence of mental occurrences: One has a headache. A little while later, one experiences a set of observations associated with finding a bottle of aspirin and swallowing a tablet. Finally, the headache is gone. How are we to account for its disappearance? Because the states we are dealing with are mental ones, our first reaction is to seek an explanation in mental terms. But it is not obvious how this is to be done. The intermediate observations cannot themselves be regarded as sufficient explanation. The feeling of swallowing an aspirin is no different from that of swallowing any other tablet, yet the effects are different. We have no recourse but to call upon the physical explanatory framework. Accordingly, we examine whatever brain activity occurs at the same time as the headache - the physical state that maps to the mental experience. Then, by following through the chemical changes that occur to the brain as a result of the chemical action of the aspirin, we arrive at the resulting later state of the brain - one that is of a type that maps to mental experiences free of headaches. The rationale characteristic of the physical domain is able to forge a continuous link between the earlier and later brain states, and then, through the mapping of the two brain states onto their respective mental experiences, we complete the explanatory connection between the two otherwise disconnected mental states - the one with the headache and the one without. Of course, in practice it is difficult, not to say impossible, to carry out such an investigation in all its detail; the development of drugs entails a good deal of trial and error.

Nevertheless, an explanation of the disappearance of the headache is generally to be thought of in terms of the chemical action of the aspirin on the brain. In effect, *one is relying on the physical explanatory framework to help out with an explanation of something happening in the mental domain.* According to those who hold to the view that the relationship between the mental and the physical is asymmetric, this need to defer to the other explanatory framework in order to fill a gap in explanation that otherwise cannot be bridged, is not something that applies to the physical domain. They are of the view that physical phenomena can be explained exclusively in physical terms. For example, a man raises his arm. The arm at first is resting by his side; the next moment it rises up. How do we account for this? Electrical currents and chemical changes in the brain trigger off other processes in various parts of the body, resulting in the contraction of the relevant muscles. Again, of course, there are practical problems in actually seeing through such a programme of investigation. But such an explanation is, in principle, possible - at least so it is claimed. This being so, an explanatory link between the two physical states - arm resting, arm up - can be forged purely in physical terms. Though there might be an alternative mental explanation for what happens - one couched in terms of the man willing his arm to rise in order to scratch an itching nose - this is entirely by the way; *the physical explanation is complete in its own terms.*

The *asymmetric view* of the relation between the mental and physical explanatory frameworks, whereby the former in its explanation of mental occurrences sometimes has to defer to the latter, while the latter in its explanation of physical occurrences never has to defer to the former, can be accounted a reasonable one. After all, our search for understanding begins with ourselves as conscious beings in the reality domain of mental experience; we do not start out from the physical domain. All understanding eventually refers back to mental experience, not to physical events. Therein lies the source of the asymmetry. Explanatory frameworks - all of them, not just the mental one - ultimately have a bearing on our understanding of the mental domain; that is the reason they are invoked in the first place. This being so, it should cause no surprise if the relationship between the frameworks is not reciprocal.

4. That having been said, however, it has to be added that there is no scientific proof that the relationship between the frameworks is as described. Admittedly no physics textbook yet written introduces mental concepts as an integral part of its description of the physical. But this signifies little. Explanations in mental terms, if they are to be required at all, would be expected to arise in the context of exhaustive studies of the physical working of the brain. These have not been carried out, at least not at the level of detail necessary to show that behaviour at the atomic level in the brain conforms in all respects to that expected from the normal operation of the known laws of physics. For all we know, it could be that when a person decides on a course of action, that act of the will results in a hiatus in the operation of the physical laws as applied to the working of the brain. Take the case of the man with the itching nose. For a time he is content to do nothing about it. The physical processes in the brain evolve in the manner expected from the operation of the laws of physics. But then he suddenly decides he has had enough and resolves to raise his arm and scratch. Corresponding to this decision, the brain now goes into a state that is different from that which would have occurred had he not so decided to act. A scientist who happened to be examining the contents of this person's brain at the time would find that the evolution of this new brain state was inexplicable in terms of the laws of physics. He would be left with no option but to defer to the mental explanatory framework's account of what was happening in order to bridge the gap in understanding. It is a possibility. The experimental evidence to date is insufficient to settle the issue one way or the other. Indeed the difficulties in-

volved in such an investigation are so great, the question might never be resolved.

This latter possibility, in which the explanation of physical events must sometimes defer to the mental explanatory framework in much the same way as the explanation of mental experiences must sometimes defer to the physical explanatory framework, we shall call the *symmetric view*. In terms of the TV quiz show analogy, it is a view that can be represented by a suitable change to the format of the game. It is arranged that among the prizes are some unusual ones consisting of cards saying things like 'Double your score!' or 'Miss the next turn!' Unlike the other prizes which simply consist of goods that are taken home, these have a direct impact upon the quiz itself. In breach of the normal arithmetic governing the addition of scores, one of the contestants suddenly acquires a bonus. In breach of the way the contestants take turns at asking questions, one of the contestants drops out for a round. These anomalies do not make sense according to the rules that normally control the running of the game; they are to be understood only by deferring to the description of the prizes.

It is important that you be clear about the asymmetric and symmetric views of the relationship between the explanatory frameworks. At the risk of labouring the point, let me spell it out:

The explanatory framework associated with a given reality domain, A, is able successfully to account for what is happening in that domain until a certain state (called State 1A) is reached. The next state is State 2A, and there appears to be no satisfactory explanation as to why State 2A should follow State 1A. It is noted, however, that State 1A is mapped to State 1B of a second reality domain, B. Using the concepts and rules belonging to the explanatory framework of domain B, one then accounts for the way State 1B evolves into State 2B. This new state in reality domain B is then seen to map to the second of our states, State 2A in reality domain A. So although the explanatory framework associated with reality domain

A provides no rational link between State 1A and State 2A, that associated with reality domain B does provide a satisfactory link between State 1B and State 2B. It is not that the framework associated with reality A borrows concepts from that associated with reality B. Rather, *a complete switch is made from one framework to the other*; there is a clean break in the description given by one framework, and the other takes over for a while to explain what is happening in its own reality domain.

According to the first of the two views we have been examining (that in which the relation is asymmetric), domain A is to be regarded as exclusively identified with the mental domain, and B with the physical. An understanding of mental experiences sometimes needs to defer to the physical, whereas an understanding of physical phenomena need never invoke the mental explanatory framework. The second view holds that, depending on the circumstances, A and B can be associated with either the mental or the physical; mental processes sometimes require physical explanation, physical processes in the brain sometimes require mental explanations. Both views strike their adherents as reasonable. Neither has been experimentally confirmed or refuted.

5. Thus, we are left in the unsatisfactory situation that we do not know, and might never know, whether physical laws alone could adequately account for all physical phenomena in the brain (the asymmetric view), or whether it is sometimes necessary to invoke the mental framework to explain what is going on (the symmetric view).

Can it be argued that one point of view is more reasonable than the other? Not really. I have already indicated why the asymmetric relation between the frameworks can be regarded as a satisfying way of looking at the situation. But a plausible case can also be made for expecting a symmetrical relation. In talking about different types of reality (or one reality addressed in complementary ways), it can be argued as aesthetically pleasing and simple that the explanatory frameworks should enjoy equal status. If one of them needs sometimes to defer to the other, then the reverse should also apply.

6. When the mental framework defers to the physical in order to fill in an explanatory gap, it is responding to the otherness of the situation. Something happens in the mental domain that cannot be explained by the mental framework. In order to account for it, we look outside for an explanation couched in terms of some other reality. But there is another entirely different reason why we might need to switch explanatory frameworks: *the type of question to be answered*. Recall that I said of explanatory frameworks, not only that they incorporate concepts, principles for handling those concepts, and rules of discussion, but that they are set up to address particular types of question. Physical explanatory frameworks are especially concerned with questions of the how-type; they are not equipped to deal with why-type questions to do with purpose. Yet sometimes it is that kind of question that interests us.

In asking why an arm is raised, for example, it is unlikely one is concerned about the mechanics of muscle movement. The answer one wants is about noses itching and the motivation to do something about it. Or take the example of a contestant getting home after the quiz show and being asked by his wife how he got on. He launches into a detailed account of the questions he was asked, how many points he scored for this, how many for that, how he missed out on the bonus - only to be interrupted: 'That's all very well. But what I want to know is: Did you win anything worth having?'

The motivation behind asking a question ostensibly about the physical domain, might well be more directed at the mental experiences that attend those physical occurrences, than with the occurrences themselves. The type of question being asked can thus determine the framework to be used. It is important to bear this in mind. Later we shall find that the need to address questions to do with ultimate meaning and purpose will be one of the motivations for setting up a spiritual explanatory framework.

7. That essentially completes what I have to say about the relationship between the physical and mental reality domains. I cannot leave the subject, however, without pointing out a potentially serious consequence arising out of the adoption of the asymmetric view. This concerns its implications for the concept of free will. If everything happening in the physical domain can adequately be accounted for solely in terms of the normal operation of physical laws, then the future is determined (laying aside quantum uncertainties). Under these circumstances how can anyone affect that future by choosing one course of action rather than another? And if there is to be no free will, does that not make a nonsense of all religious talk about our need to 'choose' to enter into a relationship with God, or to follow Christ, etc.?

Indeed this is not the only threat to free will. In Section 8.5 we saw how relativity theory presented us with a picture of the whole of physical time - past, present, and future - as being in existence together. Thus, whether or not we can predict the future deterministically from the laws of physics, the future, whatever form it takes, is already fixed waiting for us to come upon it. Again, where is the room for making choices? The question of free will is clearly one we have to face up to at some point, and this is probably as good a time as any. It involves something of a digression from the main line of argument, so if you prefer not to interrupt the train of thought we have been developing, you can skip to the start of the next chapter, returning to this section later.

Instinctively we rebel against the idea that we do not have freedom to act as we will. It is not that we always do what we want. External constraints, to say nothing of unconscious drives, sometimes force us into courses of action we would reject if circumstances were otherwise. But when faced with an apparent choice, we always act according to our will. We might decide to act 'against our better judgement' (perhaps to prove that someone else's advice was wrong), or we might act altruistically in the interests of someone else at some sacrifice to ourselves. Or we might not have the strength of character to act as we would wish, perhaps through fear, or some addiction or phobia. Nevertheless, each conscious choice is accompanied by a will so to act. We might be ashamed of our action, or disappointed at our weakness in making such a decision, but the decision is ours and we are responsible for it. The will and the act to which it leads are authentic expressions of our character. Such is the conviction we all share.

I suspect that it is largely because of the perceived need to retain this belief about ourselves that inclines so many to accept the symmetric view. On the face of it there appears no other way of respecting free will. According to this view, the human body is not to be regarded as just another physical object, the behaviour of which is bound by the laws of physics. Though the behaviour of inanimate objects is predictable, that of human bodies is not. This is because they can be affected by mental decisions. Though to some extent they obey the laws of physics, a conscious decision by the subject to act differently can interrupt the normal flow of physical events and alter the outcome. A full understanding of the behaviour of a human body requires a knowledge of what goes on in the mind; it thus lies beyond the competence of the physical sciences. Further, because the subject has yet to decide how to act on future occasions, the future has to be thought of as open, that is to say, as not yet fixed. Hence, according to the symmetric view, there is no problem over free will. The situation is exactly as our mental experience would appear to indicate: the future is uncertain because it depends to some extent upon choices we have yet to make.

This view does not stand up to close scrutiny - at least not quite in the form described. It does away with determinism by opting for the symmetric rather than asymmetric view of the relationship between the physical and the mental. But it in no way addresses the problem raised by relativity theory. Earlier we saw the need to distinguish between two types of time: mental and physical. The two are distinct from each other but correlated. Mental time certainly *appears* to have an open future; we do not *know* what it holds for us. Physical time, on the other hand, exists in its entirety. Relativistic spacetime, incorporating as it does physical time, is a complete four-dimensional existence. Granted, a particular instant of physical time is singled out for a special correlation with the present instant of mental time. But the particularity of this correlation does not mean that only this instant of physical time exists. Rather, we are to think of the *whole* of physical time as being simultaneously in existence, not only at the present instant, but at every other experienced instant of mental time. Though we do not know what the future holds, it is nevertheless fixed.

So the modern understanding of time argues against the notion of a future that is undecided. What significance does this have for the idea of free will? I would suggest, very little. To see why, consider the following possibility: Unknown to yourself, someone using a concealed camera has been filming you over the past couple of hours. Because you were unaware of what was happening, your actions were, of course, unaffected by the act of filming. The film shows you reading this book, turning the pages, yawning, going for a walk, making some coffee, and anything else you might have done. It shows the usual kinds of actions arising out of your decisions so to act. The film is a complete record of what you did during that period; it includes your earlier actions and your later ones. One can view any part of it, and see the whole film through several times. One can get to know it so well that by dipping into it at any point one knows exactly what is going to happen later. Your actions in the film are predictable. Does this mean that they must, therefore, be the actions of an unthinking robot? Of course not. The film shows someone genuinely making decisions and acting accordingly. The fact that someone examining the sequence comes to know what the later parts contain in no way detracts from it being the record of the actions of a free agent.

In similar vein, therefore, we are to think in terms of there already being in existence a record of one's complete life. It is a record etched into the fabric of four-dimensional space-time. It is the life story of a free agent. The fact that in this sense the future already exists and awaits us, does not stop it from being *our* future - one in which we make decisions for which we, and we alone, are responsible. The existence of this physical record in no way affects how we live out our lives. As conscious mental beings, we do not have access to that part of the record that relates to the future; in this we are like the person living out life before the concealed camera. That kind of foreknowledge is the prerogative of God; he is to be likened to a person who is able to view any part of the film at will. Thus, for the purposes of living out one's daily life, it is as though the record of the future did not exist. From this perspective it is as if God and ourselves act sequentially and progressively in time. It is only through reflection on the deeper significance of the theory of relativity that one comes to accept the need to put aside one's natural prejudice, and grant at least intellectual assent to the idea of a future that is in some form already fixed, and a God who in some sense transcends time.

Thus we see that the idea of free will, even according to the symmetric view, needs to be modified somewhat in regard to this question of openness. But that apart, it remains intact. What of free will in the context of the asymmetric view - that which holds that all physical behaviour is to be accounted for in terms of the laws of physics, there being no need to refer to what is going on in the mind? Under such circumstances is one inevitably forced to abandon all vestiges of the idea of free will? I hope to show this does not necessarily follow.

First we must dispose of a red herring. In order to escape the idea that we behave deterministically, some people like to invoke the indeterminism that arises out of quantum theory. It is certainly the case that at the atomic level, the future cannot be predicted with certainty; the most one can do is to give the probabilities of various possible outcomes. But when it comes to macroscopic objects, such as those we deal with in everyday life, the quantum uncertainties are so minute that they can be ignored. For such objects, the normal classical idea that the laws of physics can predict the future still hold. Of course, we cannot be sure that quantum effects are to be ignored in the operation of a human body. It could be that in the brain, the act of reaching a decision on a given course of action might correspond to a single atomic event - one that then triggers off an avalanche of processes, eventually culminating in the action of the body as a whole. If this were the case, then our actions would indeed to some extent be governed by quantum rather than classical physics, and would therefore not be entirely predictable.

But would that help the cause of free will? I don't see how. To have a decision arising out of pure chance (for that is what is happening at the quantum mechanical level) seems to have very little to do with a decision arising from choice. When a decision is based on chance, by the toss of a coin, for example, we do not consider it to have arisen out of conscious choice. Indeed, one resorts to coin-tossing as a way of avoiding having to make a conscious choice. So, from here on, for the purposes of considering free will, we shall ignore quantum theory and assume the human body to be predictable in the classical sense.

To clarify what is entailed by the asymmetric view, consider a physical system consisting of a human body and every other physical object that is capable of interacting with it and with each other. The system is to be thought of as closed off from all outside influence. From a knowledge of the nature of the objects, their positions, and their motions, and the forces acting between them, the future behaviour of all objects in this system is predictable. This holds equally for the human body as for any of the other objects. In order to determine the physical behaviour of the body, there is no need to take into account the centre of consciousness associated with the body. Mental phenomena accompany the various states of the human body, but they do not provide information concerning physical behaviour additional to that already available from an exhaustive knowledge of all the physical components of the body and how these are acted upon by the other elements of the system.

Under these conditions, not only is the physical behaviour of the body determined, but also the future states of the mind. As before, we consider there to be a mapping between the physical state of the body and the state of the mind. Corresponding to a particular state of the body (especially the brain) there will be a particular state of the mind. In particular, there will be a physical state corresponding to a mental state in which the person concerned has not made up his mind on a given issue. This is later followed by a physical state corresponding to a mental state where a decision has been made. Because the second physical state evolves from the first in a deterministic manner, we must conclude that the second of the mental states is also determined by what has gone before.

The mental state associated with the making of a conscious decision about some course of action, incorporates within it what is known as the *will* to act in that particular way. It is that aspect of the mental state that carries with it the sense of responsibility for the ensuing action. It also incorporates an expectation that the action will indeed be performed. This expectation might not always be fulfilled. Having decided to raise one's arm, for example, one might find that it fails to respond because it has been paralysed by the injection of a muscle-relaxant drug. Normally, however, the will to raise the arm would be followed by the experience of feeling the arm go up. In the same way as one physical state follows on as a natural outcome of the earlier one, so one mental state (the feeling of the arm going up) is perceived as a natural outgrowth of the earlier one (the decision to raise the arm). This is an important point. Too often the idea of determinism is coupled to the notion of compulsion against one's will - the idea that if we were subject to determinism our mental life would be one in which we would feel ourselves constantly fighting a losing battle against inexorable forces compelling us to act, regardless of our own intentions, in conformity to some preordained plan that was not of our own devising. Either that, or determinism is taken to imply that we have to go through life as an unthinking robot, passively swept along by the tide of events. Neither of these conclusions needs hold. Determinism is perfectly compatible with our invariably acting according to our will. It is not so much that we are *free* to act according to our will as *guaranteed* so to act; the necessity is one to which we voluntarily subscribe. Because our conscious actions spring from a will that is an integral part of the mental state preceding the action, and that mental state reflects the kind of person we are, those actions are to be regarded as authentic expressions of our character.

We have seen how the fact that one physical state determines the nature of the next physical state implies, through the mapping, that the corresponding initial mental state determines the next mental state. In the physical explanatory framework we regard the progressive evolution of one state into another as a natural consequence of the laws of physics; likewise in the mental explanatory framework we regard the evolution of one mental state into another as a natural consequence of acts of the will and of the person's general character. But the idea that a state (physical or mental) is what it is because of what has gone before is only one way of looking at the situation. 'Determinism', in the more general sense of that word, means that events cannot occur otherwise than they do. It is only in a more restricted sense that the term carries the further implication that this fixity of events arises *because* of what has gone before.

But there are other ways of accounting for that fixity. Let us examine the alternatives.

In the physical explanatory framework, the laws of physics operate equally in both directions with respect to time. Not only can one use the laws of physics to work out from a knowledge of the initial state what the later state will be, one can also deduce from a knowledge of the later state what the initial state must have been. (How else would we know that in the beginning there was a Big Bang?) Thus, in physics we are able to say that, not only does the present state fix the future state, but the future state fixes the present one. Both claims are equally valid. The idea of the future controlling the present might seem a little odd at first, especially if one has in mind a future that does not yet exist. But this is not how one should be thinking of future physical states. Recall what was earlier said about all instants of time in the physical domain being on an equal footing - they *all* exist.

The possibility of having rival interpretations of the data is not something confined to the physical explanatory framework. When dealing with mental experiences, it is again commonplace to use language predicated on the idea that the future exerts an influence on the present. We all speak of goals and expectations for the future and how these provide our current motivations. This is true at every level of activity. On the large scale it is the future state of being a doctor that determines that the young person is currently in medical school. On the small scale, it is the anticipated relief of having the nose stop itching that determines the earlier decision to scratch. But note that in both cases the sequence can be interpreted either way. The relationship can be thought of as operating either forwards or backwards in time. The desire to be a doctor determines that the youth is currently in medical school, but the fact that one is currently in medical school implies that someday one will be a doctor; the desire to stop the nose from itching determines that one should now scratch, but the fact that one now scratches is the reason why the nose later ceases to itch.

The existence of two alternative ways of interpreting what is going on means that acceptance of the fixity of events does not entail having to think exclusively in terms of being causally propelled into the future, the present state being simply a product of what has gone before. It is equally justified to describe the present state as moulded by what is to come, and to regard ourselves as drawn towards the future. This ambiguity of interpretation is reflected in the differing approaches adopted by the various schools of psychology. According to Freud, the reason for a person's neurotic behaviour is to be found by digging into the past and uncovering the deep sexually oriented events that have been causally responsible for the person's present condition. On the other hand, the school that owes its origins to Adler, holds that what matters most is not so much the sex instinct, as the power instinct - the desire to gain power over people. From this point of view, neurotic behaviour is adopted in order to exercise power over others, through evoking sympathy, etc. Its description as an 'instinct' implies 'drivenness', yet the fact that it is oriented towards the achievement of some future goal suggests, in some sense, a teleological interpretation. Thus, we have two widely differing approaches to the same situation. Both account for the data, each in its own way. Each is self-consistent. But placed side by side they appear to contradict each other: one holds that the reason for the present state lies in the past, the other that the reason lies in the future. How are we to choose between them? We do not have to choose. Each has its own particular insight to offer. Though in any given set of circumstances one interpretation might be potentially more fruitful than the other, both are required if one is to attain the fullest appreciation of what goes on in the mind.

We have seen that two markedly different ways of interpreting what happens in the physical domain, are analogous to two equally different ways of regarding what goes on in the mind. But there is yet a third way in which scientists interpret physical behaviour. It is an approach based on *variational principles*. To understand what these are we have to recognize that in physical explanation there are essentially three elements: (i) an initial state, (ii) a final state, and (iii) what happens to the physical system as it evolves from one state to the other. Knowledge of any two of these elements leads to knowledge of the remaining one. In the first physical interpretation, we start out with a knowledge of the initial state and of those laws of physics that determine how the physical system progressively evolves from there; hence we arrive at a prediction of what the final state will be. In the second interpretation, we start out again with a knowledge of the laws of physics governing the progressive evolution of the system, but this time coupled with a knowledge of the final state; the aim now is to deduce what the initial state must have been. In the third interpretation - the one based on variational principles - we start with a knowledge of both the initial and final states, the aim being to arrive at an understanding of what happened in between.

An example might help: Consider a bow firing an arrow at a distant target. If one knows the position of the bow and the initial direction and speed of the arrow, one can use the laws of motion to determine the progress of the arrow and hence where it eventually strikes. Alternatively, if one is on the receiving end, one can note where the arrow landed and what its direction and speed were on impact, and use the laws of motion progressively to trace back where the arrow must have come from. In the variational method we start out with a knowledge of the position, speed, and direction of the arrow at *both* its starting point and end point. The problem here is to determine which trajectory out of all those that could conceivably have linked these initial and final states of the arrow was the one actually taken. In other words, we imagine all manner of paths - smooth ones, jagged ones, paths that double back on themselves, loop-the-loop, any type whatsoever - and we ask which of all these is the actual one taken. The answer is remarkably simple: it is the one for which a certain physical quantity, called the 'action,' is a minimum. ('Action' is defined as the mass of the arrow multiplied by its speed multiplied by the distance it travels with that speed.) Thus, we calculate the value of this quantity for a tiny segment of a possible path, add it to the value we get for the next segment, and carry on doing this for every segment of the path, so arriving at the overall total value of the action for that particular path. One then imagines repeating this procedure for all the other paths the arrow might have followed. On comparison of these various total actions, it then turns out that, from the infinite number of conceivable paths, the one actually taken by the arrow is that for which the total action is the least.

Variational principles govern the motion of everything in the universe. In the case of light, for instance, one finds that in travelling from one point to another it picks out the path which takes the least time. Thus, a light beam confronted by the need to pass through an array of glass lenses, quartz prisms, and troughs containing water and oil - each medium characterized by a different speed for the light - this beam will unerringly arrive at its destination having charted the quickest path between the starting and finishing points.

Again this might strike you as odd. It would seem that the arrow, or the light beam, as it sets out on its journey, already has advance knowledge of where it will eventually be; how else could it work out which path to choose? Again we have to keep firmly in mind that as far as the physical domain is concerned, the final state is to be thought of as being as much in existence as the initial state. The fact that all three elements - initial state, final state, and the path in between - co-exist on equal terms makes possible a holistic interpretation. The variational method is holistic in nature in that it makes use of the two end states, together with a property which is a characteristic of the *whole* path. As such, it contrasts with the two earlier methods which rely on tracing out the path step by step starting from one end or the other. The variational method affords additional interpretive insight as to what is going on in the physical domain - insight that stems from this holistic feature.

So, does the variational approach have its analogue in the mental domain? It would appear so. There can be few who have not at sometime or other taken stock of their current situation in life, compared it to that of childhood, with all its aspirations and hopes for the future, and arrived at some assessment of the life that has linked these two endpoints. This kind of reflection often reveals that certain qualities and guiding principles, perhaps unrecognized at the time, have been at work throughout. These overarching principles - be they religious or secular, self-gratifying or altruistic, ambitious or self-effacing, aggressive or peace-loving, or whatever - these controlling principles are what have served to determine the shape of that life.

Like the earlier two approaches to the interpretation of mental experience, this more holistic method can also be thought of as represented by one of the established schools of psychology. In keeping with the theories of Jung, one first takes note of the state of the mind as it is at birth - a state characterized by a structure already possessing certain inclinations and patterns of potential behaviour. To this one adds an understanding of what it means to be a fully developed, mature adult in later life. This latter state involves the conscious recognition and fulfillment of the earlier potential of the individual. Armed thus with a knowledge of both the beginning point and desired end point of life's path, the aim is to arrive at the kind of life that links the two. This type of life incorporates a process of psychological development that Jungians call 'individuation'. I shall say more of this later (Chapter 15).

Let us now summarize the consequences of adopting a deterministic outlook: We have found that in the physical domain there are three very different interpretations one can put on events. We have further noted that each of these interpretations is closely paralleled by a way of interpreting what goes on in the mind. No single interpretation has any absolute claim to superiority over the others. All three are to be regarded as equally valid. Each has its own insights to offer. Though a specific situation might be more suitably handled by one interpretation than another, generally speaking, for the richest understanding of what goes on in either the physical or mental domain, one needs to retain all three.

So finally, are we to conclude that the fixity of events in both the physical and mental domains necessarily disposes of all traces of free will? Hardly. After all, what are we left with? A person whose actions are authentic expressions of his or her character, are consonant with and dependent upon the will, are in pursuit of adopted goals and aspirations, and accord with overall guiding principles. It is a person who sounds suspiciously like someone with free will!

What is missing? In the first place, openness, i.e. the undecidedness of the future. But that has gone whether or not one has determinism - a consequence of relativity. Secondly, some will hold that there really is no element of genuine freedom left. Here we must be careful. Freedom to do what? In line with the treatment given above, we are already acting according to our will. The will being what it is, to act otherwise would mean acting contrary to it. But that, by the very definition of the term 'will', is a nonsense; our conscious actions *must* be in accordance with our will. So the demand for freedom appears to require that there be alternative courses of action to the one taken, but courses of action which, by their very nature, are never taken. 'Freedom' so defined is an empty concept.

But, it might be countered, that way of arguing gets off on the wrong foot with the assumption of 'the will being what it is'. Suppose the will were not what it is. Suppose we adopt as our definition of a free agent someone who, under exactly the same circumstances, can will to do differently (and consequently can, under those same circumstances, act differently). Is determinism compatible with freedom so defined? To answer this we must go back to the idea of a physical system, containing a human body and all the other objects with which it comes into contact. Isolated from all outside influence, the state of this system at a given time determines what the future state will be. If the earlier state is one in which the brain belonging to the human body is in a condition that correlates to the person willing a particular action, then this state will evolve into one in which that action is performed. But we must be clear that when we talk of the 'circumstances' of the person, we are *not* referring to this overall system; we mean that *part* of the overall system that is other than the human body. We can consider two possible states of the overall system in which that part which constitutes the environment surrounding the body (the circumstances) is identical, but that part to do with the state of the brain is different. In one case the state of the brain is that which correlates to a mental state characterised by a will to perform a particular action; in the other, the brain is in a state correlated to a will to act in some alternative way. Can these alternative wills lead to different courses of action? Yes. The state of the overall system depends, not only upon the circumstances in which the body finds itself, but also on the state of the brain. Because this is different in the two cases, the state of the overall system will be different in the two cases. Consequently the evolution of the overall state in the two cases will be different - one leading to one course of action, the other to another.

This is not in any way to claim that the concept of free will poses no difficulties. There has always in Christianity been a tension between the notions of free will and predestination - the need to balance the seemingly opposed requirements of, on the one hand, our being free agents capable of offering or withholding our love of God, and on the other, God's already knowing what our future decisions will be, and more than that, having himself decided who is to receive salvation. Nor is this kind of dilemma specific to Christianity; closely related problems are to be found in Judaism, Islam, and certain Hindu traditions. Holding a fair balance between the seemingly competing demands is not easy.

There appear to be grounds for the claim that in recent times a shift has been made towards placing more emphasis on a perceived need to keep one's own freedom unfettered, with consequently less attention being paid to foreknowledge and predestination. The loss of the openness of the future, through the theory of relativity, might be seen as a welcome corrective to this tendency. It goes some way towards redressing the balance, at least in respect of God's foreknowledge. Acceptance of determinism, however, might be held to tip the scales too far in that direction. But what I hope the above treatment serves to show is that, even if one goes along with the asymmetric deterministic viewpoint, one does not end up as a pawn of fate, powerless to act in accordance with one's will. Indeed a great deal of what is normally meant by free will is preserved - sufficient, to my mind, to safeguard our sense of the dignity of humankind. The crucial point, as far as I am concerned, is this: Were we to be given the opportunity of operating under the conditions associated with the traditional idea of free will, would we choose to act differently to what we do. We would not. For that reason, we must be held accountable for our actions.

One might still try to escape responsibility for those actions by claiming that, although our character and personality led to those actions, we are not responsible for having that character and personality in the first place. There is no easy way of countering that argument. In it lies the mystery of predestination and God's own responsibility for the way he has made us, as well as the accountability of others for the part they have played in moulding us. All one can do is to note that this particular problem arises irrespective of whether one operates under the conditions of determinism, unfettered freedom as traditionally understood, or whatever.

CHAPTER 11

OTHER MINDS AND THE CONCEPT OF ONESELF

WE return once more to our main theme: how we might infer the existence of realities other than that of mental experiences. We have seen that there is no water-tight proof of the existence of the physical domain - only a reasonable inference based on the perceived explanatory power of the hypothesis. This is not to say that belief in a physical domain necessarily entails belief in a world-in-itself. That, as we have noted, is subject to greater doubt because such a world-in-itself would lie beyond the domain of interactions-with-the-world, a further inferential step away from direct experience. How about the existence of other minds?

1. In order to study what exists, one must take account of conscious experience. For the sake of argument we have allowed the assumption that there is direct access to the contents of the mind. But *whose* mind? Everybody's? That cannot be right. If I have direct access to mental experiences, they can only be those of my own mind. Strictly speaking, therefore, I ought to begin by accepting the existence of nothing beyond that. Before making use of information provided by the conscious experience of other people, I need to establish that there are indeed minds other than my own.

This, of course, sounds absurd. How could I possibly doubt that there are other minds! So much of life makes sense only in the context of my being one conscious mind in interaction with other conscious minds. Why else would I be writing this book if I were not convinced that there were some potential readers? But the fact that the conviction is so strong does not negate the need to see how it might be legitimized. Belief in the physical world-in-itself once seemed unshakable!

First we ought to consider the possibility of direct communication between minds through a telepathic link. Whether there is such a thing or not is, of course, the subject of perennial debate. I myself have no experience of the phenomenon, so am inclined to be sceptical. But even were one to accept the possibility, it would not greatly alter the conclusions of the following discussion. Such communication would be experienced as an input of information into my mind - a phenomenon I would still have to interpret in terms of where I thought it came from. Without more ado, therefore, I shall set aside the possibility of telepathy, and turn to the only alternative source of evidence for other minds - that provided by the normal five senses.

The idea that there might be minds other than my own comes mainly from those observations I make that are to do with other human bodies. In the physical domain there is an object of particular relevance to me: my body. (More precisely, in the domain of physical interactions there is a collection of interactions called 'interactions of my body'; this, however, is not a point that in the current context needs labouring.) This object is of especial significance because it is that aspect of the physical domain that maps to my mental experiences. But this body seems to be only one of several similar looking objects. I see these other bodies being subjected to actions (ticklings, bangs on the thumb, etc.), such that were these same actions to be performed on my own body, there would be an accompanying sensory experience. I do not, however, experience anything. And yet I receive vocal sounds from these bodies suggesting that mental experiences are nonetheless occurring. The claim is that conscious beings other than myself are having them. Moreover, from the description given of those experiences, they appear to be similar to the experiences I normally have. Not having direct access to them, I cannot be sure they are the same, but at least the behaviour of the bodies subsequent to the action (laughter at the tickling, or sucking of the thumb) are consistent with the experiences being similar.

The most natural explanation of this is to suppose the existence of other minds - minds capable of communicating with mine, indirectly as it were, through the medium of those bodies. Does this amount to *proof* of the existence of other minds? This is not a question to detain us long. Essentially we answered it in Chapter 7. There we saw that it is impossible to arrive at proof of the existence of consciousness from an examination of physical phenomena alone. When I observe the behaviour of other bodies, that is all I am doing - examining physical phenomena. It follows that there can be no proof as such of the existence of other minds.

So, just as there is no direct infallible proof of the reality of physical things, we now find none for the reality of other minds. Nor could there be any. As already noted in the case of a world-in-itself, were there to be such a reality, it would have to mediate itself to us through the domain of physical interactions - we would have to infer its existence from what is found there. In the same way, if other minds exist, they too would have to be inferred from what is found in the domain of physical interactions. Direct proof is an impossibility; its absence, therefore, counts for nothing. Instead, it is a matter of weighing up probabilities. I have to ask: Is it more reasonable to accept that there are other minds, or to accept that there are none? It is all very well a sceptic adopting a tough-minded philosophical stance, declaring that he is not prepared to accept the existence of other minds because of the lack of proof. He cannot do this without at the same time tacitly implying the opposite - that there are no other minds - for which there is likewise no proof.

2. So, let us look more closely at why it is, in the absence of proof, that we are yet led to accept the postulate of other minds as being the more reasonable alternative. Again it is a question of examining the concept of otherness.

Earlier we saw that there is an otherness to sensory observation, the explanation of which points to there being a physical domain beyond the senses. For example, I hear sounds. I do not control what I hear, so am led to postulate an explanation in terms of physical interactions - those involving vibrating air molecules coming into contact with my ear drum, those molecules having been put into vibration in the first place by some source or other. Among the sounds I hear are some called vocal sounds. These originate from the vocal chords belonging to a human body. So far there is nothing here that is different from the hearing of sounds coming from any physical source. The otherness of auditory observation simply suggests a physical reality beyond the senses.

Closer examination of the sounds coming from this human body, however, reveals an *additional* kind of otherness - one we have not noted before. As I listen to the sounds I realize that I am being furnished with information not only about physical reality, but also about mental reality. I might, for instance, hear a report warning me that a particularly attractive looking apple in fact tastes sour. This is information about a mental experience - information that does not originate with me. How am I to account for it? It appears only reasonable that this second form of otherness, being concerned about mental experience, derives from a source that is also mental in character. I might be wrong in this; there is no way of telling for certain. It is nothing more than an inference. But at least it has the merit of being more plausible than the alternative, namely, to attribute the information to some purely physical source or to some chance occurrence.

So far we have thought of this information as being associated with the actions of another human body. But this is not necessary. Searches are being made for signals from outer space that might be indicative of the existence of life on other planets. Here there is no presupposition that such life has to be human. One simply examines the radio signals for signs of an intelligible message. Such a message, were it to be found, would be regarded as evidence of a conscious mind of some sort. Information in itself, therefore, can be sufficient to lead to the inference of other minds; it does not have to be information originating from a human body.

The observation that there are indeed human bodies similar to one's own is a second, and separate, element of the argument. The fact that I know from personal experience the close relationship between my conscious experiences and what goes on in my body, is reason enough to suspect that other bodies are similarly associated with conscious minds. This would be so whether or not there was any communication from them. Essentially the argument is based on analogy. At work here is a principle of equality, by which is meant the following: I am an observer; as such I have to look outwards from a particular vantage point. This inclines me towards an egocentric view. But sometimes the observations I make are of a kind as to lead to the conclusion that were some other vantage point to be adopted, the appearance would be little different. In other words, there is no justification for the belief that I occupy a priviledged position. The need to compensate for an egocentric bias is well illustrated from the field of cosmology. There one begins by viewing the heavens from a base on Earth. This inevitably creates an initial impression of the Earth being at the centre of the universe. It is only later, through the examination of appearances as they would be from other vantage points, that one discerns the greater explanatory power to be had from the ideas that the Earth goes round the Sun, the Sun is but one of many stars in the Galaxy, and the Galaxy is but one among many galaxies. In a similar way, I as an individual must learn to emancipate myself from egocentricity. I have to come to terms with the lack of uniqueness of my body, and hence the implausibility of it being uniquely conscious. The principle of equality requires that, if physical behaviourism is inadequate to describe myself, it is only reasonable to conclude that it is likewise inadequate to account for others.

These then are the two aspects of observation that have a bearing on my acceptance of the existence of other minds: the otherness of information provided about mental experience, and the existence of human bodies similar to my own. But that is not an end to it. Not only are there these two features, but importantly they are found to go together; they are correlated. The information about mental experience invariably originates, directly or indirectly, from human bodies. The fact that the two features are correlated is further reinforcement for the conclusion.

3. It is along such lines a case can be made for a reasonable belief in other minds. Again it is important for us to be clear that what has been set out is *not* a description of how in practice one comes to a belief in other minds. I cannot recall what my first impressions were on being born, but I doubt that I began life assuming other human bodies to be mindless. It seems most unlikely that as a baby I argued along the above lines and only later concluded that, on balance, these other bodies might be accompanied by minds! Much more likely is the idea that each of us comes into the world already predisposed to relate to other human beings as persons rather than as things. This must be particularly so of the relationship in the first instance to one's mother. This predisposition is to be seen as part of the genetic inheritance. Past interactions between our ancestors and those with whom they came into contact have helped, through the process of evolution by natural selection, to determine the genetic make-up that has been passed down to us. An important survival characteristic might well have been one that predisposes us from the start to expect other bodies to be associated with minds - minds liable to have motives similar to those one would experience oneself if placed in a similar position. An appreciation of those motives could then be advantageous in allowing one to anticipate the actions of the other. It is, therefore, only for the specific purposes of argumentation that one must start off

from a position of questioning - which is what we have done.

4. We have seen how the existence of other minds is an inference drawn from observations of the physical interactions between my body and other human bodies. The domain of physical interactions-with-the-world is, therefore, acting as a mediator between myself and other minds. We saw earlier that the same domain of physical interactions-with-the-world was the medium through which one had to draw any inferences about the world-in-itself. In the latter case, it was the fact that an extra inferential step was involved that made the inference that there was a world-in-itself the riskier hypothesis. Does that mean that the inference of other minds, which is likewise a step beyond the domain of interactions-with-the-world, is also to be regarded as a particularly risky hypothesis? Indeed, isn't the situation worse in the case of other minds? If one is inclined to accept that there is a world-in-itself, ought one not to say that as part of that world-in-itself there will be human-bodies-in-themselves, and that one ought to regard other minds as revealing themselves through these human-bodies-in-themselves, which in their turn reveal themselves through interactions-with-the-world, which in their turn reveal themselves through the sensory experience? In other words, ought one not to regard the domain of other minds as an even further inferential step away from conscious experience, and consequently an even riskier hypothesis than that of the world-in-itself?

No. Indeed, it can be argued that the existence of other minds is *less*, rather than more, problematic than that of the world-in-itself, or even that of physical interactions. This is because what one is arguing towards is similar to what one initially starts out from. In arguing that there are minds other than one's own, the postulate is that there exist sets of mental experiences additional to that already known. In effect, the conception of the mental domain is being broadened to include the contents of more than one mind. Accordingly, it can be contended, one is doing no more than expand a domain of which one is already certain, and this must be seen as less drastic than the postulate of entirely different and novel domains of reality: physical interactions and physical objects-in-themselves.

5. Another point that needs to be made is that belief in other minds and belief in the physical domain have a bearing on each other. We are dependent on the physical domain for all knowledge of the existence of other minds; it is only through the physical that those minds are mediated to us. But at the same time our belief in the existence of the physical domain is largely bound up with what we learn from other minds. Suppose, for the sake of argument, there were no minds other than my own. How then would I view the physical domain? There would still be the otherness of my observations and this would incline me, as before, to believe that a physical domain was responsible for it. But how confident would I be in that belief? How, under these circumstances, for example, would I be able to distinguish between an hallucination and the real thing? I couldn't. So, if one is a figment of my imagination, why not both? Again, how am I to understand what happens when I close my eyes? The physical disappears - ought I therefore to conclude that it has gone out of existence?

Clarification of these issues can come only by reference to what other people tell me about their experiences. A consensus among them that there was no little green snake in the room when I thought there was one helps to sort out a figment of the imagination from the real state of affairs. The fact that others report having an experience of observing the Moon while I have none (because my eyes are shut) helps establish that there can be physical interactions in the absence of *my* having them. In this way the physical domain has claims to an existence that is independent of what might be going on in my mind - something I could never be sure of in the absence of other minds. In this way, beliefs about the existence of the physical domain and about other minds become mutually dependent.

6. Acceptance of the existence of other minds not only assists my understanding of the physical domain, but also makes possible the formation of the conception of my own self - what it means to speak of 'myself' or 'I'. In arriving at an understanding of what exists, the foundation upon which I as an individual am building is not the statement: 'I know that my mental experiences exist'. But rather: 'There exist mental experiences'. The mental experiences referred to are, of course, those ordinarily known as *my* experiences. But at the outset I am not able meaningfully to use the word 'my'. It is an adjective that makes sense only in the context of it delineating that which belongs to me from that which belongs to others. But initially I do not want to make the assumption that there are others. The existence of sets of mental experiences additional to that from which the start is made, is one of the things I want to establish by argument from the foundational premise. Until that is done the word 'my' cannot be used. This illustrates the kind of difficulty facing the sceptic who claims to be able to set up an empirically given data base of mental experience free from any assumption about other types of existence. All too easily implicit assumptions about other realities worm their way in. The unguarded use of the word 'my' in this connection is an obvious pitfall to be avoided; others were noted earlier in Section 8.1.

The formation of any conception of myself as a specific, differentiated part of the totality of conscious existence, depends, therefore, on the recognition of the existence of other conscious beings. We have here a further example of a reciprocal definition, that is to say, a definition of an existent entity that is integrally and inseparably a part of the simultaneous definition of some other existent entity. We came across such definitions first in connection with the physical domain (Section 4.3). There we found that the definition of the fundamental particles and their properties was in terms of spatial and temporal relationships. And yet, in the absence of the particles (to make up the clocks and rulers) there was no such thing as space or time. The recognition of particles through spatial and temporal relations was, at one and the same time, the recognition of space and time through the particles. So it is that the recognition of other minds is, at one and the same time, the recognition of one's own.

The same applies to talk of *my* body. In the absence of other human bodies, I would of course be well aware that there was a particular physical object specifically associated with sensory experiences - that normally known as my body. For this reason this object would be of especial interest. But I would also appreciate that there was no hard and fast dividing line between this particular object and its environment. Materials pass in and out, bones and tissues constantly renew themselves, all is in a state of flux. Body and environment together constitute a single inter-locking system. This being so, there would be no reason to think of oneself as being represented in the physical domain exclusively by whatever happened to make up the body at any one time. It is only through the acknowledgement of the existence of other human bodies that it becomes meaningful to designate the particular one associated with my sensory experiences as being 'my' body. Furthermore, the recognition that other bodies have as much access as my own to what is known as the environment, leads to the conception of 'myself', as it is represented in the physical domain, not extending beyond my body. The recognition of that which is not me in the physical domain, clarifies what it is to be me in that domain - another case of reciprocal definition.

Thus we see that the conception of oneself as an individual is moulded in the context of relationships to others, both in the mental and bodily sense. That having been said, though, it is difficult to go much further in the attempt to define what precisely is meant by the term 'oneself' or what is entailed in being a *person*. Is a person to be regarded as just a bundle of mental experiences, or as a mental I-in-myself which maps to those experiences, holding them together so to speak, and providing the continuity of identity? If so, what of the body? One speaks of it as *my* body. Does that mean it is simply something that belongs to the I but is not part of what it is to be I? That somehow does not seem right. The body plays such an indispensable role in how one comes to define oneself that it must surely be regarded as integrally incorporated into what it is to be a person. There is no justification for according priority either to the mental or the physical. *Personhood has its representation in both the physical and mental types of reality.* If one adheres to the view that the physical and the mental are complementary ways of approaching a common reality, then they are two equally important and necessary ways of understanding personhood. In Chapter 16 when we introduce the spiritual domain, we shall have cause to add a third dimension to personhood.

7. One final point before we leave the topic of other minds. The study of others leads to further important insights about oneself - insights that would not be otherwise obtainable. Take, for example, the finite span of one's life. How else would one know that there was a time when one did not exist on Earth, and that there will be a time when one no longer exists on Earth, were it not for observations made on others - their birth and their death? Or how else would one come to the realization of one's own potential if one never saw the achievements of others? In these and other ways, the study of realities beyond one's own conscious experience reflects back an understanding of oneself. It is through the acceptance of those realities and the study of their characteristics one comes to a deeper appreciation of what it is to be oneself.

CHAPTER 12

THE INNER RELIGIOUS EXPERIENCE

SO far we have studied those aspects of conscious experience that point to the existence of the physical domain, and through that domain to the existence of minds other than one's own. We now turn our attention to further features of conscious experience - those indicating yet another type of reality. In this chapter we begin to explore the grounds for belief in the spiritual domain. Our starting point is with the inner religious experience.

1. I had better begin by stating what I mean by religion. Various definitions have been suggested. For the purposes I have in mind, I shall adopt the following: *Religion is a felt practical relationship with that which is believed (a) to transcend or encompass humankind and the spatio-temporal physical domain, and (b) to provide a comprehensive meaning for life.* Certain aspects of this definition will become clearer later. For the moment we note that religion, thus defined, recognizes there to be more to existence than just humanity, history, and nature - there is a supernatural element to it. Thus I am excluding communism and humanism, two movements that could have been included in a wider definition. Note that I have said nothing about the nature of what is supposed to transcend space and time. It could be a something or a someone. In the latter case, where the belief is in God or gods, one speaks of the religion as being theistic. In practice it is not always easy to draw a sharp distinction between theistic and non-theistic religions.

With regard to religious experience, any experience can be so counted; it depends on the context. Just as a dull thud or an electronic whistle can be transformed from a noise to a musical sound if it is included in a musical

INNER RELIGIOUS EXPERIENCE

composition, and a pile of bricks on the floor becomes a sculpture if the floor happens to be that of the Tate Gallery in London, so it is possible for any experience to be a religious experience if it is so interpreted.

2. That having been said, certain experiences have special significance within the religious context. One is of paramount importance and lies at the inner core of most religions: the sense of the numinous - a clouded awareness or intuition that one is in the presence of an awesome something or someone. For theistic religions it is the sense of the Presence of God. This presence is experienced in different ways and to different degrees, the full mystical experience in all its elements being encountered perhaps by only a few.

The numinous is experienced as a reality that is other than oneself. It is something that is always present, impregnating the whole of existence, but only fleetingly recognized in consciousness. The experience has the quality of it being a revelation of an objective state of affairs; it is not to be thought of as a withdrawal into self-contemplation. In Western religions in particular, the experience is seen as one in which the individual is made aware of something that is set over against oneself. It is not to be thought of as a mere change of mood, although the emotions are undoubtedly involved. The experience comes and then quickly goes. One has the impression of facing an overpowering force of some kind. It is of a nature as to command respect and awe - rather than being some naked brute force. It is worthy of praise and elicits a desire to serve it. This response is what the Bible calls 'the fear of God'; it is also closely connected with the energy associated with the indwelling Holy Spirit. There is a sense of urgency about it; the power is volcanic, pent up, ready to be unleashed.

Though on the one hand the numinous is awesome and daunting, it also has a deeply attractive or fascinating quality about it. Prudence might advise caution in approaching this powerful presence, but one is nevertheless irresistibly drawn towards it. The dread aspects of the numinous might repel as they expose one's own worthlessness, but there are also present the attractive qualities of love, goodness and beneficence. References to these complementary aspects of the numinous are interwoven throughout the Bible. Though there is perhaps more emphasis on the awesome nature of God in the Old Testament and more on his love in the New Testament both are to be found throughout. Amidst the Old Testament stories of God wreaking vengeance on his enemies and of man being unable so much as to gaze upon the awesome majesty of God and live, one also learns of his love and forgiveness, for example, in the writings of the prophet Hosea. In the New Testament, Jesus is the personification of God's love, this being supremely displayed in the manner of his death on the cross; and yet the same account of the crucifixion also testifies to the stern God of Justice who yet requires the terrible sacrifice to be paid.

The numinous is ambivalent as between being a something or a someone; both aspects are present. In Christianity the emphasis is on God being personal, but the distinction between the personal and impersonal is not always clear-cut. When reference is made to the three Persons of the Trinity, for instance, the word 'person' does not have its normal day-to-day meaning; we shall have more to say of this in Chapter 16. Again, the Holy Spirit is regarded as a power as well as a person.

One has a feeling of affinity for the presence. Though the numinous is wholly other than oneself, one has a close bond with it. The relationship is perhaps best described as creaturely dependence on a Creator. Though a creature must always be accounted less than its Creator, it is an example of the Creator having given expression to himself and so has something in common with him. For this reason one speaks of our having been made in the image of God. One comes to recognize that all people, all things, have a common source in the numinous. At a fundamental level there is a unity between oneself and the world. In a sense the usual separation between one-

INNER RELIGIOUS EXPERIENCE 171

self and external objects no longer applies, although in a rational sense one still recognizes the separation.

It is along such lines one might speak of the encounter with the numinous. But having said that, it must be understood that no description can do justice to the experience. The numinous is fundamentally mysterious, lying outside human comprehension. There is that about its nature that is incommensurable with our existence - that which is beyond time and space.

3. The sense of the numinous impacts on people in different ways and to different degrees. As I mentioned at the beginning, not everyone sees it in the above terms. Though recognizing certain aspects of the mystical experience as having a bearing on their own encounter with God, most perhaps think of the relationship as more practical and down-to-earth. It is a relationship having much in common with the communications one has with other people in everyday life. The emphasis is on God as a constant companion in all daily happenings. Prayer is conversation, rather than the achievement of a deeply meditative and mystical state. This is the form of prayer that figures most often in the Bible. It requires no techniques; one just gets on with the task of talking and listening. Though the emotional intensity of the experience might not be as marked as that of the full mystical encounter, it is nevertheless sensed to be a genuine meeting and communing with God.

The awareness of God's presence might seep into consciousness over a long period of time - the progressive acknowledgement of something that has always been there in the background. Alternatively, it can come suddenly as an altogether new and unexpected occurrence - the experience of conversion, a second birth, a new start to life. But regardless of how the acceptance of God's presence comes about, the experience is generally accompanied by a sense of exaltation and delight. There is the appreciation that here lies the way to inner peace. This is not the kind of peace where one sits back comfortably and 'feels nice'. It is a tranquility that can be experienced in strong action, in anguish and in suffering. It is the sense of the rightness of things, the assurance that despite trauma and difficulty, one's life is in tune with God's will, one is doing what ought to be done, one is going through what needs to be gone through. Though still engaged in everyday activities and concerns, the turbulence they generate no longer reaches down into the deeper levels of one's being.

In theistic religions, like Christianity, the numinous is believed to comprehend the innermost depths of one's thoughts. Because it takes a mind to understand a mind, these religions look upon God as personal. Prayer is the meeting of one's mind with that of God. There are various aspects to the communication. Petitionary prayer, for example, is concerned with asking God for things. As regards the outcome of such requests, opinions differ. Many believe that God responds by intervening in nature and in the lives of others. He might not give exactly what is requested (in his greater wisdom he might know better than the petitioner what is really required). But whatever the response, it is direct and produces tangible effects. Others, reluctant to accept the normal course of nature being disrupted in this manner, are more inclined to think of petitionary prayer as a form of therapeutic meditation. It is a process of thought, carried out in the presence of God, which can lead to him effecting changes in one's own behaviour and attitude - changes that can in some circumstances be instrumental in bringing about the desired effect. But even when there appear to be no tangible results of any kind - a person dying despite prayers offered for recovery, for instance - believers will continue to maintain that it was, nevertheless, right and proper to bring the matter before God in this form. As for religions where petitionary prayer is not part of official teaching (the primitive Theravada form of Buddhism, for instance) the religion, as popularly practiced, will often incorporate it. Indeed one hears of occasions where even an atheist, under conditions of extreme danger, involuntarily gives way to prayer. There can be no doubt, petitionary prayer, as a manifestation of the creaturely-dependent relationship, is a powerful inner drive.

Prayer is by no means confined to its petitionary form. In a wider sense it can take on much the same characteristics as any kind of communication between people. Through it, one may acquire new thoughts and ideas, new attitudes, new perspectives on problems; one may receive encouragement, an admonition, a call to some special form of work for God, a challenge. In prayer one offers thanks, praise, love and loyalty; one expresses joy at being in the presence of the other, and contrition when the relationship is damaged.

4. The idea that the relationship can be harmed brings us to a further aspect of the inner religious experience. As God's creatures we bear his stamp - we are made in his image. To learn of God, therefore, is to learn of one's own potential. And learning of that potential, one is inevitably faced with one's failure to live up to it. The moral and ethical sense - the feeling that one ought sometimes to act and think differently - is perceived to have its source in God. This is not to say that the 'voice of conscience' is synonymous with the voice of God. It is a line of communication, and like all lines of communication, it can at times be faint and distorted; conscience is all too easily blunted. But if properly heeded, conscience, so it is claimed, can be revelatory of God. By this is meant not only that God is to be thought of as the source of these promptings, but also that something of his character can be learned from the content of these messages. For example, the fact that the moral and ethical code is mindful of the needs of others tells us of God's love for others. Again, the fact that we are sometimes to practice self-denial is indicative of God having a purpose for us that transcends self-interest and self-gratification.

This is not in any way to claim that religious people have a monopoly on virtue; they clearly do not. No-one could possibly deny that many agnostics and atheists live out lives that are every much as good, upright, and moral as those of believers. They do this without feeling the need to acknowledge God as the origin of their considerate behaviour or as the reason for their love of fellow humankind. Be that as it may, the religious believer maintains God to be the ultimate origin of every person's moral sense, whether or not the individual acknowledges it; God's light lights everyone who comes into the world.

5. The inner religious experience has aspects about it that are difficult to account for in terms of one's own input. There is an otherness about it. Previously we saw how each of two former types of otherness led to the inference of a type of reality lying beyond one's conscious experience: in one case, the physical domain; in the other, minds additional to one's own. Ought we therefore to conclude that this new form of otherness points to yet another type of reality - a spiritual domain? Or could there be some alternative explanation? So far we have spoken only of the interpretation put on the experience by the religious believer. But it could be that the sense of the numinous comes, not from an encounter with God, but through the workings of the unconscious. Likewise the moral and ethical code could have something to do with genetically determined behaviour, or with social conditioning, especially in the early years of life. We have yet to examine these possibilities. But before doing that, let me finish presenting the evidence upon which belief in God rests.

CHAPTER 13

OTHER EXPERIENCES OF THE NUMINOUS

GOD conveys his presence to us not only through the direct encounter in the inner being, but also less directly through other kinds of experience: through the study of nature, through other people, through the working out of history. He uses other realities - the physical, and minds other than one's own - as mediators between himself and us.

1. Take first the physical domain. We begin with the simple observation that the universe exists; there is something rather than nothing. The universe is contingent; as far as we can tell, it has no necessity to be. This is the familiar argument of God as the necessary Creator. As a deductive proof of his existence we have already seen that it does not work (Sections 3.1, 3.2). But in the more modest context of it being one indication among many, each lending a measure of support to the plausibility of there being God, it has its part to play.

Next, a simple point often overlooked: the physical world is intelligible. Here I am not referring to any specific aspect of the scientific laws, but rather to the fact that there are any laws at all - the prior requirement that the world presents science with something systematic and consistent to work on. Presumably, it need not have been that way; it could have been inherently chaotic, showing no signs of consistency. Either one accepts this intelligibility as a state of affairs not open to explanation, or one attributes it to the intellect of God.

Had the world not been constructed according to consistent intelligible laws, we would not, of course, have been here to see it. Not only that, but the actual laws and the general conditions prevailing in the world had to be just right for life to develop. All kinds of separate conditions had to be met (Section 3.4). The odds were overwhelmingly against a world happening by chance to have the characteristics necessary to bring it within the narrow band of conditions conducive to the development of life. Faced, therefore, by the improbability of our own existence, a limited number of options present themselves: We can postulate an infinitely large number of universes, all operating to different physical laws, with most of these universes, unlike our own, incapable of supporting life. Or we can pin our hopes on scientists at some time in the future being able to demonstrate that, for whatever reason, the odds against the universe being the way it is are not as great as they appear. Or one invokes the idea of the Designer. Certainly, if one already holds to a belief in God on other grounds, the notion that the world is the way it is because that is what God intended sounds perfectly reasonable. Again though, I would stress that the argument must not be used in the way the Argument from Design was originally intended - as a knock-down deductive proof; it is to be seen as just one more piece in a large puzzle that would appear to fit better were the hypothesis of God's existence to be accepted.

The attributes of the physical world provide intimations as to the character of God. The orderly operation of the laws of nature reflect his controlling purpose and faithfulness. The vast expanse of the heavens evokes God's majesty. The awesome strength of earthquakes, tidal floods, and supernova explosions display his might. The almost endless span of time over which the universe has evolved testifies to his patience. The evolution of humankind through natural selection demonstrates his willingness to accomplish his purpose through contingent events and within a framework that allows a measure of freedom. The underlying unity of nature mirrors God's desire that we be at one with the world and with him.

In short, the physical world confronts us with a set of characteristics consonant with those associated with the

God one encounters in the inner religious experience. Nature appears to be pervaded by the same kind of otherness as was discerned there. Recall that in our interactions with the physical we have so far distinguished two kinds of otherness: one that leads to a belief in a world-in-itself beyond the domain of physical interactions, the other to a belief in minds other than one's own. Both these realities are mediated to us through the domain of physical interactions. What we are now saying is that our interaction with the physical manifests a third type of otherness - one indicative of a reality which, like the others, is mediated to us through the physical domain. Furthermore, the characteristics of that reality, as we infer them from the features of that otherness, are the same as those associated with the reality inferred from the type of otherness we came across in the mental domain in connection with the inner religious experience.

2. The second kind of mediated encounter with the numinous is that which arises from contact with certain people - especially those looked upon as holy people. These individuals, having direct experience of the numinous in their own lives, impart something of the quality of that experience to others. This they do through their teaching and the conduct of their lives. God appears to use these people as a channel through which to speak to us. It is not so much that these persons are offering us their own advice, based on their own knowledge and experience. The communication with God is discerned as being more immediate, more direct than that. This is made markedly clear on those occasions when the person concerned is unaware of having been used in this way. A casual aside delivered in a sermon, for example, might have especial significance for a particular listener; it meets a specific need even though this was not the conscious intention of the preacher, his sermon having in the main been about something quite different. Likewise, a tiny act of kindness, performed in the normal course of events, can be just the assurance of

God's loving care needed at that time. In these and other ways, those who surrender themselves to the will of God are liable to find themselves used, consciously or otherwise, as his instruments.

Throughout history certain people have been especially favoured in their ability to communicate the sense of the numinous - people like the Buddha, Muhammad, and Jesus. In the case of Jesus, Christians find the sense of holiness so overpowering, so richly resonant with the sense of the numinous within, that it becomes hard in one's prayer life to differentiate an encounter with God from an encounter with Christ. The image of God in this particular man, so it is claimed, is so perfected as to place him on an altogether different plane to the rest of humankind. The events of his life, particularly the resurrection event, testify to his uniqueness. According to Christians, he is to be looked upon as the Son of God - the numinous in human form. Just how we ought to view such a claim is a matter we shall address in Section 18.12. Sufficient for the moment to note that all world religions have outstanding leaders, both founders and later followers.

Such persons carry with them the stamp of authority. So much so that the devout might come to accept these gifted individuals as being blessed with a deeper encounter with the numinous than they themselves experience. The teachings and examples of these leaders are, consequently, to be regarded as truer and more reliable revelations of God than one's own direct experience of the numinous. Trust is placed in the judgements of these persons and in the corporate wisdom handed down through the tradition of the church community. This in no way argues against the central role played by the inner direct encounter with the numinous. Religion, after all, is ultimately about one's relationship to the Divine. Unless the teachings of a religion have been appropriated for oneself in the form of a *felt* relationship, it counts for nothing. Nevertheless, the deepest, fullest understanding of God and of what he is trying to communicate to us might well on occasion derive more reliably from the encounter with other people - God using them as mediators - than from the interpretation we give to our own inner religious experience. Such encounters can be made either directly, if the person concerned is living (one's own priest or guru, say), or indirectly through reading accounts of the lives and teachings of the great spiritual leaders of the past, preserved and handed down in the wisdom of holy writings such as the Bible or Qur'an. It is through these writings one establishes a link to the founder of the religion. For these reasons, scripture takes its place alongside the inner religious experience as one of the two principal means of God's revelation of himself to us. Not unnaturally, such writings come to be venerated in their own right.

3. Next we turn to the numinous as it is to be discerned in history and in the pattern of one's own individual life. The religious believer approaches life with the conviction that everything happens broadly in accordance with a plan and is to be seen in the context of God working out his purpose. The justification for this view is not at first sight obvious. Life presents us with a bewildering array of contingent events. It is only when one examines the overall picture, relating the various incidents to each other, that one begins to discern the underlying pattern - a pattern that points to certain guiding principles at work - principles believed to stem from God. In this the religious believer is in much the same position as the scientist. Earlier we noted that the scientist too is always working with contingent data: particular particles with particular values of position or velocity. But it is not the particularity of the events that is important. The confusion of first impressions is deceptive. Science becomes science once it begins to penetrate beyond the contingent aspects of the events, to reveal the underlying universal laws governing all that is happening. So it is that, in similar vein, the religious believer seeks the order that lies behind the otherwise seeming disorder of the events

of life. It is held that meaningful patterns can be discerned both for the large scale development of humankind from the beginning of time, and for the life of the individual person. Thus the creation of the universe, the formation of life from inanimate chemicals, the awakening of consciousness, the shaping of humankind through evolution by natural selection, the first intimations of the inner sense of the presence of God and with it the beginnings of the religious quest, the prophetic message of Old Testament times, the coming of Christ as the fulfillment of that message, and the subsequent spread of the Gospel and the harvesting of souls - this is all to be encompassed in God's drama on the large scale.

It is against this backdrop that we are to see the purpose to be accorded to the life of the individual. One approach to life is to view it, by and large, as a series of disconnected facts and chance occurrences. Sometimes one is lucky - one gets a good job, has friendly neighbours, has a decent marriage, lives to a ripe old age; sometimes one is not so lucky - a bad car accident, the house is burgled, cancer. Life can be regarded as 'just one damned thing after another'. On the other hand, the same facts are open to a radically different interpretation - one that sees them as part of an overall pattern. Religious persons believe their lives have purpose. A life surrendered to God's will takes on shape - one that is revelatory of the nature of God. Such people do not let things slip by unnoticed; they are alert to the possible significance of events. In this, they are somewhat like a doctor examining a patient. The doctor is on the lookout for specific symptoms that could be significant - symptoms the patient overlooks, being unaware of their relevance. Those with a religious outlook on life constantly attend to the various ways God might be working out his purpose in them; they try to discern the development of pattern in their lives in order the better to co-operate with him.

There are similarities here with those familiar drawings that can be 'seen' in one of two ways; a cube seen from above or from below; a duck or a rabbit; an elegant young lady or the face of a hag. Exactly the same lines on a piece of paper can alternately conjure up incompatible impressions. So it is that a religious person and an unbeliever can put quite different interpretations on exactly the same facts concerning life - one sees God's hand at work, the other not. Does this mean each view is equally valid? Here the analogy of the ambiguous drawings breaks down. With the drawings there is no right or wrong way to look at them; either interpretation is as good as the other. But that is not the case when it comes to putting an interpretation on life. Either there is a God working out his purpose in one's life, or there is not.

The sceptic will be inclined to object that the believer is imposing on the facts a preconceived set of ideas. In this it must be admitted there is a measure of truth. Believers do indeed work from within an already formulated framework, one that colours what they see. But this is inevitable. One brings to every situation preconceived notions of one kind or another, the sceptic himself being no exception. Even scientists are affected. There is no such thing as a wholly objective approach to new experimental data. Although there is no denying an element of objectivity to the data - an objectivity sufficiently strong as sometimes to force a revision of the theory - all data are theory-laden. Scientists cannot but approach data from within an already formulated theoretical framework, probably one that in the past has proved of value. It is this pre-existing context that leads to judgements as to which experiments should be carried out in preference to others. In this way it acts as an invaluable guide to the exploration of nature. But there is the other side to the coin: The same context gives rise to expectations that influence the interpretation put on the new observations. The theoretical framework not only alerts scientists to significances that might otherwise have been overlooked, it also blinds them to indications contrary to expectation. The new experimental observation has to be fitted into the mould of the already formulated framework. Sometimes this cannot be done easily, in which case it is forced, and if that fails, it is laid aside as an 'anomaly' in the hopes that one day the difficulty will be satisfactorily sorted out. The accumulation of persistent anomalies might eventually lead to the formulation of an alternative theory. But until a new one presents itself, one capable of accommodating the data more comfortably, scientists will continue to persist with the old one, it being impossible to work outside a framework of some kind.

This is not at all unlike what happens in the field of religious belief. Religious believers work from within a framework of concepts and ideas that have already proved their fruitfulness as a means of marshalling and organizing experience. Just as scientists do not rest content with the mere collection of data, but create theoretical models for ordering that data and bringing out their significance, so religious believers build up a theoretical framework of their own. They extract from the particular contingent events of history, or from the events that mark their own lives, the underlying simple truths of the goodness and love characteristic of God's purpose at work in the world - the truths that make sense and bring order to the otherwise chaotic confusion of human situations.

4. Of course there is much in life that is not easy to bring into line with a neat simple idea of a loving God presiding over everything. There is evil and suffering. So much so, many would claim that not only is there no evidence for God in the pattern of our lives, the indications are to the contrary. The Problem of Evil and Suffering has potential repercussions throughout the whole system of religious belief. For this reason I propose we take time out at this stage to examine it.

The problem can be stated in terms of three apparently contradictory propositions: (i) God is good; (ii) God is all-powerful; (iii) Evil exists. One way out is to concede that the first statement is not wholly true, and attribute to God a darker side (as in Hindu thought). An alternative is to challenge the second statement. According to this, evil originates from a force opposed to the benificent God (the Devil of Judaism and Christianity), and God is not capable of fully controlling it. He is, therefore, not to be regarded as all-powerful.

Is there a third approach to the problem, one consistent with preserving the integrity of both statements (i) and (ii)? The answer, so I believe, is yes. The argument runs as follows: It is God's intention that we should be drawn into a loving relationship with him. For that love to take on meaning, it must be freely offered. A consequence of this is that we must have the option of withholding it. The concept 'love' cannot take on meaning until that to which it refers can be differentiated from that to which it does not refer - another case of reciprocal definition. Love cannot be a reality unless there is non-love to off-set it. Not even an all-powerful God can escape the demands of such a necessity. God's omnipotence is not thereby jeopardized. The concept of 'omnipotence' is not to be thought of as embracing the ability to perform that which is logically impossible. Does this mean that God creates evil? No. He creates only that which is good and loving. Yet this act - in itself perfect - unavoidably invests meaning in the concept of 'evil'. God thus gives rise to the *potentiality* for evil. But that is as far as his responsibility goes. How then does that potentiality become an actuality? That is where we come in. It is *our* responsibility - when we turn away from God and his goodness.

This approach to evil tends to lead to the idea of it being an absence of good - a negative reality, in the same way as blindness is an absence of sight, silence an absence of sound, and coldness an absence of heat. This is not to say that a negative reality is subjectively *perceived* as being less of a force to be reckoned with than a positive one. On a chilly morning we feel the cold coming through our clothes, attacking our fingers and toes; we might even have to speak of frost*bite*. Extreme cold can affect us as potently as oppressive heat. Yet in truth all that exists is heat - the energy of motion and vibration of molecules. An object is cold by virtue of its molecules having little of this energy, not by it possessing something that the hot object does not have.

Even so, a description of evil solely in terms of negative attributes strikes many as inadequate. There are situations in which evil is so prevalent and its influence so strong, that it is more appropriately thought of as a positive reality in its own right rather than a mere absence of goodness. We shall delve more deeply into this in Section 16.7 when we come to consider the Christian conception of the Devil. Suffice for the present to note that an aquaintance with evil is necessary if one is to sharpen the definition of what is meant by goodness.

What we have said so far applies to moral evil - that which arises from the exercise of the human will. What of natural 'evils'? There are many who would say that earthquakes, car crashes, diseases, etc. are afflictions that are not subject to human will, but are also to be regarded as evils. How can a good God permit them?

In the first place it must be said that not all so-called natural disasters are entirely independent of human will. Is one really free from responsibility if, lured by the California sunshine, one builds one's house on the San Andreas fault line, or one's lung cancer is induced by smoking, or the car crash is due to inattention or drinking? That said, however, there remains much suffering that can only be termed undeserved and for which no-one can reasonably be held responsible. Why, in these cases at least, does not a good God intervene? Why does he not stop the aeroplane from crashing when the component fails through metal fatigue? Why does he not prevent famines, and so on?

The trouble with such an argument is that, for God to operate in this manner, he would have to be stepping into the breach every five minutes in response to someone's request. The idea of what constitutes 'suffering' is flexible. Experience shows that, as the conditions of life improve, the threshold of what is perceived to be 'suffering' is correspondingly raised. This being so, it becomes difficult if not impossible to draw a line. An important consequence of God's constant intervention would be that nature would lose its consistency and reliability. If we are to exercise free will - to follow God or not as the case may be - then we must operate within a predictable environment, one where a particular action leads to a foreseeable outcome. There have to be natural laws, and these must be upheld regardless of the consequences. Nature must be neutral, indifferent. (At least, the laws must generally be upheld; we must not at this stage rule out the possibility of *occasional* miraculous interventions - a subject for Chapter 18.)

Granted that God ought not to be continually intervening in the running of affairs, could he not have devised a different kind of physics and biology, one that would ensure no suffering? For example, how about an alternative structure for atoms and molecules such that metal fatigue would be unknown? Such a proposal would reduce the number of plane crashes. But what of its other implications? There would be repercussions throughout physics and chemistry; the world would be radically different from the one we know in ways we can scarcely begin to imagine. Or how about a world where famine was an impossibility? That would mean the creation of a type of human being needing no food. What would be the ramifications of that? Or how about the abolition of pain? That would be to lose a powerful defense mechanism. In short, tampering with the laws of nature quickly renders life as we know it impossible. Whether there could be a set of laws that would exclude suffering and yet would make possible a recognizable form of life is hard to say.

Which brings us to the next point: It is surely wrong to speak of evil and suffering as though the two terms were synonymous. Undoubtedly much suffering is caused by evil, and suffering in its turn can lead to evil. There are those who, through suffering, become bitter, cynical, hardened, twisted in their thinking, and seeking after revenge. But it does not have to be that way. Suffering

the result obtained is at variance with that of other investigators. Does one abandon scientific objectivity, allowing reality to be one thing for one person, and something different for another? No. The anomalous result is laid aside, it being assumed that it must have arisen from some unidentifed subjective feature. The scientific community carries on as normal using only the results of those experiments that *are* consistent with each other - those considered by consensus to be authentic. It is uncomfortable to have such deviant results lurking in the background, but they are not in themselves sufficient cause to shake the scientists' confidence that they deal with a genuine form of objectivity.

Science and religion both have their social dimension. This is not in itself a cause for concern. It certainly does not warrant the view that they are *merely* products of social interaction - an expression of the way people interact with each other. The conclusions reached in both fields are partly conditioned by society, but also partly by that which lies beyond. The social dimension helps isolate the objective features of the relationships being studied.

5. *The reality of God stands or falls on the perceived otherness of religious experience.* Without this otherness the concept of God would become simply a way of referring to God-worship activities. One person's use of the word 'God' would be as valid as anyone else's because it simply relates to what he or she does or feels. According to this view, without people actively engaged in God-worship there is no God because the term 'God' has no meaning beyond what people do. Before people existed there was no God; when life in the Universe comes to an end there will once again be no God. This indeed is how certain modern theologians appear to use the term.

But such headlong fall into total subjectivity is not inevitable. It is rescued by the otherness of the experience. This is similar to what we have found before. As far as knowledge of the physical domain is concerned, for example, all one has to go on are sensory observations.

But the fact that one starts from conscious experiences does not necessarily lead to idealism. The otherness of those observations points beyond those experiences to the existence of a physical domain - a domain capable of existing independently of one's observations of it. Likewise, the fact that I am locked into the narrow confines of my own mental experiences does not entail a belief that I am alone. There is within my mental experience an otherness indicative of other minds - independently existing minds.

So it is with the otherness of religious experience - an additional form of otherness pointing to yet a further type of reality: God. As with the others, this type of reality also does not depend upon me for its existence. Like physical reality, it appears to have a nature of its own. For this reason, it cannot legitimately be held that one person's views of God must be as valid as those of another; one can be mistaken as to the true nature of God. There has to be a pooling of experience, an examination of the fruitfulness of opposing views. From the differing, subjective, culturally conditioned accounts of religious experience, a consensus is sought among the community of believers - an agreed view that has the proven ability to stand the test of time.

6. But here we come across a worry. It is all very well drawing a parallel between the formation of an understanding of God within the community of believers, and the formation of an understanding of the physical domain within the scientific community. In the latter case it generally does prove possible to form a consensus - physics is the same the world over. In religious matters, however, there is no such agreement - witness the variety of world religions, and within those religions, the further splintering into denominations and sects. How are we to account for this?

In the first place, I remind you that within the scientific community, when it comes to the truly fundamental questions of whether the world-in-itself exists, and if so, what if anything can be said about it, there is no unanimity. Views are as polarized here as they are in the discussion of the existence and knowability of God. Nevertheless, it must be conceded that at the level of experimental data there is no argument. There are no quibbles about what is found in the domain of physical interactions-with-the-world. The disagreement arises only at the level of the interpretation to be put on these data.

This is not the place to launch into a full-scale discussion of comparative religion. I am not qualified for the task, and in any case, one can anticipate the outcome of such a comparison: it would be inconclusive. Among those who engage in such studies, there is no consensus as to whether the similarities between the world religions outweigh their differences, or vice versa. But for our purposes it is not necessary to demonstrate that all religions say exactly the same thing. We are to establish reasonable belief, not indisputable proof. To that end it is sufficient to show that the religions do not manifestly contradict each other - that they have an essential common core of belief indicative of a genuine otherness.

It is not difficult to find common ground. The religions share the same three-fold structure:

* First, there is put forward an ideal - the state or condition which is the goal of life.

* Secondly, there is the assertion that our present condition falls short of this ideal.

* Thirdly, there is the means by which our potential for achieving the ideal state can be realised.

This is a structure that can be applied to 'religions' in the widest sense of the word, including secular movements such as Marxism and humanism. What distinguishes religions in the narrower sense is their agreement that the potential state to which they direct us is to be understood in the context of an unseen reality. The visible world is not self-explanatory purely in materialistic terms. The dominant view of the nature of this reality is that it is to be understood theistically. In particular, belief in a single God, though not universal, has always been much in evidence. Even when several gods are invoked there tends to be a supreme God. God is thought of in the main as relating to us personally rather than impersonally; he is a God who can be contacted through prayer. This is true even of Buddhism, a religion generally regarded as atheistic, but as popularly practised, one that often involves regular prayer.

The religions have rather different ideas as to the path to be followed to achieve the ideal state. But all are agreed that it has little to do with the fulfillment of bodily desires. The ethical codes they advocate are remarkably similar to each other: the avoidance of violence, killing, stealing, lying, anger, pride and sexual promiscuity, coupled with the need to live life moderately and with due regard to promoting the well-being and happiness of others.

Belief that the goal to which one aspires involves existence beyond death is widespread - whether this is thought of as life in Heaven or through reincarnation on Earth. The quality of that existence will depend in some measure on how one has conducted one's life this side of the grave. In regard to Buddhism one should note that the final state of Nirvana or 'nothingness' is not to be thought of in terms of a Western understanding of the word 'nothing'. In Eastern thought there is an ambivalence between nothing and plenitude. The description of Nirvana as imperishable, ageless and eternal, power, blissful happiness, incomprehensible peace, the place of inassailable safety, and the consummation of life, could strike Christians as a pretty good description of Heaven.

We could go on, but I think enough has already been said to make the point that there is much that the world religions share. Does this mean that peoples around the world have come independently to this view of God? Not necessarily. One view of the development of the world religions holds that they might have historical roots stretching back to a common past. Accordingly, it is not altogether surprising that the religions today should have similar characteristics. But this is not really relevant.

The important point is that these common features of the religions commend themselves to all peoples at all times and all places. They are regarded as true to the universal nature of religious experience. Together they constitute an otherness indicative of some other reality. This is not to deny the significant differences that also exist between the religions. These derive from varying subjective inputs to the interaction. Coming as we all do from various backgrounds, it is only to be expected that the religions reflect differences of historical tradition, culture, and temperament - to say nothing of the possibility that some religions might offer a clearer and truer revelation of God than others. One ought not to minimize the differences between the religions. But neither should they be blown up out of proportion. After all the fact that the same accidents of history and social conditioning give rise to very different attitudes towards acupuncture, surgery, psychiatry, or herbal remedies, does not mean that medical science is arbitrary - a mere product of the culture. It has its roots in objectivity. In the same way, as I have briefly outlined above, a sustainable case can be advanced that at the deeper, more fundamental levels, the world religions testify to a common otherness of religious experience.

CHAPTER 15

RELIGION AND THE UNCONSCIOUS

THE otherness of religious experience points to an origin lying outside the domain of consciousness. Before assuming that this must be God, we need to enquire whether there might be a more mundane explanation. In this chapter we explore the possibility that the unconscious mind, rather than God, is the source of this experience.

1. We saw in Section 9.1, that in setting up a mental explanatory framework dealing only in conscious mental experiences and not entities such as sensations, memories, etc., certain questions were left unanswered - those to do with the identity and continuity of the person. In response to this, it was suggested that it might make sense to think in terms of there being a mind-in-itself, something to be found in a mental reality domain beyond that of conscious mental experiences. If so, it would be included, along with any mental processes that are not conscious, in the domain of the unconscious mind.

As far back as the early nineteenth century the view began to form that the thoughts of which one is aware at any time make up only a part of the contents of the mind. In order to explain certain aspects of conscious experience, it has become helpful to postulate an additional part - the unconscious. This is held to be capable of influencing the conscious mind through the production of dreams and hallucinations, as well as accounting for involuntary acts, such as slips of speech and other faulty actions.

The unconscious is a postulate; there is no incontrovertible, deductive proof of its existence. We have no way of entering and examining the unconscious directly. As soon as one thinks about a supposed aspect of the unconscious, the very act of thinking about it means that it is now absorbed into consciousness. The existence of the unconscious can only be *inferred* - through the way it appears to impact on consciousness from outside, so to speak. The conviction derives from a perceived otherness of certain conscious experiences. Experiences such as dreams and hallucinations have features over which we do not exercise control and which do not readily lend themselves to rational explanation in terms solely of conscious processes. The otherness appears to be indicating a further type of reality beyond consciousness. As was the case over the postulate of a physical domain, and that of minds other than one's own, the value of the postulate of the unconscious lies in its explanatory power.

How pervasive is the explanatory power of this latest hypothesis? Could it be that the otherness associated with the inner religious experience has its source in the unconscious rather than with yet another type of reality - God? To those inclined to dismiss the notion of God, this is an attractive thought. After all, why unnecessarily proliferate the number of supposed realities? We know that the unconscious mind is able to mimic the experiences of the senses - in dreams and hallucinations. These experiences appear at the time to be real encounters with the physical world, but of course, are nothing of the sort. If the unconscious is thus able to mislead us in respect of our experiences of the physical, why should it not also play at least some part in creating religious experiences?

2. In order to progress further, we need to know more about the unconscious, particularly as regards what it contains. Only then might we judge how plausible it is to regard the unconscious as the source of religious experience. Because direct access into the unconscious is denied us, reliance must be placed on indirect means. Some insight is afforded by psychoanalysis, the form of treatment for psycho-neurosis first introduced by Freud. He held that an understanding of the unconscious begins with the recognition of two kinds of content: the *id* and the *superego*. The id is something we possess from birth. It

is associated with instinctual drives towards infantile gratification. These are to be thought of as essentially sexual in nature. The superego on the other hand is derived from the environment. It consists of the attitudes of mind absorbed from other people - the standards of behaviour expected by society, especially those originating from one's parents. These beliefs are acquired in early childhood by an unconscious process which leaves one unaware of their origin. A tension is then set up between the ego and the value system so assimilated, and from this is derived one's 'conscience'. Because the behaviour dictated by this set of beliefs often runs counter to that which would arise from self-gratification, the id and the superego come into conflict. This results in those thoughts regarded as shameful, painful, disagreeable, or alarming being repressed into the unconscious. Although repressed, these thoughts can, nevertheless, affect behaviour. In neurotic personalities these can have a debilitating effect, simulating organic disorders and giving rise to unreasonable fears and compulsive actions. The aim of psychoanalysis is to bring these unconscious thoughts into the conscious mind so that they can be dealt with rationally. All of us have repressed thoughts, not just those accounted neurotic. The difference is that most of us are able to channel the drive stemming from such thoughts into some socially acceptable activity.

What did Freud specifically have to say about the unconscious in relation to religious experience? Though at times he could be somewhat ambivalent in his attitude towards religion, he generally spoke as an atheist. It is important to note, however, that his atheism did not come about as a result of the development of psychoanalysis. Though certain of his followers claimed that it was psychoanalysis that had destroyed the credibility of religion, Freud himself consistently denied this. He had assumed an atheistic outlook from his earliest days. His view of religion, therefore, was something *added* to his psychological findings and theories, rather than drawn out from them.

Freud took over, and further developed, an idea originated by Ludwig Feuerbach one hundred and fifty years ago. This held that God was nothing more than an idealized psychologically projected image of man himself. It is man's own qualities of personhood, love, sense of justice, wisdom, etc. that are externalized by the mind and become an object of worship. Why should only the good aspects of humankind be so projected, rather than an image of its totality, warts and all? Wish-fulfillment. That is to say, the gratification in fantasy of that which is denied in reality. A particularly important example of wish-fulfillment, so it is claimed, concerns our natural desire to feel protected. In childhood, a sense of security is provided by the presence of one's earthly father. On reaching adulthood, however, this protection is lost. It is at this point wish-fulfillment takes over. It gives rise to a belief in a God who can assume the vacated role of the protective father-figure. Accordingly, belief in God is to be interpreted as nothing more than a prolongation of infantile dependence on an earthly father - an avoidance of the need to face up to the harsher realities of life. The loss of the earthly father-figure (either through death or through the recognition in later life of his inadequacies, at least in respect of his being able to continue indefinitely providing protection) is something that affects us all. For this reason it is not surprising that the community of religious believers is able to reach a consensus over the nature of God as a benign father-figure. Consensus, therefore, does not have to be regarded as evidence of us all being in contact with the same objective God as we earlier implied; rather, it can be interpreted as a vindication of the universal validity of Freud's theory. Having given rise to the belief in God, wish-fulfillment then goes on to endow him with further desirable attributes. We want his protection to be complete so we regard him as omnipotent. We desire justice in an unjust world, so he becomes a God of Justice. We wish to be loved, so God is a Heavenly Father who loves us. We wish to go on living, so we believe in a life hereafter, to be spent in the company of the same loving Heavenly Father.

3. How are we to assess such a theory of religious experience? As a preliminary, it needs to be remarked that the general view of the unconscious so far presented - that it constitutes, in effect, a dustbin for unwanted thoughts - straightaway casts some doubt on it being the main source of religious experience. It is hard to account for how such a morass could give rise to the sense of wonder, awe, beauty, and nobility associated with the sense of the numinous. Any discussion of the origin of religious experience must surely give due attention to the quality of the experience, and whether or not this correlates with the nature of that which is supposedly giving rise to it. Secondly, it has to be noted that although some people do admittedly develop unhealthy religious obsessions - perhaps being overwhelmed by an exaggerated sense of guilt - this is not common. It is far more usual to find religion regarded as life-enhancing and fulfilling, the very antithesis of a debilitating mental disorder. To be taken into account, therefore, is not only the quality of the experience, but the fruits to which it gives rise.

Next, we note that all Freud's pronouncements on religion were founded on assertion alone; there was, and is, no proof for them. Even if one does accept that the process of wish-fulfillment is at work, this does not of itself, of course, determine one way or the other whether that which is wished for actually exists or not.

The notion that religion is grounded in wish-fulfillment does not give due weight to the extent to which religious believers are *challenged* by their faith, rather than comforted by it. The very phrase 'being comforted', when used in the religious context, more often means 'being strengthened' (to carry out some task) than being made to feel reassured. In the lives of many great religious figures - Moses, Jonah, and others - we find them being forced into courses of action that were *against* their own wishes. Jesus himself, on the night that he was betrayed, asked that the cup of suffering be removed. So much of religious belief is to do with self-denial, not self-gratification. Again and again one confesses that one has wishes that are immoral. One asks for God's help, not that such wishes should be satisfied, but that they be resisted. Of course, it can be countered that on these occasions the super-ego has gained the upper hand. Fair enough. A victory for the super-ego is, in the language of the religious believer, a victory for God. But there is no denying that each win for the super-ego is a wish not being fulfilled.

At this point it is perhaps relevant to raise the issue of masochism. In his early work, Freud concentrated exclusively on the sexual instinctual drive. Only later did he come to recognize the importance of a second drive, one that he named the *death instinct*. This manifested itself in the form of aggressive, destructive acts. Inasmuch as this aggression is directed against others, it can be understood as the psychological correlate of the biologically based instinct concerned with self-preservation - just as the sexual drive is the correlate of the biological instinct towards self-reproduction. But then Freud went further. He claimed that the death instinct was directed not only outwards against others, but also inwards against oneself. In the latter case it manifested itself as masochism and an inclination to bring about one's own self-destruction. If this is true, then one would have here an explanation of the self-sacrificing nature of religious behaviour.

Freud, however, was quite unable to produce any convincing explanation as to how such a strange instinct could have arisen. His attempts to justify it on biological and physical grounds were dismissed by scientists in both areas. Psychologists, while immediately accepting the importance of the aggressive drive as directed against others, gave a mixed reception to his suggestion that it was also directed against oneself. Nowadays, the idea that there is an instinctive drive towards masochism is almost universally disregarded. This, of course, is not to deny that there are masochists and people who commit suicide. But these actions are generally thought not to arise in response to an instinct one has from birth. The reasons have to be sought elsewhere. There is therefore no easy explanation of the self-denying behaviour of religious believers in terms of instinctual drives.

A second reason for believing wish-fulfillment to be less important for religion than Freud imagined, comes from studying the prevalence of religion according to social status. Wish-fulfillment, as already mentioned, is the gratification in fantasy of what is denied in reality. This being so, it ought mostly to be in evidence among working class people - those deprived of both worldly goods and social esteem. Yet in those countries where statistics are the most reliable, the U.K. and U.S., working class people are, if anything, *less* interested in religion - the opposite of what would be expected according to the theory of wish-fulfillment. Rather than turn to a fantasy belief in God, they look to whatever economic system they think is likely to afford the greater material benefit, be it socialism, communism, or capitalism - 'religions' in a wider sense.

Perhaps the aspect of religious belief that appears, from the outside at least, to be the most open to the accusation of wish-fulfillment is the idea of an after-life - the belief that the future holds some form of compensation for the injustices of the present life. Only those who are themselves believers can appreciate just how little in fact the notion of 'bread today, jam tomorrow' plays in their thinking. Most of them see the religious way of life as the means of achieving one's potential and fulfillment in *this* life, and this holds good regardless of whatever the consequences might be for a future existence. Again, there are many believers who, if pressed, admit to having no belief in an afterlife - despite what they might recite in the creed week by week. Even in the Middle Ages, when thoughts of the after-life were given more prominence in preaching and teaching than they are now, it was not so much the forthcoming joy of Heaven that was held in prospect as the terrible consequences of being sent to Hell.

This is not to deny that most of us from time to time indulge in wish-fulfillment. We fantasize over our supposed abilities and importance. This being so, it would be unreasonable to imagine religious beliefs to be immune from this insidious tendency. Indeed, one has only to look back over the course of history, or at one's own personal life, to see instances of the image of God being manipulated to make it conform to some desired end - the justification of courses of action that perhaps only later come to be seen as self-interested and out of keeping with a more consistent view of the nature of God. But whilst fully accepting the need for the religious believer to be on guard over wish-fulfillment, it is only fair to point out that the atheist is equally open to the same influence. Can it not be argued that atheism might sometimes arise out of a desire to consider oneself independent and self-sufficient? Could one not find in certain atheists a wish to evade the uncomfortable, self-denying, demands of religious commitment? If even the most devout believers sometimes find themselves daunted by the magnitude of the tasks laid upon them by the sense of religious duty, to say nothing of the cost imposed in terms of time, effort, and worldly possessions, it is hardly surprising that some people, through the process of wish-fulfillment, manage to convince themselves that they have no such responsibilities. In this way one sees that the argument against religious belief on the grounds of it being merely a manifestation of wish-fulfillment is easily turned on its head.

The idea of a Heavenly Father being nothing more than a projection of childish fantasies concerning one's earthly father is likewise a claim that can be turned around. This was pointed out by Jung who held that Freud's concept of the super-ego could be regarded as just another name for the repressed and rejected God experience. In other words, it is an introjected God - 'a furtive attempt to smuggle in the time-honoured image of Jehovah in the dress of psychological theory'. Accordingly, God is not to be conceived of as a substitute for the physical father; rather the physical father is a child's first substitute for God. Whereas Freud saw religion as a symptom of psychological illness, Jung saw the *absence* of religious experience as the root of adult psychological illness.

One further point to be made about Freud's suggestion of God being a projection of one's earthly father: It goes no way towards explaining Eastern religions. Unlike Judaism, Christianity, and Islam, these do *not* draw on the father-figure image. Indeed, Western religions are little more than caricatured if they are represented as a belief in a larger than life father-figure, or if the Christian conception of a Divine Person belonging to the Trinity is confused with the way one uses the word 'person' in everyday language (more of this in Section 16.6). The projected father-figure hypothesis, therefore, at best addresses only naive versions of Western religions and cannot in any way be regarded as a comprehensive explanation of world-wide, fully developed religion.

In summary, we conclude that, no matter how justly pre-eminent Freud was in other areas of psychology, when it came to religion his pronouncements were at best arbitrary. He tended to attack particularly unsophisticated forms of religious belief, and even that was done unconvincingly. Not surprisingly, his chief works on religious subjects - 'Totem and Taboo', 'The Future of an Illusion', and 'Moses and Monotheism' - are today among the most neglected of his books among serious psychologists. The arguments they contain are rejected with remarkable unanimity by most specialists in the subjects around which they are based. In short, his assertion that religion is the universal neurosis of humanity is just that - an assertion; it is not an empirical finding. Obviously there are individual cases of neurosis linked to religion. But as pointed out earlier, the existence of a few aberrant cases does nothing to discredit the religious experience as it manifests itself in the normal, well-balanced person.

Before leaving the subject of Freud, it is only fair to point out that the study of his work does have its positive side in helping us understand better the nature of our religious beliefs. Rightly we reject his main thesis regarding the origin of the religious experience. But it would be foolish to think that he had nothing of value to offer. It has already been mentioned that wish-fulfillment can colour our perception of what God requires of us. In addition we must guard against clinging to infantile conceptions of God, opposing religion to psychological maturation. We must recognize that the unconscious can play an inordinate part in helping to shape the religious experience and hence our understanding of God himself. For those of us who subscribe to a religion that draws upon the Heavenly Father metaphor, we would do well to be alive to the possibility of that image being too heavily overlaid with possibly inappropriate connotations deriving from our view of the role of an earthly father. Surveys have shown that those who have had a strict upbringing tend to regard God as more severe than those who have been brought up by parents that were easier-going. With the wholescale changes that have taken place in society in recent times, especially regarding attitudes towards parents and figures in positions of authority in general, we could find ourselves unconsciously adopting a changed attitude towards God. This might or might not be a good thing, but at least we should be aware that it is happening. An indispensable requirement for understanding God's revelation of himself through the religious experience, is the recognition and exploration of the role played by the unconscious. In this, Freud's work has its contribution to make.

4. Someone with a more profound appreciation of religion than Freud was Jung. On the basis of his own deeply felt first-hand experience of religion, Jung sought

to incorporate religious insights into his study of the mind. His work begins with the recognition that the unconscious contains much more than had hitherto been suspected. In particular, the aspect of the unconscious that we all share - that which is innate and does not depend upon the circumstances of the individual's own life - extends far beyond basic instincts to do with sex and aggression. His studies led him to the conclusion that in a wide variety of situations, we all tend to think and act in similar ways. This is not because we have been taught to react so; from birth these predispositions lie dormant deep within the unconscious awaiting a suitable occasion to give expression to themselves. These patterns of potential thought and behaviour constitute what is called the *collective unconscious*. Thus, according to Jung, an individual's unconscious is characterized by two aspects - that which derives from the person's past experiences, and that which shapes the collective unconscious. The first is specific to the individual, the second is innate and common to us all. Though it is important for an understanding of the mind to make this distinction, it should not be thought that the personal and collective aspects of the unconscious are separate compartmentalized sections of the mind. Rather, the collective unconscious is to be seen as a pre-existing framework into which the events of the individual's life-history are received. One's experiences are moulded by the structure of that framework, as well as by whatever previous experiences the individual has had. Recall how in Section 9.1 we said that having heard the first chime of a clock, the experience of hearing the third chime was a different experience - one that incorporated expectation and recognition in place of surprise. What we are now saying is that even from birth our experiences have a shape. Our very first experiences might incorporate, for example, a measure of expectation.

That the mind should already have a structure of sorts from the moment of birth might at first sight seem a little odd, but the evidence for it is strong. This shows up in a particularly clear manner over the question of language. One of the most important characteristics of humankind is its use of speech. Why are we so much better at learning how to communicate with each other than other animals? Recent research shows that children throughout the world, irrespective of culture and upbringing, begin to exhibit language behaviour in the same way at the same age. They have the same innate readiness to absorb and make use of a language, a readiness not exhibited by other animals. It almost seems as though they are born half expecting to have to learn a language at some stage. Obviously the particular language learnt depends upon the specific culture to which one belongs, but not the readiness to learn a language. The general structure of the grammar and semantics common to all languages appears to be already preprogrammed into the child. The potentiality sits there in the unconscious awaiting the particular concrete form it will take up from the social environment.

The collective unconscious can be thought of as a cluster of distinct patterns of potentiality. To understand the collective unconscious it is necessary to identify these component forms and the circumstances that activate them. These various predispositions are known as *archetypes*. The term derives from the Greek words 'arche' meaning 'beginning', and 'typos' meaning 'imprint'. The idea is that throughout human history the same kinds of situation have arisen time and again, and these have provided the conditions for the selection of individuals carrying certain genes. In each of these situations, behaviour of a certain kind can confer some advantage in the form of an enhanced chance of survival. Those with a genetic make-up that inclines them towards this behaviour will be preferentially selected in the process of evolution by natural selection. This is how we ourselves come to have an innate inclination to behave in these ways, given the same circumstances. The imprint is in the collective unconscious that we now all share. How many archetypes are there? It is difficult to say. One expects as many archetypes as there are typical repeated circumstances conferring survival advantage on those with an appropriate genetic make-up. Jung was able to delineate many of them. He found archetypes associated with psychological dispositions towards various figures: mother, father, family, hero, wise old man, etc., as well as those associated with situations arising out of one's relationship to such figures.

As an example, let us take the mother archetype. A baby on being presented to the breast for the first time instinctively knows that it has to suck. It does not need to be taught this because this knowledge is already encoded into its genetic makeup. It is behaviour that arose in the course of evolution through natural selection in the far distant past when mammals first put in an appearance. Since that time, any mammalian offspring that lacked the appropriate gene failed to get sustenance and so did not survive to the point where they could themselves mate and pass on the gene make-up lacking in this characteristic. That is how the situation is described in terms of evolutionary biology. In the mental domain, the corresponding pre-existing psychological disposition the baby has towards the mother - the thought forms that give rise to the sucking behaviour - derive from the mother archetype. Not that this is all there is to the mother archetype. Breast feeding is but one small, rather superficial aspect of an intricate and far-reaching set of thought patterns controlled by this archetype. The archetype orients us from birth to expect a 'mother' who will nurture, protect, care, love, and it should be added, abandon, withhold, deprive, destroy, and hate. In all kinds of ways this archetype pre-disposes us in how we relate to our mother and to mother-figures; it can even affect the way we relate to women in general.

Are the images thrown up into consciousness by the archetypes to be regarded as nothing more than the psychological correlates of genetically determined behaviour? If so, it should be possible to see how each of the thought forms controlled by the archetypes in the mental domain leads to behaviour in the physical domain that is conducive to the survival of the individual or its close kin (relatives that share in large measure the same genetic material). On examining commonly held mental attitudes we certainly do see much that leads to the kind of self-serving behaviour we find in animals. These attitudes can manifest themselves in open aggression and violence, or covertly through forms of competitive behaviour sanctioned by society: competition through examinations or sports, or in the pursuit of jobs, political office, a marriage partner, wealth, prestige, etc. They show themselves in the limited extent to which we are prepared to put ourselves out to relieve the plight of those less fortunate than ourselves. Such then are the archetypal images incorporating the psychological correlates of the behaviour patterns that have been fashioned by evolutionary pressures. But having said that, it has to be added that the richness and variety of archetypal images are such that it is difficult, if not impossible, to demonstrate that they are associated *exclusively* with behaviour having survival value. In fact, as we shall see in a moment, some archetypal behaviour even appears to run contrary to such a requirement.

5. Among the archetypes there is one of particular importance for religion and religious experience. As far back in time as history will take us we find evidence of religious practice. Studies of the contents of the graves of Neanderthal man show that one hundred thousand years ago there was belief in an afterlife. Even before that time there is evidence of the offering of first fruits to a deity. Religion was a universal phenomenon. It affected all peoples without exception. True, there have been occasional reports by ethnologists of examples of peoples with no apparent religion. However, in each case where subsequent investigations have been carried out, the earlier claims were refuted. Today, we find that even in countries where religion is officially discouraged, pseudo-religious rituals are observed. It does not take much

imagination to see a parallel between the visit that newly-wed couples in Moscow pay to the tomb of Lenin, and the desire to have one's marriage blessed by the church; or between the requirement to observe a reverential hush and remove one's hat on entering Chairman Mao's mausoleum in Beijing, and the respectful behaviour expected on entering church. As for countries where organized religion is not discouraged but appears to be on the decline, one finds that decline in part compensated by a growth of interest in the occult, visitors from outer space, etc.

The seemingly irrepressible urge to give expression to religious feeling indicated to Jung that it must have an archetypal basis. He associated it with an archetype of especial significance - one occupying a dominant position at the centre of the psyche (the psyche being the totality of the conscious and unconscious mind). This archetype is different from the others in that all the other archetypes relate to it. It is called the 'self'. This can be a little confusing in that the term as used here does not carry quite its normal meaning. Customarily 'self' is thought of as being more or less synonymous with 'ego'. In the present context, however, the *self* is defined as the centre of the entire thinking individual, embracing both the conscious and unconscious processes, together with the exchanges that occur between the two. The *ego* is specifically the centre of consciousness.

The aim of inner psychic growth is to progress beyond the point where one is inclined to identify oneself simply with the ego. In the process of becoming increasingly aware of what lies in the unconscious, one comes to accept that the concept of personhood has to include the unconscious as well as the conscious. Earlier, we saw that there were both physical and mental aspects to personhood. At that stage we thought of the mental manifestation as being the ego. But now we recognize that it is the totality of the conscious and unconscious that constitutes the mental representation of the person.

The conception of one's nature as a mental being has therefore to be realigned so that it centres itself on the self rather than on the ego. This voyage of inner discovery, called by Jung 'the process of individuation', is one that is undertaken consciously so involves the ego. The end result is the recognition that consciousness is but a part of the totality of the person, and that the ego must concede primacy to the self. The self is therefore concerned with human wholeness. As the central archetype it provides the underlying purposeful drive that prompts the search for wholeness. It is the goal that draws towards itself all inner psychic growth and reorientation, a goal concerned with self-knowledge and self-realization.

Broadly speaking, we can think of Freud as having been primarily interested in studying early childhood and its effects on later life. Jung in contrast tended to concentrate more on the problems and goals of later life, and how these are to be achieved taking into account one's original archetypal orientation. He saw the purpose of the latter half of life as being one of bringing about the full realization of the potential of the individual. Because of force of circumstances - the career one has followed, the demands made by family obligations, the requirement to conform to the expectations of society, the pressure experienced by a man to act the typically masculine role with the consequent suppression of those qualities conventionally regarded as feminine (and vice versa for a woman) - because of such factors one reaches the mid-point of life with only certain aspects of one's personality developed. The remainder lie dormant within the unconscious. To move towards fuller maturity, the imbalance must be corrected. This complex process is guided unconsciously by the archetype of the self. It consists of a sometimes painful dialectical encounter between the ego and the self - one that can go on, uncompleted, all our life.

But what, you may ask, has all this talk of self-realization to do with religion? The answer lies in the nature of the outcome. The process is one in which the contents of the unconscious are progressively revealed and integrated into consciousness and one's potentialities recognized and fulfilled. But in the course of this journey one becomes increasingly aware that there lies in the unconscious that which is unreachable. The ego ultimately encounters a mysterious and ineffable element that it cannot assimilate - something intrinsically incomprehensible.

How does the ego react when confronted by these fathomless depths of the self? It responds in a way very similar to, indeed indistinguishable from, that which was earlier spoken of as the inner experience of the numinous. The discovery of one's inner self has the closest possible affinity to being confronted by the otherness of the religious experience. The same characteristics of awe and wonder are there. Thus, the process whereby a person becomes a mature well-balanced individual, fully realizing his or her potential, merges into the search for God. In Jungian thought there is an indissoluble link between the two activities.

Why is this? How can the discovery of one's own inner depths be at the same time the discovery of the evidence or image of God? Are we saying that 'my inner self' and 'God' are terms that can be used interchangeably. That is one interpretation, but by no means the only one. It is certainly not the one to which I myself subscribe. Recall what we learnt from the discussion of other minds. 'My mind' is a phrase that means nothing outside the context of there being other minds, i.e. those that are not mine. The acknowledgement of there being other minds is at one and the same time the recognition of one's own. Similarly, it is only through the acceptance of there being other human bodies that it makes sense to speak of one's own. We called discoveries of this type: 'reciprocal definitions'.

Now, in the present context, we find the same kind of thing happening again. The evidence that one is encountering God immediately reflects back the recognition of a further dimension of personhood, that which we shall later be speaking of as our spiritual nature. The acceptance of that which is *not* me is again an integral, indispensable feature of the definition of what *is* me. There is, therefore, no incompatibility in the idea of the archetypal self providing both the drive towards the full realization of oneself as a person, and the drive behind humankind's religious quest. Whether the initial motivation is psychological (the desire to understand oneself), or religious (the desire to enter into a relationship with God), the end result is the same: *the simultaneous discovery of both that which is one's inner self, and that which points to the existence of something other than oneself.*

Having said that, one ought to add a caveat. To regard the self as the sole archetype associated with religious images and thought-forms can be somewhat misleading. As I said earlier, *all* the archetypes relate to the self. Thus all conscious experience under the control of archetypes can be affected by religious overtones. For example, a hero or a mother can be regarded as a god or goddess. Nevertheless, the self is the ultimate focus of religious experience. For this reason it will sometimes prove useful for us to refer to the self as 'the religious archetype'. This is not customary, and there is a certain looseness in adopting such a name, there being more to the self than its association with religion. Our own particular interest, however, does centre on this specific association. Not only that, but the 'self' as referred to in the strictly Jungian sense can get confused with a more familiar use of the word. Hence the change in terminology.

The fact that everyone is affected by the religious archetype does not mean that at the level of the individual person there is always a manifest inclination to worship God; we have already noted this. In addition to the examples already cited of the religious instinct giving expression to itself outside the context of a conventional religion, most of us are aware of a tendency we have to devote our energies to some cause or other - one's tribe or country, a political party, a trade union, a football club, a campaign for animal rights, nuclear disarmament - often at personal cost to oneself. Jung declared that 'whenever the Spirit of God is excluded from human consideration, an unconscious substitute takes its place'. In this way there arises within humankind a readiness for individuals to bind themselves together in support of a common cause. One even speaks of the cause as being their 'religion' - a use of the term 'religion' that is broader than that which we have adopted throughout. Not only is there a tendency to devote oneself to a cause, but we also share certain basic attitudes towards, for example, death. Thus a person who believes with his intellect that dead people have ceased to exist - such a person will yet feel compelled to attend a funeral, tend a grave, speak of the dead with respect, commemorate the departed, etc. Such actions are expressions of something deeply felt, and manifest the potency of their archetypal basis.

6. We have seen how some at least of the archetypal images and thought-forms appear correlated to genetically determined behaviour arising out of evolution by natural selection. To the extent that this is true, we expect them, therefore, to be associated with behaviour that increases, or at a minimum does not decrease, the chances of survival. Can it be argued that an inherent tendency towards religious behaviour has survival value, so that the whole religious phenomenon becomes nothing more than a product of natural selection?

Certainly a readiness to form hunter groups or tribes can provide its members with benefits - more effective ways of catching and killing animals for food, for instance. In addition, inter-tribal rivalries could lead to the weeding out of the weaker tribes. Today's examples of extreme nationalism, racism, and warring football fans can be regarded as modern versions of such ancient tribal rivalry. It is reasonable to suppose that such behaviour might in part be genetically based. For this reason, it is only sensible to raise the question of whether or not belief in a god - an imaginary god - could have survival value in evolutionary terms through the way it welds individuals together into a more effective social unit. If so, religion could be merely a genetic device that helps perpetuate the species.

This might well be a plausible conclusion to draw from a study that restricted itself solely to ancient tribal religions. Worship of a tribal god would in effect be an expression of tribal loyalty and could be instrumental in binding the members of that grouping together in a common cause. There might well lie here an explanation of the darker side of modern religions and the terrible deeds sometimes perpetrated in the name of religion - fanaticism, intolerance, exclusivity, and just wars. Even so, it is not easy to see why an instinctive belief in a god of some sort would have conferred an advantage over some other tribe that believed in something more tangible: a warrior leader, the superiority of the tribe itself, or the right to a particular territory, for instance. Indeed, one can see certain disadvantages to having a god-worshipping type of instinct as the uniting principle. Because the existence of the god could not be demonstrated, there would inevitably be recurring doubts about its existence, and these would tend to undermine allegiance. The practice of placating the god through sacrifices - often of first-born and first-fruits - could be regarded as wasteful and debilitating and hence counter-productive.

When it comes to considering the modern forms of religion, the difficulties of dismissing them as throwbacks to ancient tribalism become even more acute. One of the central features of the ethical code common to the great world religions is a general commitment to altruism. Any claim that religion should be regarded as genetically determined behaviour fashioned through natural selection must, therefore, be able to provide a plausible explanation of acts of self-sacrifice. Sociobiologists (scientists concerned with providing biological explanations of social behaviour) have met with some success in accounting for certain instances of altruistic acts (behaviour in which an individual organism increases the chances of survival of another organism at the cost of an increased risk to its own survival). A mother bird, for example, might attract the attention of a predator to herself, and hence away from her young, thus incurring added risk to herself whilst reducing the risk to her young. Such behaviour - which in a human being would be commended as morally admirable - can be understood biologically through the recognition that the unit that is being subjected to natural selection is not the individual but a particular gene - a gene that determines that the mother will behave in this way. This same gene is not only in the mother, it is also in the young as part of its genetic inheritance. The gene has a greater chance of being perpetuated in later generations than some alternative gene that tended to make the mother put her own interests first, so adding to the risk of the gene being destroyed in the young, and hence not being passed on any further. Shifting the element of selfishness to the *gene* can, under appropriate circumstances, lead to the *individual* being altruistic. Thus sociobiology provides a plausible explanation of certain acts of altruism. It is important to note, however, that the mechanism just described works only for altruistic acts committed on behalf of individuals to whom one is closely related - those who share the same gene as oneself.

How about acts involving individuals between whom there are no such close ties? One can imagine, for instance, survival value in a gene that required an individual to risk itself in going to the aid of another in need if there was an expectation that the debt would be repaid were the individual itself to find that it was in similar need on some future occasion. This is called reciprocal altruism. There is a certain amount of evidence that seems to point to such behaviour, albeit on a limited scale. A male olive baboon, for example, will sometimes engage in a fight with baboon no. 2 whilst baboon no. 3 gains access to baboon no. 2's female partner - the favour being returned at a later date. The reason why such behaviour is not more common is that there seems no way of guarding against cheating, i.e. having benefited from the other's altruism, you then run away. There would seem to be an even stronger survival value in a gene that dictated the cheating kind of behaviour because one does not have to incur the risk associated with repaying the debt. In time one would expect the 'honest' variety to be taken advantage of, gradually being eliminated as they dutifully ran risks on the assumption that they might get repaid at a later date. This would leave only the 'cheating' variety, who of course do not behave altruisticaly. One way of trying to beat the greater survival value of the cheating type of gene is to have another gene that is prepared to engage in reciprocal altruism only with those who, on the basis of past experience, are known to pay back debts. In a given community, an individual that failed to reciprocate would be branded a cheater, and would be excluded from the advantages of any further acts of altruism. A gene giving rise to such discriminatory behaviour is called a 'grudger', because it bears a grudge against those known to have cheated in the past. A scenario of this kind might work, but then again, only within a fairly closed environment in which the same individuals come into regular contact with each other, so allowing the pattern of past behaviour to be known; it would not work in an open system where there was only occasional contact.

In addition to reciprocal altruism, where two individuals are prepared to act in turn on behalf of the other, there is a further possible type of altruism known as group altruism. Here the idea is that one's chances of survival might be greater if one belongs to a group in which all its members are prepared to sacrifice themselves for the group as a whole. This suggestion, of course, like that of reciprocal altruism, is immediately vulnerable to the claim that such a group would be liable to infiltration by cheaters. Benefiting from the sacrifices of others, at no cost to themseves, the cheaters would eventually come to dominate the group. It is difficult to see how one is to get round this objection, except by pointing out that the fashioning of the genes is a random process, and it could well be that for a given species, over a given period of time, there could exist the altruistic gene but not the cheating variety - there simply not having been sufficient time for the latter type to be created.

Claims to have found examples of group altruism are occasionally made. One of these concerns the behaviour of the blackbird. The blackbird, on spotting a hawk, will issue a cry of warning, whereupon the flock takes to the wing. The bird in behaving this way gives away its own position, hence increasing the danger to itself, and all this in the cause of allowing the others to escape. The bird cannot be closely related to all the members of the flock so it is not a case of kin selection. Neither is it likely to be a case of reciprocal altruism because after this incident it is not likely to be around to benefit from any repayment at a later date. This, so it has been claimed, must surely be an example of truly disinterested altruism of the type that in a human would be regarded as wholly admirable. But is it? Since attention was first drawn to this behaviour there have been second thoughts. A quite different interpretation of what is going on has subsequently been advanced. It begins by noting that the bird emits a high-pitched sound as the warning cry - a sound for which it is difficult to locate the source; the bird has not, therefore, betrayed its position as was originally thought. As the flock takes to the wing only one bird knows in which direction it is prudent to fly! What better way of looking after one's own interests than to send up a cloud of decoys? So, what superficially appeared to be an act of altruism, on closer examination is seen to be probably nothing of the sort. This example illustrates how careful one has to be about the interpretation to be put on animal behaviour.

In any event, it needs to be said that all this talk about reciprocal and group altruism is largely beside the point. An attitude that can be summed up as 'you scratch my back and I'll scratch yours' is hardly the kind of altruism we have in mind when concerned with the ethical behaviour of humans. Most often in the human field we are speaking of self-sacrificing acts committed on behalf of people who have no way of repaying. So, with neither reciprocal nor group altruism being regarded as very important today, and in any case largely irrelevant to the human situation, it is difficult to see how one can attribute the moral sense of humans to genetically determined behaviour fashioned by the pressures of natural selection. Certainly there is no way of accounting in these terms for one of the central tenets of Christianity: love your enemies. Of all the messages that might have become genetically encoded, that one must surely rank as the most unlikely to have been perpetuated down to modern times. Any animals in the past that habitually went around loving their enemies are most unlikely to have survived to the point where they could have left any descendents today. The symbol of Christianity is the cross - a constant reminder of the need of Christians to live a life of self-sacrifice. Moreover such self-sacrifice is not simply to be made on behalf of members of the Christian 'tribe' but for all humankind, including those who are against you.

Christianity, like certain other religions, is founded on compassion; it protects the weak and shows reverence for life. But in evolutionary terms this does not make much sense. It is difficult to see how the interests of the human race - seen as a species in competition with other species - is best served if much of its time, efforts and resources are increasingly devoted to reducing infant mortality in areas already over-populated, towards developing more and more elaborate and expensive means of medically treating the chronically weak and sick, and towards the prolongation of the lives of the aged and infirm. To put it at its crudest, evolution is concerned about the 'survival of the fittest', so what sense is there in lavishing care and attention on the 'unfit'? And yet there is an almost universal inner feeling in humankind that such behaviour is wholly right.

7. Thus we find that whereas certain forms of quasi-religious behaviour might have survival value and thus be encoded in our genetic material - behaviour such as tribalism - that which we today specifically associate with the higher religions and their devotion to a God who loves everyone and calls his followers to a life of self-sacrifice appears to have nothing to do with the evolutionary struggle. Although, according to Jungian thought, the unconscious is involved in religious experience, it does not appear to be the ultimate *source* of the otherness of that experience - either in the terms that Freud was thinking, or as an artifice thrown up by natural selection. We therefore need to seek the source of that otherness elsewhere. We need to ask: Who or what is the imprinter of the religious archetype?

CHAPTER 16

THE SPIRITUAL INTERACTION
FRAMEWORK

ACCORDING to the religious outlook on life, the simplest explanation of the inner religious experience, as well as of other indications of God's existence, is that these pointers genuinely attest to an objective spiritual reality. In addition to the reality domains we have already encountered, there is this further one - the spiritual domain. In this chapter we examine the nature of this domain and the explanatory framework associated with it.

1. The general motivation for proposing such a reality is the same as that for proposing any kind of reality - it helps to explain certain features of conscious experience. In the first place, it accounts for the otherness of the inner religious experience - the fact that we do not control the experience. Just as earlier the otherness of sensory observation led us to postulate a domain of physical interactions in order to fill an explanatory gap, so it will now be proposed that there is a spiritual reality domain such that a description of what happens in that domain will explain what happens in the inner religious experience.

The fact that the inner religious experience appears to be impressed on us 'from outside', so to speak, is the more obvious form of otherness. But there is a second aspect to otherness: religious experiences, of various kinds, seem to convey *information* to us - information about the ultimate purpose of life and how we should live in harmony with that purpose. This has similarities with the way one infers the existence of minds other than one's own. In Chapter 11 we saw that this was done partly on the basis of information received about mental concerns - information that presumably derived from some mental source which had to be other than one's own mind. The fact that religious experiences provide us with information, is indicative of an external authority. The information being about ultimate concerns, one assumes that the domain from which it originates is particularly associated with such matters.

2. A further reason for proposing a spiritual domain is that it forges explanatory links across a wide spectrum of different types of religious experience - those features of nature, history, and the lives of holy people, that are suggestive of God's presence. It yields the kind of integration that cannot be achieved in any other way. The nature of this integrative function and how it is performed is perhaps best illustrated by an analogy.

Working within the physical explanatory framework, one is able to recognize certain links between what initially appear to be very different physical entities. Thus for instance, water, ice, and steam are phenomenologically dissimilar. Detailed study, however, shows them to be alternative forms of the same substance. Similarly, electric and magnetic forces are but different manifestations of the one electromagnetic force. The recognition of connections such as these is largely what scientific explanation is about. But in addition to this type of integration, there is another. Additional links between elements of physical reality can be forged by mapping *out* of the physical domain to the mental domain. Only from within the mental explanatory framework can one discern a connection between such widely differing entities as, for example: a stretch of countryside, a pattern of chemical and electrical activity in someone's brain as they recall seeing that countryside, the configuration of electromagnetic waves spreading out from a TV aerial containing a coded picture of the scene, a landscape painting, the sounds of bird song and the rustle of leaves, a gramophone record of Beethoven's Pastoral Symphony, a map showing large areas of green, the written words 'a countryside', the same words spoken, the same idea expressed in a foreign language, and so on. In the physical framework one would be hard put to it to explain what was common to these disparate entities. In the mental framework there is no difficulty; the common link is the *mental* construct 'a countryside'. In the mental context the integration is simple and natural.

With the introduction of the spiritual framework, the potential for forging links between otherwise seemingly disparate phenomena takes on a new dimension. Just as the use of mental concepts within the mental explanatory framework allows us to grasp connections that are not apparent within the narrow confines of the physical explanatory framework, so the use of spiritual concepts within the spiritual framework enables the process of integration to be to be taken yet a stage further. Thus, the source of the inner sense of the numinous comes to be identified with the spiritual creator of the physical and mental domains. The physical world, owing its origins to God, has properties that reflect the qualities of its Maker - properties that can be studied with a view to learning something of his nature. The purpose behind the creation of the physical world becomes inseparably bound up with God's desire to bring human spirits into existence and have them fashioned and developed in such a manner that they can respond to him and enter into communion with him. In this way the rationale for the physical world, together with the meaning of conscious existence, become enmeshed with the destiny of the human spirit. Not only that, but through the acknowledgement of our relationship to God, we complete our understanding of the nature of personhood and of what is required if we are to fulfill our potential as mature human beings. That same acknowledgement also awakens us to the true nature of our relationship to one another: As children of the same Heavenly Father, we are brothers and sisters, and thereby have laid upon us all the obligations for each other's welfare that such a close relationship entails.

The spiritual domain allows one to integrate the component features of human existence into a pattern

SPIRITUAL INTERACTION FRAMEWORK

and to address questions to do with the overall character of life. Each type of reality is concerned with trying to answer particular questions. In order to tackle questions that begin with 'How' we postulate a physical domain. It is a domain that supplies answers to questions concerned with mechanism. In the mental domain we can begin to answer questions that begin with 'Why'; these are questions to do with motivation and the exercise of our will. But there are other questions, of a wider, more integrative nature. These also begin with 'Why', but are to be distinguished from the former by the kind of answer they evoke. These are the ultimate questions. What does 'ultimate' mean in this context? Consider the following conversation:

'Why work hard on your studies?'
'To get a good exam result.'
'Why do well in exams?'
'To get a good job.'
'Why get a good job?'
'To get a high salary.'
'Why do you want a high salary?'
'So I can buy whatever I want.'
'Why buy things?'
'Because they give me pleasure.'
'Why seek pleasure?'
'Well, that's what life is all about, isn't it?'

The sequence is terminated by an ultimate question - one that draws an answer to do with what the overall purpose of life is supposed to be. Other sequences might end with an ultimate question that prompts a statement that doing good to other people, or becoming famous or influential, or getting one's own way was 'what life is all about'. Such overall purposes are couched in terms of the mental or physical: feeling happy, being able to exercise power over others, etc. But this is not always the case. An ultimate question will often draw an answer that calls for a reference to the spiritual: 'I acted that way because I believed that was what God wanted me to do, and loving

God and doing his will is what life is all about'. For religious people, ultimate questions are always to be answered in spiritual terms. They hold that only by answering in that manner does our otherwise seemingly futile existence yield up its true meaning and purpose.

3. Thus, the justification for the postulate of a spiritual domain lies in its explanatory value in regard to issues of meaning and purpose - that and its ability to account for the otherness of the inner religious experience, together with the consonant features evinced by the various types of religious experience. Such grounds, by their very nature, cannot provide deductive proof of the existence of the spiritual domain. As we have noted previously in other contexts, whenever one tries to reach out beyond the domain of conscious mental phenomena to establish the existence of another domain of reality, the step has to be an inferential one. It must be be one based on an inductive argument, or a combination of such arguments, each lending a measure of support to the conclusion. No matter how persuasive the evidence might appear, one cannot expect water-tight proof of the existence of the spiritual, any more than one could earlier expect it of the physical, of minds other than one's own, or of the unconscious part of one's own mind. Belief in God rests on an assessment of the explanatory value of the hypothesis.

4. Turning to the explanatory framework that is set up to deal with spiritual reality, we first note that it does not attempt to justify the existence of that reality. Just as the physical framework takes it for granted that there is a physical reality of some sort, and the mental framework does not question the existence of a mental reality, so the spiritual framework is based on the prior assumption of there being a spiritual reality of some kind. Throughout the whole of the Bible not a single attempt is made to argue the reader into accepting either the existence of God or the reality of our interactions with him. Certainly there are many references to 'faith'. But by this is meant our need to have confidence in providence and to trust

God's promises, not our need to hold on to a belief in his existence. The justification for accepting the reality that underpins an explanatory framework - *any* reality underpinning *any* framework - must be sought outside the framework itself. And we have seen above the motivations for postulating a spiritual domain.

On the assumption that there is a spiritual reality, the task of the spiritual explanatory framework is to examine the contents of this reality. In the first place, it is a domain that must obviously contain God, or at least some representation of him. It may also contain angels and/or devils. In order for us to be able to interact with God, there must also be within this domain a representation of ourselves. In the same way as our mental self, consisting of its conscious and unconscious aspects, is mapped to the interactions of our human body in the physical domain, so it is now thought of as being mapped to a spirit capable of interacting in the spiritual domain.

Does this mean that we are to regard this domain as essentially consisting of three different types of entity: God, our spirit, and the interaction between them? In using the terms 'God' and 'spirit', do we have in mind entities capable of existing independently of one another, that is to say, irrespective of whatever interaction might be taking place between them? This might at first sight appear an innocent assumption. But we must be on our guard. Exactly this kind of thinking was incorporated into classical physics. There we had a mental picture of objects-in-themselves, such as electrons. They moved about, possessed properties, and generally had an existence of their own, quite regardless of what else might exist or whether they happened to be undergoing interactions. Modern physics exposed the deficiencies of that kind of thinking. We came to understand that what we had first to do was to think in terms of a physical reality domain that consisted solely of interactions. In this domain, 'objects', such as electrons, were to be thought of as the common endpoint of a cluster of interactions. The question as to whether there is a further physical reality domain (the-world-in-itself) consisting of physical objects capable of existing in their own right independently of having interactions, was then deferred for later discussion.

We found exactly the same considerations applied to the mental domain. What we have direct access to are mental experiences, not the ego existing in its own right, or memories, or sensations. So we set up a mental explanatory framework designed for dealing with conscious mental experiences, and deferred to later the discussion of what might exist outside consciousness - an unconscious incorporating the mind-in-itself.

Now, it does not follow that because we found it necessary to adopt a two-stage epistemological procedure in the case of the physical and mental realms we must do the same when tackling the spiritual. It could be that God and our spirits do have an existence as spiritual entities-in-themselves, whether or not an interaction is taking place. But I do not regard it as wise to start our discussion on such a basis. The physical and mental realms are the creation of God. As such we expect them to reflect to some degree the qualities of its Maker. Our best bet as to what would be a 'natural' approach to an understanding of God is surely to follow the line of thinking that has proved the most fruitful in the study of his handiwork. This, at any rate, is the strategy I shall adopt.

This means beginning with a domain that we shall call *the domain of spiritual interactions*. It is a domain that is to be thought of as consisting entirely of spiritual interactions or relationships, *and nothing else*. It is directly analogous to the domain of physical interactions and that of mental experiences. Recall how earlier a dynamic mental occurrence associated with the senses was mapped to something dynamic in the physical realm: a physical interaction. Now, the dynamic mental occurrence of having a religious experience is likewise mapped to something dynamic in the spiritual domain: an event consisting of a spiritual interaction.

In our discussion of the domain of physical interactions, we were at pains to emphasise that the expression: interactions-with-the-world carried no implication of there being three entities: two objects plus the interaction between them. Likewise, when discussing the domain of mental experiences this was not meant to imply that they were the experiences of an ego interacting with independently existing sensations and memories. The same holds for the domain of spiritual interactions. Just because we speak of someone's interaction with God, that does not mean there are three independently existing entities in this domain. Whether it makes sense to think of God and of our spiritual selves being able to exist outside the context of an interaction, is an entirely separate question. This will be dealt with in the next chapter when we come to consider the possibility of there being a second spiritual reality domain beyond that of spiritual interactions - a domain analogous to the physical-world-in-itself lying beyond that of physical interactions-with-the-world, or to the domain of the unconscious mind-in-itself lying beyond that of mental experiences.

If in the domain of spiritual interactions nothing exists other than interactions, what does it mean to speak of 'God' and of one's 'spirit'? In this connection we note that earlier, in the case of the domain of physical interactions-with-the-world, the term 'electron' was defined as the common endpoint of those interactions known as interactions-with-an-electron. That and nothing more. It was not something that 'had' the interactions, and so, in a manner of speaking, lay beyond that end of the interaction. It was the label attached to the end of the interaction itself. Analogously, therefore, we take the term 'God' in the domain of spiritual interactions to refer to the common endpoint of those interactions known as interactions-with-God. Similarly, we mean by a person's 'spirit' the common end point of the particular cluster of interactions which, when mapped to the mental domain, are to be associated with that person's religious experiences. The spiritual interactions map to the mental religious experiences; the spirit to the Jungian archetypal 'self'.

'Labels attached to the endpoints of interactions' is admittedly a rather crude way of talking. To put the matter more formally: The entities that exist in the spiritual interaction domain, like those of the physical interaction domain, are to be designated by a combination of *two* symbols rather than the usual single symbol. Thus, for example, in classical physics one might have referred to an electron by the symbol, e, and the apparatus for measuring its position by, P. Because the two physical entities are considered to have an existence independently of each other, the corresponding symbols can be used independently. In quantum physics, however, all that one deals with is the interaction. To remind us of this, we designate this entity symbolically by the combination, (e/P). Similarly a measurement of the electron's velocity is represented by the interaction (e/V). The measurement of a proton's position or velocity by (p/P) or (p/V) respectively. The symbols e, p, P, and V on their own do not refer to any existent entity. The symbol e, for instance, does not designate an independently existing particle as normally conceived. Rather, it refers to whatever it is that the interactions (e/P) and (e/V) have in common. The symbol V likewise does not refer to a freestanding piece of equipment for measuring velocity, but to whatever it is that the interactions (e/V) and (p/V) have in common. So it is in the spiritual interaction domain. The symbol (s/G) denotes the interaction between my spirit and God. The symbols s and G are not to be used on their own; they have meaning only in the context of their being components of the two-symbol expression. In this domain, the term 'God' refers to whatever is common to the interactions of all our spirits with God.

The conception of God and of ourselves in this domain as simply a 'label' given to one end of a relationship might strike you as entailing a rather insubstantial existence! In one sense - the strictly literal sense of the word 'insubstantial' - that is quite right; we do *not* have any substance, we are not constituted out of some stuff or other. Our existence is a *relational form of existence* - it depends entirely on our being able to relate to something or someone else. As far as this domain is concerned, we do not exist independently of interactions. But by a similar token, one should note that neither do the interactions exist without us. We might constitute 'merely' one end of a relationship, but without that end there is no relationship. A relational form of existence is not to be disparaged. After all, no-one would think of our existence in the physical realm as inconsequential. And yet, as we saw earlier, many physicists believe that in the physical realm there is only the domain of physical interactions - in other words, our physical existence is a relational one only. That being so, there is no call for dismissing a relational existence in the spiritual domain as not worth having!

5. The recognition that there is a representation of ourselves in the domain of spiritual interactions expands our concept of personhood. It is now seen to embrace not only the mental aspects (conscious and unconscious) and the physical body, but also a supernatural spirit.[*] We are to see ourselves as not just a physical body interacting with other physical objects, and a mind communicating with other minds through the agency of the physical world. We are also spirits, and through that spiritual dimension, are able to commune with God.

The spiritual interaction domain contains not only interactions between God and ourselves, but also interactions amongst ourselves - from one human spirit to another. Certain people strike us as holy; we sense the numinous in them. With such people we can, if we are

---

[*] The word 'soul' often appears in this context. Sometimes it is taken to mean 'mind', sometimes 'spirit'. In the latter case it might be called 'immortal soul'. To avoid possible confusion I shall stick to 'mind' and 'spirit'.

ourselves spiritually aware, be drawn into spiritual communion with them. A new avenue opens up that adds a further dimension to the concept of interpersonal relations. This does not happen with everyone. A prerequisite is that both parties be spiritually alive. Thus one might strike up an otherwise rewarding relationship, only to find that it fails totally to operate at this further level - because of a lack of spiritual development on one side or the other. On the other hand, one might meet someone with whom one appears to have nothing in common at the intellectual level or in terms of cultural interests or hobbies, only to discover a mutual warmth stemming from an appreciation of both being in communion with God and with each other at the spiritual level. In this context, credal differences are of little consequence. With an awareness of the numinous in one's own life, one generally has little difficulty in recognising that same numinous presence in someone else - and the lack of it in others. The conscious experience of the numinous in one's encounter with another person is the mapping into the mental domain of the interaction between one's supernatural spirit and that of the other in the spiritual interaction domain.

Earlier we saw how the conception of personhood is intimately bound up with relationships, to the extent that one might even regard a person as being simply or primarily a collection of relationships. It is important to the full development of our potential as a person, therefore, to recognize the possibility of our relating at the spiritual level. Not that it is a matter of simply noting the availability of this line of communication to God and to fellow human beings. As with other channels, it must be exploited. If one is to develop mentally it is necessary to engage actively in a meeting of minds and be open to allowing one's own mind to benefit from constant contact with others. If the physical body is to develop it too must become actively engaged in physical exertion. So it is with the spirit. If it is to be given the chance to fulfill its potential, it too must be able to benefit from active interaction with God and with other human spirits.

6. The idea of relatedness, as it applies to the spiritual domain, is taken a step further on considering the specifically Christian conception of God: The Trinity. We said earlier that God was the common endpoint of our interactions with him. If by the term 'God' we have in mind a view of him as a simple, bare, unitary being (as in Judaism and Islam), there is no problem; all our interactions with him converge to a single point: God. But such a picture does not adequately account for how Christians see the relationship. Although their interactions-with-God do indeed all converge on the one God, the matter is more complicated than that.

According to Christianity, there is within God himself an *internal* relatedness. It is a relationship that involves the Father, the Son, and the Holy Spirit. And yet, despite there being these three so-called 'Persons', there is only one God. It is a remarkable conception. It was devised by the early Church Fathers in response to the revelation of God, as they perceived it. Their study of the life of Christ led them to the conclusion that, although in some respects he was an ordinary man, in others he was not. Certain of the statements he made (for example, his claim to be able to forgive sins), together with his deeds (particularly his resurrection), served to convince them that he was to be regarded as uniquely the Son of God. On considering the nature of the Holy Spirit, they came to a similar conclusion - he too was to be thought of as God. He has been in existence from the beginning of the world, he is the power that descended upon the disciples at Pentecost, and he dwells in us today as a divine source of both power and guidance. To these two conceptions of God there has, of course, to be added the third: God The Father, the source of all. Thus, the early Church came to accept that there were three basic ways in which God reveals himself to us: God the Father, God the Son, and God the Holy Spirit - or if you like: God over us, God with us, and God in us.

But immediately, there was a difficulty. While there is no doubting that the Bible does clearly witness to these three forms of revelation, it just as clearly and unambiguously attests to the oneness of God. There could be no question of returning to the old idea of there being a plurality of gods. So the problem was how to do justice to the richness of God's threefold revelation of himself, and at the same time, to respect the requirements of monotheism. Two tendencies had to be resisted. On the one hand, there was the temptation to subordinate the status of both the Son and Holy Spirit, leaving only the Father as the one true God - an uncomplicated unitary conception of God, but one that ignores much of what God appears to have been trying to disclose to us. On the other, there was the risk of coming up with a formulation that could give the erroneous impression that Christianity was, in effect, advocating a belief in three Gods. After much debate, the Church Fathers eventually came to adopt the doctrine of the Trinity: three coequal divine Persons and one God.

The idea of three Persons is suggested by the manner in which God deals with us - the plan or arrangement under which he reveals himself to us and attends to our needs. It appears to us that we are dealing with three individuals. But straightaway it should be stressed that the word 'Person' has to be used with special care. As with the word 'person' as applied to ourselves it carries a strong sense of someone who is to be distinguished from others. But the three Persons are not three individual centres of consciousness each with a will of its own and capable of independent operation. There is only one centre, one will. Also, the fact that we talk of their distinctiveness does not mean that God consists of three parts, each part being an incomplete fragment of the whole God. In some sense the whole of God is to be found in each Person.

It is important not to subdivide God between the three Persons. When interacting with God through one of the Persons we interact with the whole of God. The Father never acts independently of the Son, nor the Son of the

SPIRITUAL INTERACTION FRAMEWORK 237

Holy Spirit. No matter how God's acts appear to human perception to be differentiated among the Persons, each interaction with one of the Persons involves all three. The concept of Personhood as applied to God takes on the connotation of a 'mask'. Like the mask used in Greek drama, whereby the actor is able to present various faces to the audience, so the Persons are the three masks that the one God presents to us. Of course, in the case of the mask used in drama, the actor is hiding behind the mask, suppressing his own personality. That is not the case here; each of the Persons reveals something of the true nature of God.

Thus, the Persons have elements about them that allow us to distinguish one from the other; in this sense they are individual. On the other hand, they have an element in common that enables us to say that each is wholly God, and yet there is only the one God. One way of putting it is to say that the kind of mathematics we ordinarily apply to the physical world does not apply. In the present context:

$$God + God + God = God$$

and not

$$God + God + God = 3\ Gods$$

Bearing in mind what was said in Section 9.4 about different kinds of mathematics, this should not strike us as *too* bizarre. There we pointed out that one has to choose the mathematics appropriate to the problem in hand. Mathematics is a handmaid to understanding; it does not dictate how things must be. Even in the physical world, normal arithmetic might not be applicable in particular circumstances. (Recall the bubbles rising in a column of liquid and coalescing.)

Three in One and One in Three. It is a difficult, not to say impossible conception to grasp in all its fullness. It strikes us as paradoxical. It does not fit neatly with the way we normally like to frame explanations. Because of this, there has recently been a growing tendency among certain religious thinkers to downplay its importance. Pointing to the strong influence Greek philosophical thought had on the early development of Christian doctrine, the suggestion is that we are now in a position to recognize, better than people at the time, that this influence was too strong. Hence the call for a more rational, streamlined understanding of God - one that does not get bogged down in mental gymnastics.

I myself find it curious that certain theologians, knowing how the church has for fifteen centuries tenaciously clung to its paradoxical Trinitarian conception, should choose now of all times to be questioning the belief. Only in this century have scientists themselves begun to move *away* from the traditional streamlined notion as to what constitutes a satisfying explanation. In reflecting upon the wave/particle paradox thrown up by quantum theory, they are having to accept that at the really deep fundamental levels of existence, explanations seem unavoidably to embrace an element of paradox. Inasmuch as physicists can legitimately say anything at all about the nature of an electron, they will today describe it in terms of both wave and particle characteristics. This is done regardless of the fact that one knows there to be something contradictory about thinking of an electron as being both a tiny localized particle, and also, an infinitely extended wave train. The best one can do is to hold both conceptions in mind, favouring neither one at the expense of the other, and simply accept that this is 'the explanation'. The fact that we might not feel wholly satisfied with the explanation is not a sign of its inadequacy; it is not a spur to try harder. Rather, it is an indication that we are under a misapprehension as to what constitutes 'explanation'. The feeling arises out of a wrong expectation. Acceptance of an element of paradox does not necessarily entail the abandonment of rationality; it can be the mark of an additional kind of rationality.

The need for a new kind of rationality is precisely what the early Church Fathers discovered all those years ago when they tried to 'explain' God. The Trinitarian doctrine was regarded at the time as the very height of rational reflection on the evidence of God's revelation as presented in scripture. Because of the difficulties in grasping the final formulation, one might be tempted to ask whether it was really necessary. For the purposes of gaining salvation probably not. But if the concern is to establish a faith with intellectual integrity, then it was certainly necessary. It is, after all, the same quest for intellectual integrity that motivates the writing of this present book.

What the Church Fathers discovered was that a simplistic streamlined form of rationalization was inadequate for the job. They found it necessary to embrace a mode of thinking that involves simultaneously holding in the mind markedly different conceptions (the Persons), and accepting that this constituted the best available explanation of a single whole (God). What modern scientists have discovered - a little late in the day - is that the same type of thinking that earlier provided the key to understanding the Creator, is necessary also to the understanding of his Creation.

So, what is the significance of this traditional Trinitarian conception for our description of the domain of spiritual interactions? In the first place it makes clear that when we speak of our spirit interacting with God, there are three types of interaction, three channels, open to us. We can relate to him as our Heavenly Father; or as the risen Lord Jesus; or as the Holy Spirit. In the formal terms in which we spoke earlier of interactions in the spiritual domain, rather than use (s/G) to symbolize the interaction between one's spirit and God, one ought to use (s/F), (s/S), and (s/H) to refer respectively to one's interaction with the Father, Son, and Holy Spirit. Thus, when standing in awe before the glory of the starry heavens, this conscious experience in the mental domain is mapped to a spiritual interaction we have with the Father, (s/F). The sense of the presence of Christ transmitted to us through a reading of the Biblical account of his life and teaching, or through the taking of the sacrament of Holy Communion, is a conscious mental experience mapped to a spiritual interaction with the Son of God,

(s/S). The conscious awareness of the inner religious experience is mapped to a spiritual interaction with the Holy Spirit, (s/H). When one becomes conscious of the numinous in a holy person, there is forged in the spiritual interaction domain a spiritual interaction between one's own spirit and that of the other, via the Holy Spirit. (The need for the Holy Spirit to act as an intermediate link is the message of Pentecost; it required the coming of the Holy Spirit upon the disciples before they could become welded together spiritually as an effective church). In this way Christianity has come to accept that there are three possible endpoints to our interaction with the Divine: one corresponding to each of the Persons. This contrasts with a belief in a God possessing a bare, unitary existence, where there would be just a single end point.

Just as our spirit is defined as the common endpoint of the cluster of interactions we have with the three Persons, so each Divine Person is defined as the common endpoint of the cluster of interactions he has with the other two Persons and with our spirits. In Christian terms, when speaking of the one God (at least in regard to this particular spiritual domain), we have in mind the totality of the three Persons and their mutual interactions. Because the Persons are themselves interacting with each other, and none of the Persons acts independently of the other two, our interaction with any one of the Persons constitutes an interaction with all three.

It is important in all this to note that the Persons are involved not only in relationship to ourselves (the so-called 'economic' Trinity) but also in relation to each other (the 'immanent' Trinity). The latter is made up of the interactions (F/S), (F/H), and (H/S). We have seen how we ourselves cannot exist in this spiritual domain except by virtue of our being integrally involved in a relationship. The same applies to the divine Persons. They too have a relational existence. *But there is a crucial difference between God's relational existence and ours.* Each of the Persons can exist by virtue of his rela-

SPIRITUAL INTERACTION FRAMEWORK

tionship to the other two. The fact that there are relationships *within* God, means that God can exist without us or the world. There is no need for God to relate to anything beyond himself; he is himself a social being. The same is not true of us. We have no internal spiritual relationships, and consequently depend for our existence entirely on our relationship across to him.

Of course, in a certain sense each of us can also claim to be an internally social being. Within each person interchanges take place between the conscious and unconscious aspects of the mind. These constitute an active mental life independently of interactions with anyone outside of oneself. To this extent we see an analogy with the way that God can carry on an interactive mode of existence without his having to interact with anyone external to himself. But the analogy soon breaks down. For there to be an internal dialogue between one's ego and unconscious there needs to be something in the unconscious with which the ego can interact. There is a need for it to have been moulded by past experiences - but experiences of what? Presumably past interactions one has had with the environment. There will be innate contents in the unconscious in the form of archetypes - but where did they come from? They arose from the experiences of our ancestors as they interacted with the environment. So, for the unconscious to have anything to contribute to an interaction with the conscious, it is dependent on there having been previous interactions. Thus one's internal social being at the mental level is *not* to be thought of as a type of existence entirely independent of other entities; there have to have been external interactions at some time in the past, even if there are none now. In this respect, one's internal social being is not a good analogy for the internal social nature of God in the spiritual interaction domain. *God does not at any time depend on us for his existence as we depend on him for ours.* He has complete freedom to exist on his own if he so chooses, or with us, if that is what he decides. Our existence, our creation, is entirely contingent upon his will.

The Trinitarian nature of God inevitably strikes us as paradoxical; we can never hope fully to grasp it. Nevertheless, it is not difficult to appreciate, to some extent at least, that it does have an internal logic of its own. The fact that the internal relations between the Persons are bound up with the fact that God exists independently of us - which surely must be the case - is but one example of that rationale. Another concerns the matter of God being a God of love. Love by its very nature has to be given and received. Love of oneself, to the exclusion of others, is the antithesis of love. While God has us to love there is no problem. But suppose we did not exist, would that mean that God could not be a God of love? Is his loving nature dependent on us? The answer is no, and again it is by virtue of the relationships that exist between the Persons. The Persons are engaged in relationships founded on the giving and receiving of love. This is the mutual love of one Person for another; it is not God loving himself. It is a form of love that exists quite irrespective of whatever additional loving ties might be established contingently between God and his creatures. The doctrine of the Trinity, therefore, is intimately bound up not only with the question of God's existence independently of ourselves, but also with his ability to be supremely the God of love, again independently of ourselves.

7. What of the Devil? How is he to be accommodated?

We saw in Section 13.4 that the problem of evil cannot be brushed aside. Despite the conviction that God is wholly loving, it is nevertheless our experience that the temptation to do wrong can be just as powerful as the desire to do God's will. In the same way as there are saints who devote their lives to God's service, there are others (Hitler is an obvious example) who devote themselves as assiduously to evil purposes. It seems only reasonable, therefore, that in order for justice to be done to the potency of evil, there has to be a representation of it in that reality domain concerned with questions of ultimate purpose. In other words, our spirit in the spiritual interaction domain can draw its relational existence through its interaction with God, or alternatively through an interaction with the Devil - the spiritual focal point for evil.

Does this mean that God has created the Devil? Yes - and no. What God does is to extend to us an invitation to enter into a loving spiritual relationship with him. Because he has given us free will, it truly is an invitation - it carries no compulsion. We can respond positively or negatively. If we choose the former, all well and good. If the latter, we enter into a relationship, not with God, but with that which is not God. This negative pole to God is what we call the Devil. It is not, of course, God's will that we make this latter choice. But, because of the inherent logical nature of the situation, even a God who is omnipotent cannot prevent this as a possible outcome to his invitation. In granting us free will, God creates the *potentiality* for there being a Devil. To this extent - this very limited extent - one can say that God creates the Devil. But in a deeper sense it is we ourselves who create the Devil. *By our choice to reject God, we actualize that potentiality, thereby giving rise to the Devil as a spiritual reality.*

The Devil's existence is a relational one, just as is our own existence in the spiritual interaction domain. As an alternative to our gaining that existence in the context of an interaction with God, we can derive it from an interaction with the Devil. The Devil for his part derives his existence solely by virtue of his interaction with our spirit. No interaction with human spirits; no Devil. This is in contrast to God's existence which, as we have seen, does not depend on an interaction with us.

For the sake of completeness, I should perhaps mention also the possibility of angels. There is nothing to prevent the spiritual interaction domain having other types of interactions to those we have already discussed. Angels and any other spiritual beings in this domain have the same type of relational existence as we ourselves - through their interaction with the Persons of the Godhead. This being so, one can easily take on board, if one so wishes, the idea of the Devil being a fallen angel. According to this scenario, the Devil starts out his existence, like any other angel, in relation to God. But then, with the advent of human spirits, he takes advantage of the opportunity afforded to set himself up as a rival endpoint to interactions involving those human spirits. In the process he severs his interaction with God, becoming now dependent for his existence on the human spirits - in the same way as they are now dependent spiritually upon him.

8. The next question to arise in connection with the description of spiritual reality concerns time. We have already seen (Section 8.5) that the concept of time takes on different meanings within the mental and physical domains. In the mental domain there is a transient 'now' that separates the future which is yet to be, from the past which no longer is. This mental 'now' has a special correlation with a particular instant of physical time. Yet it is not just this one instant, but the *whole* of physical time, that is in existence now and at every other instant of mental time. With this in mind, therefore, it becomes an important question to determine what kind of time applies to the spiritual domain.

On turning to the Bible for guidance, we find references to time that appear strangely inconsistent with each other. Woven together is a Hebrew view of God working out his purpose progressively over the course of time, and a Greek view of eternity in which all of time exists together. In connection with the first view, we get a description of the events of Jewish history - those leading up to the coming of Christ, his birth, life, death, and resurrection. It is the unfolding story of God's plan for our salvation, worked out over the course of time. It is a story that is not yet ended; the day of judgement is still to come. But this evolving narrative is punctuated by enigmatic references to eternity. Eternal life is not to be seen as a mere continuation of life beyond the grave - a sequel to the present story; it is to be experienced now. There are references to Jesus, as the Son of God, existing before the world. He is reported as saying: 'Before Abraham ever was, I am'. God is spoken of as having foreknowledge; he knows in advance what is to happen. These references to time derive from the second view.

Thus, the Father and the Son appear on some occasions to operate in the sequential flow of mental time, in much the same way as normal conscious beings do, and on others to relate to a quite different kind of time. This latter kind of time, like that associated with the physical domain, is one for which all instants appear to exist together on an equal footing - past, present, and future.

In order to understand what is going on, we have to recognize that the Bible is trying to do two things. On the one hand, it is describing how we, as conscious beings, come to learn of God and of his purpose for us through the flow of mental experience. When this is the underlying intention it uses the language appropriate to the description of the domain of conscious mental experience; this entails the use of sequentially experienced mental time. On other occasions, it is venturing to say something about what exists in the spiritual domain. That is to say, it is describing how we, as spiritual beings, relate to God in that domain. In this it has to use whatever language is appropriate to the explanatory framework of that domain. What the Bible indicates is that the kind of time incorporated into that language is more like physical time than mental time - at least in regard to all of that time being in existence together. The Bible is thus written partly in terms of the mental explanatory framework, when describing our experience of life, and partly in terms of the spiritual explanatory framework, when discussing the nature of God and how we relate spiritually to him.

We thus appear to have a very close parallel between what obtains in the physical domain and how that gets translated into consciousness, and what obtains in the spiritual domain and how that is translated into consciousness. In the physical domain, the interactions of our body with its environment are incorporated into relativistic space-time, and accordingly all the events of that physical life-story are to be regarded as existing permanently together. We were unable to say much about the kind of time that would govern a domain consisting of the world-in-itself, other than it appears not to be that of normal relativistic space-time. But if the interactions undergone by objects are to be regarded as all permanently in existence, presumably permanence is also a feature of whatever type of time obtains for the objects-in-themselves. This permanently existing life story is then mapped to consciousness where it is perceived as an evolving succession of mental events which, acording to mental time, pass into and out of existence.

Likewise, we are to regard the story of our development in the spiritual domain as also existing permanently in its entirety. Again there might be a different kind of time associated with interactions-with-God to that which applies to a God-in-himself. But with everything about our lives being known to God from the beginning of time, permanence appears to be a feature of both. As was the case over our physical life story, so the story of our spiritual development, when mapped into consciousness, takes on the character of an evolving succession of transient events. Though we experience a transient 'now' progressively associating itself with different instants of physical and spiritual time, the whole of spiritual time, like the whole of physical time, is to be thought of as being in existence simultaneously at each point in mental time.

As far as what happens in the mental domain we are for ever changing and developing through our physical and spiritual interactions. But neither the physical domain (the whole fabric of events past, present, and future as etched into four-dimensional space-time) nor the spiritual domain (including God) undergo any change. This is not to say that we have no effect on them, that our activities are futile, and our prayers unanswered. *The effects of our decisions, activities and prayers are already incorporated as integral features of the physical and spiritual fabric being revealed to us.*

What of God in connection with his creating and sustaining work in time? Just as the author of a book does not write the first chapter and then leave the rest to write themselves, so God's creativity is not to be seen as uniquely confined to, or even especially invested in the event of the Big Bang, the moment we have come to associate with the creation of the Universe. In four-dimensional space-time, the zero of physical time has no special status beyond it's happening to mark one end of the sequence of physical events. God's creativity has to permeate equally all space and all time. His roles as Creator and Sustainer lose their distinction and merge into one. Does this mean we ourselves become mere characters in a story that the Author has written into the space-time framework? In one sense, the answer has to be - yes. This perspective on human existence is that which goes under the name of predestination. But even so, as any good author will tell us, the characters in a story have a capacity to take on a life of their own, they assume a certain independence, and the story to a degree takes its own course.

CHAPTER 17

WHAT OF GOD-IN-HIMSELF?

HAVING seen how we establish the grounds for believing in a spiritual interaction domain, is there any point in asking whether there is that possible second spiritual domain - the one containing God-in-himself?
1. Our approach will be analogous to that adopted in Chapter 5 towards the investigation of the physical realm. There you recall we first inferred from the mental domain the existence of the domain of physical interactions. A second inferential step was then required in order to go from there to the domain of the world-in-itself. The justification for this additional inference had to lie in whatever was perceived to be the explanatory value of the inference. There had to be some pay-off in explaining features of the domain of physical interactions that could not be accounted for in terms of the concepts that applied to that domain. This in turn meant that it had to explain some feature of conscious mental experience (all explanation having ultimately to refer back to what is found in consciousness). It was because views differed as to what, if any, explanatory value there was to the hypothesis, that we came across different schools of thought. There were those physicists who claimed there to be no world-in-itself, the very concept being meaningless; others were persuaded of its existence, but believed it to be a world which, by its very nature, would for ever lie beyond our conceptualization; others held that not only did the world-in-itself exist, but it lay within our power one day to give a detailed description of it; finally there was the view that there was a world-in-itself, but one that could be described in only very general terms.

With these background thoughts in mind, therefore, we now turn to the question of spiritual reality domains. So far we have inferred from the mental domain that there is a domain of spiritual interactions. Acceptance of there being a second spiritual domain would likewise be an inferential rather than a deductive step. Thus, we must enquire whether there is sufficient explanatory power in the hypothesis to justify it, and if so, are we likely to be able to devise the conceptual tools necessary to describe God-in-himself meaningfully.

2. With regard to non-Christian religions like Judaism and Islam, the existence of this second domain is essential. In these religions, God is thought of as a unitary being having no relations internal to himself. Consequently, he has a representation in the domain of spiritual interactions only to the extent that he relates to *us*. But his existence cannot ultimately depend upon us, so it must be grounded in the second spiritual domain.

As we have seen, the independent existence of God is not a problem for Christianity. But even here the postulate of the second domain has value. This arises because the Trinitarian doctrine, in being applied to the domain of spiritual interactions, tends to place the emphasis on the *distinctiveness* of the Persons. This was inevitable from the way the Persons emerge as the distinct endpoints of interactions. Little has been said so far about the *oneness* of God.

In speaking of that which the Divine Persons have in common, the Church Fathers used the word 'substance'. The Persons are considered to consist of the same divine substance, or 'stuff'. (The term 'substance' has unfortunate associations to do with materiality, which are clearly out of place in the present context. But the metaphor is unavoidable.) This is not to say that the Persons merely consist of the same *kind* of substance - like three coins all made of copper, but three different pieces of copper. That would be tantamount to declaring the Persons to be three coequal, but separate Gods. No, the contention is that the three Persons consist of the same *identical* substance (equivalent to a claim that there is enough copper for one coin only, and all that copper is used to make the first coin, it is all used again to make the second, and again to make the third). The entire substance of the Son is the same as the entire substance of the Father or that of the Holy Spirit. The individuality of the Persons comes from how this identical substance is objectively presented. As seen and thought by us, God is three; but as seeing and thinking, he is one. God is one object *in* himself, but three objects *to* himself.

This is where the postulate of a second spiritual domain, lying behind the first, is helpful to Christian understanding. *The oneness of God is assured by the three Persons in the spiritual interaction domain being mapped to a common feature of the second domain, namely, the one God-in-himself.* Thus God, in addition to the relational existence of the Persons, also has a 'God-in-himself type' of existence, there being a one-to-three mapping between them. It seems to me that only through such a postulate can justice be done to the oneness of God.

Quantum physics provides a powerful analogy in this respect. Recall from Section 6.3 the two electrons that collided and moved apart to such a great distance that there was no longer any physical force between them. At first sight it appeared that we must be dealing with two entirely separate physical systems. But we were not. Somehow, because there had been that original collision between them, they constituted a single system. A later interaction with either one of the electrons constituted an interaction with the whole system, thereby leading to immediate consequences for the other electron. But there was no physical connection between the two electrons in the physical interaction domain, so how could this be? The possibility I suggested was that, from the reality domain of interactions-with-the-world, there was a mapping to another domain consisting of the world-in-itself. The two electrons of one domain were to be mapped via a two-to-one mapping to a *single* feature of that second domain. The unity of the system was ensured by the oneness of this feature.

I suggest that the same kind of idea can be helpful in considering the oneness that is God's. Although in the domain of spiritual interactions we are presented with three distinct and separate Persons, they all map to the same God-in-himself in the second spiritual reality domain. The oneness of God is *not* obvious while one's attention remains fixed upon what obtains in the spiritual interaction domain alone, any more than the oneness of the two-electron system is at all apparent in the physical interaction domain. And generally speaking our attention is indeed focused on the first of the spiritual domains because that is the one most relevant to understanding our encounter with God. God's oneness comes into its own only when we are led to reflect on the mapping link forged between his representation as the three Persons in the spiritual interaction domain, and his representation as the unitary God in the second spiritual domain.

Only so can we understand adequately how an interaction with any one of the distinct Persons involves the totality of God. It is an involvement that goes deeper than that which operates at the level of interactions directly between the Persons in the domain of spiritual interactions. After all, in the analogous case of the two electrons, the oneness of the two-electron system did not depend on *any* interaction between the electrons, apart from a momentary collision they had had in the past. The wholeness, the cohesion, of that physical system was *entirely* effected through the mapping to the single feature of the other domain. In the same way we are to understand the oneness of God, not in terms of the interaction directly between the Persons, but by their mapping to the one God-in-himself, and through him, to each other.

This similarity between the two-electron system and the Trinity I have described as 'an analogy'; we have used features of one to explain features of the other. But

there is a somewhat deeper point to be made in the comparison. An important insight to emerge from quantum theory is that it makes us re-evaluate what it means to have an 'explanation' of something. How are we, in fact, to judge when the search for an explanation has reached a satisfactory conclusion? The dilemma of not being altogether sure whether one already possesses the 'explanation' is nowhere more evident than in the consideration of the two-electron system. Is the description I have given to be regarded as *it*? Or do we carry on searching for something more closely in tune with our preconceptions of what would constitute a really good explanation? In short, how are we to recognize an explanation when we come across it? It seems to me that Christian theologians in respect of God, and modern quantum physicists in respect of the two-electron system, have both come to the same conclusion as to the type or structure of explanation that is appropriate (the theologians having got there first by some 1500 years!).
3. We have already seen how we ourselves have a relational existence in the spiritual interaction domain. Can we say that, like God, we also enjoy a form of existence in the second spiritual domain - as spirits-in-themselves? Though one cannot be categorical about such matters, it seems preferable to me to answer in the negative. I say this because of what Jesus said in respect of our relationship to God. He enjoined us to be one with the Father even as he and the Father were one. The Father and the Son are one through being mapped to the unitary God-in-himself. (Neither the Father, Son, nor Holy Spirit exist as such in the second domain - only as the unitary God.) So Jesus appears to be holding out the possibility of a mapping being established between our spirit in the spiritual interaction domain and God-in-himself. This is in much the same way as there has always existed a mapping between himself and God-in-himself. The invitation is not that we should become a separate spirit-in-itself existing alongside God-in-himself. No, the prospect is much richer than that: *We*

are being invited to participate in the Divine life and love itself. If this invitation is accepted, then just as God gives expression to himself in the spiritual interaction domain through the Persons, he can now begin to express himself through us also. When in Section 13.2 I spoke of the numinous being discerned through holy people, this is what I had in mind; God-in-himself maps to that person's spirit in the spiritual interaction domain, which then interacts with our spirit in that domain.

Does the Devil have an existence in the second domain? No. As in our own case, for him to have an existence in that domain, a mapping link would have to be established to God-in-himself; this is expressly denied. The Devil, therefore, has a relational existence only; he is to be found solely in the spiritual interaction domain. *The Devil does not have the same ontological status as God.* This is important. One of the reasons why people are reluctant to think of the Devil as real is that they are under the impression that this in effect amounts to a belief in two gods - one good and one evil. As far as we human beings are concerned, the Devil does indeed interact with us in just as real a manner as God does. This is because an interaction with the Devil in the spiritual interaction domain has the same ontological status as an interaction with God. The crucial difference is that behind the veil of our interactions with God there lies God-in-himself as a different order of reality; behind our interactions with the Devil there lies nothing.

4. But granted that we accept that there is a domain containing God-in-himself, what can be said about it? Is it not the case that all the concepts and ways of thought we have in respect of God are derived exclusively from our interactions with God, and therefore are liable to apply only to a description of interactions and not to a description of God as he might be divorced from the context of his having an interaction with us? Could we not find that the application of such concepts and ways of thought to God-in-himself constitutes a misuse of language? This was certainly the worry we encountered in the physical

realm. There we found that concepts such as 'electron', 'electric charge', 'position', etc. were part of the explanatory framework associated with the domain of physical interactions. Some physicists took exception to them being absorbed into the explanatory framework of any second physical reality domain - that of the world-in-itself. There is no agreement as to whether *any* of the current scientific terms have validity in the description of a world-in-itself. So, in approaching the analogous problem in the spiritual realm, we must be similarly on our guard. It could be that all the concepts and ways of thought we have about God are drawn exclusively from the explanatory framework associated with the domain of spiritual interactions and we have yet to find any concepts that could be correctly applied to God-in-himself.

In this regard we note the view long held that it is fundamentally beyond human power to speak meaningfully of the intrinsic nature of God. The doctrine of the Trinity states that the three Persons share the identical substance. This is the 'stuff' of which God-in-himself consists in this second spiritual reality domain. However, while asserting that the Persons do have this same substance, the doctrine does not go on to describe this divine 'stuff'. Augustine, for example, spoke for many in saying that one could not expect to know the name of the substance of God. Gregory Palamas, the 14th Century Archbishop of Thessalonica, expressed similar views. He asserted that one must distinguish in God between the absolutely unknowable essence and the knowable perceptible attributes: the 'energies' or external activities of God. Accordingly, one has to recognize an important distinction in God between his nature and his energies - between his essence and the outward revelations or interactions of the divine nature as we experience them. These ideas of Palamas significantly influenced the development of thought in the Eastern Orthodox Church. The unknowability of God was a theme taken up also by Martin Luther. He drew a distinction between God in his bare reality in Himself, which is hidden from us, and God in his reality for us - as he is revealed to us. Sören Kierkegaard was another who, in contemplating the Trinity, maintained that when the truth, thought of as something objective, appeared to be paradoxical, this was an indication that one should be seeking a more subjective kind of truth - one involving one's own active participation, one's interaction.

What seems to emerge is the general idea that there is a God-in-himself, but there is nothing one can say about him. But here we have to be careful. In our study of the physical realm we noted that there was little, if any, difference between saying: (a) that there is no world-in-itself; and (b) that there is a world-in-itself, but we can say nothing about it apart from it accounting for our interactions-with-the-world. This was because statement (b) is barely distinguishable from: We do not know anything about the cause of our interactions-with-the-world but we are calling it 'the world-in-itself'. As pointed out earlier, one does not solve a problem by merely giving it a name. Thus, there has to be something more to be said about God-in-himself than simply his being an unknowable entity that causes our interactions-with-God; if not, we are likely to have said in effect: We do not know anything about what causes our interaction-with-God, but we call it 'God-in-himself'.

In one respect it has to be true that we can say nothing about the nature of God-in-himself. There is absolutely nothing that can be said about the ontological nature of the fundamental entities that figure in *any* of the reality domains. We have seen that it is not a characteristic of explanatory frameworks to indulge in speculation over the metaphysical status of the entities in which they deal. The mental explanatory framework says nothing about the nature of mental entities as such; the classical physical explanatory framework is likewise silent about the intrinsic nature of physical entities like electrons, or their properties - mass, electric charge, etc.; and the quantum physical framework says nothing about what quantum interactions are in themselves. For this reason we could not rule out the possibility that the mental and the physical frameworks might actually be addressing, in complementary ways, one and the same reality. It is therefore only to be expected that theologians can say nothing about the metaphysical 'stuff' of which God-in-himself consists; they cannot even say anything about the metaphysical nature of the basic entities in the first spiritual domain - the interactions-with-God.

But the type of unknowability we were discussing in connection with the physical world-in-itself went beyond that universal metaphysical type of unknowability. What concerned us was this: Granted that one is not able to say anything about the kind of 'stuff' out of which physical objects-in-themselves are made, is there *anything* meaningful one can say about the behaviour and properties of these objects as manifested in that domain? So, when we come to consider the analogous problem in the spiritual realm, we need to draw a distinction between the two types of unknowability. Though one cannot be absolutely sure, one suspects that most of the references to God's unknowability mentioned above, concerned the first type of unknowability - that to do with the 'stuff' of God. The really important question is whether God-in-himself is unknowable in the second sense. If it turns out that there is absolutely nothing one can say about him, then the hypothesis of 'God-in-himself' has no explanatory power and might as well be abandoned.

This is where I see the value of the 'English compromise' I suggested in connection with our discussion of the physical realm (Section 5.9). There I pointed out a middle path between the extreme views of, on the one hand, those who denied the existence of the world-in-itself (or held that such a world was absolutely unknowable - which essentially amounted to the same thing), and on the other, those who claimed that the world-in-itself not only existed but was capable of being given a detailed explanation. What I suggested was a world-in-itself which was open to description in very general, non-

GOD-IN-HIMSELF

quantitative terms: law-likeness, consistency over time, contingency, public accessiblity, and so forth. Perhaps in the spiritual sphere this is where we ought also to be concentrating. Having inferred that God-in-himself exists, perhaps we too can make certain generalized statements about him. Indeed, this does seem to be what we do when we speak of God as the Creator, omnipotent, eternal, One, the God of perfect Justice, Mercy, and Love. Such claims do not tell us a great deal about him; much remains unsaid, leaving us tantalized and to some extent dissatisfied. But at least they go some way towards making the concept of God-in-himself meaningful.

5. We conclude that, just as there are various sustainable views in regard to the existence and knowability of the world-in-itself, so there are alternative beliefs regarding the existence and knowability of God-in-himself. Each has the right to be accounted a reasonable belief. This is not to say that each has the right to be accounted *true*. In calling the various beliefs 'reasonable', there is no implication of a retreat into the kind of subjectivity whereby one view is held to be as good as another. Either God has a type of existence apart from a relational one, or he does not. Either he is in principle knowable, or he is not. The fact that we have insufficient grounds for deciding which of the various reasonable beliefs is closer to the truth than the others, does not mean that there is no preferred belief.

6. One final point while on the subject of God's existence. The concept of existence is unlike any other. It is not to be regarded as a property possessed by something. In describing an electron one does not say that it is a particle that has a certain mass, a negative electric charge, a certain angular momentum - and existence. 'Existence' does not characterize the electron; it does not help us to understand what the term 'electron' means. Having defined 'electron' through its various properties, it is a quite separate issue to decide whether an entity so defined exists or not. So we must be on our guard over this word.

Especially is this so when it is applied to God. The question 'Does God exist?' belongs to a category of its own. The reason is that when one asks whether something exists or not, it is usually inferred that this is a question about some *aspect* of existence. The existence of one entity needs have no bearing on whether some other entity also exists. But with God it is different. God relates to the totality of existence; he is not confined to a particular part of it. In view of this, he is spoken of as the very ground of all being. He is the source of being, giving rise to all the individual existent entities, be they impersonal or personal. God, as Creator, creates out of nothing. He is the means, the channel, through which everything that exists is brought into being and kept in being. Because of this we must be cautious about applying the word 'exist' to *him*, that is to say, to the *means* of existence. The source must not be confused with one of its own end-products. He must not be spoken of as though he were just one existent entity among all others. If we were in difficulties getting a straight answer to the question 'Does the physical world exist?' we must expect to be in deeper trouble still over the question 'Does God exist'. The concept of existence very quickly takes us up to, and beyond, the bounds of meaningful language. Indeed, in the little I have said about it here, I might have already transgressed those limits.

CHAPTER 18

RELATING THE SPIRITUAL TO OTHER FRAMEWORKS

HAVING described the spiritual domains, we must now look more closely at the relationship they have to other reality domains. In doing so we shall need to consider how God makes his presence known in consciousness, how he relates to the physical world (miraculously or otherwise), and how Christians can regard Jesus as both God and man.

1. First, a problem similar to that which troubled us in trying to understand the relationship between the physical and mental domains. In Section 8.6 you recall how we questioned whether the mental and physical frameworks really did refer to different realities, as they appeared to do. We concluded that, because nothing could be said about the intrinsic nature of the entities incorporated into the two reality bases - the 'stuff' of which the entities consisted - we could not discount the possibility that the two frameworks were actually referring to one and the same reality, albeit in complementary ways. We noted that the existence of mappings between the domains inclined one to this 'common reality' hypothesis, whereas the incommensurable ways in which the reality bases of the frameworks were treated argued for their distinction.

We have now introduced what appears to be yet another kind of reality - the spiritual. But is it truly different? Could it not be that the spiritual framework is more to be thought of as a third complementary way of looking at a reality it shares with the mental and physical frameworks? Again there are no means to decide. We can say no more about the ontological nature of the 'stuff' of which spiritual entities consist than that of physical and mental entities. We cannot, therefore, rule out the possibility.

Indeed, to be more positive: The fact that in all three realms, physical, mental, and spiritual, we have found value in a two-stage approach through which we first come across an interactional form of existence and only later an in-itself type of existence - this repeated pattern might be regarded as actively encouraging the belief that we are dealing with the same reality. This view is further strengthened on noting that in all three cases, the in-itself type of existence fulfills similar functions in respect of the interactional existences: providing continuity, relating one interaction to another, and in some cases conferring a oneness that is not otherwise apparent. However, we should not read too much into this. The two-stage approach probably reflects an epistemological, rather than an ontological, structure. In learning about a reality - any type of reality - we presumably have to relate to it. This means we must first deal with a knowledge of that relationship; knowledge of the reality itself (if there is to be one) can only be derived from the first type of knowledge, so must come later.

The possibility that the three types of framework refer to a common reality does not mean that each necessarily addresses its totality. We have already noted that when the physical framework deals with what happens in the human brain, and the mental framework deals in the mental occurrences to which those physical events map, both frameworks are indeed speaking about the same part of that reality, each in its own way. When, however, the physical framework describes what is happening to the Moon in between our conscious observations, it is addressing an aspect of the common reality that lies outside the competence of the mental framework. In the same way, when we suggest that the physical world and God might belong to one and the same reality domain, that is not to say that God is merely the physical world interpreted differently. That might be how some regard the situation, but it is not the general view, nor is it what I am advocating. The physical framework addresses but a part of the common reality, just as the mental framework does. Only the spiritual framework, with its talk of God and the overall purpose and meaning of existence, can lay claim to be addressing the totality. This is not to say that the physical and mental frameworks are dispensable because they cover but a limited range of the reality that comes under the purview of the spiritual. The parts of the reality they do address are explained by them in ways that cannot be duplicated in spiritual terms, and are thus indispensable to an exhaustive account of the reality.

Earlier we illustrated the orthogonal viewpoints of the mental and physical frameworks by the front and side elevations in the architect's drawings of a building. Now we add the spiritual framework as the plan of the building. In order comprehensively to understand the building, all three views are necessary. Though some features of one drawing might be correlated to features of the other two, each has its own distinctive input to make. Each is set up to tackle its own type of question and provides information not accessible from the other perspectives. Will the proposed building harmonize with the others in the road? Consult the front elevation. Is the next door neighbour worried about his garden being overlooked and shaded from the Sun? Show him the side elevation. Is the town planner concerned about access roads? He needs the plan. In the same way, the spiritual, mental, and physical frameworks have their distinctive features as well as their correlations one with another. Each allows us to tackle questions that cannot be handled by the others. One of the consequences of adopting the common reality hypothesis is that it appears to cast the question 'Does God exist?' in a somewhat different light. If the spiritual framework sets out to address the same reality as that of the other frameworks, then, provided we believe that the physical and mental frameworks are hooked onto something real (as we obviously do), there can be no doubt about the reality of what it is that the spiritual framework aims to describe. Accordingly, the problem of the last two chapters was not so much one of deciding whether there is such a thing as a spiritual reality, but rather whether the spiritual explanatory framework is a valid way of speaking of the one universally accepted reality. In other words, the focus of attention ought to be on the framework and its claim to be an authentic interpretation of reality, rather than on whether it addresses a distinct reality of its own.

In summary, the question of whether the three types of explanatory framework address one reality in complementary ways, or three separate realities, is intrinsically undecidable. The question is unimportant. *What does matter is the recognition that, for a comprehensive account of reality, one needs three explanatory frameworks.* How these frameworks are to be used in conjunction with each other, that is a topic to which we now turn.

2. We begin by seeing how the frameworks can be combined to provide an understanding of the inner religious experience. This experience, as we have seen, is one in which we appear to be interacting with God. Does this mean that God, as a spiritual being, intrudes into the mental domain? Do we incorporate into the mental explanatory framework concepts borrowed from the spiritual framework? No. What is involved is a complete switch from one explanatory framework (the mental) to another (the spiritual). We defer to a second framework in order to explain a mental situation that could not be handled by the mental framework alone. In this we have a situation very similar to that encountered in Section 10.3; there we found it necessary to defer to the physical explanatory framework in order to account for the disappearance of the headache on swallowing an aspirin.

The fact that we start a time of prayer in one state of mind and subsequently find ourselves in a totally different and unexpected one by the end - one in which we appear to have received a message of some kind from God - this cannot be accounted for in terms of one's own input. In the context of God, a spiritual being, interacting with our spirit in the spiritual domain, however, it does begin to make sense. The explanation for the changed state of mind is that the first mental state maps to a particular state of one's spirit; there is an interaction involving God that changes the state of the spirit; this change is then reflected back into consciousness through the mapping link between this changed spiritual state and the conscious mental state at the end of the time of prayer. In the same way as the chemical action of the aspirin in the physical domain - a chain of events not perceived directly by the conscious mind but inferred to have taken place - provides the connection between the two mental states of having a headache and not having a headache, so occurrences that are inferred to have taken place in the spiritual domain provide the explanatory link between the states of the mind at the beginning and end of the prayer time.

3. Having seen that the mental framework must on occasion defer to the spiritual, we ask whether the reverse applies: Does the spiritual framework sometimes have to defer to the mental? It is difficult to say. The situation is again similar to that encountered over the relationship of the mental to the physical (Sections 10.3, 10.4). We know that the mental sometimes must defer to the physical, but it was left an open question as to whether, in respect of the working of the human brain, the physical has to defer to the mental. This was the problem of the symmetric versus asymmetric views of the relationship between the frameworks. The same problem arises in the case of the spiritual domain in relation to the mental. The mental must sometimes defer to the spiritual but it is difficult to know whether the spiritual must on occasion defer to the mental.

My own feeling is that it must. I say this because if it is God's ultimate intention to bring into existence spiritual beings capable of communing with him, why should he bother producing a mental and a physical representation of the person if the spirit alone would do? The answer seems to be that, just as a mind is fashioned through its meeting with other minds, and for such engagement to take place it needs to be physically embodied, so a spirit is shaped in the cut and thrust of daily interaction and thus requires a physical and mental representation. That being so it is only to be expected that in order to provide a full explanation of how the spirit has developed the way it has, one might need to defer to the mental and physical explanatory frameworks.

4. Not everything happening in the spiritual domain has to be mapped onto a conscious mental experience, any more than every physical event has to have a mental correlate. It is precisely because there are uncorrelated events in the physical and spiritual domains, and these can be explained in terms of the frameworks of those domains, that the postulate of these domains carries explanatory value in respect of those conscious experiences that otherwise do not appear to have explanatory links between them.

This suggestion that the spiritual domain can have an autonomous existence independent of what happens in consciousness is closely allied to the possibility of life after death. What we know of death is that it marks the end of the physical functioning of the body. That is *all* we know about it. The fact that we are accustomed to associate mental activity with physical activity in the body, inclines us to the view that physical death is accompanied by the cessation of ourselves as conscious beings. But this does not necessarily follow. There is no proof that conscious mental phenomena are *invariably* correlated to physical activity and cannot exist in the absence of such physical activity. The symmetric view of the relationship between the physical and mental explanatory frameworks (according to which occurrences in the physical domain are to some extent contingent on what is happening in the mental domain) accepts no such tight correlation.

But suppose there is indeed an indispensable link between the conscious ego and the functioning of the body. Suppose physical death marks the termination of the ego. Would that mean that we as persons cease to exist after physical death? The answer depends on the significance to be attached to the idea of personhood being manifested in reality domains other than that of conscious mental events. First, let us take the physical domain. In physical terms, one's life story - that is to say, one's existence - is etched into the fabric of four-dimensional space-time. In this domain nothing passes into or out of existence. All instants of physical time exist on an equal footing - those belonging to the stretch of time that marks one's life, and those that are earlier than one's birth or later than one's death. The fact that the events of one's life are confined to a small region of the time axis has no more significance than the fact that the events of one's life are similarly confined to a small region of space. Thus, at each instant of mental time, including those we imagine extrapolated beyond our death, *all* of physical time exists. Hence all the events of one's life exist, even after the flow of conscious mental phenomena has ceased. Our existence in the physical domain is permanent.

What of the possibility of a continuing existence in the domain of spiritual interactions? We have noted that there appear to be strong similarities between physical time and the time which applies to the spiritual domain, at least in respect of all time being permanently in existence at each instant of mental time. In the spiritual domain there is no coming into being, neither is there any passing out of existence. Nothing changes. This is why God is spoken of as transcending time. Belonging as he does to the spiritual domain, he lies beyond those temporal categories to be found only in the mental domain: the past that is no more, the future that is yet to come, and the ever-changing, transient 'now'. In our manifestation as spiritual beings, we likewise are transcendent. Physical death and the accompanying termination of normal consciousness no more affects the permanence of our existence in the spiritual domain than it erases our lives as manifested in the space-time of the physical domain. Just as we could learn of our impending death only from the observation of other human beings (Section 11.7), so we can learn of our immortality only from God.

Of course, it will be argued, that it is of small comfort to know that one goes on existing in the physical and spiritual domains beyond the termination of consciousness, if we are unaware of this wider existence, and hence unable to enjoy its benefits! It does not follow, however, that just because the normal flow of consciousness ceases, there cannot be some other kind of awareness. It is obviously difficult to conceive of what form such an awareness might take. But the Christian belief that eternal life can be entered into *this* side of the grave, should afford us an opportunity of catching a glimpse of it. Even before death, we can experience at least something of the contentment and inner peace, the sense of healing and wholeness, that comes of being at one with God. Communion with God is experienced as a distinctive state of mind. It is a condition best experienced at times of stillness and quietness. It comes through the shutting out of distracting sights and noises that otherwise clamour for our attention. Such changes might, of course, be nothing more than a modification of normal consciousness - a mood change. But possibly not. Perhaps these are manifestations of a separate and distinct form of awareness - one that overlays, and has to compete with, the normal on-going conscious experience of life. Whereas the latter form of consciousness is mapped to events occurring in the brain in the physical domain, the former is mapped to what happens to one's spirit in the spiritual domain. If this were the case, one would expect that with the coming of death, those conscious events associated with our normal physical existence would cease, leaving those concerned with our spiritual interactions with God to continue. Because the latter would then no longer have to fight for our attention, they might henceforward be more readily appreciated and enjoyed.

If there is any truth in the above, neither physical death nor a concomitant cessation of normal consciousness need mean the end of our existence. We continue to have an existence in the spiritual interaction domain, and moreover, one of which we would be aware. Some people - even religious people - find it hard to accept that there is life after death. They cannot shake off the thought that life is exclusively associated with, and dependent upon, the physical body. But does this really make sense? If it is believed that the physical world is itself dependent for its existence on God, then any dependence our own existence has on the physical domain must also be ultimately rooted in him. This being so, why should not God sustain us in existence directly, rather than having to operate through the physical domain? The physical domain is a 'vale of soul-making'; our spiritual selves are developed and shaped in the context of our earthly life. But once formed, a mapping is established directly between this spirit and God-in-himself. We become one with him who is the ground of all being. From here onward the physical can be cast off.

What is the nature of our resurrection body? Our existence in the spiritual interaction domain is of a relational nature only. The term 'spiritual body' is simply a way of referring to the common endpoint of our interactions with the Persons (or with the Devil). It has nothing to do with an ethereal diffuse substance, which during life inhabits the physical body, and at death detaches itself to linger on in an independent but diminshed type of existence. Even our physical body is not to be thought of in such concrete terms; in the physical interaction domain it too is simply the common endpoint of interactions. Metaphysical discussions as to the nature of the supposed spiritual substance are fruitless. In the picture I have presented, there is no such thing as a spirit-in-itself. The only form of 'in itself' spiritual existence open to us is that which comes from the establishment of a mapping between our spirit in the spiritual interaction domain and God-in-himself.

What of Heaven? That is to be found in the spiritual interaction domain. It consists of the continuing interactions that take place between our spirits and the Persons, together with those between the Persons themselves. Hell is likewise located in this domain. It is to be equated with the continuing interactions between our spirits and the Devil - the negative pole of God.

Finally as regards eternal life, we ask how the subject is approached from the standpoint of the mental, physical, and spiritual frameworks being three complementary ways of interpreting the one common reality. In this context, the question of how the spiritual can outlive the physical as a separate and independent reality does not arise; there is only the one kind of reality, and this continues in existence without interruption. It is a matter of matching specific questions about that reality to their appropriate explanatory framework. If the questions are about the conduct of a person's earthly life, then one uses the physical and mental frameworks. If they are about what might happen to that person after death, the physical framework is of no relevance - it has nothing further to say. From here on the questions are to be dealt with exclusively in terms of the spiritual framework and the mental framework - the latter to the extent that it addresses conscious awareness of spiritual rather than physical events.

5. Let us now look at the question of how the spiritual domain relates to the physical. There are basically two alternatives. Either one is prepared to accept the possibility of miracles or one is not. Here by the word 'miracle' I refer specifically to occurrences where the course of nature does not follow that expected on the basis of the laws of physics. As such it is a fairly narrow definition. It excludes remarkable events that are considered to be especially revelatory of God, but which are still covered by the known laws of physics - a providential escape from a car crash, for example. Such events might

be accounted miraculous according to a broader definition of the term, but not according to ours. In this and the next three Sections we take the line that miracles *are* possible; later we examine the implications of assuming that they are not.

How ought we to incorporate a miracle into our discussion of domains of reality and their associated explanatory frameworks? Are we to account for it by saying that God, the spiritual being, has entered into the physical domain and by some pseudo-physical force pushed the system into its new and unexpected state? No, the connection between the two states is to be seen at the level of explanatory frameworks, not at the level of the reality domains. The fact that the physical framework is unable to provide an explanatory link between the initial and final states means that one has to defer to the spiritual explanatory framework. Just as previously there was no satisfactory explanatory link in mental terms between the mental states with and without a headache, and one had to defer to the physical framework with its description of the action of the aspirin, so here there is no satisfactory explanatory link in physical terms between the two physical states, and one has to defer to the spiritual framework for an explanation.

This procedure entails some kind of mapping from the physical domain to the spiritual; without the mapping what happens in one domain is unrelated to anything in the other. Does that mean the physical world maps to some correlate in the spiritual domain, just as we conscious human beings map to our spirits in that domain? If so, God could interact with that spiritual counterpart, this being reflected in what occurs in the physical domain. It is impossible to say for sure. Initially, one's reaction is likely to be against the idea of there being a spiritual counterpart to the world. Is not spirituality something reserved to human beings? But let us not be hasty. The unique spiritual status of humankind was a view adopted at a time when it was also thought that we were unique biologically. In the light of our current knowledge of evolutionary history, we now know there to be no hard and fast dividing line between ourselves and the lower animals, nor between them and inanimate matter. Our lineage, therefore, is likely to go back to inanimate matter. This means that in order to maintain a clear distinction between ourselves and the rest of creation in regard to spirituality, we are faced with the problem of deciding at which point in the history of our ancestors the spirit is supposed to have put in an appearance. Surely it is more in keeping with the current state of our understanding of human origins to think of a spirit that evolves gradually over the course of evolutionary history in parallel to the development of the physical body, rather than one that suddenly comes onto the scene at some arbitrary point. That being the case, the lower animals, and indeed inanimate matter, can be regarded as having at least a spiritual potential of some kind. It is along such lines one can argue that it is not entirely unreasonable to think of there being a representation of the physical world in the spiritual domain, as well as one of ourselves.

But this is not the only possibility. I prefer an alternative: Recall how, according to the symmetric view of the relationship between the physical and the mental domains, the laws of physics are inadequate to explain all that goes on in the brain. This is because the mind maps to the brain and, so it is held, one has sometimes to seek an explanation of physical processes occurring in the brain in terms of what is happening in the mind. In the same way, rather than viewing the relationship between God and the world as one in which there are interactions taking place in the spiritual interaction domain between the Divine Persons and a spiritual representation of the world, God as he is in the spiritual domain is thought of as mapping *directly* to the physical world as it is in the physical domain. In other words, the entirety of the physical world *is* the representation of God in the physical domain; it is a created analogue of himself. Accordingly, certain aspects of the physical behaviour of that world might be understandable only by deferring to its spiritual counterpart - God himself. This mapping of God to the physical world would certainly explain why one sometimes senses the numinous in and through nature, much as one senses another mind mediated through the human body to which that mind is mapped. I hasten to add, however, none of this is meant to imply that the world and God are synonymous (though there are those who think of God in those terms). Not everything that is God is mapped to the physical world.

6. Having described a miracle as an occasion where one must defer to the spiritual framework to make the explanatory link between two physical states, we next ask whether there is anything in the study of science that demonstrates that miracles cannot and do not occur. The answer is no. Science is the study of the normal operation of nature - physical behaviour in accordance with laws. For the purposes of conducting scientific investigation, the presupposition has to be that the world operates in an orderly fashion. But just because that is the assumption under which science of necessity works, it does not mean that the physical laws hold *invariably* - that they must be obeyed in all circumstances. All that science can do is show that such exceptions are rare.

At the time the Bible was written, people generally delighted in stories of marvellous happenings. Miracle stories were looked upon as legitimate vehicles for expressing truths about God and his relationship to us. It was the deep inner spiritual insights that mattered, and not so much whether the events actually happened as literally described. But with the passage of time, attitudes towards miracle stories changed. Today, under the influence of scientific reasoning, we are accustomed to think much more pragmatically than was common two thousand years ago. We regard it as a matter of some consequence whether the events happened or not - an attitude, which to us seems only natural and sensible, but one that would strike people of former times as inappropriate. It is as well to bear this in mind when reading the

Bible. What I am saying is that Biblical scholars who have studied the role of miracle stories in ancient cultures, have for a long time been pointing out that miracles have never been as common as one might suppose from a literal reading of the Bible - it did not need science to tell us this. It is the spiritual truths conveyed by these stories that are of relevance to how we should see our relationship to God and how we should conduct our lives. Whether these stories additionally describe actual physical events is a separate and probably less important matter. Not that this means one should now go to the opposite extreme and say that *none* of the miracle stories were intended to be read literally. In respect of the resurrection of Jesus, for example, Christians need to consider very carefully before reaching any decision to discount the physical side of the event. All that is being pointed out is that, just because one is prepared to accept the possibility of miracles, one does not thereby incur a commitment to believe in the literal interpretation of *all* miracle stories in the Bible.

7. Belief in miracles means that one accepts that certain physical events cannot be accounted for in terms of the physical laws. Does this entail us regarding miracles as totally unpredictable, maverick events that 'violate' the laws of physics? Not really. In order to appreciate why, we first note that physical laws are always at risk when applied to areas of experience not previously tested. Sometimes the assumption of their validity in the wider domain proves to be false. The laws of classical physics, for example, were once thought to have universal validity. But, in fact, they do not apply to situations involving speeds close to that of light, nor those involving behaviour at the atomic level. Neither of these areas had previously been checked experimentally. When they were, it was discovered that classical physics is but an approximation to the truth - it is subsumed under the more exact and comprehensive theories of relativity and quantum physics. These in their turn were later shown to be subsumed within relativistic quantum dynamics. Thus,

classical physics, like other physical theories, is to be seen as an explanatory framework embedded within a *hierarchy of physical frameworks.* The hierarchy is such that, occurrences which appear impossible according to the more limited theory at the lower level of explanation, can be readily accommodated by the more powerful and comprehensive theory at the higher level. It is not that we think of Newton's laws being 'violated' or 'interrupted' by such events. Rather we think of these events as lying outside the area of applicablity of classical laws.

So far we have considered the risk encountered when applying a physical theory to a wider domain, one involving higher speeds than before, smaller or larger objects, etc. But there is an additional risk when assuming that the same laws are valid for those physical phenomena having some close connection to another type of reality. We have already drawn attention to the not inconsiderable assumption that is made when it is held that the normal laws of physics can be applied as well to the working of the brain as to that of any other physical system. The assumption that, despite the close connection with mental occurrences, there is no need at any time to defer to the mental explanatory framework (for instance, by making specific reference to an act of the will) might well be justified. But its validity has yet to be demonstrated experimentally.

In similar vein we ought to be alive to the possibility of there being an extra risk involved in situations that have a special association with the spiritual realm. Christians, for example, believe that Jesus had a unique relationship to God. That being so, why should there not be aspects of the physical behaviour of his body (his virgin birth and physical resurrection) and the behaviour of his immediate physical surroundings (acts of healing and the nature miracles) that lie outside the province of normal physics, and which can only be explained in terms appropriate to the spiritual framework?

If such miracles did occur at that time, and still occur today, it would not be necessary to look upon them as 'violations' of the laws of physics. We have just seen that when we come across events that classical physics cannot handle, we do not speak of them as interruptions to the normal flow of nature. They lie outside this particular framework's area of competence, but they still come under the purview of a higher law. The same idea can be applied to miracles; they are events that lie outside the area of competence of our physical laws - *all* physical laws. But this does not necessarily mean that they are not law-like. There is nothing to stop us looking for an even higher law - one that embraces all physical laws, even the most powerful still to be devised. If there were such a law, and miracles were seen to be embraced by that law, then they would have as much right to be regarded as being part of the normal predictable flow of events as any other. According to this view, all physical laws, even the most powerful, would have to be thought of as approximations to the truth, each with a limited area of validity.

This is an important point, but one too easily overlooked. Part of the natural reaction we have against the acceptance of miracles today is that they appear to point to a God who gets things going according to the laws of physics, and then changes his mind. From a superficial reading of the Bible, one can get the impression of a God forever tinkering with the world, almost as an afterthought. He seems constantly interfering in order to get it back on the rails again when something has unexpectedly gone wrong. This surely cannot be right. God has foreknowledge; he is never taken by surprise. God has ordained that this should be a world run on orderly lines; he is not by nature capricious. If there are to be miracles at all, they only make sense if they can be seen as an integral part of his overall plan; they too must conform to law-like behaviour of some kind.

Having recognized the need for there to be such a law, it is not difficult for us to identify it. It is the law of love.

Love is God's supreme characteristic. Jesus, being the Son of God, was the perfect personification of love in human terms. When during the course of his life there arose a conflict of interests between, on the one hand, allowing the laws of physics to work inexorably, and on the other, being true to his perfect loving nature, the latter had to prevail. Faced with human suffering, the requirement on Jesus to express God's love in all its fullness took precedence over his normal custom to work within the scope of the normal operation of the physical laws. God, as the creator of those laws, is not himself constrained by them. If the expression of love, through an act of healing, for example, requires physical events to take a course different to that which would otherwise have occurred, so be it. There is nothing capricious about such an event. It accords with the rationale of the higher law of love, the law that embraces and subsumes all others - including the physical laws. That healing event is to be seen as an integral part of God's eternal plan for revealing himself to us and helping us to glimpse the nature of his kingdom. And if it was natural for Jesus to perform such miraculous acts of healing in accordance with that law of love, why should not other devout people be able to do the same today?

8. We have spoken of the way God interacts with our spirit in the spiritual interaction domain, and how this is correlated to our conscious religious experience in the mental domain. But so far we have said nothing of what might be going on at the physical level of the brain when we are engaged in prayer. If all our mental states are correlated to brain states, and God produces a change in our conscious mental state during prayer, what happens in the brain? Does it now move into a state other than that which it would have moved to had God decided not to communicate with us? Does the experience of the Presence of God in the mind entail the brain moving to a different state to that which would have developed from the normal operation of the laws of physics? In other words, does a small-scale miracle take place in our brain?

It depends on the nature of the relationship between the mental and physical domains. According to the view that not all thoughts in the mind are correlated to processes occurring in the brain, there is no problem; God can change our mental state without affecting the brain state. But if it is the case that every change to the mental state is correlated to a changed physical state of the brain, then the new and unexpected thought derived from God will presumably be accompanied by an unexpected twist to the chain of physical events occurring in the brain. This new physical development will lie outside the competence of physics to explain. It can only be accounted for by deferring to the spiritual explanatory framework, which means that the communication from God has indeed been marked by a small-scale miracle in the brain.

Another way in which we might be affected by small-scale miracles concerns the origin of the religious archetype - the archetype that predisposes us from birth towards seeking God. One supposes that this archetype, like others, is probably the psychological counterpart of genetically determined behaviour owing its origins to an encoding within the DNA molecule. With the other archetypes, or imprints, we know who the imprinters were. In the case of the mother archetype it is to be identified with the mothers our ancestors interacted with. The changes to the encoding happened at random, but then the mothers were part of the environmental conditions that preferentially selected out that encoding associated with the appropriate behaviour towards mothers. With the religious archetype, we have already pointed to the apparent lack of survival value in acquiring a gene that leads one to love one's enemies and sacrifice oneself for those who do not necessarily share the same gene. How then does such an encoding, even if it does arise by chance, manage to get selectively preserved. Once again, if one subscribes to a viewpoint that accepts miracles as part of God's overall plan to draw us into an active, loving relationship with him, there is no difficulty; God as the imprinter simply augments the normal laws of nature by ensuring, through miracles if necessary, that the coding does arise in the course of the evolution of humankind, and having arisen, is subsequently preserved.

Thus, we see there can be several ways in which miracles could be a normal on-going part of the running of the physical world. I say 'normal' inasmuch as they all conform to a rational orderly plan embracing the overall purpose of existence and God's scheme for dealing with us. It is a purpose that only manifests itself at the spiritual level. That is why the rationale behind miraculous events can only be adequately understood by deferring to the spiritual framework.

9. Until now we have taken the line that miracles are possible and that God does indeed reveal himself in ways that science cannot explain in its own terms. But suppose this is *not* the case. Suppose the workings of the physical world are invariably open to description in terms of physical law - perhaps not by the laws as they are currently formulated, but as they might be understood at a future date. In other words, it is *never* necessary to defer to the spiritual or the mental framework in order to account for physical behaviour. Under these circumstances, would it still be possible for God to make his Presence known to us?

Certainly. He does it in a way that is directly analogous to that by which one human mind communicates with another human mind. In our normal encounters with people, the meeting of minds is exclusively mediated through the interaction of physical bodies in the physical domain. Moreover, for this mental interaction to take place, there is no need to have the mental interfering in the normal running of the brain; all the physical behaviour of these bodies can be describable in terms of the normal operation of the physical laws. And yet one mind makes itself known to the other.

Normally of course we are barely conscious that this meeting of minds is being conducted through a physical medium. We do not think of it in those terms. We do not analyse our sensory observations and decide on the basis of their otherness that they are indicative of quantum interactions; that there is in turn something about these interactions indicative of a human body out there; that there is something about the behaviour of the body which convinces us that it is associated with a mind. On the contrary, the end product of the chain of inferences being a mind - one that is presumably similar to the one we start out from - it becomes second nature to think in terms of a direct line of communication between one's own mind and that of the other person. We habitually think of someone else's thoughts and feelings directly influencing one's own thoughts and feelings. It is only when we stop to think out the matter in detail that we come to accept that all mental transactions are, in the final analysis, physically mediated.

This being how we communicate one with another, why should God not do the same? If we have no need of a non-physical channel in order to communicate with someone else, why should he? Of course, he does not have a human body like ours. But interactions do not have to involve direct interaction between two such bodies. When we read a book, look at a painting, listen to music, enter a building, or walk down a street, we are all the time being influenced by other minds - those of the author, painter, composer, architect, and town planner. All this without us ever having met them. It is sufficient that we come into contact with their handiwork. If it is thus possible to influence one another through nothing more than the simple rearrangment of physical objects (ink on paper, paints on canvas, etc.), how much easier it must be for God, the Designer and Creator of all physical things to communicate with us through the physical world. God does not need a distinctive body. The whole of the created world is mapped to him, the events of history are mapped to him, holy people are mapped to him. He stands behind all things and uses all things to disclose himself to us.

But if that is the case, what does God actually *do*? If the laws of physics carry on regardless, is not God superfluous? In a sense, yes - the same sense as other minds are superfluous. After all, what do other minds *do*? As far as the behaviour of the body is concerned - the body thought of purely as an object of physical interest - the answer is: nothing. The laws of physics take care of everything. But in another framework of discourse, one in which one is asking different kinds of question, the answer is that minds do everything. It is the same with God. As far as the study of physics is concerned, he too is superfluous. But when it comes to other kinds of discussion he is everything.

If the laws of physics are operating normally, what is it about our experiences of the physical that encourages us to interpret them as instances of God revealing himself to us? The situation is again analogous to that involving other minds. The reason we interpret the behaviour of human bodies as minds that are revealing themselves to us, is that we are aware of our own mind in relation to our own body. We know what it is to be a mind. The recognition of ourselves as having a representation in the mental reality domain is what alerts us to the possibility of the existence of other minds. Actually, it is not quite that straightforward; we have already pointed out the reciprocal nature of the discovery of other minds. But the important point is that, without an awareness of our own mind there can be no awareness of other minds. In the same way, it is the recognition of ourselves as having a representation in the spiritual domain that sensitizes us to those features of physical experience which, although readily lending themselves to explanation in perfectly pragmatic physical terms, are yet indicative of a non-physical spiritual reality. Acceptance of the existence of God and of the spiritual natures of others is conditional on there being an awareness of ourself as a spiritual being. Just as it takes a thief to catch a thief, so in a manner of speaking, it takes a mind to catch a mind, and a spirit to catch a spirit.

10. According to the non-miraculous viewpoint, brain activity is governed, without exception, by the laws of physics; it evolves in a predictable manner. If there is a one-to-one mapping from brain states to mental experiences, it follows that the progression of mental experiences will also be determined. In particular, during a time of prayer, the mental state at the end of the prayer time is the one appropriate to the brain state that has evolved deterministically from the brain state at the beginning of the prayer time. This state, in its turn, has developed from those that existed before it was even decided to engage in prayer. In other words, there is no 'outside interference' from God. We ask: Under these circumstances, how can God still make his Presence known to us through prayer, and what is the origin of the otherness of the inner religious experience?

The bogy of determinism again! I can well imagine the reactions of some readers at this point - those opposed to the very notion of determinism. I ask them to be patient. Though they personally might feel the idea to be mistaken, it is not demonstrably wrong; indeed, one day it might even be shown to be correct. In the interests of intellectual integrity, therefore, we ought to take the trouble to examine how damaging, or otherwise, such a development might be for belief in God. (As was the case with free will, we shall find that things are not nearly as bad as one might at first fear!)

But, it might be countered, determinism simply *cannot* apply here. In the case of free will, our act of the will flowed naturally as an authentic expression of our character, the new mental state being an unforced, inevitable development out of the previous one - analogous to the way the corresponding brain state developed naturally and predictably out of what had gone before. In contrast, what marks the encounter with God in the inner religious experience is its ability to surprise us - the otherness, the unexpectedness of the experience. The mental state at the end of the prayer time does *not* flow in any natural way from what has preceded it. There seems to have been an injection from outside - the input we attribute to God. Any explanatory approach to prayer must be able to do justice to the perceived sense of otherness. This is true, but in fact, there is no problem. The otherness originates with the unconscious mind. During a time of prayer, when one is effectively divorced from outside physical influences, the otherness that is perceived in the conscious mind must derive from the unconscious - there is no other possible source. Unlike a direct input from the spiritual explanatory framework, which would require a miracle in the brain, that from the unconscious requires nothing untoward occurring at the physical level. Unconscious processes, like conscious ones, map to aspects of the normal working of the brain.

To an hypothetical outside observer furnished with a knowledge of all the brain states involved and of how these are to be correlated to conscious and unconscious activities in the mind, such an observer would have no difficulty predicting the development of the mental events; for him there is nothing unexpected or surprising about them. Only to the subject himself does there appear to be an unexpected element. This is because when we talk of 'the subject', we specifically mean the ego, the consciousness of the subject, not the totality of the mind. The conscious part of the mind does not have all the information that is available to the outside observer. He is ignorant of what is going on in his unconscious, and so is liable to be taken unawares by it. It is this unanticipated input from the unconscious that manifests itself as the otherness of the religious experience. In looking beyond the domain of consciousness for an 'outside' explanation, it is not to the spiritual explanatory framework he must defer, but to that associated with the description of the unconscious.

But haven't we already disposed of the idea of the unconscious as a source of the inner religious experience (Chapter 15)? Did we not there come to the conclusion that shameful thoughts repressed in childhood, along with basic instincts to do with sex and aggression, were unlikely to give rise to the uplifting quality that characterizes the sense of the numinous? Yes. But what I have in mind here is not so much the unconscious being the ultimate *source* of the experience, as it being a *channel* through which God, as the true source, communicates with us.

This possibility comes about in the following way: We have seen how God can reveal himself through nature, history, scripture, holy people, etc. Thus, the unconscious contains not only instincts and repressions, but also the effects of past experiences, *some of which bear the stamp of God's revelation.* It is not that we were necessarily aware of the revelatory nature of those experiences at the time. This is something that might emerge only over a lengthy period of unconscious assimilation and processing.

The unconscious mind has a remarkable ability to work on past experiences, sifting and sorting them out. Thus, for instance, we might temporarily be unable to recall someone's name. We put the matter aside and turn our attention to something else - only to discover a little later that the name is now readily to hand. While we were consciously thinking of other things, the unconscious mind was apparently getting on with the job of readying itself to produce the name later. Or we might be wrestling with some seemingly intractable problem. We decide to try the time-honoured solution: sleep on it. In the morning, there is the answer awaiting us. The fact that the unconscious mind, in these and other ways, appears to lead a life of its own, raises the possibility that it might also be mulling over past experiences that carry the stamp of God. These will include not just our own first hand experiences, but those of past generations as they have become encoded into our DNA. All these will be worked on by the unconscious, the process of evaluation being motivated and controlled by the archetypal self.

And what of the end result of this activity? Out of it there emerges a conception of what is common to all these experiences - the character of the numinous. *It is this conception, distilled in the unconscious, that is then offered up by the archetypal self to the ego, and is there in consciousness perceived as the Presence of God.* This is how the sense of the numinous could arise - that mysterious something that is set over against us (entering the conscious mind unexpectedly from 'outside'), and yet is also perceived as an integral part of one's own very depths (a part of one's own unconscious).

But this cannot be the whole story behind the inner religious experience. It is all very well saying that the otherness derives from an unconscious interpretation put on past events. But how come those events lend themselves so readily to that interpretation in the first place? From whence came this type of intelligibility? It is here we must defer to the spiritual framework. The intelligibility we speak of has to do with meaning and purpose, and as we have seen before, questions of this kind can only be addressed in the conceptual terms of the spiritual framework. Though earlier I said that one should seek to explain the consciously perceived otherness of the religious experience by deferring to the explanatory framework of the unconscious, rather than to that associated with the spiritual domain, the latter does have the final say.

This is a tricky point that needs to be spelt out: Recall that there are two possible reasons why one should wish to switch from one explanatory framework to another. The first is to account for otherness of the type where there is a gap in understanding why one mental state should follow another (switching from the mental to the physical to explain the disappearance of the headache was an example of this). Just now we were concerned to explain why the religious experience appeared unaccountable. This form of otherness was explained in terms of what is happening in the unconscious. But then we moved to a different sort of otherness. Through the experience we are supplied with information. We gain knowledge about ultimate questions and the meaning of life. The situation is analogous to that which led to the inference of other minds. Earlier we saw how on listening to someone's voice there was in addition to the otherness associated with the physical impact of sound waves on the ear drum, a second type of otherness to do with the information being conveyed concerning mental experiences - a warning that an apple tasted sour, for instance. We concluded that such information had to have a mental source, even though it was being conveyed through the physical medium. In a similar way, we find with the religious experience that we are again being supplied with information. This time it is about spiritual matters. This indicates a spiritual source - one that uses the unconscious as the medium of transmission. Thus, having switched out of the conscious mental framework to the unconscious one in order to account for the first type of otherness, we must then switch from that to the spiritual one in order to deal with the informational type of otherness, and thus complete the explanation.

According to the picture presented, the mapping link between the spiritual domain and that of consciousness is an indirect one via the unconscious. This contrasts with the previous picture (the one that permitted small-scale miracles in the brain) where the link was regarded as a direct mapping into consciousness. The view that the spiritual domain might be somewhat removed from consciousness in no way detracts from its significance. Were the postulate of the spiritual domain devoid of explanatory power, the unconscious would have nothing to distill from past experiences, and would thereby have nothing to offer to the ego as an experience of the Presence of God.

So far so good, but does such a conception really do justice to the experience of prayer? A reservation one might have is that it appears to be solely concerned with reflecting on past experience, whereas much of prayer is directed towards seeking guidance about future courses of action. Down through the ages God has 'spoken' to humankind; he has passed on messages to his people as to what he requires of them in current and future situations. Does an unconscious digestion of past events adequately deal with this aspect of prayer? It is here that we must remind ourselves of the 'timelessness' of God. To know how God was in the past is to know how he is now and how he will be in the future. To know God is also to know the kind of life he intends us to lead. Admittedly, in specific situations it might be difficult to discern the particular course of action he wishes us to take. But we do know the general frame of mind we should be in and the kinds of factors we should be taking into account in arriving at our decisions. Provided we approach decisions with a genuine openness to act in whatever way we imagine Jesus, or Muhammad, or Moses would have acted (as judged on the basis of our accumulated knowledge of that person), then that is all that God can require of us. If the preferred choice of alternative paths before us is still not clear, it is probably an indication that to God it is immaterial which one we select; he can make use of either course of action. It is important to recognize that where the revelation of God is concerned, it is not so much that one enters into communication with him, as one enters into *communion* with him. The aim is to know him and to be at one with him - not to reach him on the end of a spiritual telephone line. If we are at one with God, we do not need specific messages. Having surrendered our will to him, it is up to him to make use of us. So, in conclusion I would say that the conception of the inner religious experience we have presented probably does do justice to the full experience of prayer, even in respect of those aspects that seem to us to be future-oriented.

11. Continuing our investigation of the consequences of accepting a non-miraculous, deterministic view of the physical domain, we turn next to the question of the origin of the religious archetype as encoded in the DNA molecule. The problem is how it got there, and once having arisen, how the gene was preserved despite it conferring no survival advantage to those possessing it.

One approach is to suggest that the gene has originated in the same way as all DNA codings do: by chance. Through mutations, an individual, at some particular point in the past, came to acquire a sequence of molecules along the DNA helix that produced the pattern of behaviour associated with the religious archetype - the urge to seek after ultimate meaning and purpose in terms of spiritual realities, and to live a life of self-sacrifice. When I say it formed 'by chance', I mean that this is how it would appear in the context of a discussion on evolutionary biology. But that does not prevent it from being also an event covered by God's foreknowledge, and thus, in another context, an indispensable link in his overall plan for human existence. In this latter connection it would not be correct to regard it as a chance event.

Once formed, this gene would be at a disadvantage in regard to its being handed on to future generations. Individuals possessing it are likely to be less promiscuous than others, some take vows of celibacy, others are killed in religiously inspired wars, etc. There is, therefore, a generally reduced chance of such individuals mating and producing offspring sharing the same gene. So, how is it preserved?

One possibility is to say that the mutation is a recent one and there has not yet been sufficient time for its marginally negative survival value to have taken its toll. The trouble with this is that it is difficult to see why the gene, far from being an isolated fluke teetering on the brink of immediate extinction, has been remarkably successful in propagating itself throughout the whole of humankind. We have already noted the universality of the religious phenomenon.

It seems to me that we are probably on the wrong track thinking in such terms. For a more plausible account of the origins and history of this genetically determined behaviour, we must take our cue from the observation that the religious archetype is not like the others. As we have said previously, it is one concerned with the *whole* person. Unlike the other archetypes, this one - the self -

stands at the centre of the psyche. All the other archetypes relate to it. Until now we have looked upon the biological counterpart of the religious archetype in the same way as we have the counterparts of other archetypes. We have thought of them as encodings of small constituent molecules along the DNA helical chain, in much the same way as it is known that the codings related to physical characteristics of the individual's body are stored. But suppose, in keeping with its special nature, the religious archetype is not encoded in that way at all.

There is no reason why psychological predispositions have to be exclusively associated with codes along the DNA chain. For example, it is sometimes held that the human mind has an uncanny ability to anticipate scientific discovery. To the extent that this might be true, it could arise out of the way the mapping is established between mental processes and physical interactions occurring in the brain. The form of the mapping could result in the mind tending automatically to adopt a pattern of thought which, in some analogical sense, mirrors the physical interrelationships of the brain processes, which themselves are examples of the interrelationships that one is trying to understand. In this way we would be endowed with an innate mind-set having nothing specifically to do with DNA molecules.

In similar vein, therefore, we seek some feature of the physical domain, other than a DNA coded sequence, that could conceivably be associated with the religious archetype. It might, for instance, have something to do with the universal helical configuration that DNA molecules possess regardless of the exact make-up of their individual sequences. Such a hypothesis has the merit that, qualitatively at least, the overall structure of the helix has a relationship to its component sequences somewhat similar to that between the religious archetype and the other archetypes. If this is indeed the manner in which the self is encoded, then we can begin to see that the religious behaviour characteristic was bound to put in an appearance early in the evolution of humankind. The very nature of the bonds that can be forged between the relevant chemicals dictates that an overall helical structure will be adopted. Moreover, once formed, this helical structure is certain to be preserved. The evolutionary pressures are solely concerned with weighing up the relative survival values of DNA molecules possessing alternative sequences. But all DNA molecules have the helical structure.

Now I hasten to say there is not a scrap of evidence to confirm what I have just suggested; there is no way I can think of for demonstrating how the overall structure of the DNA molecule would produce the behaviour characterised by the self. But then again the whole subject is very much in its infancy; we do not even know how different sequences within the DNA molecule succeed in controlling genetically determined behaviour. The sole purpose of making such a suggestion is to demonstrate that it does not require a great deal of imagination to come up with at least one plausible way as to how God could have implanted in us a religious archetype that orientates us towards him, without his having to act outside the normal operation of the laws of physics. Inasmuch as God is the designer of the atoms that go to make up the DNA molecule, and has foreknowledge of what is to come, he is to be seen as the imprinter responsible for the religious archetype.

12. Finally we must look to the implications of the present viewpoint for the unique status Christians accord Jesus - the claim that besides being a man, he was also the Son of God. According to this assessment, he is not simply to be venerated as someone particularly distinguished from birth to be a great prophet and servant of God, which is how Islam views him. It is not that he was 'the best man who ever lived', which is an assessment many are happy to accept. To Christians he is someone *qualitatively* different from the rest of us. But how can this be? If everything happening in the physical world is to be considered explicable in purely physical terms,

what room is there for assigning Jesus a special spiritual nature? The key lies in this concept of mapping. *The man Jesus in the physical and mental domains, maps to the Son of God in the spiritual domain.* Whereas we map to spirits which lie outside of, and distinct from, the Godhead, the man Jesus was mapped to one of the Persons of the Trinity. This means that in order to understand certain aspects of Jesus, it is necessary to defer out of the physical or mental frameworks and think of him in the spiritual domain represented there as the Son of God. On what occasions should we so defer? We have already noted the two general reasons why one would want to switch frameworks. First to fill a gap in explanation. If one is not thinking deterministically, then one might want to defer to the spiritual framework to provide an explanation of certain otherwise inexplicable events surrounding the life of Jesus - his virgin birth, the healing and nature miracles he performed, and his physical resurrection. On the other hand, if one is thinking deterministically, as we currently are, then there are no gaps in physical explanation. Provided that further advances in the physical sciences do not come up with natural explanations of these events, one must assume that such events did not take place as literally described. The accounts of these events must be seen purely as vehicles for conveying spiritual truths.

Which brings us to the second reason for switching frameworks. Even though, according to the deterministic view, there are no gaps in explanation to be filled as regards the way the physical and mental domains function, there are nevertheless questions to do with purpose and meaning - questions that involve the spiritual. It is in the discussion of the significance of the life of Jesus in the context of God's overall plan for humankind that one sees his distinctiveness. God chose from the beginning of time this one particular man to convey to the world a special revelation, one that has not been entrusted to anyone else.

What is this message? It is the revelation of God's *concerned* love for us, his will to overcome our alienation from him and be reconciled to us. He is not a God who stands aloof from his creation, presiding over it in a detached manner from outside so to speak. He is not a benign ruler sympathetic to the problems of his subjects, yet personally detached from them. Instead, he knows exactly what it is to be a part of that creation, what it is to be human. He loves us so much that he suffers alongside us, indeed suffers to a degree we ourselves shall never be called upon to endure. He loves us so much that he will forgive us anything, even our putting him to death on a cross - provided only that we repent and sincerely love him in return. Sin is not an unbridgeable gulf between him and ourselves; he assures us of this by himself crossing that gulf and becoming one with us.

No other religion, no matter how clear a conception it has that God is good and loving, offers the same understanding of God. *This is the one kind of message that cannot be conveyed with authority other than by the one human being who is mapped into the Godhead itself.* Without that mapping, first hand experience of what it is to be human cannot be incorporated into the Godhead, neither can God genuinely suffer with us.

But, it might be argued, have I not previously indicated that we too have been invited to participate in the Divine life and so establish a mapping between our spirit in the spiritual interaction domain and God-in-himself? Would not that mapping be similar to that between the Son of God and God-in-himself? True. But although we at that stage become 'one with the Father' in the same way as Jesus is, it was not always so. Recall that the concept of time as applied to the spiritual interaction domain means that the whole of the domain is in existence. From that perspective we see that Jesus was always mapped to the Son of God and from thence to God-in-himself; we on the other hand have at least part of our existence lying outside the Godhead in a sinful condition, in fellowship with the Devil. It is this that marks a qualitative difference between him and ourselves. We must not lose sight of the fact that we partake of the Divine life only at Christ's invitation and through his saving work on the cross.

Note that the distinctiveness of Jesus in no way rests on the notion of the spiritual and physical realities being mixed up with each other. Jesus is not a spiritual entity walking the Earth masquerading as a human being. In the physical and mental domains he is just as much physical and mental as we are - no more and no less. In the context of discussions conducted within the physical or mental explanatory frameworks he *is* man. But, in the context of discussions conducted within the spiritual framework, because of his unique mapping, he *is* God. Talk about Jesus being both God and Man sounds paradoxical. But it is only so if one does not clearly understand that all discussion must take place within a particular explanatory framework - one cannot simultaneously sit astride two or more frameworks. Depending upon which framework one is using at any particular time (that choice depending upon the type of question one is asking) Jesus will be spoken of *either* as God *or* as man, whichever is appropriate to that framework.

The situation has its parallel in quantum physics. There we were faced with the problem of how to describe an electron: it was both a particle and a wave. But the conceptions are mutually exclusive of each other, so how can they both apply at the same time? The answer is that they do not apply at the same time. If one asks one type of question (where an electron will probably interact next) one has to use the wave concept; if one asks a second type of question (how the electron behaves when it does interact) one has to use the particle concept. The two concepts are inextricably tied to one or other of the two types of question; they are meaningless outside the context of such a question. But one cannot be asking both questions at the same time. Therefore, there is no call to use both concepts at the same time. The impossibility of reconciling the two concepts is merely a reflection of the impossibility of asking the two questions at the same time. If in the face of the difficulties one, nevertheless, persists in trying to form a unified conception of an electron, the best one can hope to do is to hold simultaneously in the mind both the wave and particle ideas, acknowledging their incompatibility, not confounding them with each other, nor emphasizing one at the expense of the other.

This is very similar to what we have just found with Jesus; either we are asking questions about him from within the physical or mental framework, in which case he is to be regarded as man, or from within the spiritual framework, in which case he is to be thought of as God. We cannot be in more than one framework at a time. If despite this fundamental difficulty we insist on forming some kind of unified conception of him, then again, the best that can be done is to hold simultaneously in the mind two conflicting ideas: a limited, vulnerable, crucified man, and an omnipotent, exalted Lord and Saviour. Again, understanding comes, not through finding a neat resolution of the paradox, but by acceptance of a juxtaposition of opposites. Any sense of dissatisfaction this generates arises not from some supposed inadequacy of the answer given, but from the falseness of our expectation as to what form the answer should have taken.

Because of the special nature of the revelation of God that comes to us through Jesus - God's intimate involvement in the particularity of human existence - it is appropriate that we should respond to that revelation in a special way. This we do by worshipping Jesus. In so doing, it is not that we worship the man Jesus, but the Son of God for whom Jesus is his Earthly representation, through that unique mapping. It is not blasphemous to worship Jesus as God, as it would be to worship anyone else in that way. No matter how holy an ordinary person might be, no matter how much that person is revered, it is never appropriate to worship such people as God. Therein lies the difference between Jesus and ourselves.

13. How ought we to conclude this discussion of how the spiritual relates to the physical? There appears to be no clear-cut way of deciding the nature of the relationship. We have explored two basic standpoints. The first holds that one must defer to the spiritual framework in order to explain certain aspects of physical behaviour not covered by the laws of physics, and to explain the otherness of the inner religious experience. Such a viewpoint accepts the occurrence of miracles. It seems to me to be a reasonable point of view. There is nothing in science to gainsay such an idea. Miracles can even be regarded as law-like and natural within the scope of a hierarchy of laws that embraces the physical laws as a sub-set of the total.

The second standpoint holds that one never needs to call upon the spiritual framework for that kind of reason. God is perfectly capable of making his presence known to us, and also his will for us, using as mediator a physical domain that invariably operates in accordance with the physical laws. Even the otherness of the inner religious experience can be accounted for satisfactorily in terms of the operation of the unconscious part of the mind. According to this view, the reason for deferring to the spiritual domain is to tackle questions of ultimate purpose and meaning - a reason which also applies to the first standpoint. This non-miraculous approach is, I would say, again to be accounted a reasonable one.

As for where I personally stand, I would say that the second viewpoint clearly indicates that there is no *need* for God to invoke miracles to get through to us. My training as a scientist tends to orient me towards economy and the non-proliferation of unnecessary hypotheses. But such spartan thinking, while understandably a part of the methodology of scientific investigation, does not necessarily apply to other areas of investigation. A bountiful, all-powerful God is not constrained to raise parsimony to the level of an inviolable principle. Though he can and does reveal himself to us through the normal operation of nature, if he can also do it in special ways that do not so conform, like for example through the physical resurrection of Jesus, why not? I am happy, therefore, to accept that certain miracles did occur, and indeed occur still today - but I would not be seriously disturbed to learn that this was not so.

CHAPTER 19

THEOLOGY AS SCIENCE

THIS completes our study of the grounds for believing in God. I hope the preceding chapters have served to show how science, far from disproving God's existence, finds itself facing rather similar problems when addressing the really fundamental questions of existence and knowledge. Psychology is in much the same boat. This being so, it is not surprising that science, theology, and psychology have insights to offer each other as they tackle their respective difficulties in analogous ways. This is not to say that the conclusions arising out of these several studies carry the same measure of conviction. There can be differing perceptions as to the weight to be accorded the various inferential arguments. There are people who accept the existence of the physical world but not that of God; likewise there are those who accept the existence of God but not that of the physical world (at least, they do not accept a physical world-in-itself). Even among those who believe in a given type of reality, there is room to accommodate a number of more detailed viewpoints.

Building on what we have already learned, I would now like to examine more closely the relationship between theology and science. Not only are there parallels in the answers they come up with in response to questions of similar type, there is much they have in common in respect of how each is pursued as a human endeavour. One might even say that theology has some claim to be regarded as a science in its own right. Not that this assertion needs to be pressed too far. There is no reason to bend over backwards to establish theology's scientific credentials. This chapter is devoted to highlighting the

similarities between theology and science, the next to those features that remain distinctive to each.
1. Science is confronted with a bewildering array of contingent events. But first impressions are deceptive. Behind this multiplicity of events there are a few overriding laws at work. It is the task of science to make sense of this intelligible pattern. To do this one cannot just sit back, passively surveying the scene and indiscriminately collecting data. Some guiding principle or methodology must be adopted to decide which of the infinite number of experiments that could conceivably be done, are those most likely to yield fruit. Not only that, there needs to be some system for organizing the raw data as they are collected. Although in former times it was thought that scientists dealt in plain unvarnished facts - the raw material produced by their experiments - it has more recently come to be accepted that all data are 'theory laden'. The mind is never free of suppositions. As scientists decide what experiments to do in new and unfamiliar situations, and how to regard the data so acquired, they already have expectations in mind based on some theoretical model. This model gives direction to the line of investigation and draws attention to significant observations that might otherwise get overlooked. Created by an imagination informed by past experience, the model consists of modes of thought in which provisional concepts are linked in provisional ways. These ideas might be highly tentative and later rejected. But often they turn out to be in tune with nature.

Turning to theology, we again find what at first appears to be a meaningless array of events - this time those that make up our lives. The religious view holds that behind this surface confusion there lie patterns of meaning. These are most likely to be discerned if one knows the kind of thing one is looking for. The exploration is, therefore, conducted in the context of certain hypotheses - for example, that God is good, or that inner peace is more readily found through self-sacrifice than self-gratification, or that the Presence of God is to be sensed in prayer.

The approach to God is always through some religious system; in these matters there is no such person as an entirely independent thinker. And yet despite there being these preconceived structures of thought - models that help mould the perception of what is found - theology, like science, is set on empirical foundations. What finally counts is whether or not the ideas conform with experience. Because expectations have not always been borne out, theology has evolved through the ages. In this respect it has some claim to be regarded as an empirical science.

2. As we have seen, the value of working from within an already formed theoretical framework is that it gives direction to the investigation and alerts one to patterns of intelligibility that might otherwise get overlooked. There is, however, the reverse side of the coin: the danger that these same presuppositions will act as blinkers, preventing due weight being given to those indications that do not conform with expectation. They may also distort one's perception of what is found. The most one can do about this is to examine closely the nature of the chosen viewpoint and try to anticipate the type of bias to which it is likely to lead. In theology, for example, when describing God as 'personal', we have in mind a theoretical model in which God is being likened to ourselves. Clearly, if we are not careful, we get caught up in a tendency to be *too* anthropomorphic, assigning to God features of human existence that are not appropriate, as well as those that are. We must try not to lose sight of this danger, making what corrections we can.

3. Although the adopted viewpoint can blind us to those experiences that do not fit with expectation, nevertheless, in science, contra-indications sometimes arise that simply cannot be ignored. In response to these, the model gets refined and modified to bring it more closely into line with actuality. Some data might not fit at all into the model. The pressure from these awkward results can become so great as to cause a wholescale, radical change in viewpoint - a so-called 'paradigm shift'. The

changeover to relativity and quantum theory from classical theory were examples of this.

The fact that scientific theories yield expectations that can be confirmed or refuted, has in the past led certain enthusiasts to claim that the only meaningful statements are those that lend themselves to some practical test whereby they could be verified. This came to be known as the 'verification principle'. It was further asserted that only scientific statements passed that test, so only scientific statements could be accounted meaningful. All metaphysical statements, including those of theology could be discounted as having no content. Although this view is no longer taken seriously in philosophical circles, it still exerts a powerful influence on those unfamiliar with the way thought has progressed meanwhile. There are a number of reasons why the principle has fallen into disrepute. One is the recognition that the statement of the principle itself could not be verified; on its own terms, therefore, it is not to be regarded as meaningful! Secondly, it came to be recognized that even scientific statements are not open to verification - or indeed verification in principle, given that there might be practical difficulties involved. They are only ever tested on a limited number of occasions, under particular circumstances and to a limited level of precision. There consequently remains a risk of the statement being proved wrong whenever the supposed domain of applicability of the law is extended to physical circumstances not previously tested. As we have seen, the laws of classical physics do not in fact apply to conditions involving speeds close to that of light or to sub-atomic particles. They do not even apply to everyday situations if one tightens up the demands on the level of precision.

In response to these objections, the emphasis swung away from verification to the opposite extreme: falsification. Accordingly, the criterion a statement had to meet in order to qualify as a genuine scientific statement was that there had to be, in principle, some way in which the statement could be shown experimentally to be false.

This revised principle was certainly preferable to the earlier one, but even this has subsequently come in for a good deal of criticism. One difficulty lies in the way the laws and concepts of science are inextricably enmeshed with each other. This enmeshing is an integral feature of the theoretical framework through which any new experimental data is approached. If an observation goes against expectation then something somewhere has been falsified. But what? It is not always clear. Let me give an example. There was the case of the radioactive decay of a certain atomic nucleus that appeared not to conserve energy. A linchpin idea that holds much of physics together is the law of conservation of energy: whatever energy is around at the beginning of an interaction must still be around in some form or other at the end. This preconception prevented the scientists from jumping to the obvious conclusion from this experiment, namely, that energy had disappeared. The cherished theory biassed them in the direction of asserting that there must be some hitherto unknown, invisible sub-atomic particle carrying off the missing energy - despite the fact there was no evidence for making such an assertion. But sure enough, in the course of time the hypothesis came to be vindicated through the subsequent discovery of the elusive particle (the neutrino). This example demonstrates the usefulness of approaching data from within some pre-existing theoretical framework that allows one to place the specific experiment under study within a context of wider experience. But it does create problems for anyone who believes there to be some neat, definitive way of falsifying a statement, and thereby sorting out whether it is scientific or not. Openness to falsification is certainly an important feature of science, but exactly how it is to be incorporated can be problematic.

How about theology in relation to verification and falsification? As already stated, there is no deductive proof of God so we can rule out the hope of verification. But that, as we have now seen, is no different from the case of science. With regard to falsification, can it be argued that theological statements can be challenged experimentally and shown to be false? The problem of evil obviously has relevance here. Religious people, as we have seen, do not accept the existence of evil as a falsification of the ideas of an omnipotent, good, and loving God. Does this point to blind faith, held in the face of contrary evidence, so nullifying any claim of theology to be regarded as a science? It would seem to me that the situation here for theology is very similar to that which confronted physics over the apparent loss of energy in the radioactive decay of the sub-atomic nucleus. In that case the explanatory power of the law of conservation of energy was so great in other areas, it justified a continuing belief in it, despite the apparent anomaly. Scientists are sometimes prepared to cling to their faith in a law in the expectation that one day that faith will be justified. So it is in theology. The idea at risk through the problem of evil (the omnipotent, good, loving God, as shown concretely in the life, crucifixion, and resurrection of Jesus) is no ordinary idea; it is key to the whole framework of Christian thought. It is even more central to the overall theological structure than the law of conservation of energy is to physics. The idea has such great explanatory power in so many respects, it cannot be abandoned lightly without severe repercussions throughout the whole system of thought. Thus, there arises a willingness to lay aside anomalous occurrences - those that appear on the surface to falsify the statement - in the expectation that such trust will eventually be vindicated. Of course, this would be a dubious attitude to adopt if there was absolutely *no* notion as to how the problem might eventually be resolved. Recall that the scientists did at least entertain the possibility of the unknown, invisible particle, implausible though that might have seemed to some at the time. The same is true of theology. The problem of evil is *not* an insurmountable difficulty. We have already glimpsed a possible resolution: the requirement for at least a measure of evil in order to off-set, and thereby give meaning to, the concept of goodness (Sections 13.4 and 16.7).

So does this mean we are to regard the theological statement of God's goodness as not falsifiable? One of the difficulties with such a question is that God is bound up with the totality of existence. It is not that there are several universes, some made by good gods, others by evil gods; some made by gods who exercise unlimited power over their universe, others who are not fully in control. If that were the case we could compare our universe with all the others and see whether ours came within the category of those made by the good, omnipotent gods. But there is only the one universe, so the statement is not open to falsification in that way. There is, however, nothing to stop us *imagining* what other universes might be like if made by other types of god. It is not difficult to conceive of a chaotic, ugly, squalid universe, steeped in evil and suffering - one where life is so hideous and unbearable that no-one living in it could possibly conclude that it was being run by an omnipotent, good God. In this imaginary universe, such a claim would be dismissed as false. So, in this sense the statement *is* open to falsification. It just so happens that our universe, fortunately, is not of a kind that does falsify it.

4. We have spoken of paradigm shifts in science in which the overall view of physical reality undergoes a radical change. These large scale changes are brought about within the scientific community as a whole. To an extent that has only recently been appreciated, science has to be regarded as a community activity. Though scientific investigation prides itself on being more objective than most human endeavours, there is nevertheless an important social factor to be taken into account. At any one time, certain views are regarded with favour - the 'orthodox position'; others are branded as heretical, or unsound. Prestige, funding, jobs, and Nobel Prizes go in the main to those who contribute to the lines of research that are currently in favour with the scientific establishment and conform to the wider interests of society as

a whole. These factors obviously influence the outlook of the individual scientist.

Apart from these social pressures, the individual becomes dependent upon colleagues in another way. Life is too short for any one person to work through all the theories and perform all the experiments to one's own satisfaction. In any case, a facility for working out a difficult mathematical theory does not necessarily go hand in hand with the practical skill to carry out the experiment needed to test the theory. So it is that, to some extent, the individual has to take on trust what other people do. This is not to be mistaken for blind faith and gullibility. Theories and experimental results are subjected to rigorous checks before being accepted by the community at large. In the process, many false claims and rogue results have to be weeded out. In this way a body of knowledge, representing the accumulated experience and wisdom of the community, is progressively compiled and refined. It is to this accepted body of knowledge that the individual turns when needing guidance and information that cannot be obtained at first hand.

Just as the individual comes to rely on the community of scientists, so the community in turn looks to those individuals within it that are particularly gifted and have most to offer. Certain scientists gain reputations for having especially powerful intellects, or for having intuitive flair suitable for making theoretical breakthroughs. Others establish themselves as skilful, reliable experimenters; they become the heads of large teams capable of attracting funding for expensive projects. Such people emerge as the leading figures of the community; they are respected, trusted, and honoured; the younger generation of scientists tries to emulate them.

All of which is a far cry from the conventional picture of the solitary scientist working in the privacy of his laboratory, collecting purely objective data free from any bias or extraneous influence, and drawing unerringly the inescapable conclusions to which the data point. One must not be misled by the dehumanized, desiccated manner in which scientists choose to present their results in scientific journals; these accounts bear little relation to how the work was actually carried out. Scientists are creatures of their time, products of the culture in which they live; they see the world to some extent the way they are trained to see it. There is within scientific circles today a new and welcome sense of humility. No doubt this is partly because scientists are no longer held in quite the esteem they were a few decades ago - before the realization that scientific progress is a mixed blessing, bringing with it problems as well as benefits. But also it is due to a growing awareness of the extent to which human qualities and fallibilities are as much a part of science as they are of other areas of human activity.

Turning again to theology, we find that religious believers, like scientists, develop their subject from within a community. They too need to have recourse to like-minded people if they are to disentangle from their own personal experiences those aspects of otherness that are common. Through discussion and the sharing of experience and insight, the community homes in on an agreed body of belief. In the process many ideas are tested and discarded as distortions of the truth - the distinction between orthodoxy and heresy. In the same way as scientists, considered as individuals, are responsible for making few (if any) original discoveries of their own, and thus have to take on trust the findings of fellow-workers past and present, so the individual religious believer is informed by the corporate wisdom handed down in holy writings and made manifest within the living church. As in the scientific community, so in the church there emerge leaders in whom reliance can be placed - those commonly recognized as having sound judgement and good insight in spiritual matters: the saints of yesterday and today.

5. Science is cumulative in its findings; it progresses. Give or take the odd blind alley, and the occasional loss of some insight of the past, today's theories are more

powerful in terms of explanatory value than those of the past. Is the same true of theology?

In one sense, it might be argued, religions do *not* progress. This stems from their tendency to anchor themselves in the truths expounded by their original founder. Christians, for example, see in Jesus a standard of truth that cannot be bettered. Truth is to be found in uncovering the facts of what the founder said and did, freeing the accounts as they have come down to us from any distortions that might have accreted around them in the course of time, and making due allowance for cultural differences between then and now. Having so arrived at the long-established truths, the concern then becomes one of interpreting them in the context of contemporary problems and situations (abortion, contraception, test-tube babies, genetic engineering, the prolonged use of life-support systems, industrial pollution, conservation of Earth's resources, etc.) In this, theology is perhaps to be likened more to technology than science. It is more concerned with the application of understanding than with its advancement. The teachings of Jesus are unlikely to be superceded in the way that those of Newton were.

If this is a fair distinction to draw between science and theology, it is presumably one that will not be perpetuated indefinitely. One day in the far off future, our descendents will reach the point where they will have the best, the most comprehensive understanding of the physical world that humankind is capable of possessing. That being the case, there will be nothing left for science but to see its knowledge applied to whatever new practical situations arise. Indeed, there are certain branches of science that appear to have reached that stage already. Perhaps theology should be regarded as a science that has already passed through its transitory growing pains and reached this state of maturity!

This static view of present-day theology is not one that everyone would share. It is unlikely to commend itself to theologians themselves. The reason is that in Christianity, for example, it is not simply a matter of referring everything back to what happened 2000 years ago. All truth must indeed refer to Christ in the final analysis, but not just to the historical Christ. We have an on-going relationship with a *living* Christ, one whose Spirit is leading us into all truth. We must, therefore, hold open the possibility of Christ progressively revealing more and more of God to us. Why do it in this progressive fashion rather than all at once whilst he was on Earth? Because no-one was ready for it at that time. A knowledge of evolution in the biological sphere, coupled with an understanding of modern cosmology, are prerequisites for appreciating certain aspects of God's role as Creator. The doctrine of the Fall of Man could perhaps do with some reworking in the light of the theory of evolution, as could the supposed spiritual status of other animals. The recognition of the possibility of intelligent life on other planets raises the question of salvation in respect of those life-forms and how it is to be brought about. A modern understanding of physical time through the theory of relativity widens our horizons as to the possibilities open to God in relation to time, as well as having implications for the notions of free will and predestination. The changing role of women in society sensitizes us to qualities of God that are perhaps best addressed in terms of feminine-based metaphors, rather than exclusively masculine ones. Today one is unlikely to hear theologians speaking of Hell in quite the way it was discussed in medieval times. Whilst still maintaining the uniqueness of Jesus as the one Son of God, Christians are now less dismissive of other world religions as they once were, and see them now as potential paths to salvation.

In these various ways theology, using contemporary thought-forms, reworks the faith in order to bring it alive for the current generation. Are these changes mere whims of fashion, or do they constitute genuine progress? It is hard to tell. My own view is that some at least of the shifts are to be seen as progress. They may not amount to the startling changes that science is currently undergoing. There is no doubt that we are living through the golden age of scientific progress, whereas the equivalent period for Christianity was during the earthly life of Christ and the following centuries of the Early Church. But the fact that the main activities in the two enterprises are displaced in time relative to each other is unimportant. The main point is that a good case can be made for the progressive nature of both theology and science. One certainly would not want to exchange the modern theological position for a former one (say, one in which we went back to a belief in a multiplicity of gods), anymore than one would think of putting back the clock in science. This is because those involved in both activities are convinced that they are, in the main, drawing ever closer to the truth about an objective state of affairs.

6. Modern physics has come to recognize that what it deals in are relationships, rather than things-in-themselves. Moreover, the relationships being studied involve the participation of the observer. The choice of experimental investigation (whether to go for precise position or precise velocity, for instance) helps create and shape what is observed. Does this mean reality is simply whatever I decide it should be? No. As we have seen, what rescues the objectivity of science is the residual otherness of the interaction - those features of the interaction that cannot be interpreted as due to one's own input. It is this otherness that betokens a reality other than oneself, so halting the slide into total subjectivity.

Theology has always recognized the problem of subjectivity - the human element in the data in which it deals - to the extent that sometimes one hears the opinion voiced that there is nothing more to the concept of 'God' than what humankind does religiously. (In other words, if no-one is thinking or doing anything related to a belief in God, then there is no God.) But this is to deny the otherness of the relationship - that aspect that is not explicable as an input from oneself. Otherness holds the key to objectivity in theology as in science.

7. In our study of quantum physics we saw that to meet the need to speak of interactions-with-the-world rather than of things-in-themselves, it was not a case of creating a new vocabulary. Rather it was a matter of finding new ways of handling the old concepts. Concepts such as 'position', 'velocity', 'wave', 'particle', and 'electron', were taken over from the language of classical physics but in the new context acquired a somewhat different meaning. Thus, for instance, the familiar concepts of a 'precise position' and 'precise velocity' were retained, but were now no longer to be used simultaneously. Likewise, the concepts of 'wave' and 'particle' were found to arise in response to different questions - questions that could not be asked at one and the same time. An 'electron' came to have a relational existence only; if one insisted on having a mental picture of an electron, it became necessary to hold simultaneously in the mind the incompatible concepts of 'wave' and 'particle' and learn to accept that this combination somehow constituted the explanation.

So it is in theology. In trying to describe God one has to fall back on the familiar language of everyday life - we have no other. The novelty, as in quantum physics, comes not from generating new words, but from the unusual and seemingly paradoxical manner in which familiar concepts, used metaphorically, are handled. Thus we regard God as personal, but then immediately speak of him as infinite and all-encompassing - which seemingly negates much of what one normally associates with an individual person. We speak of him as working out his purpose in time, and yet in another sense he is to be regarded as transcending time. He is thought of as Three, but also as One. Our best understanding of the nature of Jesus is to hold simultaneously in the mind the contradictory conceptions of God and man. At the frontiers of knowledge in both science and theology, therefore, language is being taken to the limit.

8. Often one hears a contrast drawn between, on the one hand, the sure and certain findings of science and their

tangible outcome in terms of technological benefits, and on the other, the much more speculative and tentative conclusions of theology. The comparison is not a fair one. Science deals in raw data consisting of interactions-with-the-world. While it sticks to handling such data it proceeds with confidence and does indeed produce tangible results as witnessed by technological change. The raw material of theology is religious experience in all its various manifestations. Like the data of science, a great deal is known about religious phenomenology. It is widespread, well documented, reproducible, predictable. Religion has tangible outcomes that are just as well attested and valued, if not more so, than those of science - the benefits of peace of mind, courage in adversity, the sense of personal fulfillment, etc. Religion is well understood and 'works', just as science is well understood and 'works'.

Where religion becomes less sure of itself is when, through theological reflection, it seeks to go beyond the handling of raw data and speaks of a reality lying beyond - the spiritual domain to which the religious experience supposedly refers. This is where divergent schools of thought emerge. But this is no different from what happens in physics. Physicists are agreed over the nature and handling of raw material. It is when they try to go beyond that level and say something about what might lie beyond in a domain of the world-in-itself, that there is no agreement. In this regard, views are just as polarized and stoutly defended as they are in theology. The trouble is that when people compare scientific knowledge with religious knowledge, all too often what they are doing is weighing the confident handling of scientific data against the more difficult exercise of speaking about God himself. But surely one must compare like with like. In other words, one must set the confident handling of scientific data against the equally confident handling of religious data, the more philosophical speculations about the world-in-itself against those concerning God-in-himself. (Not that the comparison is quite as symmetrical as it might sound from that statement. Science starts out from the assumption of a domain of physical interactions, i.e. from that which lies beyond conscious mental experience; theology in dealing with religious experience begins with the domain of consciousness, i.e. it does not take the domain of spiritual interactions for granted.)

9. I think enough has been said to indicate that in at least certain respects, there are grounds for claiming theology to be a science. It certainly has the right to be regarded as such if by science one means the systematic, ordered collection and critical study of a set of empirical data, with explanations offered in the form of theoretical models that are open to modification in the light of further experience. But, as I said at the opening to this chapter, the claim ought not to be pressed too strongly. The value of a system of thought does not have to hang on the degree to which it can be regarded as a science. I hope, however, the discussion has served to demonstrate that the distinction between science and theology, in respect both of methodology and the status of their findings, is not as marked as commonly supposed.

CHAPTER 20

THEOLOGY BEYOND SCIENCE

HAVING seen how theology and science have certain features in common, we must now turn to those ways in which they retain their distinctiveness.
1. Just now we saw how an unfair comparison can be made between the status of knowledge in science and in theology - the tendency to set the more certain knowledge of physical interactions against the less sure knowledge of God himself. For the reasons already given the comparison is not valid, nevertheless, it is not difficult to see why it is often made. Scientists work with physical interactions with the general aim of learning how to control the environment - an environment that impacts on us through interactions. The concern of science, therefore, not only begins with the domain of physical interactions, it also ends there. Very few scientists give a thought as to whether the world-in-itself exists or not; for their purposes, it is irrelevant!

Not so with theology. One of the crucial differences between science and theology is that the former studies an object that is impersonal, the latter one that is personal. The one deals with an It, the other with a You. When dealing with things, it is usual to think of how they can be manipulated to one's own ends. When dealing with persons, consideration must be given to the wishes of the other. This is especially so when the other is God. The aim here is the exact *opposite* of making the other conform to one's own wishes. Whereas the focus of concern in the I-It relation is on the desires and needs of the I, the emphasis in the I-God relation is on God and his requirements of me. Whereas scientific study is generally content with a knowledge of interactions, theological study cannot settle for an understanding of religious experience; it must go beyond experience as such, towards a knowledge of God himself and of his will for us. Theology is thereby forced into the less certain areas of discussion more often than science.

2. When speaking of God we use metaphors. These are drawn from situations arising in the mental and physical spheres. The use of metaphor is not unique to the spiritual framework. The statement 'My car is acting temperamentally' is a description of physical behaviour using a metaphor drawn from the mental sphere. In this case, however, it was not necessary to use a metaphor; had I so chosen, I could have described the car's behaviour less colourfully in purely physical terms. When it comes to talk of the spiritual domains, however, there appears little or no alternative.

Another feature of the language of the spiritual is that the concepts are always *pointing* to their referents rather than encapsulating them. When stating that God is Love, for example, the metaphor we have in mind is clearly the love between two people. But this is not to say God simply loves us in this way. We talk of our imperfect partial acts of love in order to point to the perfect, infinite love of God. Yet the love of God remains unique as the love of *total* commitment. As we imagine ever better and fuller examples of human love, so the concept of 'God' is more insistently evoked. But no matter how close this process might take us to the love characteristic of God, one never actually reaches it. In the same way we speak of God as being all-wise, all-good, and all-powerful. Again, in order to convey some idea of what is meant, we invoke examples of human behaviour - those that to a degree participate in that quality of God to which we refer. But even the very best examples still leave us with a gap that cannot be spanned. There remains a qualitative difference between the way we apply words such as 'wisdom', 'goodness', and 'power' to God, and how they apply to ourselves. This is why we say that the concepts can merely act as pointers to the truth about God.

As the opening line of the *Tao Teh Ching* puts it: 'The Tao that can be expressed is not the eternal Tao'.

In trying to reduce theology to a science, one loses sight of an essential quality of God: his mystery. By 'mystery' we do not mean a puzzle waiting to be cleared up, a temporary difficulty to be resolved by further study. We refer to that which is fundamentally hidden from us, that which is inaccessible and will forever lie beyond human understanding unless God chooses otherwise to reveal it at some appointed time. One of the attendant difficulties of an exercise like ours is that we end up with a rational scheme of argument and exposition that sounds *too* cut and dried. Our talk of the Persons being found in one spiritual domain, God-in-himself in another, mappings between them, etc. can be thought *too* neat. Don't get me wrong. I believe that what we have done is valuable. It is only right and proper that we should pay God the compliment of using the intellect he has given us to pursue our understanding of him as far as it will go. It is all too easy to throw up one's hands and say 'Right, that is as far as we can get; the impenetrable mystery begins here.' I am sure there is yet more ground waiting to be explored by the intellect. But what is important is that such attempts be undertaken in humility, and in the knowledge that God's richness is ultimately inexhaustible and beyond grasp.

Science has no need to acknowledge comparable limits in its exploration of the physical realm. As long as science sticks to its task of dealing with physical interactions, it aims to fashion a language that can successfully encapsulate a comprehensive explanation of that reality.

3. There is a problem concerning the accessibility of the raw data from which theological reflection starts - a difficulty not shared by the data given to science. In the case of physics, we all have access to the physical interaction domain and are agreed upon what we find there and how it should be described. The situation in religion is not so clear. The problem is that an integral part of the

raw data of religion is the inner religious experience. This lies one step removed from the public arena in the consciousness of the individual - the domain of private access. Any discussion between a religious person and one who has had no first hand experience of the inner sense of the Presence of God is bound to encounter difficulty; the latter does not have access to all the data.

4. Of course, the inner religious experience is not the only way in which the numinous is discerned; God is to be found in nature, history, and in other people. Because these belong to the public arena rather than the private interior world of the psyche, there will not be the same difficulty in communicating with others about the sense of the numinous in this context. But even here there are problems.

We can illustrate this by taking an analogous situation from the world of music: Beethoven is held to be a great composer. But what exactly is it about his symphonies that raise them above the level of other works? Among Beethoven-lovers there is little difficulty in discussing such matters. They can argue whether the odd-numbered symphonies really have turned out to be greater than the even-numbered ones. But when talking with someone who does not appreciate Beethoven, it is not at all easy to put one's finger on just what aspect of the works makes them great. Here, unlike the situation over the inner religious experience, we are no longer speaking of two people, only one of whom has had the experience. Both listeners hear the notes being played; as far as the reception of the basic sound is concerned there is no difference. And yet one listener is transported with delight, the other bored to death. One perceives and responds to a synthesis of the individual sounds that the other does not. In an attempt to find out what it is all about, the latter might turn to a book on musical appreciation. Such books undoubtedly have their place; they provide pointers to the kinds of thing one should listen for. But reading about the greatness of a Beethoven symphony does not guarantee that the next time you hear the work you will *appreciate* that greatness.

Similar difficulties are encountered in respect of those aspects of religious experience arising from the synthesis of overall patterns in nature, history, and one's life. One can talk about them, as we did in Chapter 13, in ways that might be helpful. Such talk might possibly evoke in another person a parallel response. But there is no inevitability about it. No-one can be forced into accepting the religious outlook on life as the one and only way of seeing things. Either one perceives it that way, or one does not.

Once again, science is not like that. Science is to do with intellectual argument and rational explanation grounded in the results of experimentation. Though the individual scientist might from time to time sit back and reflect appreciatively upon the beauty of the synthesis so achieved, this is beside the point; one can be a perfectly good scientist without such a feel for the overall picture.

5. What this means is that for someone to progress towards an understanding of spiritual matters, there has to be *personal involvement*; one must have first hand experience of the Presence of God within, together with an appreciation for the numinous in other aspects of life. One cannot expect to be argued into a belief in God, or even to understand fully what talk about God is really about, unless one is prepared to invite a religious experience of one's own. In a way, all the argumentation of this book has been strangely distant from its subject matter. The most that can be claimed for our discussion - in respect of those who do not presently believe in God - is that it might have cleared away a few intellectual obstacles in the way of taking religion seriously. What is ultimately required is not argument but an act of the will. There has to be a will to give religion a try. A leap of faith must be made. One must accept, provisionally at least, that God exists, and live life that way and see what happens. Only so can one hope to have for oneself the

personal religious experiences necessary to enter fully into the religious dialogue.

Integral to an understanding of the spiritual aspects of existence is the need to become immersed in the language applied to the spiritual domain - its concepts and the way it is used. This is not unique to the language of the spiritual explanatory framework. *Any* language that purports to be true to a reality must gain its sense by being grounded in some appropriate aspect of human experience and activity. Take, for example, our normal everyday language as it is applied to the physical world. How does one come to understand the meaning of a simple physical concept like 'cup'? Presumably someone begins by pointing to an object and says the word 'cup'. The learner repeats the word. Has he thereby learnt the meaning? Probably not. Asked to demonstrate an understanding he points to other cups. So far so good. But then he points to saucers and plates and says 'cup'. Obviously something is wrong. Perhaps he has in mind what we would call 'crockery'. We put him right about that, but then find he hesitates over pointing to an enamel cup; he is unsure whether it being made of pottery is an integral part of an object being a cup. We assure him that it is not and the new object is, therefore, also to be regarded as a cup. We then point to a picture of a racing driver holding up a trophy. He is once again surprised; he did not know that cups were still cups out of doors, that they were allowed to be that big, or that they could have two handles rather than one. He has also to be told that a chalice - with no handles - is also a cup. Having seemingly learnt all there is to be known about cups, he is dismayed next morning to learn that the receptacle for holding his egg is a cup, but the mug out of which he is drinking is not!

We thus find that even with a simple physical concept like 'cup' the explanation of the word and the demonstration of understanding involves an intricate complex of actions - pointing to many objects (including those that are *not* cups), holding them, using them, etc. Understanding comes only through the interplay of words and actions.

This being the case when acquiring a language about what is readily accessible to us all in the physical domain, it must be even more the case when trying to share a language about the private experiences we have in our individual consciousnesses. In order for words like 'love', 'joy', or 'pain' to take on meaning, there must be a personal experience of them. Not that we can ever be sure that when I talk of 'pain' I am referring to exactly the same kind of experience as you have, but at least the circumstances for having the experience must be comparable (for example, we each refer to whatever we experience when our respective thumbs are banged). So it is over the acquisition of a religious language. I cannot be sure that someone else's sense of the numinous exactly matches mine, but at least we can discuss the matter meaningfully if we do both join in the activity of prayer and thus lay ourselves open to the possibility of each having an experience of that kind. Discussion with someone who does not participate in the activity of prayer, and consequently has no experience of the numinous, cannot get beyond first base.

It is not my intention to delve further into the nature of language and how it comes to acquire sense. It is a complicated business and goes much beyond the simple naming of entities. The point I wish to make is a simple one: in coming to terms with a language, *actions as well as words are needed*. Actions are needed as explanation; actions are needed to demonstrate understanding. In the religious context, the actions involve prayer, meditation and generally living one's life according to the precepts of that religion. There is no middle path. Either one lives one's life as though there is a God, or as though there is not. Those who have not made up their minds, and so have yet to respond positively to God's call to devote their lives to him, are to be found in the latter class. As Jesus said, those who are not with him are against him. In this respect, life has more in common with an English court of law than a Scottish one. In Scotland a jury can, in cases of doubt, opt for a non-proven verdict; in England this is not allowed. Regardless of what doubts the jury might still harbour, it has to come off the fence and declare for or against the defendant.

The decision over the attitude to be adopted towards God is similar to that encountered over other minds. Though from a strictly philosophical point of view it is justified to hold that there is no deductive proof for or against the existence of other minds, when it comes to living out one's life one is faced with a stark choice: one either lives life as a social being or one does not. In the same way, one either devotes one's life to God, or one does not. Only by responding affirmatively does one gain confirmation of the rightness or otherwise of one's choice.

What marks out the religious way of life from other human activities like the pursuit of science, is that it involves *total* commitment. A necessary requirement for coming to any kind of experience of God is that there should be no holding back. This is because of the manner in which the discovery of God is at one and the same time the discovery of one's own true inner nature. To know God is to know also the image of God - which is the ultimate depths of one's own being. To know that image is to know one's potentialities, and what God requires of us. We thus come to know God to the extent that we are prepared to surrender ourselves to him. Though there be compartments to life - even the life of the most devoted scientist - where the adoption of a purely scientific outlook would be inappropriate, the religious orientation must be allowed to inform every aspect of life without exception; with God there can be no half measures.

6. But, it might be objected, there are many people who have attempted to live life in a spiritual context - and got nowhere. How is one to account for their lack of success? There are two possibilities to be considered. In the first place we must note an important difference between the

scientific and religious endeavours. In the former, the object of enquiry is something passive that can be brought under one's own control. If the experimental conditions are right, it has no alternative but to yield up its secrets to the investigator. But with religion (theistic religion at any rate) the object of inquiry is not a thing at all but a Person - a Person with a will of his own, capable of revealing himself or not as he chooses. There is no guaranteed outcome to this kind of experiment. Perhaps God has reasons for not revealing himself. All one can say is that, on the basis of what is known of God, it would seem unlikely he would withhold a revelation of himself indefinitely from someone who truly persists in seeking him.

Which brings us to the second possible reason for lack of success: the appropriateness or otherwise of the attempt. In science we know that the result of an experiment depends critically on the experimental conditions being set just right. With an unsuccessful attempt to reach God, one cannot but question in similar vein whether the approach was made with a suitable set of mind, including a fitting degree of commitment and humility. As already pointed out, being engaged in a relationship with God means nothing less than total immersion in the religious way of life. Mere curiosity is not enough.

7. We have seen some of the difficulties that affect religious inquiry more deeply than science. There remains yet one further problem. Throughout this book we have tried to answer the question 'What exists?' through the setting up of appropriate explanatory frameworks. These assume the existence of a certain type of reality. More than that, they make the assumption that one can expound on that reality - it can be described in words. But are we right to assume that there is no other approach to reality other than through some means of articulating it?

Already we have come across hints that there might be aspects of reality that cannot be put into words and are thus not encompassed by *any* system of articulated explanation. We encountered problems, for example, in speaking of the world-in-itself and how it brought about the 'connectedness' of the two-electron system, and of God-in-himself and how he ensures the oneness of the three Divine Persons; we found difficulty in accounting for the greatness that marks a Beethoven symphony. In each case, the root of the problem appears to have something to do with synthesis - seeing things holistically.

This should not altogether surprise us. I can illustrate why by setting you a task: Describe whatever scene is before you at this present moment - but do it *holistically*, that is to say, give a description of it in terms other than those involving reference to the component parts of the scene. You might, for example, begin by pointing out the chair you are sitting on and the book you are reading. But this will not do; you have begun to break down the scene into component parts, the chair and the book. You are engaged in a process of differentiation; you have separated that which is the chair from that which is not the chair, that which is the book from that which is not the book; you have highlighted the distinction between book and chair, i.e. what they do not have in common. But the point of the exercise is the precise opposite of this. The aim is to put across the *unity* of the scene - what everything has in common. Certainly, having taken the picture before you apart, you can in your mind's eye reassemble the pieces to see how one part relates to and interacts with the others within the total scene. Even so, you are left with a picture that is understood in terms of component parts.

Any attempt to use language inevitably brings about a fragmentation of our conception of the world. We saw this whenever we came across the idea of reciprocal definition. For a concept to take on meaning it must be made clear not only what it refers to but also what it does not refer to. The concept of 'my mind' took on meaning at one and the same time as the concept of 'other minds'; the concept 'cup' required a distinction to be drawn between cups and other items of crockery. Thus we see that language is indissolubly wedded to a fragmentary form of explanation - the very antithesis of what is required when seeking a holistic view.

This limitation on rational articulation is likely to be especially severe when it comes to questions to do with God. One of the reasons for advocating a spiritual domain in the first place is in order to allow us to address questions of overall meaning and purpose - in other words, to look at life holistically.

The fact that something lies beyond words, however, does not mean it cannot be encountered and known some other way. To clarify this, it might be helpful at this point to introduce a convenient distinction that has come to be drawn between 'left-hemisphere thinking' and 'right-hemisphere thinking'. These terms arise from the fact that the human brain is constructed in two halves. When the connection between the two is surgically severed, the two halves operate in isolation from each other. In this state one can more readily determine the role played by each half. It is found that the left hemisphere is primarily concerned with verbal and mathematical thinking; it is logical, analytical, intellectual, and operates much like a digital computer in the way it manipulates sequences of discrete symbols. In contrast, the right hemisphere adopts a holistic approach; it synthesizes sensory data into continuous wholes rather than analyzes them into component parts. It deals with information in a parallel rather than a sequential fashion. It identifies patterns and allows one instantly to recognize a face, even though it might be difficult to describe in words exactly what it is about that face that distinguishes it from similar faces. It forms intuitive judgements about people and events. It is the seat of musical appreciation and is responsible for most of our emotional responses.

Neurological patients who have had the two halves of their brains disconnected behave, to some extent, like two persons, one associated with each half. Each tackles problems in quite distinct ways using markedly different strategies. Normally both types of thinking are employed, one overlaying the other. Just as earlier we speculated on the possibility of there being two types of conscious mental experience - one mapped to the activities of the physical body, the other to the interactions of the spirit - so here we find that even within the former category one might meaningfully speak of two forms of mental experience - one mapped to the left-hemisphere, the other to the right. (This, however, is not an analogy to be laboured: in the unsevered state of the brain there are physiological connections between the two halves of the brain, as well as some overlapping of functions.)

It is customary to emphasize the abilities associated with verbalized, numerate, and rational thought. It is therefore not surprising that the split-brain results were at first interpreted as showing that we possessed a 'major' and a 'minor' hemisphere, most of the thinking being done by the left half. However, more recent studies have revealed just how important are the non-verbal activities of the right hemisphere. Years of testing have demonstrated that the mute hemisphere has an inner conscious experience of much the same order as that of the articulate hemisphere. These days, therefore, one tends no longer to think in terms of an inherent dominance of left over right hemisphere; rather, the activities of each half are seen to have comparable significance.

For our purposes we have no need to quibble over the exact allocation of specific thought processes to one half of the brain or the other; that must be the object of continuing work by the scientists involved in this field. For us it is sufficient to recognize that these interesting experiments have highlighted two distinct modes of thought, and given us a short-hand way of referring to them: left- and right-hemisphere thinking. In making this distinction we cannot help but note that, for whatever reason, Western civilization, through the emphasis laid by society's educational system on skills of literacy, numeracy and scientific investigation, has come to focus its attention on the development of those activities we associate with the left hemisphere, to the neglect of the equally important abilities of the right.

A concentration on left-hemisphere thinking has been a hallmark of the approach adopted in this book. Throughout there has been an assumption that it is possible to do justice to our beliefs through rational discussion. But perhaps it is not. The reliance we in the West are prepared to place on this type of thinking is not to be found in certain other civilizations. Eastern thought has continued to recognize the importance of the mystical. It accepts and values those aspects of experience that cannot adequately be articulated. It recognizes that knowledge can be gained not only as the end link of a long serial chain of rational argument, but also by a process of infusion or absorption.

This is not to say that we in the West are totally bereft of this kind of thinking. We have, perhaps, an inkling of the same type of insight in the Biblical reference to the most intimate of human embraces as 'having knowledge of each other'. The early Christian church, in its formulation of the creeds, eschewed attempts to produce a simplified serially rational conception of God. Instead it came up with the doctrine of the Trinity as a framework within which discussion on the nature of God was to be conducted - a doctrine that forces simultaneously into the mind the ideas of God as revealed in his creation, as revealed in man through the Son of God, and as encountered in our own interior being through the Holy Spirit. Seeing these three Persons holistically as the one God is a mode of thought that normally rests uneasily with modern Western thinking. However, as we have seen, there are now parallels to be drawn from modern quantum physics, and from the Jungian school of psychology.

What I am saying is that left hemisphere articulation offers *explanation* - to the extent that explanation can be taken. The mute right hemisphere offers *appreciation* - a form of understanding that cannot be articulated, but can only be felt or sensed. Another way of putting it is to describe the former as knowledge of the intellect, the latter as knowledge of the heart; or again, the one as explicit, the other as tacit knowledge. Because of the especially close link between God and holistic questions to do with the ultimate significance of life and existence in general, appreciation rather than explanation is likely to play a more important part in religion than it does in science.

Not that I want to give the impression that your reading of this book has been a waste of time! Just as a book about music or art can be a gateway to the appreciation of a great symphony or painting, so in the religious context, left hemisphere rational explanation, such as that offered here, is to be thought of as the handmaid to right hemisphere appreciation of God. As I said in the context of our discussion of prayer, what matters most is not communication from God, but communion with him. Though it is only right and proper that our involvement with God should lead us to speak of him to the very limits that language will allow, we must be prepared to accept that there are ways to God that lie outside *any* explanatory framework.

Religious language is in some respects like poetry: it aims to evoke a state of mind, touching resonant chords deep down within the listener, opening up new perceptions of reality. The suggestion of such a comparison is not to be taken as a licence for sloppy thinking and the casual use of words. On the contrary, a poet will take infinite pains over the choice of words in order to capture the right nuance of meaning. A poem is a pointer to the truth, requiring the listener to complete the process of understanding by following the direction indicated. For the pointer to be helpful, it must be accurately aligned. The language of the spiritual explanatory framework points us in the direction of God, but the journey is one that must be completed by the whole person, not by the intellect alone. It is a journey that ends not so much in the acquisition of a solution to a rational problem, as in the offering of praise and thanksgiving through a life of sacrificial love inspired by the love of God in Christ.

CHAPTER 21

REVIEW

THIS is a chapter by chapter, section by section, summary of the argumentation of the book.

1. Introduction

The main aim has been to establish whether, in the light of scientific thought, it is possible to hold to a belief in God with intellectual integrity. The evidence for there being a spiritual dimension to human existence is examined in the light of how one might try to justify belief in the physical and mental aspects of existence

2. The Viewpoint of Classical Physics

But first we look at a claim to be able to disprove God's existence on scientific grounds. It is a view based on classical physics.

1. According to this type of physics, objects exist in a three-dimensional spatial arena, changing their positions with time. Space and time are treated separately. An explanatory framework is set up to account for the properties and behaviour of the objects. The concepts and laws that figure in the theory are assumed to stand in one-to-one relation with the properties and behaviour to which they refer. The picture presented is one in which all behaviour is determined by prior causes.

2. To gain the necessary information for setting up the explanatory framework, we must perform experiments. The effects of these interactions on the physical system, however, are negligible, so we can regard ourselves as detached observers. The laws as formulated apply to the behaviour of the world whether or not it is being observed.

3. *Composite objects are to be described in terms of their basic constituent parts and the forces between them. It is held that such descriptions provide a complete understanding of the object. The aim is to reduce the number of types of constituent particle and the number of different types of force to a minimum.*

4. *Scientific discussion is governed by rules. Firstly, it deals only with how-type questions, i.e. how things behave; it does not deal in why-type questions - those to do with purpose. Secondly it assumes that all occurrences within the world are open to description in accordance with physical law; it has no place for miracles. Thirdly, theories are valued for their simplicity in relation to the range of phenomena they set out to explain. In accordance with Ockham's Razor, it discounts the existence of any entity deemed unhelpful or unnecessary to such an understanding of physical occurrences.*

5. *The view so described can be called 'classical materialistic reductionism incorporating representative realism'. An extreme version of this holds that one day we shall know everything and, moreover, will at that time come to recognize that the world could not have been otherwise than it is.*

3. The Exclusion of God

What might be said of the existence of God on the basis provided above?

1. It might be argued that the very existence of the physical world needs to be accounted for; God is its Creator. But in the physical explanatory framework, the existence of the world is taken for granted; it is not a subject for discussion. In any case, postulating God as the source of the world only raises in its turn the question of where God comes from.

2. An alternative way of dispensing with God's creative role is through the suggestion that the universe is oscillating. Accordingly, it has no beginning and no end.

The Big Bang did not mark its start, merely the most recent of its Big Bounces.

3. Science does not admit of the need of an agency for holding the world in being. So the notion of God as the Sustainer of the universe is also unnecessary.

4. The argument for God's existence from biological Design was undermined by Darwin's Theory of Evolution by Natural Selection. A new version of the argument, this time based on the physical features of the universe and how these seemingly 'conspire' to create conditions conducive to the development of life, is intriguing. But it would be unwise to place too much store by it.

5. Arguments of the God-of-the-Gaps type fail to convince; science progressively closes the gaps in knowledge.

6. The idea of God revealing himself through miracles is pre-empted by one of the rules of scientific discussion.

7. The claim that one must postulate God in order to invest the existence of the world with meaning and purpose is likewise discounted by the rule that confines discussion to the how-type questions.

8. Uncritical acceptance of classical physical reality and the kinds of rules that normally govern scientific discourse - particularly the rule associated with Ockham's Razor - automatically leads to the conclusion that there is no God.

4. Towards the Modern Physical View

To see what is wrong with this kind of thinking, we begin by asking whether classical physics is competent at its prime task: the provision of a valid description of physical reality.

1. The natural language for expressing physics is mathematics. But there are different kinds of mathematics, each built on a different set of axioms. Empirical observation of the physical world dictates which mathematical assumptions are the appropriate ones. All mathematical structures have properties in common, however. So, regardless of which particular type of mathematics is involved, we can state that physical theory - any physical theory - will be subject to certain general constraints. In the first place, the choice of basic mathematical axioms (corresponding to the physical laws) cannot be justified from within the mathematical (or physical) structure itself. Secondly, Gödel's theorum places further restrictions upon what can be said from within the structure. Thus, the extreme view described earlier, that one day our understanding of the physical world will be complete and we shall then know that this is the only kind of world there could have been, is unsustainable.

2. Neither physical objects nor their properties are observed directly. Their existence can only be inferred from what is observed: spatial and temporal relationships. A fundamental particle, such as an electron, is the end-point of a cluster of relationships - an end-point that has no size or shape.

3. Not only do these relationships occur in space and time, they themselves define space and time. Objects and their properties, space and time - all are mutually dependent on each other. We call this 'reciprocal definition'. It applies to situations in which the meaningfulness of a term becomes clear only in the context of some other term simultaneously acquiring meaning.

4. On turning to relativity and quantum theory, we find the idea of relationships further developed with the integral involvement of the observer.

5. According to relativity theory, space and time are not to be thought of as separate; they form a single four-dimensional space-time continuum. A consequence of this is that different observers will assign different values of lengths and time intervals to the same events, the values depending on the speed of each observer relative to that which is observed. The observer thus enters into a relationship with whatever is being observed, and,

to some extent, helps determine what is found. But note this is not a signal to retreat into wholescale relativism; the observer has an input to make, but so does the observed.

6. Quantum physics shows that all physical entities have a wave and a particle nature. How can an electron, say, be both a wave and a particle? We cannot answer that type of question. Rather than speak of what an electron is, we must concentrate on its behaviour within the context of a particular kind of question. If we are asking about how the electron interacts, we use the particle concept; if we ask how it behaves between interactions, we must use the wave concept. The observer, by choosing the type of question to be asked, again affects the answer.

7. The waves involved are probability waves. They introduce an element of uncertainty, such that one cannot simultaneously measure both the precise position and precise velocity of an electron. A consequence of this is that one is able to predict only the probabilities of various possible outcomes of an interaction. The physical world is not strictly speaking, deterministic.

8. For the reasons given above, classical physics is exposed as an inadequate forum for the discussion of fundamental questions to do with physical reality.

5. What of the Physical World-in-itself?

Quantum physics deals solely in interactions-with-the-world, not with a world that exists independently of interactions. Can we be sure that the physical world-in-itself actually does exist?

1. Intuitively we feel the physical world must exist independently of us, but how come we have this intuition?

2. We are taught classical physics at school and are able to verify that it works well in the description of the physical environment with which we are familiar - that of macro-sized objects. This is one reason why the classical approach strikes us as 'natural'.

3. We do our thinking with a brain that has been fashioned in response to evolutionary pressures concerned with survival. What has emerged is a machine adequate for solving pragmatic problems involving macro-sized objects; it does not follow that its analogical approach is also suited for doing philosophy.

4. The structure of the language we use - which was developed within the same ethos as gave rise to classical physics - helps influence and structure the way we think.

5. These causes of the intuition that there is a world-in-itself are all spurious; the intuition is not to be trusted.

6. The reason why some physicists believe there is no world-in-itself is that we only ever deal in interactions-with-the-world. On trying to 'look through' the interactions to see what we might be interacting with, we get bogged down in paradoxes. These difficulties suggest that the very conception of a world-in-itself is meaningless. Through quantum theory, we have come to recognize that all our familiar scientific concepts apply to the description of interactions, not, as was originally thought, to the world itself. As such they have no validity outside the context of interactions; it is a misuse of language to try and apply them to what might exist in between interactions. Precise position and precise velocity cannot be measured simultaneously because they do not exist simultaneously. The postulate of a world-in-itself adds nothing to our understanding, so by Ockham's Razor it should be eliminated. In other words, the weapon that earlier got rid of God, has now removed the physical world.

7. A somewhat less radical view holds that the world-in-itself does exist, contributing to the interactions those aspects that cannot be accounted for in terms of one's own input (the so-called otherness of the interaction). However, there is nothing meaningful that can be said about it.

8. Finally, there is the view that not only is there a world-in-itself, but the task of science remains what we

always thought it was, namely, to describe it. Some believe moreover that such a description, when finally accomplished, will reinstate strict determinism.

9. My own position is that there is a problem in accepting the existence of interactions and nothing else. Quantum interactions occur instantaneously. If nothing at all exists between these events, how is the information on the previous interaction stored ready to be incorporated, if needed, into a subsequent interaction? A postulated world-in-itself could act as such a store. Granted there were such a world-in-itself, would there be anything one could say about it? Clearly there are obstacles to a comprehensive description. But likewise there is a problem if absolutely nothing can be said about it. In this latter case, it can be argued that the term 'world-in-itself' has no meaning. It appears, in fact, that we can make a few statements about the world-in-itself, albeit of a very general nature only. Perhaps we should be content with such generalizations.

10. The question of whether the world-in-itself exists or not, and if it does, what one might be able to say about it, has divided scientific opinion. This is not to say that all views are to be thought of as equally 'true'. It is accepted that there must be an objectively correct view, the others being wrong. This is not altered by the fact that we may never know which is which. Again, there is no retreat into subjectivity.

6. The Inadequacy of Nothing But...

Next, we turn to the element of reductionism. Is a description in terms of component parts the only type of understanding one should seek?

1. Reductionism describes a human being in terms of the structure and behaviour of the human body - a physical object essentially no different from any other object, inanimate or otherwise. Clearly, it is important to decide how comprehensive such a description might be.

2. *Examples of the inadequacies of reductionism come easily to mind, provided one is prepared to lift the arbitrarily imposed ban on why-type questions concerned with purpose.*

3. *Quite apart from this, quantum theory has shown that two isolated electrons with no force connecting them, can under certain circumstances behave as a single system. Accordingly, an interaction with one of these electrons constitutes an interaction with both. There is a wholeness to the system that cannot be accounted for in terms of component parts and whatever forces there might be between them.*

4. *Thus, reductionism has its problems within science, let alone elsewhere.*

7. The Exclusion of the Mental

Suppose one takes on board all that has been said about modern physics, and adopts a suitably non-reductionist outlook, can one still maintain that a discussion in purely physical, materialistic terms is an adequate forum in which to examine all that exists?

1. No. A discussion on these lines cannot embrace mental experiences.

2. It is impossible to decide from the physical behaviour of objects such as computerized robots, animals, or even human bodies, whether they are associated with conscious minds. In the case of human beings, one can only infer the existence of other minds - this being done primarily by analogy with the way one knows one's own mind to be associated with a body. But this is not a deductive proof.

3. The suggestion has been made that one day it will be possible to show that consciousness arises as a necessary consequence of physics at a certain level of complexity in the brain - an emergent property similar to other emergent properties such as 'liquid', 'temperature', 'life', etc. But this claim is unfounded. Although mental experience and brain function are correlated, knowledge of this can be incorporated into the discussion only through injecting information about the mental as an empirical fact originating from outside physics. Emergent properties, properly understood, are themselves always describable in physical terms; mental experience is not.

4. It does not help to suppose that the mind can make its presence felt by interrupting the normal flow of physical events occurring in the brain - by an act of the will, for example. The description of such anomalous physical events says nothing about the experience of pain, emotions, etc.

5. From the point of view of physics, the postulate of consciousness is unnecessary; by the rules of the game, therefore, Ockham's Razor gets rid of it. This is obviously absurd. Unnecessary though consciousness might be for the description of physical reality, it nevertheless does exist. Ockham's Razor may have its value in curbing the number of hypotheses used in the description of physical reality, but it is not qualified to pronounce on the existence or otherwise of non-physical types of reality.

6. So concludes our critique of the attempt to explain everything in terms of physics alone.

8. Explanatory Frameworks

We now turn to our main task of seeing how belief in God and other realities might be justified.

1. The aim is to address questions concerning existence, as they might be raised by a sceptic. The chosen starting point is a given basis of mental experience. Though it is problematic whether such a basis is truly free from hidden assumptions about other realities, it is a position we concede for the sake of argument. Our discussion therefore shifts from the physical to the mental explanatory framework. Before proceeding, however, we need to be clear about the nature of such frameworks.

2. An explanatory framework presupposes a certain general type of reality the ontological nature of which is not a subject for discussion. The existence of such a re-

ality can be inferred only from outside the framework in question. The framework is made up of concepts and procedures for handling those concepts which, taken together, describe the detailed nature of that reality and what goes on in it. Also incorporated are rules governing the discussion and assumptions about the kinds of question to be answered.

3. We are about to introduce a mental explanatory framework to deal with conscious mental experiences. But are we quite sure that the physical and mental are different realities and so call for separate frameworks?

4. For instance, what about the insistence in relativity and quantum theory that the observer be drawn into a relationship with that which is observed? This appears to mix conscious beings with physical objects. The term 'observer' in this context, however, does not refer to a conscious being; rather, it is a way of referring to a particular set of apparatus by which measurements are recorded. The relationships are purely physical ones.

5. A second reason for being unsure of the separation of the physical from the mental is that both physical and mental events are spoken of as taking place in time. Do they not, therefore, have this in common? No. Two different types of time are involved. Physical time is integrally bound up with space; mental time is not. All of physical time exists at each instant of mental time; the special instant 'now' separating the 'future' which is yet to be from the 'past' that is no more, is a feature only of mental time. The 'flow' of time comes from the comparison of one type of time with the other. Although mental and physical times are distinct from each other, there is, nevertheless, a close correlation between them. It is for this reason that they are both (rather confusingly) called 'time'.

6. The third reason arises from the fact that at no time do we specify the ontological nature or 'stuff' of which the physical and mental realities consist. This objection to the dual-reality hypothesis, unlike the other two, cannot

be dismissed. A single reality would account for the correlations that are sometimes seen to occur between physical and mental occurrences. However, it gives no indication of why that reality has two such different and mutually exclusive manifestations. The problem of whether the physical and mental frameworks each have their own separate reality, or alternatively are to be regarded as complementary ways of looking at a common reality, cannot be resolved. In a sense this does not matter. What is important is not that there are two realities, but that there is a need for two explanatory frameworks.

9. Inferring the Physical from the Mental

Starting from the acceptance of there being a conscious mental reality, can one establish the existence of other types of reality? We begin by trying to establish the existence of the physical domain.

1. What exactly is the reality base assumed by the mental explanatory framework? Conscious mental experiences incorporating the active participation of the ego (the centre of consciousness). That and nothing else. Whether there are entities like raw sensations and memories, capable of an existence independent of their involvement in an experience, is problematic. Indeed, the modern theory of the mind has come to look very like the quantum view of the physical domain: the emphasis is on a relational, interactional type of existence. Arguments for the existence of a further reality domain consisting of the mind-in-itself closely parallel those made earlier in respect of there being a world-in-itself.

2. Knowledge of the physical domain enters consciousness through sensory observation. Does that mean the physical domain must exist as the necessary cause of those observations? No. The nature of the causal links within the physical domain beween like physical entities is not understood, much less how one type of reality (physical) could affect another (mental).

3. Do we have knowledge of the physical domain independently of the use of our senses? If so, this might open up the possibility of proving the existence of the physical in some other way. For example, are we not born with a prior understanding of physical space? Relativity theory shows this not to be the case.

4. Likewise, a priori information about the physical world is not to be had through mathematics or logic.

5. Information inherited through our gene make-up, though not gained through our own senses, is nevertheless dependent on the senses through the way it is selected out from the interactions of our ancestors with their environment.

6. We conclude that there is no deductive proof as such of the physical domain, only a reasonable inference based on induction. By 'reasonable' we mean that the belief satisfies a number of criteria: it makes use of rationality as far as the nature of the problem allows, it does not ignore contra-indications, it is adjudged the most plausible of the various alternatives. Inductive arguments are not to be undervalued; they, and not deductive arguments, are the ones we have to deal with in most situations.

7. When, from arguments based on what one finds in one reality domain, one tries to establish the existence of some other reality domain, the best one can hope for is a reasonable inference. The inference that there is a physical domain is based on the otherness of sensory observation - that aspect not attributable to one's own input. Successive observations are, by their nature discontinuous. The postulate of a physical reality helps to account not only for the contingent nature of observations (their ability to surprise us), but also for the consistency of successive observations (the law-like character of their variations), and the concurrence of input from different senses.

8. In short, it is the perceived explanatory power of the hypothesis in accounting for the otherness of sensory observation that leads us to make the inference. By 'explanatory power' we mean the hypothesis allows predictions to be made on the basis of some coherent theoretical model; the model is economic in the number of concepts and principles used (always bearing in mind the range of phenomena being explained); also to be taken into account is an affective response we have to the proposed theory.

9. Finally, let me reiterate: What we have described is how we might justify the belief in the physical; it does not account for how we in practice come to acquire that belief in the first place.

10. Relating the Mental and the Physical

Having inferred that there is a physical reality beyond sensory observation, what is the relationship between the mental and physical domains?

1. We use the idea of a mapping. Certain entities in one domain correlate, or map, to certain entities of the other. Relationships that apply between entities belonging to the same domain, are reflected in relationships between entities belonging to the second domain. The two domains exist on an equal footing, to the extent that what happens in one domain, though correlated to what happens in the other, is not to be regarded as the cause or the effect of the other. The mapping link is neutral in this respect. In speaking of the entities that make up the mental or physical domains, we refer to the total state of the mind or body as it is at different times, rather than their component parts at some particular time.

2. A TV quiz game provides a useful illustration of this mapping concept, with its two domains: point scores and their corresponding prizes. Likening the point scores to physical events and the prizes to mental events we see an analogy. Point scores and prizes each follow a rationale of their own, just as physical and mental events follow their separate rationales.

3. However, to some degree, what happens to the prizes can be understood only by referring to what is happening

to the point scores. *The accumulation of points, on the other hand, can be fully understood solely in terms of the rules of the game. This asymmetric relation between the two domains is similar to that which is held by many to apply to the mental and physical - what we call the asymmetric view of the relationship. Thus, in order to explain certain mental experiences one must defer to the physical explanatory framework, whereas it is never necessary to defer to the mental framework in order to explain physical phenomena.*

4. It has yet to be proved that this view is correct. The alternative, the symmetric view, maintains that the explanation of the physical sometimes does need to defer to the mental framework; this would be particularly the case over the explanation of processes occurring in the human brain accompanying mental experiences to do with decision-taking.

5. Either of these views can be accounted a reasonable one.

6. But filling explanatory gaps is only one reason for switching frameworks. A second is that we might wish to ask a different type of question - one that the original framework is not designed to handle. Even under the asymmetric view of the relationship, where there are no gaps in understanding the physical, one would still need to defer to the mental framework if the question is one to do with motivation and purpose.

7. Finally, we turn to the question of free will. According to the symmetric view, the description of physical reality is contingent on acts of the will. But relativity theory disposes of an open, undecided future - the results of future acts of the will are, in some sense, already incorporated into space-time. Something of the traditional idea of free will has, therefore, been lost. But the greater threat to free will appears to be posed by the asymmetric view founded on physical determinism. Determinism at the physical level implies, through the mapping, determinism at the mental level. What then is left of free will? To answer this, we note that there is not one, but three ways of interpreting how a physical system evolves from its present state to a later one. Corresponding to these, there are psychological counterparts which cover such aspects as: (i) an act of the will being a natural outgrowth from one's present state of mind, and hence an authentic expression of one's character as it is manifested in that state; (ii) the act being in the pursuit of goals; (iii) the path taken through life being governed by certain holistic, overarching principles. It can be argued that these, considered together, cover the essentials of free will. What is missing is freedom to act against one's will. That type of freedom, however, is meaningless. Also lost, as already stated, is the openness of the future. But there is nothing new in this; it has always been recognized that predestination and God's foreknowledge must involve an element of fixity for the future.

11. Other Minds and the Concept of Oneself

Having seen what is involved in trying to infer, from conscious experiences, the existence of a physical reality, we now turn to a different reality: other minds.

1. Discounting a possible telepathic link, the only way of establishing that there are minds other than my own is through the senses and what they tell me about the physical domain. In the physical domain there is an object that appears closely related to conscious experience: 'my' body. There are further bodies similar to this one. When these are acted upon, there is no direct mental experience - and yet it is reported that experiences are taking place. Credence is given to the idea that there are clusters of mental experiences associated with those bodies in the same way as the experiences of direct awareness are associated with my body, ie. there is more than one centre of consciousness. The argument relies on analogy; it does not amount to a deductive proof. But the inference is a reasonable one.

2. The postulate of other minds explains a second kind of otherness: how one comes into possession of informa-

tion about mental events - information that can be checked out by subsequent experience. Together with a principle of equality - which holds that, all other things being equal, there is no reason why my body alone among bodies should be uniquely associated with a mind - the evidence for other minds combines to be as strong as it could be, given the nature of the problem.

3. Though this is how one might argue for the existence of other minds, it must not be confused with the way we in practice come to form that opinion. Past interactions between our ancestors are likely to have left us with a genetic make-up that orients us from birth to expect other minds.

4. Other minds are mediated to us through the physical domain. They are inferred to lie beyond the physical. But the existence of the physical domain is itself an inference. The postulate of other minds, however, is not to be thought of for that reason as being doubly risky. Unlike the physical, other minds belong to a type of reality essentially no different to that from which we start out - our own mind.

5. Our knowledge of other minds depends on the physical, but so also does our understanding of the physical depend in large measure on the acceptance of there being other minds.

6. Acceptance of the existence of other minds is integral to the formation of the concept of oneself - another case of reciprocal definition. Personhood is to be thought of as transcending the mental and physical domains, but having a representation in both.

7. Finally, we note that we learn from others certain things about ourself that could not otherwise be known, for example, the finite span of life.

12. The Inner Religious Experience

Here we begin to explore the grounds for inferring the existence of a spiritual reality.

1. We shall take a religious experience to be any experience that implies a supernatural connection.

2. The inner religious experience is the awareness of being in the Presence of God. The numinous is perceived as a reality other than oneself, but one for which one has the closest possible bond. It has an awesome quality, but also an attractive, loving nature; it has both personal and impersonal aspects. It is the source of all that exists and the underlying principle uniting all people and all things.

3. In addition to mystical experiences, there are forms of prayer conducted at a more down-to-earth, practical level. In particular, petitionary prayer is to be seen as an expression of creaturely dependence.

4. Being made in his image, to learn of God is to learn of one's own potential. Conscience can be a channel through which God makes us aware of our failure to live up to that potential.

5. Is the otherness of the inner religious experience truly indicative of a spiritual domain? Before attempting to answer that, let us look at other indications of God's existence.

13. Other Experiences of the Numinous

In addition to the inner religious experience, God appears to mediate his Presence to us through nature, history, and other people.

1. The fact that the world exists at all, that it is intelligible, and that its nature is consonant with the type of God perceived through the inner religious experience, are inferential arguments in favour of God's existence.

2. The numinous can be discerned in other people - in the case of those who lived in the past, through accounts of their lives and teachings as set down in holy writings.

3. God's nature is revealed through history - through the overall pattern of human history, as well as that of one's own individual life.

4. *This is not to say that everything fits easily and naturally into this picture - there remains the problem of evil and suffering. There is no simple answer to why an all-powerful and loving God permits them, but we can at least glimpse a possible underlying rationale: In order that the positive virtue of love should take on meaning, there is a certain logical necessity to there also being its opposite, evil. A requirement of love is that it be freely offered - but such freedom can be abused, so giving rise to evil. In order to have free will, we must operate in a reliable, consistent environment, such that to initiate a certain action will lead to a predictable outcome. The same consistent operation of the laws of nature is liable sometimes to lead to consequences associated with suffering. Finally, one should note that suffering is not to be thought of wholly in negative terms. Without the opportunities it affords, love would find it virtually impossible to give expression to itself.*

5. *The various indications of God's Presence in the world provide a coherent pattern of revelation that is consonant with, and confirms that which comes from the inner religious experience. Together they invite a belief in God.*

14. The Otherness of Religious Experience

But what are the reasons for thinking that the inner religious experience is anything more than a subjective psychological condition?

1. *Certainly the experience 'works' at the subjective level; it confers positive benefits on those who have it. But we are now interested in looking beyond the experience itself.*

2. *The experience is likely to be attended by the emotions, and emotions are generally mistrusted as being subjective. Emotions, however, are normally evoked as a response to some external stimulus; to this extent they point to that which is objective.*

3. *The experience yields knowledge and wisdom, the value of which can be attested through putting it into practice. In order to account for how one comes into possession of such knowledge, an external source is postulated.*

4. *The knowledge is acquired only in the context of having a relationship with God - one that involves both a subjective and an objective element. In distinguishing the commonly perceived objectivity attributable to God from the differing subjective inputs of individuals, a consensus view is sought within a community of believers.*

5. *The reality of God, as an existence beyond and distinct from humankind's God-worship activities, stands or falls on this perceived otherness of the religious experience. In religion as with physics, we are unavoidably drawn into a relationship with that which is observed. What rescues such situations from total subjectivity, is the recognition of those features of the relationship that are not explicable in terms of one's own input.*

6. *In physics, however, there is universal consensus over the nature of the otherness of scientific experiments. Given the variety of world religions, can the same be said of the otherness indicative of God? Though the situation is ambiguous, the claim that the similarities between the religions outweigh their differences is certainly one that can be defended.*

15. Religion and the Unconscious

Given that there is a commonly perceived otherness to religious experience demanding an explanation in terms of a reality other than that of conscious mental experiences, could not that other reality be the unconscious mind rather than God?

1. The unconscious is a postulate inferred on the basis of its power to account for otherwise inexplicable features of conscious experience - the otherness of dreams and hallucinations, for example. We must enquire whether the unconscious could be the source of the otherness of religious experience as well.

2. To decide this we need to know what is in the unconscious. Freud suggested the mind had a structure consisting of the ego, the id (an instinctual drive), and the superego (a system of values and attitudes absorbed from society). The id and superego come into conflict, and as a result, shameful and disagreeable thoughts are repressed into the unconscious. These later manifest themselves as neurotic behaviour. Specifically in regard to religion, Freud described God as a projected father-figure, created by wish-fulfillment in response to a perceived need to prolong into adulthood the sense of being protected.

3. For a variety of reasons, Freud's atheistic pronouncements on religion are today largely rejected. Nevertheless, his work continues to provide useful insight into the way religious conceptions can be coloured by psychological factors.

4. Jung expanded our understanding of the contents of the unconscious by drawing attention to the collective unconscious, a set of predispositions we all possess and which are present from birth. The collective unconscious helps to shape our perception of later experiences. It is described in terms of a cluster of archetypes, each of which is concerned with a particular type of recurring human situation. Some at least of the archetypes can be regarded as the psychological correlates of genetically determined behaviour evident in the biological context. The latter come about through evolution by natural selection, and so are primarily characterized by having survival value for the individual or for close relatives sharing the same genetic material. Some archetypes have this characteristic, others appear not to. The latter might require an explanation outside biology.

5. An archetype of especial significance is known as the self. It is central to the psyche, embracing both the conscious and unconscious. The process of psychic growth, called individuation, is one that culminates in the ego coming to accept that the individual's true nature is to be aligned, not with itself (the centre of consciousness), but with the self (the centre of the totality of consciousness and unconsciousness). In coming to terms with the self, the ego is ultimately confronted with that which is unfathomable. This encounter is indistinguishable from the inner religious experience. The process of self-realization, therefore, becomes one with the religious quest; each ends with the simultaneous discovery of both one's inner being and the otherness indicative of God. Again a case of reciprocal definition - the recognition of that which is not us being, at one and the same time, the recognition of a new dimension of one's own personhood. The self, therefore, is an archetype that motivates and controls man's religious behaviour. This is so whether that behaviour is in overt acknowledgment of a relationship with God, or is diverted into some alternative activity pursued with 'religious' commitment.

6. Could the religious archetype be nothing more than a spurious phenomenon thrown up by the process of evolution by natural selection? This proposal does not hold up. The altruistic behaviour to which religion leads is prejudicial rather than helpful to survival. Though sociobiology has had some success in explaining certain forms of altruism, it has not been able to account for altruism in its true and widest sense.

7. We conclude that the unconscious, though playing an important role in the conduct of the religious life, is not to be seen as the ultimate source of the religious experience.

16. The Spiritual Interaction Framework

We turn now to the postulate of a spiritual domain.

1. The first reason for making this proposal is that it helps to explain a feature of conscious experience that cannot otherwise be easily explained: the otherness of the inner religious experience.

2. *Secondly, it fulfills an integrative function. It explains why the same numinous quality is manifest in many ways, not just in the inner religious experience; it allows one to address questions concerned with the overall purpose and meaning of life.*

3. As with the existence of other types of reality - the physical, other minds, and the unconscious - that of the spiritual domain has to be inferred; it cannot be deductively proved. The justification for the inference must rest on its perceived explanatory value.

4. What are the contents of this spiritual domain? Taking our cue from what we found in the physical and mental domains, we begin by assuming that religious experiences map to a domain of spiritual interactions-with-God. Each of us is represented in that domain as a spirit, defined as being the common endpoint of a cluster of interactions-with-God. God likewise lies at the other end of those interactions.

5. The concept of personhood has now been expanded to include representations not only in the physical and mental domains, but also in the spiritual interaction domain. The spiritual domain opens up a further way in which we, as persons, may interact with each other.

6. The idea of relatedness is taken a step further through the Christian doctrine of the Trinity. This holds that God consists of three Persons: Father, Son, and Holy Spirit. Though these Persons are to be thought of as distinct from each other, they do not constitute individual centres of consciousness; the whole of God is to be found in each, and no Person acts in isolation from the other two. Despite there being three Persons, God remains One. This is a difficult conception, requiring the acceptance of a different kind of 'rational explanation'. But this type of explanation now has its parallel in modern physics. The significance of the Trinitarian conception for the way we view the contents of the spiritual interaction domain, is that our interactions-with-God do not converge on a single endpoint representing God. Rather, one needs to think in terms of our interactions-with-God converging on three separate endpoints, one for each Person (the economic Trinity), the Persons in turn being connected by interactions amongst themselves (the immanent Trinity). A consequence of this is that although God has but a relational existence in this domain, his existence is not contingent on our being there to provide him with something to relate to. He can exist independently of us by virtue of the interactions within the Godhead itself. In contrast, we being the endpoint of interactions with him, do not have an independent existence - hence the sense of creaturely dependence on him.

7. God cannot grant us free will without raising the possibility of our rejecting him. When we do this we relate to that which is not God - the Devil. The Devil derives his relational existence through our willingness to relate to him.

8. Previously we saw that time in the mental explanatory framework is not the same as the time referred to in the physical framework. What of time as it is applied to the spiritual? It appears to have much in common with physical time, at least in respect of it all being in existence at each instant of mental time. Essentially God's creating and sustaining roles are merged.

17. What of God-in-Himself?

Is there any point in postulating a second spiritual domain consisting of God-in-himself?

1. We have postulated a spiritual domain of interactions-with-God, analogous to the physical domain of interactions-with-the-world. Whether one should infer a further spiritual domain containing God-in-himself, analogous to a physical world-in-itself, depends on the perceived explanatory power of the hypothesis.

2. Religions that regard God as a simple unitary being must postulate this additional spiritual domain, otherwise God, having only the relational kind of existence characteristic of the spiritual interaction domain, be-

comes dependent on us for his existence. Although for Christianity God's independent existence is already guaranteed, there remains value in making the further inference. This is because it provides the most natural way of ensuring the oneness of God. The three Persons in the spiritual interaction domain map to the same unitary God-in-himself in the second spiritual reality domain. The situation is analogous to that of the two-electron system we considered earlier.

3. Our spirits are not to be thought of as mapping to spirits-in-themselves in this second domain. Rather, we are invited to map to God-in-himself. The Devil has no representation in this second domain, his ontological status being fundamentally different to that of God.

4. Granted that it does make sense to think of there being a God-in-himself, what if anything can be said about him? All knowledge of God comes through our interactions with him, and the concepts we use are all devised in the context of explaining interactions. Are we not, therefore, misusing the language if we apply them to God himself? Here we face the same difficulty as was encountered in the study of modern physics. Just as some physicists say that nothing meaningful can be said about a world-in-itself, so there have been theologians who have long held that it is intrinsically impossible to speak of God-in-himself. Again the problem is not only the universal one of making statements about the metaphysical nature or 'stuff' of an existent entity, but more importantly whether one can say anything at all about it. It appears that there are, in fact, certain generalized statements that can be made - those to do with God's qualities of love, justice, oneness, etc.

5. In summary, we conclude that various standpoints regarding the existence and knowability of God-in-himself can be accounted reasonable - which is not to say they are all equally valid.

6. A final word of warning. In asking whether God exists we must realize that such a question is unique; it is not asked in the same sense as we ask whether things, or even whole types of reality, exist. God is to be thought of as the very source of all existence rather than one existent entity among others.

18. Relating the Spiritual to Other Frameworks

We now need to look more closely at the way the spiritual domain relates to other types of reality.

1. First, we must realize that the spiritual, physical and mental explanatory frameworks might be three complementary ways of addressing a single common reality, each framework concerned with different questions. It is the need for three frameworks, not three realities, that has to be stressed.

2. The otherness of the inner religious experience is to be explained, not by having spiritual realities intruding into the domain of conscious mental entities, but by deferring from the mental explanatory framework to the spiritual framework, making use of the mappings between the domains.

3. Not only do we defer to the spiritual framework to account for the otherness of the religious experience, but the reverse is probably also true: there is a need for the spiritual explanatory framework to defer to those associated with the mental and physical domains.

4. The whole of physical and of spiritual time is to be thought of as being in existence at all instants of mental time - both those mental instants contained within the span of our earthly lives and those extrapolated beyond our death. In that our personhood has its representation in those domains, we have, therefore, an eternal existence. But is it one that we shall be consciously aware of beyond physical death? Only if there is a form of consciousness specifically mapped to our spiritual rather than physical functioning. There is no reason why this should not be. This second type of consciousness could come into existence and overlay the other during the

course of our earthly life, and then remain after the cessation of the physically related consciousness.

5. Turning to the relationship of the spiritual to the physical, we first take the line that miracles are possible. By miracles we mean occasions where one has to defer to the spiritual framework in order to explain what has happened physically. We can regard this as coming about either through God interacting in the spiritual domain with some kind of spiritual representation of the physical world, or through God mapping directly to the physical world in the physical domain.

6. Is there anything in science that says miracles cannot happen? No. The most it can do is to indicate that they are likely to be less common than would be supposed from a literal interpretation of the Bible, a view which many Biblical scholars share.

7. Physical laws are arranged in a hierarchy of explanatory frameworks, the higher the framework the broader its field of application. Events that can be understood only by relativity or quantum theory are not spoken of as 'violations' of classical physics; rather we regard them as lying outside the competence of classical physics. In the same way, we can envisage even the most powerful physical law as having but limited applicability, it being subsumed under an all-embracing law, such as the law of love. A miracle, while being unaccountable in terms of physical law, might then appear perfectly law-like as far as the higher law is concerned.

8. The acceptance of miracles means there need be no problem over what happens in the physical brain when receiving an input from God during prayer. If to each mental experience there has to be a corresponding action in the brain, the religious experience can be accommodated by a small-scale miracle in the brain. Likewise God can ensure by miracles that the gene representing the religious archetype, once formed, is preserved despite its lack of survival value.

9. *But suppose miracles never occur. Under these conditions can God make his presence known? Yes, in the same way as other minds are able to make their presence known to to our mind through the normal operation of human bodies and other physical intermediaries, so God can disclose himself to our spiritual natures through the same normal physical channels.*

10. According to this non-miraculous view, the otherness of the inner religious experience must derive from the unconscious. The unconscious distills from past experiences the essence of God as he has revealed himself through the physical. This distillation is then offered up to the conscious mind, it being perceived there as the Presence of God. Can such an origin for the inner religious experience, rooted as it is in past events, do justice to those aspects of prayer concerned with the future? Yes - if we recall the timeless nature of God and of his will for us.

11. How are we to explain, non-miraculously, the preservation of the religious archetype, given its lack of survival value in the context of evolution by natural selection? One suggestion is that its biological encoding has a different form to that of other types of innate behaviour. It could be associated, for example, with the overall helical structure of the DNA molecule, and hence be universally present.

12. How are Christians to understand the unique status of Jesus? Not as a spiritual being invading the physical, but in terms of mapping. Whereas we ordinary human beings map to the spiritual interaction domain as individual spirits lying outside the Godhead, Jesus the man, maps to the Son of God. Through this unique mapping to one of the Persons of the Trinity, Jesus alone has the authority to reveal God's concerned love for us, his intimate involvement in the particularity of human life, his sharing in our suffering, and his forgiveness of our sin.

13. We conclude that both the miraculous and non-miraculous views of the relationship between the spiri-

tual and physical frameworks can be accounted reasonable. Though God does not need miracles to make himself known to us, being all-powerful, there is no reason why he should not use such means if he so chooses.

19. Theology as Science

We have seen various ways in which science and theology shed light on each other. Just how similar are these endeavours?

1. In both science and theology, one tries to discern patterns of intelligibility lying behind what at first seems a bewildering array of contingent events. In approaching the data one already has preconceptions in mind - a theoretical framework to give direction to the investigation, and through which the data are organized. The theory is often able successfully to anticipate the intelligibility being sought. But in both enterprises, the final verdict is that of empirical test.

2. The adopted theoretical model can help shape what is found, or thought to be found. It can be difficult disentangling one's own input from that which genuinely originates with the other. But there is no avoidance of a model of some kind. The best one can do is to try and anticipate the type of bias to which it is likely to lead.

3. The fact that scientific theories are sometimes modified or abandoned in the light of experimental findings, led some to put forward the 'verification principle' as a means of determining whether a statement was meaningful. It was held that only scientific statements passed this test. This has since been replaced by the 'falsifiability principle' as a means of determining whether a statement is to be accounted a scientific one. But this too has come in for criticism, scientists having shown themselves reluctant to abandon certain of their laws even in the face of apparently contradictory evidence.

This is similar to what happens in theology. Despite the existence of evil, religious believers are not prepared to abandon the notion of an all-good, all-powerful God. They maintain that this way of understanding God has such great explanatory power in other respects, it is not to be laid aside lightly. This is not to conclude that the statement of God's perfect goodness is unfalsifiable; one can imagine worlds of such a nature that the idea of God's goodness would be universally regarded as untenable. It happens our world is not like that.

4. Both science and theology are social activities. The individual influences, and in turn is influenced by, the community of colleagues. The community acts as the repository for accumulated wisdom and knowledge and defines the orthodox standpoint.

5. Science progresses; today's theories are generally an improvement on those of the past. Theology to some extent anchors itself to the wisdom revealed in former times, but it too is constantly reworked according to contemporary thought-forms, and to some extent might be seen as progressing under the on-going guidance of the Holy Spirit.

6. In both theology and modern physics, we are inescapably drawn into a relationship with that which is under study; we help create the spiritual and physical interactions upon which knowledge of God and of the world depends. In both cases, the slide into subjectivity is halted by the otherness of those interactions.

7. At the frontiers of knowledge in science and theology it is not a matter of generating a new language in order to deal with new situations. It is more a case of taking familiar concepts from everyday life and using them in unconventional and seemingly paradoxical ways.

8. In comparing the confidence with which one can make statements in science and in theology it is important to compare like with like. This means comparing the confident handling of scientific interactions with the equally confident statements that can be made about the phenomenology of religious experience; it means comparing the less sure statements that can be made about

God himself, with the equally tentative statements that can be made about the world-in-itself.

9. The above considerations serve to demonstrate that, to some degree, theology can be regarded as a science.

20. Theology beyond Science

In certain other respects theology and science retain their distinctiveness.

1. Science deals in interactions with an impersonal It. Theology deals with a You. To shape the environment, science needs go no further than an understanding of interactions. To shape ourselves in conformity to God's will for us, theology must try to understand God himself. It is therefore more often forced into the less secure realms of understanding.

2. For this reason, theology cannot hope to encapsulate the truth as is the aim of scientific discussion. It eventually comes up against the mystery of God.

3. There is a problem speaking of an important aspect of the raw data upon which theological reflection is based: the inner religious experience. Unlike the results of scientific experiment, this experience is not publicly accessible. Without personal acquaintance with it on both sides, it is difficult for dialogue to take place.

4. This is not a problem with those features of nature, history, and holy people that religious believers regard as indicative of the numinous. These are readily accessible to all - but not all discern the alleged numinous quality. Such discernment requires a holistic synthesis of the data, and this is not a perception shared by everyone.

5. These considerations point to the need to be personally involved in religious experience. To make sense of the spiritual explanatory framework, one must become immersed in the life that attends the use of that language.

6. What of those who make the attempt but do not find God? God reveals himself to whom he chooses. Granted

he would not withhold himself from those who earnestly desire him, one must question the appropriateness of the approach adopted. Knowing God is at the same time to know oneself and what God requires of us. What God requires is total surrender to his will - a price some are not prepared to pay.

7. Spiritual matters are concerned with the whole pattern and purpose of existence. But articulated explanation is always in terms of fragmented components. An additional form of understanding is required - a holistic one based not so much on explanation as appreciation. This kind of thinking is that associated with the right-hemisphere of the brain. Western civilization has become preoccupied with rationalistic, scientific thought characteristic of the left-hemisphere. The balance needs to be redressed in favour of the complementary, more holistic approach. The religious journey needs to be undertaken not by the intellect alone, but by the whole person.

INDEX

action, principle of least, 150-151
Adler, A., 149
altruism, 218-222
angels, 229, 243-244
appreciation, 313-314, 320, 322-323
archetypes (see self and religious archetype), 119, 210-217, 241, 276, 285-288
Argument from Design, 17-20, 176
arguments
  based on analogy, 161
  based on deductive proof, 61, 120, 122, 159, 188, 196, 199, 228, 249
  based on induction or inference, 61, 121-122, 124, 160-162, 188, 200, 228, 248-249, 278, 284
  asymmetric view of relation between the mental and physical (see determinism), 135-140, 142, 144-156, 263
atomic structure, 7, 10, 31
Augustine, 254

behaviourism, 161
Bible, the, 179-180, 228, 236, 239, 244-245, 271-272, 274, 322
Big Bang, 7, 15, 18-19, 148, 247
bodies, human, 7, 9, 17, 46, 48, 69-70, 76, 78-80, 83-86, 103, 129-130, 136-138, 142, 145-146, 154, 158-163, 166-167, 215, 229, 233-234, 246, 264-268, 270-271, 277-279, 321
Bohr, N., 53
brain, 47-48, 81-86, 131-132, 134-138, 145-146, 154, 260, 263-264, 266-267, 270, 273, 275-277, 280-281, 284, 287, 320-321

Buddhism (The Buddha), 172, 178, 197

cause and effect, 111-113, 130-131
Christianity, 154-155, 170, 172, 183, 207, 222, 235-240, 249-250, 252, 266, 272-273, 288, 304-306, 322
collective unconscious (see archetypes), 209-210
common reality hypothesis, 102-105, 130, 139, 167, 256, 259-262, 268
community of believers, 178, 193-195, 202, 303
comparative religion, 195-198, 218, 222-223
complementarity, 103-105, 130, 139, 167, 256, 259, 261-262, 268
conscience, 173, 201
consciousness (see mental experiences), 146, 157, 161, 165, 168-169, 171, 180, 199-200, 213-214, 229-230, 245-246, 248, 259, 263, 265-267, 281-284, 309, 313, 321
contingency, 58, 62, 64-66, 124, 175-176, 179-180, 182, 242, 257, 264, 296
Copenhagen (or standard) interpretation of quantum theory, 53-60, 63, 86
correlations (see mappings), 61-63, 123-124, 130-132, 143, 162, 204, 261, 264, 275-276

determinism, 9, 44, 59, 62-63, 141, 144-156, 280-281, 285, 289
Devil, the, 183-184, 229, 242-244, 253, 267-268, 290
DNA molecule, 17-18, 276, 282, 285-288
dualism, 102-103

357

INDEX

ego, 106-109, 213-215, 230-231, 241, 264-265, 281-284
Einstein, A., 13, 27, 31, 35, 59, 96
electric charge, 19, 31, 90, 92, 254-255, 257
electron, 10, 13, 30-32, 38-44, 52-54, 59, 62, 65-66, 69, 92, 94-95, 104, 110, 112, 192, 229, 231-232, 238, 254-255, 257, 291-292, 307
two-electron system, 71-76, 85-86, 250-252, 319
emergent properties, 80-84
emotions, 169, 190-191
energy, 57-58, 61-62, 64, 109, 299-300
eternal life, 205-206, 244-245, 264-268
evolution by natural selection, 17-21, 47-48, 70, 118-119, 125, 128, 162, 176, 180, 186, 211-212, 217-223, 270, 276-277, 285-288, 305
explanation, 238-239, 252, 322
explanatory frameworks (*see* mental, physical, *and* spiritual interaction explanatory frameworks), 8-9, 10, 13, 15, 88-105, 136-137, 255-256, 261-262, 268, 291, 323
explanatory power (or value), 61, 68, 122, 125-128, 157, 161, 200, 228, 248-249, 256, 263-264, 284, 300, 304

falsification principle, 298-301
Feuerbach, L., 202
free will, 141-156, 185, 243, 273, 280, 305
Freud, S., 119, 149, 200-208, 214, 223

genes (*see* DNA molecule), 17-18, 128, 210-211, 219, 276
genetically determined behaviour, 117-119, 162, 174, 204-205, 210-212, 217-223, 276, 286-287
God (*see* Trinity, Persons, numinous, *and* spiritual interactions)
as Creator, 15-16, 20, 170, 175, 226, 230, 239, 247, 257-258, 270, 275, 278, 290, 305
as Sustainer, 16, 20, 247, 267
fear of, 169
his existence, 15-24, 56, 87, 120, 176, 191, 194-195, 224, 232, 240-243, 257-258, 261-262, 295
his foreknowledge, 144, 154-155, 274, 286, 288
his love, 170, 182-183, 186-187, 193, 203, 223, 242-243, 253, 257, 275-276, 290, 300, 311
his mystery, 312
his oneness (*see* God-in-himself), 75, 196-197, 236-240, 249-251, 257, 307
God-in-himself, 75, 246, 248-258, 290, 308, 312, 319
Gödel, K., 28-29

Heaven, 268
Heisenberg, W. (*see* uncertainty principle), 54, 59
Hell, 206, 268, 305
Hinduism, 155, 182
holism (wholeness *or* integration), 76-77, 85-86, 151-152, 214, 225-227, 251, 260, 266, 286-287, 313-314, 319-320, 322-323
Holy Communion, 239
Holy Spirit (*see* Persons of the Trinity)

id, 200-201
idealism, 120, 125, 195
imagination, 114-115
individuation, process of, 152, 214-215
information derived from other realities, 160-162, 191, 224-225, 283-285
inner religious experience, 168-174, 177-179, 189-198, 215, 224-225, 228, 230-232, 240, 262-263, 275, 280-285, 293, 308-311, 313-315
interactionism, 84-86
interactions-with-God (*see* spiritual interactions)

INDEX

interactions-with-the-world,
  45-46, 49-51, 53, 56-58, 60-68,
  74-75, 90-91, 94-96, 107, 111,
  122, 157, 159, 163-164, 177,
  196, 229-233, 246, 250-251,
  254-256, 267, 277-278,
  306-307, 309-312
intuition, 45-46, 50, 58
Islam (Muhammad), 155, 178,
  207, 235, 249, 285, 288

Jesus Christ (see Persons of the
  Trinity)
Judaism, 155, 183, 207, 235, 249,
  285
Jung, C., 119, 152, 206-217, 223,
  322

Kierkegaard, S., 255

language (see explanatory
  framework), 49-50, 210,
  253-254, 258, 307, 311-312,
  314-316, 319-320, 322-323
law-likeness, 63-67, 257, 274-275
left-hemisphere thinking,
  320-323
life, 69-70, 81-82, 176, 179-182
light,
  wave/particle nature, 40
  principle of least time, 151
localization, problem of, 51-52,
  62, 238
logic, 115, 117
Luther, M., 254

mappings (or correlations),
  75-76, 81-84, 100, 103,
  129-135, 138, 146-147, 158,
  225, 229-231, 234, 239,
  250-253, 259-260, 263-264,
  266-267, 269-271, 278-280,
  284, 287, 289-291, 312, 321
mass, 30-31, 33, 255, 257
materialism, 13-14, 69, 81, 196
mathematics,
  in relation to physics, 25-30,
    237
  nature of, 25-30, 113-117, 131,
    237
  incompleteness of, 28-30

measurement of precise position
  or velocity, 43-44, 53-55, 57,
  65-66, 72-75, 192, 307
mediation of reality domains,
  61, 67, 163, 175, 177, 188, 233,
  277-278, 284, 293
memory, 106-109, 124, 199,
  230-231
mental experiences (see inner
  religious experience and
  sensory observation),
  78-93, 101-132, 135-137, 140,
  142-143, 148, 152, 158-160,
  164-167, 230-231, 245, 248,
  264, 280
mental explanatory framework,
  89-93, 102-104, 109, 130,
  134-140, 147, 199, 225-226,
  228-230, 245, 255-256,
  259-264, 268-269, 273,
  291-292
mind-in-itself (see unconscious
  mind), 109-110, 167, 199,
  230-231
Minkowski, H., 114
miracles, 12, 21-22, 259, 268-269,
  271-277, 281, 284, 289,
  293-294

Nirvana, 197
numinous (Presence of God),
  sense of the, 169-190, 203,
  215, 226, 234, 253, 271,
  275-277, 280, 282-284, 293,
  296, 313-314

observer, role in
  classical physics, 9, 34, 46-47
  quantum physics, 34-35, 38-41,
    50, 57, 71-77, 93-96, 307
  relativistic physics 34-38, 50,
    77, 93-94
Ockham's Razor, 12-13, 16, 18,
  20, 24, 56, 86, 126
oneself (see personhood)
other minds, problem of, 78-80,
  157-167, 174, 195, 215,
  224-225, 264, 271, 277-279,
  284, 317, 319
otherness
  of mental experience, 140, 162,
    164, 174, 177, 188, 200,
    283-284

of physical interaction, 57-58, 61-64, 68, 122-123, 177, 306
of religious experience, 174, 177, 187-199, 215, 223-224, 228, 280-285, 293, 306
of sensory observation, 122-123, 159-160, 194-195, 224, 278

Palamas, G., 254
personhood, 165-167, 199, 213, 215-216, 226, 233-234, 265, 286-287, 320
Persons, of the Trinity, 75-76, 170, 207, 235-244, 249-254, 267-268, 270, 289, 312, 319
Father, 202-203, 206-208, 226, 235-236, 239-240, 245, 250, 252, 290
Holy Spirit, 169, 235-237, 239-240, 250, 252, 305, 322
Son (or Jesus Christ), 170, 178, 180, 186, 204, 235-236, 239-240, 244-245, 250, 259, 272-273, 275, 285, 288-294, 304-307, 316, 322, 324
physical
concepts, 8-9, 13, 34, 102, 307
forces, 7-10, 13, 19, 31, 90, 92, 225
interactions (see interactions-with-the-world)
laws, 9, 12-13, 22-23, 57-58, 61-66, 84-86, 91-92, 137, 141-142, 144-145, 147-148, 150, 175-176, 179, 185, 268, 270-274, 277-280, 293, 296
properties, 8, 30-33, 44
world (see world-in-itself)
physical explanatory framework,
classical, 7-15, 25, 44, 46, 55, 86, 90-93, 99, 126-127, 255, 272-274
in general, 130-132, 134-140, 147-148, 157, 181-182, 225-226, 228-229, 259-264, 268-269, 291-292, 311-312
modern (see quantum theory and relativity), 25-44, 50-68, 87, 89-90, 93, 102-103, 127, 253-256

prayer, 171-173, 178, 197, 247, 262, 275, 280-281, 284-285, 296, 316, 323
predestination, 154-155, 247, 305
probability waves, 42-43
Problem of Evil, 182-188, 242, 300

quantum events (see interactions-with-the-world), 41, 44, 67, 93, 109, 112, 123
quantum theory, 38-44, 71-77, 93-96, 107, 232, 238, 250-252, 272, 291-292, 298, 306-308
quark, 10, 13, 30, 32, 44, 69, 92
questions,
how-type, 11, 23-24, 140, 227
ultimate, 15, 24, 70, 140-141, 186, 227-228, 283, 286, 289, 293, 323
why-type, 11-12, 15, 23-24, 71, 76-78, 87, 140, 227

reasonable belief, 120-122, 136, 139-140, 157, 159, 162, 187, 196, 293
reciprocal definition, 34, 165-166, 215-216, 279, 317
reductionism, 13-14, 69-76, 86
relational existence, 232-235, 240-244, 249-250, 252-253, 267, 306-307
relativity theory, 27-28, 31, 35-38, 44, 46, 50, 74, 77, 93-94, 96-97, 99, 126-127, 272, 298
religion, 168, 201-223, 296-297, 303-304, 308, 312-314
religious archetype (see self), 216-217, 223, 276-277, 285-288
representative realism, 13-14, 69
resurrection, 178, 235, 267, 272, 289, 294, 300
Riemann, G., 27-28, 114
right-hemisphere thinking, 320-323
rules of discussion, (see explanatory framework), 10-13, 15, 70, 91

scepticism, 88-89, 120, 122, 159, 165, 181, 200

INDEX

science as a human endeavour,
45-46, 67, 193-196, 295-309,
317
second law of thermodynamics,
97
self (see religious archetype),
213-216, 232, 283, 287-288
sensory observation, 106-128,
160, 166, 194, 230, 278
space
in classical physics, 7, 27,
33-34, 90, 113, 117
in relativistic physics, 27-28,
35-37, 44, 74, 113-115
space-time, 36, 96-97, 101, 144,
246-247, 265-266
spatial and temporal
relationships, 30-35, 44, 50,
165-166
spirits, human, 226, 229-235,
239-240, 243-244, 252-253,
263-270, 275, 279, 289, 321
spiritual interactions, 67-68, 90,
172-174, 229-233, 239-240,
246, 249, 253-254, 256,
265-267, 270, 321
spiritual interaction
explanatory framework,
104, 141, 181, 244-247,
253-254, 259-294
strangeness, 31-32
subjectivity, 37-38, 67-68, 127,
191-195, 198, 257, 306
superego, 200-201, 204, 206-207
symmetric view of the relation
between the mental and
physical (see interactionism), 137-140, 142, 144,
263-264, 270

telepathy, 158
theism, 168, 172, 196, 318
theology as a human endeavour,
295-324

theory-laden data, 181-182,
296-297, 299-300
time
in classical physics, 8, 90
in relation to God (see
transcendence), 101,
244-247, 265-267, 307
in relativistic physics, 35-38,
44, 74, 96-97, 99, 141, 143,
148, 151, 155, 244-247,
265-266, 305
instant known as 'now',
98-101, 244-246, 265
flow of, 97-98, 100-101, 265
mental as opposed to physical,
96-102, 131-132, 143, 148,
244-246, 265-266
transcendence, 168, 171, 265, 285,
307
Trinity, doctrine of (see
Persons), 75, 235-242,
251-255, 322

uncertainty principle, 42-44,
54-55, 59, 84-85, 145
unconscious mind (see
collective unconscious,
archetypes, and mind-initself), 91, 110, 141, 174, 199-223,
229-230, 233, 241, 281-285,
293

variational principles, 150-152
verification principle, 298-299

wave/particle duality,
38-42, 44, 46, 51, 54, 104, 238,
291-292, 307
wish fulfillment, 202-208
world-in-itself, 50-68,
74-75, 86, 109-111, 122,
157-159, 163, 177, 195,
230-231, 246, 248, 250,
254-258, 295, 308, 310, 319